CRIMINAL JUSTICE

CRIMINAL JUSTICE

A Carrie Shatner Mystery

Randee Green

coffeetownpress

Kenmore, WA

A Coffeetown Press book published by Epicenter Press

Epicenter Press
6524 NE 181st St.
Suite 2
Kenmore, WA 98028

For more information go to:
www.Camelpress.com
www.Coffeetownpress.com
www.Epicenterpress.com
www.randeegreen.com

This is a work of fiction. Names, characters, places, brands, media, and incidents are either the product of the author's imagination or are used fictitiously.

ISBN: 978-1-94207-886-9 (Trade Paper)
ISBN: 978-1-94207-887-6 (eBook)

Produced in the United States of America

To my "son"
Alexandr Schmitt
Mama loves you, Bubba J!

Acknowledgements

MANY THANKS TO MY AGENT, JESSICA ALVAREZ, for believing in both me and Carrie Shatner. And for finding the two of us a home at Camel Press.

And, of course, to Jennifer McCord, and everyone else at Camel Press, thank you so much for all of your hard work and support.

Much love to Alex Schmitt, my son from another mom. And to the rest of my haunt family—you crazies know who you are!

Limitless thanks and smooches to Molly, Daisy, and Snookums for the love and support that only pets can provide. Thank you to my mom for (mostly) not complaining every time that I've handed you a new manuscript with the expectation that you find and correct all of my grammatical and punctuation errors. And thank you to my dad for subjecting me to professional wrestling, *Star Trek: The Original Series* NASCAR, The Doors, and Neil Diamond at such a young age.

I'd also like to thank William Shatner for no other reason than for being William Shatner.

And, of course, Carrie Shatner . . . Thank you for letting me tell your story.

Acknowledgements

CHAPTER ONE

"Tell me, Carrie . . . How much murder and mayhem have the Shatners been involved in since our last meeting?"

"No murders," I said as I turned my back on the dilapidated lake house that had been the scene of a murder over fifteen years earlier. And yes, two Shatners were responsible for it. As far as I knew, it was the last time any of my relatives had killed anyone. Blocking the rush of bad memories, I leaned against the rear bumper of my Jeep and faced Lieutenant Alexander Schmitt. "And no mayhem aside from the usual."

"That you know of . . ." Alberto Ramos grumbled as he slipped a hoodie over his head. The sleeves concealed the tattoos that covered his arms from wrist to shoulder. "There's a whole heck of a lot going on that you don't know about."

"Oh, yeah?" Challenging Alberto, I asked, "And what don't I know about?"

"Did you know Dale and Dickie jacked a car last night?"

I groaned. "Seriously? No one tells me anything."

Heat spread across my chest, traveling up my neck to my face as I battled a rising wave of anger and embarrassment. When I got my hands on my cousins, I was going to strangle them. Dale and Dickie were not supposed to steal cars without talking to me about it first. That way I could run the license plate numbers through the system and figure out who the car belonged to.

"How do you know they stole a car?" Schmitt asked his agent.

"Because I helped them steal it," Alberto said. "And I helped them tear it down and load the parts into a moving van bound for the ports in Houston."

"What the heck, Alberto?" I balled up my fist and thumped him on the shoulder. "I thought we were supposed to be in this together. But you're as bad as the rest of them. Committing crimes and not telling me about it until afterwards."

For about two months now—ever since I had agreed to turn over evidence against my family's criminal operations—I'd been having weekly meetings with Lieutenant Alexander Schmitt and Agent Alberto Ramos. They both worked for Texas's Department of Public Safety's Drug Unit, and they were overseeing the extensive investigation into my family. Alberto was working undercover, and he had done an excellent job duping my family. They had quickly accepted the undercover officer who was masquerading as a career criminal. The name my family knew him by was Beto Sánchez.

"And I thought you were supposed to be the head of your family's criminal organization," Alberto mocked me as he swatted my hand away. "But, as far as I can tell, not a single one of them takes you seriously. Okay, maybe three or four of them take you seriously. And that's only because they like you. The rest of them think you're a joke."

"Thanks for the confidence boost," I said as I shuffled my feet in the loose stones. "I'm doing the best that I can. Besides, it's not like I want to be in charge. You know the only reason I'm doing it is to help you bring down my family and put a stop to their crimes."

And to protect my innocent family members.

"Yeah, I know," Alberto said. "I also know that the only reason you agreed to help us is because we had you backed into a corner. It was either help us and get your slate wiped clean or chance a lengthy stay in prison for all the crimes you've committed over the past few years."

"The only reason I committed those crimes was to keep my family out of trouble," I hissed. "And, up until recently, it's not like I really did anything all that horrible. I just shredded speeding tickets and talked people out of pressing charges against certain family members. It's Murph that covered up the more serious crimes."

My uncle Murph was the Sheriff of Wyatt County. Before that he was a deputy and then the chief deputy. For over three decades now, he had been using his position to cover up our family's crimes.

"Sure . . ." Alberto rolled his eyes. "What about the time Naomi shot that guy in the foot?"

"It was barely a flesh wound," I said, jumping to my cousin's defense. "And the guy happened to be cheating on his wife. When Naomi found out that she was the 'other woman', she took a shot at him. The guy deserved it."

"I doubt a judge would agree with you," Alberto said.

"Now, children." Lieutenant Schmitt clapped his hands and drew our attention to him. His shoulders shook with silent laughter. "Carrie's right. The two of you are supposed to be working together. Knock off the squabbling before I have to put both of you in timeout."

I glared at Schmitt. "I'm beginning to think you're enjoying this, Lieutenant."

"Oh, I am. Immensely." Schmitt chuckled. "Every meeting with you is like an episode of my own personal reality show. Actually, it's even better because it's real."

"That's because we only tell you about the good stuff," I said. "You don't have to live with the stress or suffer through the boring parts."

Personally, I don't watch many reality shows. I think they're stupid. But one of my cousins had been a contestant on *The Bachelor*, and she had told me about all the uninteresting stuff—like the long hours stuck in the mansion or a hotel room—that never make it on to television.

"Carrie's right," Alberto said. "Reality shows are only fun to watch because it's entertaining to observe someone else's train wreck or dumpster fire. Considering my recent experiences, I can guarantee it's not fun to live it."

"Excuse me? You have no room to talk. You've only been undercover with my family for two months." I stuck my hand in Alberto's face and held up two fingers. "Count them. Two months. One. Two. Sixty days or so. That's nothing. I've been living with this 'train wreck' or 'dumpster fire'—"

"More like a train wrecking into a hundred dumpster fires."

Since I still had my hand in Alberto's face, I lowered my index finger and left the middle one raised. "Whatever you want to call it, I've been living it for almost thirty-two years. If anyone gets to complain about how sick and tired they are of it, it should be me. Plus, trying to run my family's criminal operation while turning over evidence to y'all is stressing me out. Last week I found my first gray hair."

"I'm surprised you don't have a head full of gray hairs thanks to your family. Just be glad you don't have my problem." Schmitt removed his white cowboy hat to show me his bald head. "I don't know how you do it, Carrie. I really don't."

"I was born into it," I reminded him. "When you grow up in a . . . I don't know if toxic is the right word . . . but when you grow up in the type of toxic situation that I did, you grow immune to it. Like I always say, I come from a long line of criminals. To you, it might seem crazy. To me, it's normal. For the Shatners, breaking the law is a family tradition."

Some of my ancestors—and several of my living relatives—were moonshiners, rumrunners, and drug dealers. I also had horse thieves and carjackers in the family . . . plus bank robbers, burglars, pickpockets, and con artists. And then there has been the occasional murderer. You name it—whether it's a felony or a misdemeanor—somewhere along the line a member of my family has committed it.

As far back as the Shatner family can be traced—from southern England in the 1500s, to the mountains of western North Carolina, and now to the Piney Woods of East Texas—we have been breaking the law—and running from it, too.

Prior to moving to Texas in the late-1800s, my ancestors were only breaking the law on occasion. Given, some of the laws that those Shatners broke and the crimes they committed were serious ones—like murder, assault and battery, destruction of property, and illegal distillation of alcohol. At least they weren't doing any of it on a regular basis . . . except for the moonshining.

Not counting any of the kids who are under the age of sixteen, there are currently seventy-four Shatners and Shatners-by-marriage. It pains me to admit that just over half of my adult family members are actively breaking the law on a regular basis.

I—like Alberto so nicely pointed out—only knew about a fraction of the crimes that were taking place around me. My family members were purposely keeping me in the dark while I was trying to bring their criminal ways into the light and expose them once and for all.

Back when I was a kid, I had known that several of my uncles and older cousins were criminals. No, I wasn't quite sure what all they were up to aside from the moonshining. I was also somewhat proud of them for getting away with their crimes. But that didn't mean I wanted anything to do with my family's various transgressions.

Since I hadn't wanted anything to do with the Shatners' criminal enterprises, I moved away from Wyatt County not long after I graduated from high school. First, I moved to Huntsville, Texas, to attend Sam Houston State University. And then—after I graduated with my Bachelor of Science in Criminal Justice—I moved to Tennessee and went to work for the Nashville Crime Scene Investigation Section.

I had never planned on coming back home except to visit, and I had done my best to remain ignorant of my family's various crimes. That was up until four years ago when my great-aunt Emily Morgan demanded that I immediately return home to Wyatt County, Texas.

I could have said no.

I knew that no one—and I mean no one—said 'no' to Emily Morgan Shatner-Mount; if they did, they didn't live to tell about it.

Until she died just over two years ago, my great-aunt had been running the Shatner family's illegal endeavors. After Great-Grandpa Shooter was arrested for brewing moonshine in the early-1950s, Emily Morgan took over running the family's illegal operation despite only being in her late teens. Even after Great-Grandpa Shooter was released from prison, Emily Morgan continued to run the family's criminal operation.

My great-aunt had been a terrifying woman, and she had kept the family in line for over seventy years. Sure, the Shatners were breaking the law on a regular basis during all those years. But everyone respected Aunt Emily Morgan, and they always asked for her permission before they broke the law. Emily Morgan set the rules, and the rest of the Shatners played by them.

Even as she was dying—her body wasting away from leukemia—Emily Morgan had ruled the Shatner family with an iron fist.

It was the leukemia diagnosis that had prompted Aunt Emily Morgan into requesting that I return home to Texas. She knew she didn't have much time left, and she had wanted to do whatever she could to make sure the family would be protected after she was gone. Because of my degree in Criminal Justice and the years of experience I had working for the Crime Scene Investigation Section, Aunt Emily Morgan had deemed me useful. She demanded that I return home so that I could take a job with the Wyatt County Sheriff's Department.

I accepted the crime scene technician job—and, later, the promotion to detective—knowing full well that Aunt Emily Morgan and the rest of my family expected me to help them cover up their crimes.

Fortunately, there isn't a whole lot of serious crime in Wyatt County.

Unfortunately for me, most of the crimes committed are perpetrated by Shatners.

Yes, I will admit that I have occasionally abused my position with the sheriff's department to cover for my criminally inclined family members.

No, I am not proud of it.

When I first started working at the sheriff's department, I hadn't been fully aware of what all criminal activities that my family was involved in. Yes, I knew about the moonshine . . . and the marijuana . . . but I didn't know the extent of either operation . . . nor had I known about the insurance scams, money laundering, frequent assaults, or any of the other various crimes that my family members committed on a regular basis.

But, once I had accepted the job, I had no choice but to run around after my family members to clean up their messes. Okay, no one forced me to cover up any crimes. I just did it. I'm not sure I want to know what that says about me as a person.

Before she died, Aunt Emily Morgan begged me to take a more active role with the family. But I couldn't bring myself to do it. I had what most of the other Shatners lacked—a moral compass. Not that my moral compass had ever pointed true north. But at least it pointed somewhere in the general direction of northwest.

After Aunt Emily Morgan died, her brother—my great-uncle Houston—took over as head of the family. It quickly became clear that he was better at committing crimes than orchestrating them. Going against his sister's instructions, Uncle Houston loosened the reins and basically let everyone do whatever they wanted. The younger generations of Shatners began to run wild. Uncle Houston also expanded the criminal operations.

I've always regretted standing back and letting Uncle Houston take control of the family. The rest of me was relieved that I wasn't the person in charge.

Until now.

Because now I am the person in charge.

After acting as the grand marshal of the parade that led the Shatners straight down the road to ruin, Uncle Houston admitted defeat two months ago. He finally accepted that he couldn't handle being in charge, and he asked me to take over running the family.

The only reason I reluctantly accepted was because a couple weeks before that—after Alberto caught me breaking up my cousin Wesley's drug selling operation at a local bait shop—he and Lieutenant Schmitt approached me with a deal. They made it clear to me that the Shatner family's time was almost up, and then they offered me the opportunity to get away with anything illegal that I'd done if I turned over evidence against my family.

Sometimes I hate myself for betraying my family, and I have to periodically remind myself that the Shatners have done this to themselves. They broke the law, and they had to know that their misdeeds would eventually catch up to them. Furthermore, thanks to Uncle Houston letting the family run wild, the Department of Public Safety's Drug Unit was finally able to acquire some solid evidence against us. With or without my help, the Shatners were about to go down.

I was not about to go down in a blaze of glory with them. I had to look out for myself.

By agreeing to help the DPS acquire evidence against my family, I would be able to protect myself and some of the other innocent Shatners.

Also, by taking over as head of the family, I would be able to acquire even more evidence against the Shatners and bring them down from the inside.

I was playing both ends against the middle—which was turning out to be a whole heck of a lot harder than I originally thought.

"Can we just hurry up and get this over with?" I asked.

"Got somewhere you need to be, Carrie?" Schmitt asked.

"Yeah. I do. And so does Alberto," I said. I glanced at my phone and sighed. It was just after four o'clock in the afternoon. "The Hayride of Nightmares is going to open around six-thirty and we both need to get into our costumes and makeup before the first wagon rolls out."

The Hayride of Nightmares was one of the four haunted attractions that my uncle Elvin McCarty owned and operated. I worked there as an actress. Getting to scare people was an outlet for all the pent-up stress and frustration that I was currently dealing with.

"No, you're the one who *needs* to get over to that stupid haunted attraction," Alberto said. "Unlike you, I've got better things I could be doing on Saturday nights than scaring people."

"Don't pretend like acting at the Body Farm isn't fun, Alberto," I said.

"Yeah, all right, it's kinda fun. I'll admit I get a sick thrill out of making grown men cry."

"And remember, Alberto, we both agreed that you volunteering at the Body Farm was a good way to make friends with the Shatners," Schmitt said as he drummed his sausage-sized fingers on the hood of his car. "They've come to accept you a lot quicker than they would have had you not been helping out at the Body Farm."

"You're practically one of the family now, Alberto," I said.

"Yeah, yeah. I know I had to win over the Shatners. I just think it's stupid dressing up and scaring people. But Carrie's right. We're here to talk about the Shatners, so let's talk about the Shatners." Alberto paced back-and-forth across the cracked remains of the asphalt driveway. He wasn't much taller than I was, but he carried himself in a way that made him appear bigger. "Carrie, is there any truth to the rumor that your cousins Wes and Waylon have been selling drugs to people at the high school football games?"

Out of all my criminally-inclined family members, Wesley and Waylon were the biggest pains in my butt. Wesley was reckless, arrogant, and stupid. The boy didn't have enough common sense to fill a bottle cap. Since the age of fourteen, he had been getting busted by the police on a regular basis. Waylon wasn't quite as bad as his older brother, but he frequently got caught up in Wesley's many wrongdoings. I'd lost count of how many of their messes I'd had to clean up over the past four years. They sold drugs and moonshine, and they had been caught doing it multiple times by me and by others. Neither of them seemed to understand the concept that they should be secretive about their crimes. Instead, they would sell their wares right out in the open where everyone—including law enforcement officers— could see them.

"Yeah, it's true. I confronted Wes about it at the game last night. Allegedly they've been doing it all season," I said. When Alberto and Lieutenant Schmitt both opened their mouths, I held up my hands and waved off their comments. "And, before you ask, I had no idea what they were up to until last night."

"I thought the point of you taking control of your family's criminal operation was so that you could keep tabs on what your family members are up to," Lieutenant Schmitt said.

I kicked a rock and sent it tumbling across the asphalt. How was I supposed to know what crimes my family members were committing when none of them felt the need to fill me in about what they were doing?

"Can we please just arrest Wes and take him out of the equation?" I asked. At almost every one of my weekly meetings with Alberto and Lieutenant Schmitt, we argued about Wesley. "I've given y'all so much evidence against him, and so many opportunities to take him down. But y'all haven't done anything."

"Carrie, I'm only going to explain this one more time," Lieutenant Schmitt said. "We want to wait until we have all of our evidence compiled before arresting anyone. We need to have an ironclad case. I understand you want Wesley out of the way, but we'd be moving too soon. We need more evidence."

"Evidence that you are supposed to be getting us," Alberto said.

"I'm doing the best that I can. But I'm fighting an uphill battle." I pushed away from my Jeep and joined Alberto in pacing back and forth across the driveway. "Uncle Houston is pulling the strings behind my back. As long as he's doing that, no one is going to listen to me. And it's hard for me to get any new information when Uncle Houston is purposely keeping it from me."

"Is there *any* new evidence you can give us since last week's meeting?" Schmitt asked. "Where, may I remind you, you gave us next-to-no new information."

"Ummm . . ." I thought about it for a few seconds. Like I had said earlier, I was unaware of anything other than the usual mayhem that my family caused. Schmitt probably would have been better off asking Alberto if he knew anything. "Nope. I got nothing."

"What about the Devereuxs? Do you have any new information on them?"

"Not really," I said.

Leslie "Catfish" Devereux had been Uncle Houston's partner in crime since childhood. They'd been breaking the law together since they could walk, and, over the years, Catfish had played a significant role in my family's criminal endeavors.

Catfish had been married six times, and he had eleven children— all of whom he named Leslie after himself. Catfish then gave each of his kids a nickname so that none of them went by their given name. Both of Catfish's daughters and three of his sons had married into the Shatner family. One of his grandsons had also married into the Shatner family, and I doubted that he would be the last. Of the

Devereuxs who had joined the Shatner family, I had a fairly good idea of what crimes they were involved in. I was clueless about the other half. They could be breaking the law on a daily basis—or they could be completely innocent.

"Carrie, you have got to give us something," Schmitt said.

"I keep telling you that Uncle Kinky is selling moonshine out of the back of the liquor store. It wouldn't be hard for Alberto or any of your other agents to go in and buy a couple jars."

Kinky Devereux was Catfish's third son by his first wife. He was married to my aunt Margaret. Kinky ran Catfish's Fine Liquor and Beer Emporium, and he had been selling homebrewed moonshine there since before I was born. Almost everyone in Wyatt County knew that he did it, and no one really seemed to care.

"Already have," Alberto said. "Multiple times. Kinky told me that I'm becoming one of his most loyal customers."

"Please don't tell me Uncle Kinky has a frequent buyer's program where you get a free jar of moonshine for every ten that you buy," I said.

"It's for every twelve," Alberto said. I couldn't tell if he was being sarcastic or not. Before I could ask, Alberto stopped pacing and turned to face me. "I also bought an eight-ball of cocaine from Levi Palmer at the Dancing Cowgirl on Thursday night."

"Son of a . . ." I muttered.

"I'm guessing you didn't know the Palmers were back in business down at the strip club," Lieutenant Schmitt said.

I shook my head. "No one tells me anything."

Up until a few months ago, the Shatners and the Palmers had been mortal enemies. But then—much to my horror—after a hundred plus years of feuding with each other, the Shatner and Palmer families banded together and combined their respective criminal operations.

The feud started after the Civil War when the widow of my many-times-great-granddaddy went and married a Union deserter named Palmer. The offspring from their first marriages started the feud after the combined family moved to Texas. Aside from a brief truce during Prohibition, the two families had been feuding up until this past January.

After the Shatners and Palmers had combined forces earlier this year, the circle of people I had to worry about had grown even larger. I had no loyalty to the Palmers, and I gladly would have arrested them if I had caught them breaking the law. But I had to sweep their indiscretions under the rug because protecting them meant I was also protecting my family. I might have partially hated myself for betraying my family, but I felt no such remorse when it came to turning over evidence against the Palmers. The problem was that some of my family members were now linked to many of the Palmers' crimes.

"Carrie, you keep giving us crumbs—"

Cutting Lieutenant Schmitt off, I said, "I've given you a whole heck of a lot more than crumbs. I've told you all I know about the family's moonshine and marijuana operations."

"But you still haven't told us where the still or the grow houses are located."

"That's because no one will tell me," I said. "But I've confirmed that the El Rio Cartel has been supplying the Palmers with harder drugs."

"And that's good to know—"

"Not to mention I've told you about how my family illegally obtains the prescription pills," I said. "I've told you about how we launder the dirty money. Alberto has learned firsthand about the chop shop. And then there are the insurance scams and other con jobs that my family members are involved in. I've told you everything I know about that."

Okay, maybe I hadn't told them everything . . . but I'd told them *almost* everything.

"But, Carrie, it's not—"

"And what about all those cold cases I solved for you?"

"Technically you haven't 'solved' any cold cases. All you've done is give us the alleged identity of some bodies that we may or may not find buried on your family's property. But we can't consider those cases solved until we've located the remains and confirmed the identities." Lieutenant Schmitt said. "Your stories are interesting, but they're not enough. And no judge is going to sign a warrant based solely off your stories. We need solid evidence. And the longer it takes for you to help us get what we need, the longer this investigation is going to drag out. You need to get us irrefutable, physical evidence so that we can move on to the next phase."

"And I keep telling you that it comes down to a trust thing," I said. "Not everyone trusts me. And I can't blame them. Until recently, I have never supported my family's crimes. And I left it up to Uncle Murph to cover up most of their mistakes. When there is some sort of problem, my family members go to Uncle Murph to clean up the mess or fix things. They're not coming to me despite the fact that I'm now in charge. And that's because most of my family members don't trust me. If either of you have any ideas on how to get them to trust me . . ."

"It's up to you to get them to trust you, Carrie," Schmitt said.

"Yeah, Carrie," Alberto said. "I keep hearing about what a great leader Emily Morgan was. That she was a woman no one messed with. Maybe it's time you start acting more like her."

"I don't think anyone's ready for that."

"But we're ready for it, Carrie," Schmitt said. "Whether you want to be in charge or not doesn't matter. What matters is that we *need* you to take charge. And if you've got to wrestle control away from Houston or do something drastic, then do it. It's time to stop tiptoeing around and take the clichéd bull by the horns. I don't care how you do it. But you need to do it. You want this to be over and done with? Then it's up to you to finish it."

CHAPTER TWO

IT WAS ALMOST FIVE-THIRTY WHEN I ARRIVED at the Body Farm. The main customer parking lot was packed full of cars, and the parking lot attendants were directing the latest arrivals into the overflow lot. The entertainment area—which consisted of food trucks, carnival-type games, and live entertainment—had opened at five, and the two haunted houses would start admitting customers around six. The hayride and trail would start up after the sun set around six-thirty. That gave me about an hour to get ready.

The Body Farm was open every Saturday and Sunday night from the beginning of September through Halloween. We weren't open on Friday nights because Uncle Elvin didn't want to compete with Texas's unofficial religion—high school football. The closer we got to Halloween, the busier we were at the Body Farm. Tonight was the Saturday before Halloween. In the past, this was always the busiest night of the season. Thousands of people would come through the Body Farm in a matter of hours tonight.

Fifteen years ago, when Uncle Elvin—who was married to my great-uncle Houston's only daughter—decided to open a haunted hayride, everyone thought he was nuts. Haunted hayrides were an East Coast thing. There were a few out in California, but hardly any in between and none in Texas. And—aside from the occasional fly-by-night haunted houses—there weren't any established haunted attractions in East Texas. The closest to Wyatt County were in Dallas, Austin, and Houston. There were also a couple across the state line in Louisiana.

But Uncle Elvin had the land, the tractors, and the flatbed wagons. He was also obsessed with Halloween. He believed that if he built it, customers would come.

All the actors, tractor drivers, and other volunteers during the Hayride of Nightmares' first season were either Shatners or Devereuxs—myself included. We wore costumes that Uncle Elvin bought on clearance from various retail and party stores the year before. The props were either store-bought, handmade, or picked up at flea markets or along the side of the road. Everything about the hayride's first season had been chaotic. There were only a couple of scenes—such as the guillotine and the alien abduction. The rest were just actors in cheap costumes randomly popping out of the woods and cornfields to "attack" the wagons.

Despite only barely breaking even, and the hayride receiving some scathingly horrible reviews, Uncle Elvin refused to quit. During the off-season, he worked on the hayride and opened the "new and improved" attraction for a second season.

Over the years, Uncle Elvin has made countless changes to the hayride. The only thing that hasn't changed is the wagon path. What Uncle Elvin did was develop more scenes—some of which are now housed in buildings that the tractors drive through. He invested in Hollywood-quality costumes, makeup, and props. He also added animatronics and special effects.

Even though the Body Farm has expanded to include two haunted houses and a haunted trail, the main workforce continues to consist of Shatners and Devereuxs. Not only are we actors and tractor drivers, but Shatners and Devereuxs also operate the ticket booths, game stands, and food trucks. We make the costumes and some of the props, and work as makeup artists. Shatners and Devereuxs also serve as security guards and the maintenance crew. Several of the Palmers have also joined us this season.

I have been working at the Body Farm off and on for the past fifteen years. Since the Moonshiners' scene was first developed during the hayride's fifth season, I had wanted to act there, but Uncle Elvin had deemed it a male-only skit. For years, he stuck to his guns and refused to let any females act at Moonshiners' Grove. Then, four seasons ago—not long after I moved home to Texas—I finally wore down his resistance. Uncle Elvin told me I could act at the Moonshiners scene on opening night if it would shut me up. It was only supposed to be a one-time deal, but Uncle Elvin thought I did such a good job that he let me stay at Moonshiners permanently. It took him a while to admit it, but he eventually conceded that a female character was crucial to the skit. I have played the role of Mama Moonshine ever since.

After parking in the staff lot, I looped around the entertainment area and then ducked through a hole hidden in the wooden fence that surrounded part of the hayride.

Hidden in the grove of pine and cottonwood trees in the center of the hayride path was a double wide trailer in which costumes, masks, and props were stored. Racks of costumes that were separated by the four attractions took up much of the floor space. The costumes only got replaced when they were ruined beyond repair, and the closest they came to getting washed was either a rainstorm or the occasional spritz of Febreze to mask any odors. The building reeked of stale sweat, dirt, and mildew. I grabbed my costume—which consisted of distressed, faux blood-and mud-spattered jeans and a flannel shirt.

Once I was in costume, I rushed next door to the makeup trailer that Uncle Elvin had bought at auction when an Austin production company declared bankruptcy and was forced to sell off all its assets. Originally the trailer had six makeup stations, but Uncle Elvin gutted part of the interior space and added six more.

"'Bout time you got here," Veda Houser-McCarty said as I walked through the door. She grabbed me by the shoulders and shoved me into a chair. She then yanked the elastic band out of my hair and attacked my curls with a comb. "Where were you? You're never late."

"I went to see a man about a horse."

Veda smacked me on the head with the comb.

Veda is my best friend, and she has been for going on thirty years. We met way back in preschool, and had formed a sisterly bond. We had been best friends up through high school when Veda started dating my cousin, Bubba McCarty. After that, neither of them had time for anybody else. Veda and I drifted apart. She stayed in Wyatt County while I went off to college; then Bubba and I—along with a few other Shatners—moved to Nashville.

During the time that I lived in Nashville, my friendship with Veda depended on her relationship with Bubba. If Veda and Bubba were good, then Veda and I were good. If Veda and Bubba were on the outs, then she and I either talked every day or we went weeks or months without talking.

Bubba was Uncle Elvin's and Aunt Loretta's younger son. We were close in age and had grown up together. Earlier this year, Bubba finally came to his senses. He quit the country band that he had been part of to come home and marry Veda.

Veda—who was a hairdresser and stylist—co-managed the Body Farm's makeup department. Bubba was training to take over running the entire attraction. Uncle Elvin planned to hand over operations of the Body Farm to Bubba at the end the current season. After fifteen years, Uncle Elvin had had enough. He wanted to dedicate more time to his expanding alpaca farm and breeding program.

"I'm worried about you, Carrie," Veda said as she teased my hair. "Ever since you found that body in the dumpster on New Year's, this year has been kicking your butt. It's just been one thing after another. But these past couple of months—"

"Veda, there's no need to worry."

I turned my head and stared into Veda's green eyes. Her blonde hair was pulled back in a bun, white makeup had been airbrushed over her face to give her a ghostly pallor, and her costume was a distressed vintage wedding gown.

"How can I not worry about you?" Veda dropped her voice to a whisper. "Something is up with you. I'm your best friend. I know you better than you know yourself. I can tell something is wrong. You're always stressed out. Your hair's going gray."

Veda plucked one of my hairs and held the white strand in front of my face.

"Not another one . . ."

"Your taste in men has taken a nosedive," Veda continued. "You went from dating a Texas Ranger to dating a criminal. Given he's a good looking criminal."

Veda and I looked over to where Alberto was having his makeup done. The artist was sponging makeup around his left eye to make it look like he had a black eye. Alberto was dressed in a sleeveless orange jumpsuit that showed off his muscular, tattooed arms.

I wanted to tell Veda that the man she knew as Beto Sanchez wasn't really a criminal. But then I would have to explain that he was an undercover agent. I also wanted to tell her that there was nothing between me and Beto. Our "relationship" was just part of the ruse to get my family to trust him.

Of all people, Veda would most likely understand and support what I was doing, but she was also a Shatner-by-marriage. While her loyalty was mostly confined to Bubba and me, I couldn't risk telling her that I was helping the Department of Public Safety bring down my family. Inevitably, she would say something to Bubba, then Bubba would tell someone else. It was bad enough that my grandparents knew what I was up to. I couldn't take the chance of anyone else finding out. Lives depended on it—especially mine. If certain family members found out that I was betraying them . . . well, let's just say I had no intention of joining the other bodies that were scattered about the Shatner's collective property.

"At least we don't have to worry about this boyfriend arresting any of the family," my cousin Naomi said. She flicked a glob of gooey silicon on my forehead and began to spread it out using a small metal spatula. "Though we do have to worry about him getting busted alongside the family."

Naomi was a makeup artist, and she co-managed the Body Farm's makeup department alongside Veda. Naomi—who looked like a Barbie-doll come to life—had her long blonde hair tucked up under a frizzy gray wig. Her heavily applied theatrical makeup made her look like an old woman. Out of all my female cousins, I was closest to Naomi. She was a few years younger than me, and, growing up, she had practically been my shadow.

"Everything is okay," I said. "Neither of you have to worry."

"What a load of crap," Veda said. "Just a few months ago you were telling me how you couldn't take much more of your family and their antics. Now you're running the family. What happened? Aside from losing your damn mind."

"Do I have to remind you that you're the one who compared my family to the mob? Once you're in, there's no getting out. I figure if I can't beat 'em, I may as well join 'em," I said, giving the same excuse that I had been using for the past two months. "Besides, it's my circus and they're my monkeys. I realized that it was time I stepped up and took over as ringmaster."

Veda snorted. "Well, your circus is out of control and the monkeys are the ones running the show. Not you. You might not want to admit it, but your family is falling apart."

"Yeah, Carrie, my dad says it's only a matter of time until one of us gets busted," Naomi said. She finished spreading out the silicon across my forehead and began airbrushing a layer of white makeup over my face. "And he's not the only one who thinks that."

"Then tell your dad to stop breaking the law," I mumbled. I had to keep my mouth and eyes shut while Naomi used the airbrush.

"Daddy hardly ever breaks the law anymore. He's too busy working at the outdoor store," Naomi said. Uncle Leroy—along with his brother Delmar—owned the Guns 'n Stuff Outdoor Emporium. "These days Daddy only helps make the occasional batch of moonshine."

"Sure…" I said, cracking open an eye wide enough to look at Naomi.

According to Uncle Houston, his son Leroy, was involved in a whole heck of a lot more than just the "occasional batch of moonshine." One of these days, I would have to burst Naomi's happy little bubble and reveal exactly what kind of crimes her father was caught up in.

"Bubba and I have been talking to the guys in Nashville," Veda said. "We all want you to move back there for a while. At least until things calm down."

"And what could I possibly do in Nashville?" I asked. "Go back to managing the Flaming Outhouses and chasing off groupies?"

During the years that I had lived in Nashville, I had managed a run-of-the-mill country band and sang backup vocals for them. Bubba, along with his brother, two of our cousins, and the older of my two half-brothers made up the band. When I wasn't at work for the Nashville Crime Scene Investigation Section, most of my time was spent either keeping the guys from doing something stupid or chasing off the pack of groupies that seemed to follow the band everywhere. I hadn't exactly hated it, but I hadn't enjoyed it either.

"I don't know," Veda said as she sprayed half a can of hairspray around my teased-out hair. "Get your old job back as a crime scene investigator. I'm sure they'd hire you again. Or take over lead vocals for the Flaming Outhouses. You're a better singer than Andrew. Either way … just get out of Wyatt County for a while."

"I'm not going back to Nashville. There's nothing for me there," I said as I waved away the cloud of hairspray. "Can you just trust me when I say that everything is going to be fine?"

"No. I have this gut feeling that something bad is going to happen."

"So do I," Naomi said.

"You're not the only ones," my cousin, Tate Shatner said. Tate was Naomi's older brother, and he was one of the handful of Shatners who I knew was not involved in the family's illegal activities. "You should just quit while you're ahead, Carrie."

"I didn't realize I was ahead."

"Because you ain't. In fact, you're behind. If this were a NASCAR race, you'd be about ten laps down with a busted-up car," Tate said. "Way I see it, you're like that Sissy Puss guy."

"Who?" Veda, Naomi, and I asked.

"You know . . . that super-old dude who's stuck trying to push a boulder uphill for eternity. Every time he gets to the top, the darn thing rolls back down on him."

"You mean Sisyphus?" I asked, referring to the figure from Greek mythology.

"Yeah. Ain't that what I said?" Tate asked as Naomi used the air-brush to spray black paint around his eyes. He was dressed in a leather tunic and carried an executioner's hood and axe. "Besides, it's weird having you in charge. I mean, you've spent the past four years trying to shut us down—"

"No, I've spent the past four years trying to keep y'all out of jail."

"And you did a surprisingly good job at it. But it's hard for any-one to trust you when you go from trying to shut us down to running things," Tate said. He opened his eyes just as Naomi sprayed an alcohol-based sealing agent to the makeup. Tate hissed and frantically waved his hands in front of his now watering eyes. "Take it from someone who's never been involved in the family business but knows enough about it . . . Those that are involved ain't ever gonna take you seriously. Our grandparents' generation sure as hell ain't gonna listen to you. And our parents' generation won't listen to you either. They're all stuck in their own ways, and they won't take too kindly to you messing with their system. They know way more than you could ever hope to learn. So why should they take you seriously? And our generation don't want you involved since you've been lecturing us to stay out of the family business since we was in grade school. Way I see it, the older genera-tions are too far gone, Carrie. Forget about saving them. Focus on the kids. Try to keep them from making the same mistakes that their par-ents and grandparents have been making."

"Amen to that," Veda said.

"I'll do my best," I promised Tate.

"Sometimes our best isn't enough," Tate said.

Somewhere nearby, a radio crackled and then Uncle Elvin announced that Camp Quarantine was now open and that he was about to send out the first hayride wagon.

"Got to go," I said.

"We are not done with this conversation," Veda said.

"I know. To be continued."

I slipped out of the chair, grabbed my backpack and thermos, and headed for the door. On my way out of the makeup trailer, I paused by the floor-to-ceiling mirror to check out what Veda and Naomi had done to me. Veda had teased my naturally curly brown hair out to Texas-sized proportions, and she'd streaked faux blood through it. Slashing across my forehead were claw marks made from silicon. Naomi had enhanced the claw marks with makeup and faux blood. It looked like I had been in a fight with either a bobcat or Bigfoot—both of which were native to Eastern Texas. Okay, so no one has been able to prove Bigfoot's presence in East Texas, but I know what I saw when I was a kid.

The sun had set while I was in the makeup trailer, and I had to use the flashlight on my phone to light up the narrow path down to Moonshiners' Grove. A thick layer of fog that was produced by the strategically placed fog machines drifted between the trees.

Emerging from the trees and the fog, I glanced around my scene. My half-brother Elijah Song Patterson was seated on the front porch of our shack. He was the younger of my two half-brothers. When I was a teenager, my dad had an affair with my oldest sister's best friend. Elijah was the result of that affair.

Sitting alongside Elijah were my second cousins Cletus and Festus Devereux. Their maternal grandfather, James Bowie Shatner, was my granddaddy's younger brother. Bowie's daughter Margaret had married Catfish's son Kinky. Both Festus and Cletus were involved in selling the moonshine and marijuana. Cletus had been doing it since he was a teenager. Festus had only recently gotten involved when his wife encouraged him to get a second job. Jolene had realized that their daughter's diapers and clothing were expensive, and that Festus wasn't making enough money as a landscaper to afford all of their bills.

Elijah and Festus were both dressed in distressed NASCAR shirts and jeans. Cletus had on tattered overalls that showed off his narrow, hairless chest. Their makeup made it look like they'd just got finished fighting each other over the last piece of possum pie.

Across the path from the shack was a moonshine still, an outhouse, and a rusted-out 1950s Ford F-1 farm truck. The old truck was up on cinderblocks, the frame was twisted from a long-ago accident, and the windshield was a spiderweb of cracks.

"Thank God, you're here!" Elijah jumped off the porch and gave me a hug. It was a rare show of affection from the fifteen-year-old. "Why didn't you tell us you were running late."

"Because I was busy."

"We'll, we've got some bad news," Festus said as he tucked his long blonde hair up underneath a ratty coonskin cap. He then handed me a sawed-off shotgun. "Billy Bob ain't here. You're gonna have to run the show."

My cousin-by-marriage, Billy Bob Lawrence—known as Pappy Moonshine—was supposed to be the person who came busting out of the shack to start the show. He was a lot louder than me, and his voice was much deeper. And, at two-hundred pounds, he was considerably bulkier and more menacing looking than me.

"Is Billy Bob planning to show up?" I asked.

"He better," Elijah said. "Nothing against you, Carrie, but Billy Bob is scarier than you. Not that you ain't scary. He's just more intimidating. Plus, your voice ain't gonna last all night."

"I'm aware my voice won't last all night." Turning to Festus, I said. "If Billy Bob doesn't show up, you'll have to take over for me when I lose my voice."

On a slow night, when there were lengthy gaps been wagons, I could run the show from start to finish without a problem. But, when the wagons were coming back-to-back with roughly two to two-and-a-half minutes in between, it wouldn't be long before I lost my voice.

"I just hope Billy Bob didn't get busted," Festus said.

"Busted doing what?" I asked as I jammed the first of three shells into the shotgun. "What is Billy Bob up to?"

"Makin' a moonshine delivery," Festus said. "I figured you knew."

"No, I didn't know. How am I supposed to know what's going on with this family when no one tells me anything?" I asked.

As far as I knew, Billy Bob was only involved in the family's moonshine business. He helped his father-in-law—my uncle Delmar—with brewing, bottling, and selling the moonshine. Like Festus, I could only hope that Billy Bob didn't get caught, because, if he did, I'd get the phone call in which I would be encouraged to use my position with the sheriff's department to help get him out of trouble.

In the distance, a diesel engine revved as a tractor slowly made its way down the rutted dirt path towards us. I glanced towards where the sound was coming from. Our small clearing was dimly lit by firelight and whatever weak light from the three-quarter moon managed to filter through the leaves and the thick strands of Spanish moss that hung from the surrounding trees. Between the lack of light and the dense fog, I couldn't see more than a few feet down the path.

"Get in your hiding spots before they see us," Elijah hissed before he darted to the other side of the path and climbed into the bed of the truck.

Cletus ducked behind the moonshine still, and Festus gave me a cheeky salute before disappearing into the outhouse that was next to the truck. The outhouse was nonfunctional, but it was a crappy hiding spot since it was cramped, dirty, and inhabited by bugs and mice.

Grabbing my stuff, I headed into the rundown shack that had been thrown together out of scrap wood and sheets of rusty metal. As far as hiding spots go, the shack was obvious. Anyone with even a small amount of common sense would assume that someone would be hiding in the shack—but would they expect that person to have a sawed-off shotgun or that person to be a petite woman who physically didn't look all that intimidating? Despite the shack being an obvious hiding spot, the shotgun had an element of surprise.

"Here we go. I got this. I got this. I got this."

A surge of adrenaline flooded my body and shot out to all my nerve endings. I hated feeling this nervous. I squeezed my eyes shut, sucked in a deep breath, and willed myself to calm down. I had done this a few hundred times before. Make that a few thousand times. But I always had a stomach full of butterflies before the first wagon.

With one hand, I grasped the door handle. With the other, I held the shotgun propped on my hip. I waited until I heard the tractor's engine throttle down before I threw my weight against the door and shoved it open. The door slammed against the side of the shack with a *bang!* As I stepped through the open doorway and onto the porch, I swung the shotgun up to my shoulder.

"Y'all got a lot of nerve trespassing on my land!" With my left hand, I yanked back on the shotgun's forearm. The shotgun made a loud, definitive click as the first round was chambered. I then pulled the trigger and fired the shotgun harmlessly above the customer's heads. "Consider that your warning shot."

"Holy shit! They're shooting at us," shouted a guy who looked big enough to play guard for the Dallas Cowboys. He dove face-first into the straw that was spread out on the bottom of the flatbed farm wagon.

The wagon was hooked up to the back of the tractor. "Get us out of here, Mr. Tractor Driver."

Welcome to Moonshiners' Grove, I thought as I bit down on my lip to keep from laughing. *Thanks for coming on the haunted hayride.*

There were forty-five to fifty people packed into the wagon, and all of them reacted differently to my sudden appearance followed by the gunshot. A couple people laughed, and some cheered. Most of the people screamed.

Even though I have worked as a haunt actor since I was a teenager, scaring people has yet to get old. I especially love scaring "tough guys" who are twice my size. Hearing their screams makes me smile.

"Now which one of y'all wants to stick around for dinner?" I yelled.

"Whatcha having?" asked a teenage boy near the back of the wagon.

"Deep fried trespassers." I chambered the second round and then fired another shot into the air. "Find Mama a tasty one, boys. We're eating good tonight."

On the other side of the wagon, Festus kicked open the outhouse door and fired his rifle. "Meals on Wheels, boys! Come and get it!"

Over top of the wagon, I watched Elijah scramble out of the back of the old farm truck and Cletus come barreling out from behind the moonshine still.

Elijah, Cletus, Festus, and I leaped onto the wagon's running boards at about the same time. Over the customer's screams, I could hear my cohorts using skit lines that were meant to either terrify the customers or make them laugh.

"Your head's gonna look real nice hanging above my fireplace," I whispered in the ear of a cowering, middle-aged woman. I moved over to a giggling young boy and said, "I bet you'll taste real good with mashed potatoes and gravy."

The tractor driver revved the engine, signaling to us that he was about to pull out of our scene. I jumped off the side of the wagon before it jerked forward. I then grabbed my discarded shotgun off the porch and fired the third round just as the wagon pulled away.

"Off my land!"

The boys and I lingered in the path and stared menacingly after the wagon as it disappeared into the thick haze at the far edge of the clearing.

"One wagon down." Elijah pulled his cell phone out of his jeans pocket and held it up. The screen illuminated his makeup covered face.

"Mom says that the queue lines for all four attractions are packed. And the line at the ticket booth is out into the parking lot."

Elijah's mom, Shelia Patterson, worked at the Body Farm as a ticket taker. Nightly she kept us informed on the length of the queue lines.

"It's going to be a long night, boys," I said. "Conserve your energy and stay hydrated."

Leaving the boys standing in the middle of the path, I headed towards the shack. I needed to reload the shotgun before the next set of "trespassers" arrived.

I had just enough time to load the gun and send Billy Bob a text message asking where he was before the second tractor of the night pulled up to the shack and I had to go through the act a second time . . . and then a third . . .

Every two minutes, a tractor would pull into the clearing, and I would burst out of the shack with the shotgun. I tried to change things up each time, otherwise it became monotonous. I would also play off what the customers yelled at me.

Finally, after what was probably the twentieth wagon of the night, a 'yee-yee' heralded Billy Bob's arrival. I found the light switch and turned on the single bulb that dangled from the ceiling. The interior of the shack was dirty and mostly empty aside from a ratty recliner—but it's not like anyone lived there, so there was really no point in sprucing the place up. I swung open the door and Billy Bob barreled inside.

"Where have you been?" I asked.

"Ain't none of your business," Billy Bob said as he yanked his costume out of his bag.

"It is my business if you were breaking the law."

"You ain't the boss of me."

"Oh, yes, I am." I jabbed Billy Bob in his flabby stomach with the barrel of the shotgun. "I'm the one running this family now. You need to get used to it and start listening to me."

Billy Bob snorted in response.

"How am I supposed to protect y'all if you don't tell me what you're doing?"

Instead of answering, Billy Bob asked, "You gonna take care of that wagon? Because I don't think anyone wants to see me out there in my underwear."

"Yeah, yeah, yeah," I mumbled. I had been so caught up in arguing with Billy Bob that I failed to notice another tractor was pulling into the clearing. "We are not done talking."

"You might not be. But I am." Billy Bob reached around me and turned off the light. He then shoved open the shack's door. "Now git."

"I thought I told them to stop bringin' y'all onto my land," I yelled as I stepped out onto the porch. I then fired the shotgun, causing a teenage girl to burst into tears. "I guess your tractor driver don't read so good since he missed the sign about trespassers gettin' shot in these parts."

Billy Bob came out to stand next to me on the porch. "Y'all got a lot of nerve coming 'round here and interrupting me making babies with my cousin."

Apparently, Billy Bob had changed his mind about showing off his camouflage print boxers. Over them he had on a ratty tank top and a sleeveless flannel shirt. Since he hadn't had a chance to get makeup, he'd opted to pour fake blood over his head. The viscous liquid was slowly rolling down his forehead and cheeks. His brown hair and beard would be a sticky, matted mess by the end of the night.

I followed Billy Bob off the porch and headed for a young man who was screaming hysterically and begging the tractor driver to get him out of there.

After the wagon pulled out of Moonshiners' Grove, I held out the shotgun to Billy Bob. "In the future, you need to run everything by me first. If you want to run product, then you need to tell me when and where beforehand."

"You know, this ain't my first rodeo, Carrie. I've been running moonshine for Delmar since I started dating Ellie May back in high school. You're the newbie at this. Not me." Billy Bob grabbed the shotgun, but I refused to let go. He took a step closer to me, and, since he wasn't any taller than me, we were nose to nose. "Besides, Houston knew what I was doing."

"Houston isn't in charge anymore. I am."

Without responding, Billy Bob yanked the gun out of my hands. He then went in the shack and slammed the door.

"Lose the battle," I whispered as I fought the urge to go after Billy Bob. "Win the war."

I went over to my hiding spot—which wasn't really a hiding spot considering I would be sitting in a rocking chair on the porch. I would be in full view of the customers as the tractor drove into the scene. I had just enough time to grab an empty whiskey bottle before the next tractor arrived. I slumped over in the rocking chair as if I were passed out drunk. A couple of customers yelled at me, but I didn't react until Billy Bob kicked open the shack door. Then I jumped up and fumbled with the whiskey bottle.

"What in the name of cousin kissing, NASCAR watching, moonshine brewing, Walmart shopping, cornbread eating, pickup truck driving, 'hell yeah' yelling, shotgun toting, y'all better not be fans of that polished pop country crap do y'all think you're doing trespassing on my land?" Billy Bob rattled off before firing the shotgun. He then turned to me. "And you, woman! What in tarnation do you think you're doing letting these varmints on our land? Are you drunk?"

"Only a little," I slurred, causing a few of the customers to laugh.

"Typical no-good woman," Billy Bob said. "Drinking our assets when she should be inside making me a sandwich and minding her own damn business."

Sure, it was one of the skit lines that we had come up with for Moonshiners. But I had a feeling that this time Billy Bob meant it personally.

I knew that most of the Shatners were not happy that I was now in charge—and I was about to be up Shit Creek without a paddle if they didn't start listening to me.

The problem was that—thanks to their various crimes—almost the entire Shatner family was already up Shit Creek. They had no idea where they were headed, they'd long ago lost the paddle, and the dilapidated boat was taking on water faster than we could bale it out.

I was the closest thing my family had to a lifeboat, however.

CHAPTER THREE

"**L**AST TRACTOR IS IN THE PATH," my cousin Bubba McCarty announced just before two o'clock in the morning. He'd parked his mud-spattered four-wheeler in front of the Moonshiners' shack and sat slumped over the handlebars.

"Hallelujah," I muttered as I collapsed on the edge of the porch. "It's been a long night."

The first wagon had rolled out around six-thirty, and it had been almost nonstop since then. That was over seven hours ago. On busy nights, the hayride averaged a wagon every two to two-and-a-half minutes. We had hit over two hundred wagons since we'd started.

I was physically and mentally exhausted. My entire body ached—though my knees and ankles were the worst. Mama Moonshine had been moving at half speed and with a pronounced limp for the past two hours. My voice was shot, and I was also hungry. I would never admit it out loud, but I was getting too old for these shenanigans. Maybe next year I'd retire from acting and go take tickets or something.

At least all the screaming, running around, and scaring people had worked off most of my stress and aggravation.

"You think you had a rough night?" Bubba lifted his head long enough to glare at me. "At least all you had to do was act. You have no idea how hard it is to keep this place running smoothly. I don't know how my dad's done it for the past fifteen years. I've been dealing with problems almost non-stop since we opened."

"What happened aside from the garage door coming off the track at

Psych Ward?" Elijah asked, referring to the incident that had shut down the hayride for almost fifteen-minutes.

"Figures it had to be the exit door that came off the track. And there was a wagon in the barn when it happened. But we got the door muscled back on," Bubba said as he held up one of his arms to show off his over-developed muscles. "But a drive shaft broke on a tractor, and we had a flat tire on another. We put on a fresh tire while we were loading the wagon. I had to break up a brawl in the hayride queue line. One of my actors in the Haunted Mine broke a finger. Cooter Devereux spit his dentures out into a customer's lap. Some idiot stood up in the wagon and ripped one of the dolls out of the trees in Doll Forest. The werewolf animatronic kept malfunctioning. I lost count of how many times I had to fix it throughout the night. And I had to break up a cat fight between two teenage girls in the Witch Coven."

"Let me guess . . ." I said. "They were fighting over a guy?"

"And he does not look like he's worth fighting over. The boy didn't just fall out of the ugly tree. He did the hundred-meter dash through the ugly forest and hit every tree on the way through. Twice. It's rare to have an actor who's so ugly he doesn't need a mask or makeup."

"Are you talking about the kid with all the acne?" I asked.

"The one who looks like he's got a case of smallpox?" Bubba asked. "Nah, that kid is over in Camp Quarantine playing an infected camper. But he doesn't need a mask either."

Butting into the conversation, Billy Bob said, "Look on the bright side, Bubba. You didn't have any problems at Moonshiners' Grove. My shotgun worked all night, and Festus's rifle only jammed a few times."

During my four seasons at Moonshiners, we'd had countless problems with our prop guns. Not only did the guns jam and misfire, but the inner spring would also frequently slip out of place. One night we accidently broke off the trigger guard. Another night the gun fell apart in my hands and I had to duct tape it back together.

"I didn't have any physical problems down here," Bubba said. "But multiple customers claimed that you were saying 'offensive' stuff, Billy Bob. How many times do my dad and I have to tell you that Carrie is the only one who can threaten to take the customers out back and make them call her 'daddy'?"

"Yeah, Billy Bob. Stop stealing my line," I said.

"It's scarier when I say it," Billy Bob said.

"But it upsets people," Bubba said.

"And it excites some people when Carrie says it," Billy Bob argued. "Tonight, we had a guy try to get out of the wagon and follow her. Cletus and I had to shove him back in."

Bubba rolled his eyes. "The drunks were also out in full force. Three intoxicated customers tried to start fights with my actors in the cemetery. Two drunks fell out of the wagon at unloading. One went head-first over the side, and the other one rolled down the steps at the back of the wagon. My actors over in the alien abduction scene took a bottle of whiskey from a customer. Another drunk lost his shoe in the wagon and was wandering around without it for at least two hours before he went over to the ticket booth to claim it."

"How drunk do you have to be to not realize you're missing a shoe?" Elijah asked.

Bubba shrugged. "But those are just problems I had to deal with on the hayride. Both haunted houses, the trail, and the entertainment area had their own issues. Not to mention I had to help the parking lot staff chase off people from Calvary Baptist again. They were going around sticking pamphlets for Hell House under the windshield wipers of every car in the lot."

Calvary was an Independent Baptist church that followed strictly fundamentalist and conservative beliefs. They believed that Halloween was about Devil worshipping, and they were vehemently against the Body Farm because they believed it promoted Satanism. For close to ten years—starting in the late-1990s and continuing until the mid-2000s—Calvary Baptist Church put on their own version of a haunted house every year on the weekend either before or after Halloween. Like the haunted attractions at the Body Farm, Hell House was meant to terrify the patrons. Unlike the Body Farm, Hell House focused on real life situations like the consequences of drinking and driving and the seven deadly sins. Even though the main goal of everyone at the Body Farm was to scare the customers, we wanted them to ultimately have a good time and leave with a smile on their face. Calvary Baptist's main goal was to terrify people with the threat of eternal damnation, and then save their souls.

"I can't believe Calvary Baptist started that up again," I said. The last time they had put together a Hell House was when I was sixteen.

"Maybe someone needs to vandalize Hell House like back when we were kids," Bubba said as he gave me a very pointed look.

"Good times. Good times." Billy Bob nudged me in the side. "Maybe we should get the band back together and relive our youth."

"Absolutely not. That was kids' stuff. We're adults now." I smacked Billy Bob upside his head. I then turned to Bubba and said, "Don't let your dad hear you complaining. He'll just lecture you about how this was a normal night and then bore you to death with stories about all of the problems that he's had to deal with over the years."

"Yeah, yeah, yeah . . . I know I really don't have anything to complain about. No one pretended to go into labor because she wanted to get off the hayride. No one was seriously injured. And nothing was too severely damaged. Knock on wood." Bubba pulled off his baseball cap and then rapped his knuckles against the side of his head. "But I did have to deal with Wesley, Waylon, and Hank. And I am going to complain about those dumbasses."

"Oh, no. What kind of trouble did the Three Stooges get in to?" I asked, using the nickname I had bestowed on my cousins and their friend.

Hank Garrett the Third was the latest person that Wesley had drawn into helping him break the law—not that Hank hadn't already been committing crimes on his own prior to teaming up with Wesley. Hank was one of Ophelia Palmer's grandchildren. Like me, he was descended from a long line of criminals and their feloniously-inclined DNA flowed through his veins.

"I caught them selling moonshine, pot, and other drugs at the ring toss game up in the entertainment area. Wes told me he's been doing it all season," Bubba said. His neck muscles tightened, and a vein by his temple pulsed. "I was so mad I could have kicked their butts across the entertainment area and back. But there were too many witnesses. Instead, I confiscated what they had and sent them back to work."

"Whatever happened to don't shit where you eat?" I asked rhetorically.

One of the Shatner family's main rules was that we were not to jeopardize any of the family's legitimate businesses—such as the Body Farm—with criminal activities. The legal and the illegal were to be kept separate—not that Wesley and Waylon were the first Shatners to break the rule. Recently, a lot of Shatners, Devereuxs, and Palmers had been breaking the rule.

I pulled my cell phone out of my pocket and fired off a text message to Wesley.

"WTF Wes?!?!? R u kidding me? Selling f'n drugs from the game stand? What the hell is wrong with u? I've had about all I can take of ur BS. If u don't knock this shit off, I'm gonna make u stop. And ur not gonna like what I do to u."

Wesley's response—which was made up of a string of laughing smiley faces—was almost immediate.

"Carrie, you need to do something about the three of them," Bubba said.

"I'll talk to them."

Bubba sighed. "Carrie, talking ain't gonna get anywhere with Wes. You've been 'talking' to him for the past four years, and it's accomplished nothing. It's about as productive as beating a dead horse. No matter what you say to him, Wes keeps doing stupid stuff. And Waylon and Hank just follow his lead. It's time you did something about the three of them. Before they piss off the wrong person and it ends badly for them."

"What do you want me to do, Bubba? Arrest them?" I asked. "I've tried that, but, every time I do, Uncle Murph just lets them go or cancels the arrest warrants."

Wesley's and Waylon's father, Woodrow, was Uncle Murph's younger brother. My great-uncle Bowie was Murph's and Woody's father. Uncle Murph might be tired of cleaning up after his nephews—he'd told me so repeatedly—but he would continue to do it out of misguided family obligation.

"I think you should just leave the boys alone," Billy Bob said. "The reason Wes is getting more reckless lately is because you keep chasing him down and forcing him to move his set-up somewhere else. If you just left the boys alone, they probably wouldn't be a problem."

"That's a load of bull crap," Festus said to Billy Bob. "I'm with Bubba. Wes and Waylon are a liability."

Cletus raised his hand. "Yo, they needs to go."

"And we ain't the only ones who think that," Festus said. "Some of us have been talking, and we all want Wesley to either knock it off or go away."

"Y'all need a lesson in family loyalty. Heck, I ain't even related to y'all by blood, but I've got more loyalty to this family than y'all do combined," Billy Bob said before he went into the shack and slammed the door.

"No, what Wes needs is a lesson in how not to be an idiot," Bubba muttered. He then looked over at me and said, "Carrie, promise me you'll do something about the Wes situation. Aside from talk to him."

"I'll do what I can," I said.

Dealing with Wesley was like a never-ending game of Whack-A-Mole. I would shut him down in one place, but he would just pop back up somewhere else.

The sounds of whirring chainsaws and people screaming warned us that the final wagon of the night was in Slaughterhouse.

"Shut everything down and lock up when you're done," Bubba said before he fired the engine on the four-wheeler and sped off down the path.

"All right, boys. Last wagon. Then we can get out of here," I said before I climbed onto the porch and collapsed into my rocking chair.

We hit the final wagon of the night with a lot less energy and enthusiasm than we had when the first wagon came through almost eight hours earlier.

Leaving Billy Bob, Festus, and Cletus to shut down the power, the fog machines, and the propane tank that fed the fire under the still, Elijah and I grabbed our bags and then trudged up the dark path to the final scene on the hayride.

Ever since the Hayride of Nightmares first opened, Torture had been the final scene. The original Torture scene had been a guillotine set up on a platform. An executioner would pretend to chop off a victim's head while other victims tried to escape the cages and shackles. After a couple years, Uncle Elvin put up a prefabricated metal building with garage doors at each end. Around the outside of the building, Uncle Elvin and his crew had constructed a faux stone façade that resembled a micro-sized medieval castle. Six-foot-tall pikes that were topped with mannequin heads lined the path to up to the Torture barn, and cages with rotting skeletons hung on either side of the doorway. Inside the building were stages that ran the length of each side.

Just after the last wagon pulled out of the Torture scene, Elijah and I walked in. I looked around the dimly lit building and spotted my cousin Ellie May climbing out of the cage that she had spent the night "trapped" in.

"Did you know your husband was delivering moonshine tonight?"

"Of course, I knew. Daddy and Billy Bob tell me about everything that's going on," Ellie May said as she jumped off the three-foot high stage. Her voice was hoarse from a night spent screaming and rattling the bars on the cage. Her shoulder-length brown hair was hidden by a long, black wig, and she was dressed in a French Revolution-era peasant costume.

"Is there a reason no one bothered to tell me?" I pounded my fist against my thigh and fought the urge to scream. I was aggravated with most of my family members, but I didn't want to take it out on Ellie May. Sure, she was probably guilty of something, but she hadn't been directly involved in her husband's latest criminal endeavor. "I'm supposed to be in charge, but it seems like I'm the only one who never knows what's going on."

"If it makes you feel any better, I didn't know what Billy Bob was up to," Elijah said.

"And I don't want you to know because I don't want you involved in the family's crimes," I said to my half-brother. Recently, some of the Shatners had tried to draw him in to their illegal activities. "If I find out you're involved—"

Interrupting, Elijah said, "Mom would kill me before you got a chance to."

"You got that right," I said to Elijah. I then turned to Ellie May and asked, "Is there a reason Billy Bob didn't feel the need to inform me of what he was doing?"

"Because he doesn't need a babysitter. Plus, Billy Bob says you have no idea what you're doing. That's why he and most of the family don't trust you," Ellie May said. "You can't just go from constantly telling us to stop breaking the law to suddenly helping us do it. You keep demanding the family's trust and respect instead of doing something to earn it."

"Regardless of how everyone feels about me, I am in charge now. I need to know what's going on," I said.

"Whatever. I'll say something to Billy Bob, but I can't promise that he'll listen." As Ellie May headed over to the other side of the Torture barn to join her husband, she called over her shoulder, "I don't know why Gramps put you in charge and not my daddy like he and Aunt Emily Morgan always said they would. My daddy would know what he's doing. And everyone would listen to him because they trust him. Unlike you."

"Ellie May makes a good point," Elijah said. "The family trusts Uncle Delmar. And they don't trust you. And you really haven't given them a reason to."

"I'm aware, Elijah," I said.

I hated being lectured to by someone who was half my age—even if he was my brother. What I hated even more was that Elijah was right.

Elijah gave me a quick hug before darting off to join a group of teenagers who had straggled in from the other hayride scenes. The Torture barn was quickly filling up with exhausted actors and actresses. Some of them had already changed into their street clothes while others had yet to take off their costumes or masks.

"All right everyone, listen up," Bubba shouted as he climbed up onto one of the stages.

Every night, after each attraction shut down, Bubba had a meeting with that attraction's actors. Uncle Elvin had done the same thing. Bubba was not as taciturn as his father, and the length of his meetings tended to test everyone's patience.

Bubba took up a stance next to the guillotine. Also on stage was a cage and the Iron Maiden. When activated, the Iron Maiden would rock back and forth. Inside was a speaker that emitted screams and howls of pain. On the opposite side of the barn was another stage featuring a second cage, a pillory, and the torture device known as the rack. The rack was tilted almost straight up so that the customers could see the animatronic dummy that was stretched out between the four corner posts. The dummy got pulled apart at the arm and leg joints countless times a night. When the lights were low, the dummy could be mistaken for a real person. In daylight, the dummy was laughably fake.

Above us, seven mannequins hung from the ceiling. All of them were severed in half at the waist, and rubber entrails hung from the torsos.

"It's been a long night, and I know y'all want to get out of here before what's left of Hurricane Nestor hits. But we've got some stuff to talk about," Bubba said.

Hurricane Nestor had struck the Texas Coast near Corpus Christie earlier in the day. She had been a Category One hurricane when she made landfall. Upon making landfall, Nestor had dropped down to a tropical storm and broke apart without causing too much damage aside from some flooding. As Nestor broke apart, part of the storm curved towards the northeast and headed for East Texas. Local meteorologists predicted that the line of storm cells would hit Wyatt County between three and four in the morning.

"I don't have time for this," I said to myself before I hustled out of the Torture barn. I couldn't imagine that Bubba had anything all that important to say—and, even if he did, I doubted it would directly affect me.

Around the side of the Torture barn was a path that led to the costume barn and the makeup trailer. Walking into the makeup trailer, I caught sight of my reflection in the floor-to-ceiling mirror that hung just inside the trailer's door. My costume had acquired some new rips and stains throughout the night, my hair was a tangled and sticky mess, and the fake bruises and contouring that Naomi had flawlessly applied using an airbrush and sponges was now a sweat-streaked, flakey mess. One of my silicon slash marks had also peeled off sometime during the night. Overall, it was not an attractive look.

"No wonder the customers kept screaming when they saw me," I mumbled to myself. "I look like I just walked out of someone's nightmare."

"That you, Carrie?"

I spun around and came face-to-face with a zombified Buffalo Bill. Uncle Elvin was dressed in an Old West-style costume and his face had been painted to resemble a zombie. Now that he was no longer running the Body Farm, Uncle Elvin had decided to take up acting. He roamed the entertainment area throughout the night.

"My boys call me 'Mama.' But I'll make you call me 'daddy.'"

"Ha ha. You're *so* funny." Uncle Elvin smirked. "You hear about Wes and Waylon?"

"Yeah, I heard."

"What are you gonna do about them? I can't have them breaking the law around here. They get caught . . . There goes the Body Farm. And I worked too darn hard to make this place what it is for those punks to destroy it by being stupid."

"Do I have to remind you that this place was paid for by dirty money?" I asked. I had recently discovered that the Body Farm had been used to launder the family's dirty money. For all I knew, it was still being used to launder money. Learning that had been a blow, and it continued to sting whenever I thought about it, but I refused to let it ruin any of my good memories of working at the Body Farm. "And I'll deal with Wes and Waylon."

"It's a darn good thing that Bubba caught them and not me," Uncle Elvin said. "I'd have dragged them out behind the woodshed and given them the butt whooping that their daddy should have a long time ago."

Sidestepping around Uncle Elvin, I grabbed two slices of pizza from the boxes that had been set out at one of the makeup stations. "Uncle Woody has always been a softie."

"More like soft in the head," Uncle Elvin said. He ripped off his black cowboy hat and slammed it down onto a chair. "And Wes and Waylon don't need a talking to. Between their parents and now you, they've had enough of those to last a lifetime. What those boys need is some sense beat into them. And, since Emily Morgan ain't around to handle it, I aim to do it."

"First of all, Aunt Emily Morgan would never have gotten her hands dirty. She would have had someone else dole out the can of whoop ass for her," I semi-coherently mumbled around a half-chewed piece of pizza. "Second, you'd probably wind up beating them to death before you managed to beat any sense into them."

"Is that an option?" Uncle Elvin gave me a rare smile. "'Cause it would definitely solve the Wes and Waylon problem."

"Don't tempt me."

"You know, Carrie, the family might take you a little more seriously if you took a few pages out of Emily Morgan's book. No one messed up . . . or they tried real hard not to . . . because they knew there would be consequences. And those consequences were not good." Uncle Elvin winked at me. "You're too diplomatic when it comes to dealing with them. Just do what she did and order everyone around. And if they won't listen, you gotta make them."

"I'll get right on that," I said.

Now two people had told me that I needed to start running the family like my great-aunt had previously done. Maybe it was time I gave it a try. I really had been too soft on them over the past four years. Of course, if I had been a little more forceful four years ago, we might not be in this current predicament.

Uncle Elvin glanced at his watch and groaned. "I better get cleaned up and then go check on my alpacas one more time before the storm hits."

I waved off Uncle Elvin and then grabbed a double-chocolate chip cookie. I had just taken a bite of the cookie when a horde of hayride actors swarmed into the makeup trailer. They fell upon the pizzas and cookies like a pack of starving wild animals.

"Where'd you disappear to?" Bubba asked me as I bumped into him on my way out of the trailer. "I was looking for you at the meeting. You have got to talk some sense into those two lovestruck girls from the Witch Coven. They're still fighting over that boy."

"The season is almost over, Bubba. We've got tomorrow and next Saturday, and then we're done. I say we let the girls fight it out. Heck, knowing how teenage girls are, they'll be in love with someone else by tomorrow," I said. Personally, I was in no mood to deal with squabbling teenagers now or in the future. "And I'll talk to the Three Stooges tomorrow."

"Oh no, you are talking to those dumbasses right now."

Bubba grasped my upper arm and dragged me up the path towards the area where the hayride wagons were unloaded.

"You really want me to go out there looking like this?" I asked. There was a longstanding rule that—aside from the actors who worked there—no one was allowed out in the entertainment area while in costume and makeup.

"It's dead out there. Any customers left are going through the haunted houses or over by the food stands," Bubba said. He shoved aside the wooden gate that had been pulled across the exit of the hayride. "While you deal with them, I'll go shut down Camp Quarantine."

I walked out into the nearly deserted entertainment area and glanced around. To my right, a stage took up the space between the entrance and exit of the hayride. On stage, the band Bubba had hired to perform was packing up their equipment.

On the far side of the hayride's entrance was the Terror of Shadow Manor haunted house. Two years after he started the Hayride of Nightmares, Uncle Elvin transformed an old, three-story barn into a haunted house. Around the outside of the barn, Uncle Elvin constructed a façade that resembled a decaying Southern plantation. The inside of the barn was designed to depict the interior of the house. In the kitchen, the cook served up human flesh and poisoned concoctions. Skeletons dined in the formal dining room, the dolls and other toys came to life in the nursery, and a crazy lady portrayed by Naomi occupied the attic. There were a few customers standing in the queue lines. Once they were through, the Manor would shut down.

Directly across the entertainment area from the hayride was the Body Farm's newest attraction. The Carn-Evil of Chaos—which had opened last season—was housed in a red and white stripped, three-story building that was supposed to look like a circus tent. The entrance to the haunted house was through the mouth of a gigantic clown face. Two tufts of orange hair that resembled devil horns stuck out of the top of the satanic looking clown's head.

To the left of the Carn-Evil was a row of food trucks. Despite it being two in the morning, the food trucks were still dishing out cheeseburgers and funnel cakes.

Tucked in between the Carn-Evil and the Manor was the entrance to Camp Quarantine. The haunted trail took visitors through a recreated summer camp that was overrun with menacing campers and counselors. A trail cut through the camp—passing through and around cabins, tents, the dining hall, campfire areas, the boat shed, a faux cave, and along the shore of a small lake.

I turned to my left and headed for the row of rigged carnival games. The football and basketball games were almost impossible to win. The holes and hoops through which customers attempted to throw the football or basketball were barely bigger than the balls. The balloon bust game was almost always winnable. But the prizes were candy and cheap trinkets.

The Three Stooges worked at the ring toss game. While it was possible to land one of the plastic rings around the top of a glass bottle, it was rare that anyone did. Waylon and Hank were gathering up the scattered plastic rings while Wesley goofed around and flirted with the young woman who ran the balloon bust game.

Wesley and Waylon both had ghostly pale skin and bright red hair. They were tall and scrawny, and neither looked like they would last exceptionally long in a fight. Hank Garrett the Third was short and pudgy. His blonde hair was overdue for a cut, and it hung in his eyes.

"Uh oh, guys. Here comes Carrie to lecture us for the trillionth time," Wesley shouted when he saw me headed his way. He bounced around in some sort of spastic dance and waved his arms around in the air. "Better cover your ears before she talks them off."

I rolled my eyes. "Good. You know why I'm here—"

"Yeah, Bubba tattled on us," Wesley said. "So now you gotta yell at us."

"Then we can skip the preamble."

"Just get on with it. Ain't like you're gonna do anything other than lecture."

I don't know what came over me—either I'd finally had all I could take of Wesley's arrogance or Emily Morgan's ghost possessed me—but I reached up and slapped Wesley across the face. His green eyes widened in shock.

Aside from smacking certain family members upside the head, I'd never gotten violent with any of them. Okay, that's not quite true. I've smacked Bubba around on multiple occasions. But that's because he excels at pushing all of my buttons. My intention had never been to hurt Bubba—but I wanted to hurt Wesley. I wanted to hurt him badly. Wesley was the only other one of my family members who pushed all my buttons, and he constantly jabbed those buttons on purpose. Recently, just hearing Wesley's name made my blood boil. Looking at his smug face . . . well, I figured someone had to wipe the haughty expression away.

"What the fu—"

"Enough." I grabbed Wesley's wrist and yanked it behind his back. I then threw myself against him and shoved him up against the front of the ring toss game. I pulled his arm upward, forcing him to bend over the counter. I then leaned against his back and held him down. "At what point did you think selling moonshine and drugs at the game stand was a good idea?"

"It was a perfectly good idea until I got caught," Wesley mumbled.

"Y'all aren't supposed to be breaking the law at the Body Farm. What if someone other than Bubba had caught you? Not only would you have gotten into trouble, you would have put the Body Farm at risk," I hissed in Wesley's ear. I then looked over at Waylon and Hank. Waylon was clinging to one of the oversized stuffed animals, while Hank ducked down behind the bottles. "You boys have anything to say for yourselves?"

"I . . . I told Wes it was a . . . a bad idea," Waylon stuttered.

"Shut up, Waylon!" Wesley snapped as he struggled to get away from me. "No one forced you to help."

Hank peeked at me over the tops of the bottles. "I'm real sorry, Detective Carrie. We won't sell nothing at the Body Farm ever again. We all knew we was being stupid, ma'am. But Wes figured with all the customers coming through, it was an easy way to sell product and make some money."

"We were making at least a grand a night since opening weekend," Wesley added. "Probably would have cleared five grand tonight had Bubba not stopped us."

"You boys are done selling. Period," I said in a voice that sounded deadly serious. I pushed away from Wesley and allowed him to stand up. His left cheek was chafed from the rough wood countertop. "As of now, you are done. No more breaking the law. You're too obvious about it, and you've been caught way too many times. Y'all's stupidity is going to get the rest of the Shatners, Devereuxs, and Palmers in trouble. You're going to screw up and bring the law down on all of us."

What none of them realized was that they already had.

"I don't gotta listen to you, Carrie. And you ain't gonna make me," Wesley said. He flipped me the middle finger before vaulting over the counter of the ring toss game. He grabbed Waylon and Hank by the arms and dragged them out the back of the stand. "I do what I want!"

"Oh, I'll figure out a way to make you behave, Wesley . . ."

CHAPTER FOUR

IT FELT LIKE MY HEAD—ALONG WITH MY FRESHLY WASHED and conditioned hair—had just hit the pillow when the severe weather alert siren on my phone went off and just about scared the living daylights out of me and my pets. Either Wyatt County was in for another round of bad weather or Uncle Houston was calling me. Neither option was all that appealing.

I pushed Manny, my chubby orange cat, away from my head so that I could sit up. My four-year-old dog, Molly, rolled across my legs and then jumped off the bed.

"I guess Uncle Houston is better than a tornado," I muttered after I fumbled around on my nightstand and grabbed my phone. The damage that Uncle Houston could cause usually wasn't as far-reaching or destructive as a tornado. "What do you want?"

"Is that any way to greet your favorite uncle?"

"No, I'm much nicer to my favorite uncle," I said. I was so tired, and my brain was so fogged, that I had to give it some serious thought to determine if I even had a favorite uncle. By default, Uncle Elvin came in first place since I genuinely liked him—which was more than I could say for a lot of my other family members. He also wasn't actively involved in any crimes—unlike the rest of my uncles. "And my favorite uncle would have the courtesy not to wake me up this early in the morning unless it was for an emergency. Is this an emergency? Did something happen during the storm?"

What was left of Tropical Storm Nestor had hit Wyatt County not long after I got home around three o'clock in the morning. I had slept through the worst of it, but, if the drumming sound on the roof was any indication, it was still raining.

"No. Far as I know, everyone is fine," Uncle Houston said. "But I need you to come out to my house right now. We're going on a field trip."

"Can't this wait?" I was having trouble keeping my eyes open. "It's six o'clock in the morning. I need more than two hours of sleep."

"Oh, I guess it can wait until another day," Uncle Houston said. His tone of voice conveyed his annoyance with me. "But, by then, your aunts, uncles, and cousins might change their minds and decide they don't want to show you the moonshine stills and the bomb shelters. This could be a one-time opportunity, Carrie, and I wouldn't want you to miss out on it because you need your beauty sleep."

I punched my pillow in frustration.

"I'm on my way," I said before I hung up.

I rolled out of bed, threw on a sweatshirt and jeans, and then stumbled down the dark hallway after Molly. Manny—who was the smartest of the three of us—had elected to stay in bed. Knowing him, he'd spend the whole day sleeping and then be up all night running around the house and driving me nuts.

My house is the same one that I had lived in from the day my parents brought me home from the hospital until I was almost seventeen. It was haunted with bad memories from my childhood. My mom was an alcoholic who had spent more time drunk than sober. My dad had rarely been around. When he wasn't covering up the family's crimes or at work at the sheriff's department, Dad could usually be found with one of his many girlfriends. I had preferred it when Dad stayed away. When he was home, all he and Mom did was scream at each other. My home life might have been more bearable had I gotten along with my two older sisters, but, more often than not, they had shut me out and left me to suffer by myself.

I tried not to think about any of that too much.

At the end of the hallway, I tripped over Molly and then crashed into something blocking the doorway into the kitchen. I screamed before I remembered that I had hauled most of my outdoor Halloween decorations inside prior to the storm. I flipped on the light and came face-to-face with a six-foot-tall T-rex skeleton.

Scooting around the skeleton, I stepped into my kitchen. After making sure that Molly and Manny had food and water, I grabbed something to eat and then headed for my garage where I knocked over a stack of Styrofoam tombstones and was leered at by my life-size Grim Reaper.

In my Jeep, I plugged the auxiliary cable into my phone and then queued up my favorite playlist. Some people used caffeine or drugs as a stimulant; I listened to Pat Green. I figured his music was the only thing powerful enough to keep me awake during the drive. With the music blaring and food in my stomach, I felt ready to face whatever adventure Uncle Houston had planned for me.

My neighborhood was near the eastern border of Wyatt County, and it was surrounded by trees and fields. Typically, it would take me about fifteen minutes to drive to Uncle Houston's house in the northern part of the county. Today it took almost twice as long because I had to detour around a flooded section of roadway and drive around some storm debris. At least the rain was letting up.

I didn't encounter much traffic during my drive. Aside from a couple gas stations and a coffee shop, none of the local businesses were open that early on a Sunday morning. Most of Wyatt County's twelve thousand residents were probably taking advantage of the weekend and sleeping in an extra hour or two. The largest town in Wyatt County was Holler, and about a third of the county's twelve thousand residents lived within the city limits.

The Shatners owned roughly five thousand acres in the northern part of the county. Uncle Elvin's alpaca farm, the Wild West town tourist trap he operated, and the Body Farm took up a third of those eight square miles. The rest of the land was occupied by various Shatners and their businesses—both legal and illegal. Just past the Shady Grove Baptist cemetery was the old barn that housed Guns n' Stuff. Farther up the road was the Wyatt County Animal Shelter that two of my aunts ran. The no-kill animal shelter was meant for dogs, cats, and other small pets, but, over the years, they had taken in everything from horses to a capybara.

Uncle Houston's property was on the eastern side of the two-lane highway that split the Shatner land nearly in half. A "NO TRESPASSING" sign the size of a billboard marked the beginning of his driveway. Similar warning signs were posted all around the edges of the five thousand acres—and the signs weren't just idle warnings. There were booby traps scattered about to snare or harm anyone who was dumb enough to climb over the barbed-wire fencing that encircled almost the entire property. Uncle Houston had also installed security cameras and high-tech surveillance equipment throughout the property to keep an eye out for two-legged intruders.

I drove slowly down the narrow, half-mile dirt road towards Uncle Houston's farmhouse. The hint of sunrise in the east wasn't quite strong enough to penetrate the cloud layer or the thick foliage that surrounded me, and I had to rely on my headlights. On either side of the lane, I could make out the hulking shapes of abandoned cars and piles of junk scattered among the pine trees.

I knew I had reached my destination when I pulled into a small clearing that was lit up by three blindingly bright floodlights that were mounted on the farmhouse, the barn, and another outbuilding. In the middle of the yard was an old Soviet tank. For years, Uncle Houston had sworn that the tank was non-operational. He proved that was a lie almost three years ago when he got drunk and then took the tank out on a joyride. Uncle Houston caused twenty thousand dollars' worth of damage before Uncle Murph was able to get him to stop.

Running around the tank and splashing in mud puddles were Uncle Houston's fifteen hunting dogs and a potbellied pig named Mr. Giggles. They swarmed around me as soon as I climbed out of my Jeep. My jeans and jacket were instantly covered in muddy paw prints.

Granddaddy—who had been standing near the tank along with Houston and Bowie—waded through the pack of dogs and gave me a bear hug. The three brothers all looked similar—except Granddaddy was a lot skinner than Houston and Bowie, he had less hair, and his beard wasn't as bushy. All three of them—as well as their sister and a younger brother who died a long time ago—were named after heroes of the Texas Revolution. Granddaddy's full name was David Crockett Shatner.

Granddaddy had worked for the Wyatt County Sheriff's department most of his adult life, and he had been the sheriff for several years. Like me and Uncle Murph, Granddaddy had used his job to cover up the Shatner family's crimes. He had been more aware of what the family was up to, but he had never really stepped in and tried to stop any of it. It had taken some persuasion—mainly from my grandmother—to convince Granddaddy to accept a deal with the Department of Public Safety. Granddaddy knew more than me about what was currently going on, but he was reluctant to share some of what he knew with me or anyone else. We remained close but working with the DPS continued to cause tension between me and Granddaddy.

After letting go of Granddaddy, I turned to Houston and Bowie and said, "We need to talk about Wesley and Waylon. Did you know they were selling drugs at the Body Farm?"

"I had no idea until Bubba called me last night," Uncle Houston said as he ran his gnarled fingers through his beard. He may resemble Santa Claus with his plump belly and white beard, but Uncle Houston was rarely jolly.

"Neither did I. If I'd known what my grandsons were up to . . ." Uncle Bowie trailed off. He had always been Uncle Houston's lackey, and he most likely wouldn't have done anything to Wesley or Waylon without his older brother telling him what to do.

"Don't worry about the boys, Carrie," Uncle Houston said. "Wes and them ain't gonna be a problem for much longer."

"What's that supposed to mean?"

"Means the boys are becomin' a serious problem. And I plan to take care of it so that they ain't a problem no more," Uncle Houston said ominously. He then slung his arm around my shoulders and roughly pulled me against his side. "What's also becomin' a problem is all these meetings you're having with Beto and the bald man. I hear you met up with them over at George Masters' old lake house yesterday afternoon."

"You spying on me, Uncle Houston?" I asked.

"Just keepin' an eye on you. Same as I do for everyone else," Uncle Houston said. "It was bad enough when you were datin' that Texas Ranger. Now you're spendin' time with that Beto guy—"

"What's going on between me and Beto is none of your business," I said.

"Everything you do is my business, missy," Houston snapped. "And I just don't trust that boy. I'm only tolerating him because you're knockin' boots with him."

Alberto and I were not "knocking boots"—though I was certain that he wanted to. I had nothing against Alberto; I just wasn't interested in him. Even though nothing was going on between me and Alberto, we had led my family to believe that we were in some sort of relationship for the past two months so that they would be more accepting of him.

"You don't have anything to worry about Uncle Houston."

"Oh, yeah? Well, maybe your love life ain't none of my concern. But I want to know who the bald guy is that you and Beto was meetin' with yesterday afternoon."

I bit back a string of swear words. I had told Alberto and Lieutenant

Schmitt from day one that the weekly meetings they insisted on were a bad idea. Just because we had them at out-of-the-way locations didn't make it impossible for someone to follow me.

"He's, uh, the bald guy is a cocaine supplier that Beto knows from when he was in prison," I said, coming up with a lie that I hoped sounded plausible. Lieutenant Schmitt probably wouldn't be too pleased when he found out that I had claimed he was a drug dealer. "Beto wanted me to meet with him to see if we could make a deal to get some of his product."

"You're as bad as Wes. I heard he's been talkin' to other dealers, too." Uncle Houston sighed. "Didn't realize that I also had to remind you that we already got a guy. My guy. Well, he's the Palmers' guy. But they've been doing business with him for years."

"Yeah, well, it doesn't hurt to look for another guy," I snapped. I had met the Palmer's guy a few weeks earlier, and he had given me the creeps by repeatedly hitting on me. "I told you, I don't like El Lobo."

El Lobo—Spanish for The Wolf—was an enigma. He was also wanted by numerous law enforcement agencies throughout parts of southern and eastern Texas, Louisiana, and northern Mexico. No one knew El Lobo's real name, how old he was, or where he had come from. He had no criminal record, but he was linked to half a dozen murders and various other crimes. El Lobo also had ties to the notorious Rio Cartel. According to the rumors, he was either the son or the nephew of the cartel's leader. The Rio Cartel had been smuggling drugs and people back and forth across the border for years. Several law enforcement agencies from the United States and Mexico were working together to stop the Rio Cartel, but, so far, they'd had little success.

"Oh no, we're sticking with El Lobo. We made a deal with him, and we ain't breakin' it," Uncle Houston scolded me. "We can't be switching dealers. You've heard about what happens to people who cross El Lobo."

"Yeah . . . They wind up dead or missing." A shiver ran up my spine as I thought about the string of gruesome murders that El Lobo had allegedly committed. Changing the subject, I asked, "What's with the sudden change of heart? I've been asking to see the moonshine still and the bomb shelters for years. Why show them to me today?"

"Well, you see, while you were talkin' with Beto and his bald-headed drug dealer, we had a little family meeting—"

Interrupting, I asked, "You had a family meeting without me? You do remember putting me in charge of the family, right? That means I should be attending all family meetings."

"The meeting was about you." Uncle Houston rocked back-and-forth on his heels. "And it was only for select people. I know I ain't been making it easy for you to take control—"

"Kinda hard when you keep pulling the strings behind my back."

"I told you and told you that you couldn't just take charge overnight. The family's gotta get used to you being the new person in command. You might not see it, but they're slowly warmin' up to you. Most of them know you're the smartest of the bunch. They just have to trust you. That's why none of them wanted you to know where the still and bomb shelters are located," Uncle Houston said. "But, yesterday, some of us sat down and discussed things. And we've come to the decision that it's time for us to share the locations with you."

"Yippie!" I said, faking the excitement that I was too tired to feel. "Does that mean we'll be starting with the bomb shelter under your barn?"

Uncle Houston laughed, but the dry, hoarse chuckle quickly turned into a cough. After clearing his throat a few times, he asked, "You really think I'm that dumb, Carrie? I don't grow pot on my own property. At least, I don't do it anymore."

"Then why do you tell everyone that you grow pot in your old bomb shelter?" I asked. Okay, maybe Uncle Houston didn't tell *everyone* that he grew marijuana in a bomb shelter on his property. But he didn't seem to be making a secret of it.

"That's to keep people off our scent," Uncle Houston said.

"Like a decoy," Uncle Bowie added. "If we ever got raided, they'd go straight for Houston's bomb shelter. And they won't find nothing illegal in it."

"What is in the bomb shelter?" I asked.

For almost my entire life I had heard stories about how Uncle Houston grew marijuana in the bomb shelter that was under his barn. I knew where the entrance to the bomb shelter was, but I had never been inside. And that wasn't for a lack of trying. I'd attempted to break in on multiple occasions, but hadn't been successful.

"What's in my bomb shelter ain't none of your business," Uncle Houston said.

"Oh, just show it to her," Granddaddy grumbled. He gave Houston a shove towards the barn. "Carrie isn't going to believe you until you prove it."

"Yeah, all right."

Uncle Houston whistled for his dogs and the pig, and then led the way into the barn. The interior of the barn was nicer than some people's houses. Since his wife refused to let the dogs or Mr. Giggles into their farmhouse, Uncle Houston had turned the barn into their home. The floor was covered in dog beds, and there were multiple food and water stations. He had even installed heating and air conditioning to keep his pets comfortable.

In one of the back corners of the barn was a set of cellar doors. Uncle Houston swung the doors open and then headed down the crumbling, concrete steps. I followed him, while Granddaddy and Uncle Bowie stayed up top. At the bottom of the steps was a steel door. Uncle Houston punched in a code on the electronic pad that was above the door handle.

Glancing over his shoulder at me, Uncle Houston said. "You gotta promise you won't tell no one about what you see in here."

"I promise," I said.

Excitement was beginning to overtake the exhaustion. I reached around Uncle Houston and shoved open the door. I had no idea what I was expecting to find in the bomb shelter—especially after I had been assured that there wasn't anything illegal inside—but I definitely was not expecting to see a television, a worn leather couch, and a well-stocked mini-bar.

"Welcome to my Man Cave."

"What about the Man Cave in your house?" I asked, referring to the second-floor bedroom where Uncle Houston spent most of his time. It was the room where he had meetings with the criminally-inclined Shatners about their illegal activities. I'd also had multiple meetings in the Man Cave with Uncle Houston over the years.

"This is my private Man Cave. This is where I go when Mabel gets to naggin' me. Which seems to be all the dang time." Uncle Houston leaned closer to me and winked. "Mabel don't know about this, so I'd appreciate it if you don't say nothin' to her about it."

"You should be ashamed of yourself." I turned around and headed back up the narrow steps. "Now let's see the rest of these bomb shelters and the still."

Uncle Houston finished locking up the entrance to his Man Cave. He then led the way out of the barn and over to the all-terrain vehicle that was parked next to the tank. The vehicle had two rows of seats, and a short, deep bed. Houston and Bowie sat up front while I sat in the backseat with Granddaddy.

"Where y'all off to?" Aunt Mabel yelled as she shuffled across the muddy yard towards us. Her white hair was piled up in her trademark beehive, and she was all gussied up in her Sunday best. "We've got church later this morning."

"We ain't goin' to church today. We're goin' on a field trip," Uncle Houston snapped at his wife of sixty-four years. "Now why don't you tend to your own knittin' and stop worryin' about what I'm doin' all the time."

"God keeps track of how many times you miss church, Samuel Houston," Aunt Mabel scolded as she took up a stance in front of the ATV. "And you skip church more times than you go. God don't like that. He wants your butt in a pew every Sunday morning."

"God probably don't like a lot of things I do. And skippin' church ain't nowhere near the worst of what I've done." Uncle Houston hit the gas and kicked up mud as he swerved the ATV around Aunt Mabel. I could hear her screaming at us as we raced down the driveway to the road. When we got to the two-lane highway, Uncle Houston slammed on the brakes. He then turned around and handed me a red bandana. "I'm goin' to need you to wear this, Carrie. We're gonna show you everythin'. But this first location . . . well, we need to keep it a secret till we get there. You gotta be blindfolded."

"Fine." I snatched the bandana out of Uncle Houston's hands, and Granddaddy helped me tie it around my head.

Once Uncle Houston determined that I couldn't see anything around the blindfold, he resumed driving. He seemed to be driving in circles, and it felt like he hit every bump and pothole that he could find. I was thankful that the ATV had seatbelts—otherwise I probably would have wound up getting ejected.

After ten to fifteen minutes of driving around, Uncle Houston stopped the ATV and announced that we had reached our destination.

I whipped the bandana off my head and looked around. We were sitting in a familiar-looking clearing in the woods. On the left side of the ATV was a rundown shack, and on the right was a nonfunctional outhouse, an old farm truck, and a hulking moonshine still.

We were parked in the middle of the wagon path that cut through the Moonshiners' scene on the Hayride of Nightmares.

"Is this a joke?" I scrambled out of the ATV and landed ankle deep in a puddle. Looks like we would be having the Redneck Yacht Club in Moonshiners' Grove tonight. Slogging across the rutted path to the moonshine still, I asked. "Seriously? This is a joke, right?"

"No, this is for real," Uncle Houston announced as he trekked over to join me.

"Oh my God . . . Y'all are stupider than I thought." I turned to Uncle Houston and screamed, "What happened to don't shit where you eat?"

"Admit it, Carrie. This here is a humdinger of a hidin' spot." Uncle Houston pounded his fist against the side of the moonshine still. "Who would ever think that we'd hide the still in plain sight? I mean, it's been here for about ten years, and no one—not even you, Miss Smarty Pants—has figured it out."

"Does Uncle Elvin know that y'all use this to make actual moonshine?" I asked.

"Of course, he knows," Uncle Houston said. "He ain't never been happy about it, but he leaves us alone as long as we don't use it during September and October."

I circled the still. For all these years I had believed that it was fake. Okay, I had never really believed it was fake. I had always figured it was one of the family's old stills. But I had never once suspected that it was a functioning still.

"What about the moonshine that Billy Bob delivered somewhere last night? Where did that come from?" I asked.

"That was stuff Billy Bob made himself. He's got a hundred-and-fifty gallon still hidden in one of his sheds. Delmar and a couple others got 'em, too," Uncle Houston said. He stepped in front of me to stop me from circling the still for a third time. "Carrie, we ain't been using this still all that often anymore. Just for the occasional big run. Moonshine just ain't as popular as it used to be. Not when they're sellin' that commercial crap in stores."

"Then why don't you get a permit and make it commercially?" I asked. "That way you wouldn't have to worry about the law catching up to you."

"But where's the fun in that?" Uncle Bowie asked. He had gotten out of the ATV and walked over to join me and Uncle Houston next to the moonshine still.

"Where's the common sense in this?" I asked as I wildly gestured towards the moonshine still. "Have any of you ever thought about how many felonies you're committing? Like unlawful production of distilled spirits, possession of an unregistered still, and engaging in business as a distiller without registration. Transporting and selling the moonshine is also illegal. Not to mention all of the tax fraud involved."

"We know, Carrie. Crockett's been preaching the same line to us since we all was knee-high to a grasshopper," Uncle Houston said.

"And I'll say it again," Granddaddy yelled from the back seat of the ATV. "Each felony y'all are committing is punishable by up to five years in prison. And y'all could get fined up to ten-grand for each offense."

"Have y'all forgotten about what happened to Randy?" I asked, referring to my cousin who had recently been released from Forcht-Wade Correctional Center in Keithville, Louisiana. "He spent five years in prison after the Louisiana State Troopers caught him running 'shine."

Uncle Houston swatted away Granddaddy's and my protests as if it were an annoying fly buzzing around his head. "I ain't worried 'bout none of that."

"Well, you should be," I snapped. "As of today, y'all are done. I'm gonna have Bubba come down here and mess with the still so that y'all can no longer use it. You're not jeopardizing the Body Farm any longer."

"Darn it, Carrie! If you're gonna be like this, then our field trip is over," Uncle Houston said. He then stomped through the puddles on his way over to the ATV. "I ain't showing you where the bomb shelters are if you're gonna get your feathers all ruffled over it."

"We started this field trip," I said. "We're going to finish it."

I climbed into the front seat next to Uncle Houston. Uncle Bowie slid into the back beside Granddaddy. After a few minutes of arguing, Uncle Houston relented and drove us past the Torture barn and out through the Body Farm's entertainment area. He then headed out to the road and over to Uncle Bowie's house.

My burly, mustachioed Uncle Ted was waiting for us by the old barn that housed Uncle Bowie's vast model train display. A dirty bandana covered the top part of his mullet along with his enlarging bald spot. Theodore Bohannon was married to my grandparents' only daughter. While Aunt Eileen had never had anything to do with the family's crimes, her husband had revitalized our marijuana production not long after they got married. Ted was the one who moved the marijuana plants into the bomb shelters and worked on cultivating the strains. Out of everyone, Uncle Ted had been the most adamant against me taking over as head of the family. I was shocked he had finally agreed to show me the bomb shelters.

"Let's get this over with," Uncle Ted said as he disappeared into the old barn. "Come on, Carrie. Don't drag this out by lagging behind."

I followed Uncle Ted into the barn and walked past the model train display that Uncle Bowie had been working on since he was in his early twenties. Nearly sixty years later, and he was still tinkering away at it. The display was laid out on a table that was fifteen-feet-wide by fifty-feet-long. Urban, suburban, and rural areas were set up on the eight-hundred square foot table. Eight model trains ran around the multiple tracks.

In the back room of the barn was Uncle Bowie's Christmas-themed model train display. It was much smaller than the other one, but equally detailed. At the far end of the room, Uncle Ted shoved aside the pocket door that hid the control room. He then opened a hidden panel in the floor and gestured for me to follow him down a rickety looking ladder.

I peered down into the dark hole where Uncle Ted had disappeared. "You're telling me that there's a bomb shelter under here?"

"I ain't telling you nothing. I'm showing you." Uncle Ted's voice echoed up at me. "Now git down here."

By the time I made it down the ladder, Uncle Ted had the lights on, and he had opened the door to the bomb shelter. This bomb shelter appeared to be twice the size of the one under Uncle Houston's barn, and it was full of marijuana plants. The leafy plants were about three feet high and were supported by trellises. Grow lights and fans were mounted to the ceiling.

"This here is my strain of Purple Kush. It's my most popular strain, and I've been cloning the same plant since before you was born," Uncle Ted explained. He guided me over to the plants closest to the door. "These babies are ready to be harvested. I'm planning to do that tonight. Once I've got all the buds harvested off these plants, I'll start all over with a new crop in here. Meanwhile, I'll work on drying these buds out and getting them ready for sale."

I knelt and examined one of the plants. I had seen marijuana plants up close on multiple occasions. The Shatners weren't the only people in Wyatt County growing marijuana, but this was the first time I had seen a grow house that wasn't in someone's spare closet.

"Are they all like this? Are all of the bomb shelters under houses or barns or whatever?"

"It's a good way to hide them," Uncle Ted said. "Between the grow lights and the fans, we use up a lot of electricity. Most of the bomb shelters have barns or other outbuildings built over top of them, so I had the owners convert those places into something that will also use a lot of electricity. That way, we can use our legal ventures to hide our illegal ones."

"Show me."

CHAPTER FIVE

IT WAS ALMOST LUNCHTIME WHEN WE FINISHED UP the "field trip" and arrived back at the farmhouse. The five of us had spent the morning driving from one Shatner family's residence to another so that Uncle Ted could show me where the other bomb-shelters-turned-grow-houses were located. Of course, Uncle Ted had a grow house located under his woodworking shop. There was a grow house under the greenhouse where Ellie May grew flowers and plants for her floral shop, and another was under the barn that housed Aunt Bunny's herd of dairy goats. My cousin Rooster Devereux had a grow house under the garage that he had converted into a blacksmith shop, and Uncle Leroy had a grow house under the barn that he used as a taxidermy workshop. The final grow house was under Aunt Deidra's art studio.

Uncle Houston also showed me the hundred-and-fifty-gallon moonshine stills that Uncle Delmar, Billy Bob, and a couple other Shatners had hidden in buildings on their properties.

My family's operation was a lot larger than I had ever suspected. I had to applaud my family for keeping everything so well hidden, but I was not happy to see that so many of the family's legal ventures were being used to hide the illegal ones.

After bringing the ATV to a stop next to the tank, Uncle Houston turned to me and asked, "Well, Carrie, are you happy you finally know where the stills and grow houses are located?"

"No. Quite frankly, I'm not happy at all," I said as I climbed out of the ATV. "I don't know if y'all are idiots or geniuses. Well, I know y'all are idiots. I've known that my whole life. But after what all I saw this morning . . . I just . . . I don't know anymore."

"Pretty impressive, huh?" Uncle Houston asked.

"No, 'impressive' is definitely not the word I would use," I said as I stomped across the muddy yard. "I'm leaning more towards 'asinine.'"

"Carrie, wait," Granddaddy said as he followed me to my Jeep. "Let's talk about this."

"No," I snapped as I whirled around to face Granddaddy. Because my dad hadn't been that great of a father, Granddaddy has always been the strongest male influence in my life. What I learned this morning felt like a major betrayal and I was furious at Granddaddy for keeping secrets from me. "I have nothing to say to you right now. Or at least nothing good."

Actually, I had a lot I wanted to say. I just didn't think I was capable of saying any of it without screaming or swearing. I needed some time to think and to calm down before I would be ready for a rational conversation.

After knocking some of the dried mud off my boots, I climbed into my Jeep and floored it down the driveway. When I reached the road, I slammed on my brakes and slid through the mud until I came to a stop. I then dug my cell phone out of my jacket pocket and called Bubba.

"It's real," I said when Bubba answered. "The still at Moonshiners' Grove is real."

"What?" Bubba asked. "No . . . For real? Does my dad know?"

"Yes, for real," I said. "And, yes, he knows."

Bubba muttered a few choice words.

Continuing, I said, "We've got to do something about it, like, right now."

"I'm over at the Pumpkin Patch," Bubba said. "I have to run the piggy races at twelve-thirty. We can take care of the still after that. Meet me by the racetrack."

Bubba hung up on me before I could ask him where the racetrack was located. I hadn't been to the Pumpkin Patch since it opened eight or ten years earlier. I didn't remember there being any pig races that year. What I did remember was a small corn maze, a petting zoo featuring a few docile alpacas, and a hayride around the farm.

It was Aunt Loretta—Uncle Elvin's wife and great-uncle Houston's only daughter—who created the Pumpkin Patch as a non-scary, kid-friendly alternative to the Body Farm. Yes, it had a Halloween theme, but it was meant to be cutesy instead of scary.

After slipping in through the staff entrance, I could immediately see that the Pumpkin Patch had changed quite a bit since I had last been there. The corn maze was larger than before, and—according to the sign—the hayride now stopped at an actual pumpkin patch so that families could pick their own pumpkins. There was also a station set up for the kids to paint their pumpkins. Nearby was another activity station where kids could make their own scarecrows out of hay and donated clothing. There was a gemstone mining area as well as a jungle gym and other play areas. The petting zoo had also grown and now included miniature ponies and donkeys, goats, sheep, and rabbits.

I got a cheeseburger and a Coke from one of the food trucks and then wandered around in search of the racetrack. Despite the earlier bad weather and the fact that everything was still soaked, the Pumpkin Patch was packed with families.

I finally came across a signpost pointing towards where different activities were located. I had just determined that the racetrack was behind the petting zoo barn when I heard someone shouting my name. I turned around and spotted Roxanne Devereux forcing her way through the crowd as she headed in my direction. She had two little redheaded girls in tow.

Despite being only twenty-one years old, my cousin Wesley had four children by three different women. The oldest child was five, and the youngest child was a few months old. Roxanne was the mother of Wesley's two daughters—five-year-old Summer and two-year-old Autumn. Wesley and Roxanne had been off-and-on since high school. I'd long ago lost count of how many times they had broken up and then gotten back together.

"Where is he?" Roxanne screamed at me. Her face was flushed red, and her green eyes were bloodshot. "What have you done with Wes?"

"I haven't done anything with him," I said before stuffing the last bite of cheeseburger in my mouth and tossing the balled-up wrapper into a nearby trashcan.

"Then where is he?"

I finished chewing and then swallowed. "How should I know where Wes is? I haven't seen him since last night."

"Well, he was supposed to meet us here when the Pumpkin Patch opened at noon," Roxanne said. "It's almost twelve-thirty, and he's not here."

"Are you sure?" I asked. "I just saw his car in the staff parking lot."

Wesley had a yellow junker that he had nicknamed "the pineapple." It was hard to miss.

"If he's here, then where is he?" Roxanne asked.

"Knowing Wes, he's selling drugs out of the handicap portapotty."

"I already checked there. I checked everywhere. He's not here. I don't know if I should be worried or mad."

"Have you tried calling him?"

"He's not answering his phone." Roxanne shot me a blistering look. "And what are you doing in here? Shouldn't you be out front chasing off the protestors from Calvary Baptist or arresting them for harassment. I'll file charges against them if you need me to."

"They're protesting here, too?" I asked. Was nothing sacred anymore? "What does Pastor Kemp and his flock have against the Pumpkin Patch?"

"Apparently it promotes Satanism."

"It's meant for kids . . ." I glanced around and tried to spot something that looked even remotely Satanic. The cartoonish fiberglass pumpkin that was perched on top of the ticket booth was creepy. But it was hardly demonic. And the volunteers dressed in various Halloween costumes weren't even the tiniest bit scary. "What did you say about harassment?"

"Pastor Kemp . . . the young one, not the old one . . . He and his wife and some other people are out in the parking lot handing out brochures for Hell House and calling people sinners for coming to the Pumpkin Patch."

Roxanne handed me a brochure for the Hell House. I skimmed over it before tossing it the trash.

"What did they say to you?" I asked Roxanne.

"Pastor Kemp accused me of being a sinner because Wes and I had 'premarital relations.' Then he told me I'm a whore because I'm an unwed mother. And he called the girls bastards. He said I should come to Hell House and learn about the 'errors of my ways.'"

Above my head, a high-pitched piggy sequel blared out of a speaker. A robotic sounding voice then announced that the pig races were about to begin.

Autumn began oinking, and Summer announced she was done looking for her daddy and begged her mother to take them over to see the pig races.

"Forget about Pastor Kemp. And forget about Wes, too. He'll show up if he wants to," I said. "Now let's go see some piggy races."

I took Summer by the hand and allowed her to pull me towards the racetrack. Roxanne picked up Autumn and followed us.

The racetrack was a steel-framed enclosure that had been set up in a short oval. Sawdust had been sprinkled over top of the mud to make for a better racing surface. Lined up at the starting line were four juvenile Yorkshire pigs. Each wore a different colored vest to differentiate them.

Leaving Roxanne and her daughters, I walked over to the far side of the track and joined Veda and Naomi by the shed in which the pigs were kept prior to the races. I was honestly surprised to see that Veda and Naomi were up and about considering how long we had been at the Body Farm last night.

"Bubba told us," Veda said. "He's about ready to kill his father."

"He's not the only one," I said.

"I told him that if he kills Elvin, I'm finally taking out Loretta."

Veda has been threatening to kill Bubba's mom for thirteen years now. For whatever reason, Loretta hated Veda and had always made it clear that she didn't think Veda was good enough for her son. To keep Loretta from protesting at the wedding. Uncle Elvin had drugged her with a couple brownies that were laced with marijuana. Since the wedding, Loretta had been begging Bubba to divorce Veda. The fact that Veda has put up with my aunt Loretta for all these years was proof that she was truly in love with Bubba.

"What did Aunt Loretta do this time?" I asked.

"She's done a complete one-eighty in the past couple days. She's gone from begging Bubba to leave me to bugging him about getting me pregnant so that she can be a grandma. Loretta came up to me last night at the Body Farm and told me that my biological clock is ticking, and that I better hurry up and get pregnant."

"What did you say to her?" I asked.

"I told her that Bubba and I don't want to have kids. Never have. Never will. I mean, can you imagine me and Bubba as parents?" Veda asked. She didn't give me a chance to answer before she plunged ahead in her story. "Loretta flipped out and accused us of being selfish. She thinks we're not going to have kids for the sole reason of depriving her of being a grandma. But she doesn't even want to *be* a grandma. She just wants to be able to *tell* people that she's a grandma. She flat out said that she wouldn't really do anything with the kid and that she wouldn't help us out by babysitting or anything. So, the only person being selfish is Loretta—which is exactly what I told her. She had a conniption and stomped off. I don't know how much longer I can put up with her. She's driving both me and Bubba nuts."

"Oh, Veda . . ." I patted her on the arm. "Remember, if you kill her, I will help you get rid of the body. That's what best friends are for."

"Don't joke, Carrie. I might just have to take you up on the offer."

In the middle of the racetrack, Bubba stepped up onto a platform and began hyping up the crowd. "Who's ready to see the swiftest swine . . . the hastiest hogs . . . the world-famous Pumpkin Patch Porkers? In the first race, we have Hamlet, Porky, Hogwash, and Mademoiselle Piggy."

After Bubba had picked four kids to be the official supporter of each pig, he kicked open the starting gate and the pigs were off. As they raced around the track to the finish line, the pigs kicked up sawdust and tripped each other up. The race was over in a matter of seconds, and Mademoiselle Piggy was declared the winner.

While Bubba told lame jokes to keep the crowd entertained, Red Devereux herded the four pigs into the shed and brought out the next set of racers. Red was Catfish's youngest son and the second youngest of his nine children. We had been friends since we were kids. Up until recently, Red had been a professional wrestler, but, after injuring his back, he decided to heed his doctor's advice and hang up his wrestling boots.

Red had started dating Naomi earlier this year, and he had just recently moved in with her. The two were practically inseparable. The only times when they weren't attached at the hip was when they were at work or when Naomi started acting like a drama queen and Red stormed off because he couldn't deal with her. Almost every time Naomi and Red got into an argument, I got dragged into the middle of it. Somehow, I had become their relationship counselor. I was tempted to start charging them for my advice—not that I was in any way qualified to give relationship advice.

The pig races were entertaining—especially the third race that featured four Vietnamese pot-bellied pigs that were all descendants of Mr. Giggles. By the time Bubba and Red had the pigs rounded up and back in the petting zoo area, I was feeling slightly less homicidal than I had when I'd arrived at the Pumpkin Patch.

"You know," Bubba said to me. "I asked Dad about the still down in Moonshiners' Grove at the beginning of the season. He swore to me it was fake."

"Well, he lied to you," I said. "Uncle Houston assured me it's real."

Bubba made a disgusted face. He then led the way out of the Pumpkin Patch and over to the Body Farm. Veda, Naomi, Red, and I followed him past the ticket booth that resembled a mausoleum, across the entertainment area, and then through the Hayride of Nightmare's queue lines and out onto the path near the loading area. The entertainment area was covered in gravel, but the hayride path was dirt. After the copious amount of rain this morning, the path was now a thick layer of mud that squelched under our feet.

Across the start of the hayride path was a wooden gate that would slide open to admit each tractor and then slide closed after the back end of the wagon had passed through. Scrawled across the gate in red paint were the words "Abandon all hope ye who enter here."

"We may as well walk the path and check for damage. I'll have to do it sometime before we open tonight." Bubba strode over to the electrical box that was hidden behind a bush next to the gate. A few seconds later, the gate slowly slid open. "I'll take that as a good sign."

"Don't speak too soon," Veda said after the gate had slid completely open. "You've got a piece of fence down."

Bubba swore under his breath as he stomped through the puddles to where a pine tree had fallen onto the chain link fence that ran along each side of the path until it reached the first skit.

"And your prison guard blew away," Naomi said as she pointed to the empty guard tower on top of the prison. The exterior of the building was covered in gray stucco, and the faux windows all had bars on them. A sign declaring "Welcome to Death Row" hung above the doors.

"Nah, I took the mannequin down before the storm," Bubba said. "Y'all wait out here while I open up the doors. Then I'm gonna run the show to make sure everything works."

Bubba ducked around the side of the building and entered the prison barn through a hidden access door. A few seconds later, the garage doors slid to the side.

Red, Naomi, Veda, and I walked into the barn, climbed up onto the tailgate of the wagon that was parked inside, and looked around at the interior of the prison scene. There were stages on each side of the barn. On the stage to my left were four cell blocks, and on the right were two cell blocks and a replica electric chair. During the show—once the wagon was parked in the barn and the garage doors had closed—two actors dressed as prison guards would drag an inmate out of one of the cells and strap him into Old Sparky. The wires on the electric chair would light up and then malfunction, casting the interior of the prison into complete darkness. The cell doors would then slide open with a loud clang and the inmates would rush out of the cells and jump on the sides of the wagon while strobe lights flashed.

The garage doors, electric chair, cell doors, and strobe lights were all operated from a control panel next to Old Sparky. Bubba flipped the switches and ran through the show. After confirming that all the electronics in the prison scene worked properly, the five of us closed the doors and then set off down the path to the haunted mine.

Unless something went wrong, it took the tractors between eighteen and twenty minutes to make the mile-long loop around the hayride path. It took us a little longer to walk it since we had to thoroughly check each of the scenes.

Most of the damage that we came across was minimal—a piece of sheet metal had been ripped off the roof at the insane asylum, multiple sections of the path were now small lakes, and a downed branch had shattered the windshield of the old farm truck at Moonshiners. While Naomi, Veda, and I cleaned up the worst of the broken glass, Bubba and Red permanently disabled the moonshine still. No one would be using it to make moonshine again.

"As long as everything is okay in Torture, I'd say the hayride came out mostly unscathed," Bubba said as the five of us trudged up to the final scene on the hayride. "We'll be good to go tonight."

After inspecting the exterior, Bubba entered the Torture barn through a doorway that was hidden in one of the corner towers. He popped back out a few seconds later.

"There's something rustling around inside," Bubba said. "Probably an animal crawled in to get out of the storm and got stuck. Y'all might want to get away from the door and give it some room to get out."

Veda, Naomi, Red, and I backed away from the garage door as it started to rise. The door was halfway up when the interior lights flashed on and Bubba screamed.

CHAPTER SIX

"**B**UBBA!" My boots slid in the mud as I charged towards the open doorway. I would have slipped and fallen on my face had Red not grabbed the back of my jacket and dragged me along with him as he raced to Bubba's aid.

As we rushed into the Torture barn, I expected to see Bubba getting attacked by an angry possum or a rabid squirrel—maybe even mauled by a bobcat. Uncle Elvin had spotted a bobcat stalking his alpacas a few weeks earlier.

Instead, Bubba was standing in the wagon and holding on to one of the mannequins that dangled from the ceiling.

Except it couldn't possibly be one of the mannequins since all seven of them were severed at the waist, and the body that Bubba was holding on to had legs.

"What the . . ." I mumbled as my brain tried to catch up to what my eyes were seeing.

"It's Waylon!" Bubba yelled. "Help me get him down."

Like the mannequins, a thick rope had been wrapped around Waylon's wrists. The rope had then been strung over one of the rafters that ran the length of the barn, and Waylon had been hauled up until his toes just touched the bottom of the wagon. The other end of the rope was tied off to the side of the wagon.

I grabbed onto the back of the wagon and hauled myself over the metal tailgate. Clods of mud flew off my boots and pelted Veda and

Naomi in the face and chest. Veda cursed, and Naomi screamed. Ignoring them, I trampled over small mounds of straw to get to Bubba's side.

"Is he alive?" I asked.

Waylon's left eye was swollen shut, and there was dried blood around his nose and mouth. Judging by the odd angle of his shoulders, both had to be dislocated.

"Waylon's got a pulse. But he's unconscious." Bubba used his head to gesture towards where Hank Garrett the Third hung a few feet away from Waylon. "I don't know about Hank. He ain't moved or made a sound yet."

I moved closer to Hank to get a better look at him. His head slumped forward, and his chin touched his chest. The right side of his face was covered in blood and, he had a sizeable gash above his ear. Head wounds tend to bleed a lot, but it looked like Hank had lost a dangerous amount of blood. The blood had turned part of Hank's gray sweatshirt a dark red, and it had dripped down onto the straw around his feet. He was in desperate need of medical attention.

Beyond Hank, painted in red spray paint on the interior side of the garage door were the words "This is just the beginning." *The beginning of what*, I wondered. *The beginning of assaults against my family members? The beginning of the end?*

"It looks like someone strung them up and beat them like piñatas," Red said.

If two of the Three Stooges were here, the other one couldn't be too far away. A third rope was tied off to the side of the wagon, but it had been cut near the knot. I felt safe in assuming that the rope had been used to suspend Wesley from the rafters.

"Where's Wes?" I asked Bubba. "Is he in here?"

"Over there," Bubba said as he gestured over my shoulder. "In the pillory."

I looked over to where the pillory was half hidden in the shadows behind the rack. Wesley stared back at me from where his head was stuck in the center hole of the crude, wooden framework. His hands poked out of the holes on either side of his head. To prevent him from pulling his head and hands out of the holes, someone had looped rope around his neck and both wrists. His back was bent at roughly a forty-five-degree angle, and he had to tilt his head back to look at us. Having once filled in for the pillory victim, I knew how painful it was to stand with my back and neck at such an awkward angle for even a short period of time. I had no idea how long Wesley had been forced to suffer.

"We'll get you out in a minute, Wesley," I said.

Because a gag had been stuffed in his mouth, Wesley could only grunt in response.

"Help Bubba support Waylon while I cut him down," Red said. He knelt next to where the rope was tied off to the side of the wagon and used a pocketknife to saw through it. "Don't let Waylon fall. He's hurt bad enough, and we don't want to make it any worse."

Veda, Naomi, and I crashed into each other as we moved to help Bubba. Naomi slipped and went down on her butt. A pile of straw cushioned her fall.

"Oh my God! Oh my God! Oh my God!" Naomi shrieked.

Naomi, who suffered from high functioning anxiety, was starting to lose it. She had never been able to remain calm in high pressure or stressful situations. After all, this is the woman who overreacted and shot her ex-boyfriend in the foot when she found out that he was married.

I could see that Naomi was on the verge of a breakdown. I could feel my own panic attack building, but I was much better at controlling my anxiety than Naomi.

"Naomi," I snapped at her to get her to focus on me and not Waylon. I wanted to shake her, but that was impossible to do while I helped Bubba hold up Waylon. The last thing I needed was for Naomi to lose control. "Listen to me. I need you to use your phone to take pictures. This is a crime scene, and we're about to destroy evidence. Document what you can."

"I can . . . yeah, I can, like, do that," Naomi said as she pulled her phone out of her jacket pocket. She aimed the camera at us and nearly blinded us as she snapped a picture.

It took Red a minute or two to saw through the rope that was as thick around as my wrist. When the final strands of rope gave way, Waylon tumbled limply into Bubba's arms. Naomi put her phone down so that she could help me, Veda, and Bubba lower Waylon down into the wagon and stretch him out on top of a pile of straw.

I knelt next to Waylon and gently tugged up his sweatshirt to get a look at the physical damage that had been done to him. Waylon's abdomen and chest were covered in bruises.

"It feels like some of his ribs are broken," I said as I ran my hands along Waylon's sides. "He's also not breathing too well, and his pulse is pretty rapid."

"Shit . . ." Bubba mumbled. "Who could have done this to them?"

"That's what I plan to find out," I said. A wave of anger crashed over me, smothering the mounting anxiety. Regardless of my personal feelings for Wesley and Waylon, no one messed with my family. I was going to find whoever it was that had hurt my cousins and Hank, and I was going to make that person pay. "But, first, we have to get these guys to the hospital. Veda, call 911 and get them to send three ambulances out here."

"Have the ambulances meet us in the parking lot," Bubba said to Veda. "There are tractors blocking parts of the path. And I don't want to risk the ambulances getting stuck in the mud. Once we get the boys free, I'll drive the tractor out into the parking lot. Red, I'll need you to open the gate into the overflow lot."

"Can do," Red said as he began to saw through the rope that held Hank. "Hang in there, buddy. We'll have you down in a minute."

After the rope gave way, Hank flopped down onto Bubba's shoulder. Bubba stumbled backwards a few steps, but, with help from me, he managed to remain upright.

Once Bubba and I had Hank laid out in the wagon, I pressed my fingers to the side of Hank's neck to confirm if he was unconscious or dead. I could just make out a pulse that was both weak and rapid.

"I think Hank's in shock. And he's lost a lot of blood." Turning to Veda, I asked, "Where are my ambulances?"

"They're on the way," Veda said.

"What are you guys standing around for? Go get Wes," I snapped at Bubba and Red. I then walked across the wagon and approached Naomi. She stood motionless next to Waylon, clutching her cell phone between shaking hands. "Did you get pictures?"

Naomi nodded. "I got a bunch of Waylon and Hank. And some of Wes, too."

"That's good, Naomi. Real good." Hopefully, she had been able to get some decent pictures that I would be able to use as part of my investigation. "Can you keep it together for another few minutes? I need you to call the sheriff's department and tell them about what's going on. Tell whoever answers that Detective Shatner said we've got a crime scene out here and that the sheriff needs to send everyone he can out to the Body Farm."

"I can do that," Naomi said.

I pried the phone out of Naomi's trembling hands, punched in the sheriff's department's emergency number, and then handed the phone back to her. As soon as someone answered, Naomi started stammering on about an assault at the Body Farm. Naomi wasn't quite coherent, but she managed to pass along the pertinent information.

"Little help, Carrie?" Bubba shouted.

I spun around to see what was going on. Bubba and Red had freed Wesley from the pillory, and they were helping him around the rack that took up the entire middle section of the stage. Wesley hobbled along, bent over with his left arm held tightly against his chest.

"Give me your hand," I said to Wesley as I reached out and clasped his left elbow to help hold him steady as he stepped over the narrow gap between the stage and the wagon. Wesley howled in pain and recoiled from me. "What's wrong? Is your arm broken?"

"No. It ain't broken," Wesley screamed at me. "They cut off my finger!"

"What?!?"

"They. Cut. Off. My. Fucking. Finger!" Wesley shrieked as he held up his left hand. His wrist was swollen and bruised, and his hand was wrapped in a bloody bandana. Fresh blood seeped through the old blood that had dried and crusted over the dingy fabric. "The assholes used a pair of pruning shears to cut off my pinkie!"

I shoved a pile of straw into the one corner of the wagon and helped Wesley get settled back against it. Behind me, either Veda or Naomi gagged and then emptied the contents of her stomach. I couldn't blame whichever one of them threw up. I was feeling nauseous myself.

"What happened, Wes? Who did this to you guys? And why?"

"I screwed up, Carrie," Wesley sobbed. "I should have listened to you."

"No shit, Wes. I kept telling you it would blow up in your face and look what happened."

I immediately regretted what I said. Wesley had been through enough. He didn't need me berating him. I could do that later—after Wesley had received medical attention.

"We good to go, Carrie?"

"Yeah. Get us out of here, Bubba."

Bubba, followed by Red, jumped over the side of the wagon, raised the other garage door, and then hurried out of the Torture barn. Bubba climbed onto the tractor and started the engine. Meanwhile, Red rushed down the path to open the gate. Just beyond the Torture barn was a narrow pathway that cut through the grove of trees that separated this section of the hayride from the overflow parking lot. A ten-foot-tall wooden fence ran along the perimeter of the parking lot to keep customers from wandering through the trees and onto the hayride path.

"Hold 'em steady, girls," Bubba shouted at me, Veda, and Naomi as he released the brake. "It's going to be a bumpy ride to the main parking lot."

The tractor rolled forward, jerking the wagon along with it. Bubba then gently pulled the wagon out of the Torture barn. He almost immediately turned left and sideswiped a pine tree as he turned off the hayride path and onto the trail through the trees.

"It's my fault," Wesley kept mumbling as he rocked back and forth on the pile of hay. Sobs wracked his body, and tears streamed down his cheeks. His nose was mashed to one side, and both of his eyes were partially swollen shut. Also, the skin around Wesley's neck and wrists was raw and bloody from rubbing against the coarse rope. He didn't appear to be as severely beaten as Waylon or Hank, but he was in poor shape.

"I should have listened. Stupid. Stupid. Stupid!"

"What happened, Wes?" I asked. I gently gripped him by the upper arms and forced him to stop rocking. "Tell me what happened."

"I was stupid. These guys . . . they told me they could get me cocaine."

"Are you talking about drug dealers? Like El Lobo?" I asked.

"Yeah. But not El Lobo . . . Honduran."

"You've been talking to someone from a Honduran cartel?" I asked as I tried to clarify what Wesley was disjointedly saying.

Wesley nodded. "His name is Facundo . . . He told me he could get me better quality cocaine . . . And for less money than El Lobo . . ."

"Where did you meet this Facundo guy?"

"I didn't. He texted me. Said he got my number from a mutual friend."

"Which mutual friend?" I asked. A low hanging branch brushed the top of my head and snagged a few of my hairs. I batted the branch away.

"I don't know. He didn't say, and I didn't ask. He just said—"

"Hold on," I snapped, cutting Wesley off. "Some random person texts you about supplying you with cocaine. And you weren't suspicious that it might be a setup or a scam?"

"You're dumber than I thought, Wes," Red said as he climbed over the side of the wagon. We had just passed through the gate and were now out in the parking lot. "And I always thought you were dumber than a box of rocks. What Roxanne sees in you I'll never understand."

"I was pretty freaking stupid, I know. But the guy sounded legit . . . at the time." Wesley slid down the pile of straw and stretched out his back. "I've been talking to this Facundo guy for the past week or so. He was pushing to meet. So, I agreed to meet him last night."

"And you met him out here at the Body Farm?" I asked. "During a storm?"

Wes shook his head. "No. We met at the Roadhouse."

The Roadhouse was a cheap motel located next to the Pumpkin Patch. The staff parking lot butted up against the back of the motel. The Roadhouse was an ideal place for a clandestine meeting since no one willingly stayed at the motel unless they had no other choice. Personally, I would sleep in my car before spending the night at the Roadhouse.

"Then how did you wind up here?" I asked Wesley. "What happened?"

"There were three of them." He struggled to push himself up on his elbows. "Me, Waylon, and Hank . . . we went in the room. The room I rented to meet these guys."

"They were already in the room when you got there? How did they get into the room before you if you're the one who rented it?"

"I don't know," Wesley said. "I opened the door, turned on the light, and there they were. Three of them."

"Did you recognize any of them?" I asked.

"They were wearing cheap devil masks. I barely got a glimpse of them before they jumped us. One of them got me with a taser." Wesley pulled up his shirt and showed me the two round spots on his chest where the taser had burned him through his sweatshirt. Like Waylon, Wesley had multiple bruises on his abdomen. "You have any idea how painful a taser is? 'Cause it freaking hurts! Not as bad as having a finger cut off. But it still hurt."

"I know, Wes. I've been hit with a taser before," I said. And I had not enjoyed the experience. "Did they get Waylon and Hank as well?"

"I dunno. Probably. I was passed out for at least a few minutes."

"That'll happen," I said. I glanced over my shoulder to make sure that Veda and Naomi were okay. Red was helping Veda hold Hank steady. And Naomi was doing the same for Waylon. It appeared that both Waylon and Hank remained unconscious. Turning back to Wesley, I asked, "What happened after you came to?"

"They had me blindfolded and tied up. They were arguing about what to do with Waylon and Hank. They weren't supposed to be there. Facundo told me to come alone. But I ain't stupid. I mean, I'm a freaking moron. But I ain't stupid. I wasn't going to the meeting alone," Wesley said. He swiped at the tears still streaming down his cheeks. "They held us a gunpoint and threatened to shoot us if we didn't cooperate. Then they made us walk down to the Torture barn. Except I had no idea where we were headed until we were in the barn and they had strung us up to the rafters. That's when they took the bag off my head and I figured out where we were."

"Did these guys take their masks off?" I asked. "Did you recognize their voices?"

Wesley shook his head. "They were disguising their voices whenever they talked."

"What did they do after they tied you up?"

"Like Red said . . . they beat us like piñatas."

"Why? What did they want?"

"Info. On the family. They kept asking about our crimes and what all we're involved in," Wesley said. The wagon went over a dip, and Wesley grabbed at his back and groaned in pain. "They knew things, Carrie. Things that only certain Shatners should know. Stuff I don't know about. Stuff you probably don't even know about. Like about the money laundering. And some of the scams. Stuff that happened in the past."

"If they already knew about our crimes, why were they asking you about them?"

"I dunno . . . Maybe for proof or something."

"Did you tell them?"

"Not at first." With his right hand, Wesley grabbed the front of my jacket and yanked me towards him so that we were nose to nose. "I didn't want to tell them, Carrie. I really didn't. But I had to. They said they were gonna kill my brother and Hank. I told them what they wanted to know so they wouldn't. After I talked, they cut me down and stuck me in the pillory. That's when they cut off my finger. They said it was what I deserved for talking. Then they beat up Waylon and Hank some more."

"You did the right thing, Wes."

"But Uncle Houston is gonna kill me. He always says—"

"Fuck what Uncle Houston says."

"But I talked, Carrie. Yeah, most of it was a load of bullshit that I made up. But some of what I said was true. And now the whole family is in danger. I don't know who these people are, but they ain't members of no Honduran cartel."

"That seems fairly obvious," I said. "Sounds to me like this was a setup."

"Hell, yeah, it was," Wesley said. "And now these people are coming after us. They told me our time is about up and we're all gonna go down. They said that what I told them is gonna help them bring down our family. They said the Shatners are done."

"We were already running out of time," I said. My grandparents and I were the only ones who knew that the DPS was closing in on our family. Even though I was helping them, I was still worried about the outcome of the DPS's case. Now I had to worry about this unknown, but clearly aggressive and violent entity coming after my family. Who were these people and what did they want? What would they gain by bringing down the Shatner's criminal operation? "Wes, how long did this go on? When did these three guys leave?"

Wesley shrugged. "It went on for a couple hours. Or at least it felt like hours. At some point I heard something with an engine go by—"

"Like an ATV?"

"Yeah, maybe."

I ducked my head and bit down hard on my lower lip. The engine that Wesley had heard was most likely the ATV carrying me, Granddaddy, Uncle Houston, and Uncle Bowie as we left the Body Farm after checking out the still in Moonshiners' Grove. We had driven right past the Torture barn while the Three Stooges were being assaulted.

"It wasn't long after the ATV or whatever drove by that they left," Wesley said. "I tried to get out of the pillory, but the ropes were too tight. If you guys hadn't—"

The tractor came to an abrupt halt and the tailgate at the back of the wagon crashed down. I looked up and saw that Bubba had driven us out into the Body Farm's main parking lot. Three ambulances raced towards us, and they were followed by four sheriff's department cruisers.

Within seconds, the wagon was swarmed by EMTs, Wyatt County deputies, and Shatners. The Shatners must have been working at the Pumpkin Patch and had run over to see what was going on when they heard the sirens. I yelled at my well-meaning family members to get out of the way and then directed the EMTs to help Waylon and Hank first. Wesley needed medical attention, but not as immediately as his brother and their friend.

"Listen to me, Wesley. I know you have a hard time doing that, but, for once in your life, I need you to listen to me." I leaned over him and forced him to look me in the eye. "Do not talk to anyone about what happened unless it's me or Uncle Murph, you understand? If any other law enforcement officer questions you, you give them the bare minimum and then say you don't remember what happened. I'm going to handle this. I will find the people who did this to you, and I will take care of them. You got it?"

"Yep. If anyone asks, I don't know jack shit."

"Tell them you got hit in the head and you don't remember anything. That excuse should work. At least for a couple days." I leaned closer to Wesley and whispered, "Now, quick. Before the EMTs come over. Tell me what I have to clean up at your place."

Wesley and Waylon shared a townhouse on the outskirts of Holler. I had never been there, but I was positive that there was plenty of evidence of their criminal activities lying around. I wanted to get it cleaned up before anyone went to search the townhouse.

"Wes!" Roxanne screamed as she scrambled over the side of the wagon and sank into the straw next to Wesley. "What the hell happened?"

"It's a Code Red, baby. I need you to get rid of everything," Wesley said as he pushed Roxanne away from him. "And tell Jason he was right. I should have listened to him."

Jason Devereux was Roxanne's twin brother. Wesley and Jason had been best friends from when they were toddlers up until they were teenagers.

"Don't you dare die on me, Wes."

"I'm not planning on it."

Roxanne gave Wesley a quick kiss. She then leaped over the side of the wagon and took off running across the parking lot. I didn't see Summer or Autumn anywhere, and I could only hope that Roxanne had left them with a Shatner or Devereux at the Pumpkin Patch.

"Is Jason here?" I asked Wesley, panicking because I was afraid that we had missed seeing Jason and left him behind in the Torture barn.

"He's not here. He was supposed to come with us, but he got called in to work this morning so he went home to get a couple hours of sleep," Wesley said as he wrapped the fingers of his right hand around my wrist and pulled me back down onto the hay beside him. "Jason told us not to come. He said it sounded fishy. I should have listened to him. Tell him I should have listened to him."

Before I could respond, one of the EMTs yelled at me to get out of the way. I scrambled backwards and surrendered Wesley to the EMTs.

Hank was being loaded into the back of one of the ambulances, and three other EMTs were working on Waylon. The EMTs had placed a neck brace on Waylon, and they were in the process of strapping him to a backboard.

I climbed out of the wagon and was instantly surrounded by deputies and Shatners. All of them were shouting questions at me. I fought back another wave of anxiety, and then I started handing out instructions on what I needed everyone to do. I sent Veda to ride in the ambulance with Wesley in case he had anything more to say. I tossed Naomi my keys and told her to follow the ambulances to the hospital. I sensed that Naomi was still on the verge of a panic attack, and I could only hope that she didn't crash my Jeep. I instructed Red and Bubba to close the gate and make sure no one went down to the Torture barn. The area was now a crime scene, and I didn't want to risk having evidence get trampled because people decided they wanted to have a look. I also told Bubba to put up announcements that the Body Farm was closed tonight.

"What the hell is going on?" Uncle Murph shouted as he shoved his way through the crowd of Shatners and deputies. "What happened to the boys?"

"That's what I'm trying to figure out," I said. I gave Uncle Murph a summary of what I knew. "I need you to go over to Uncle Woody's and Aunt Deidra's place. Tell them about what happened and get them to the hospital. And then do the same with Hank's parents."

"Considering how many Shatners are here, Woody and Deidra probably already know. Same with Hank's parents," Uncle Murph said before he took off running for his cruiser.

"What would you like me to do?" asked Chief Deputy Juan Quaranta. His Fu Manchu mustache was uncombed, and his brown uniform pants were soaked from the knees down.

Quaranta and I didn't always get along—he was aware that Uncle Murph and I cleaned up after our family's criminal misdeeds, and he did not approve—but he and I worked well together at processing crime scenes and investigating the cases.

"Let's get the crime scene secured and start processing it," I said to Quaranta. He gestured for me to lead the way, but I wasn't quite ready to face the Torture barn. "Give me a minute. I need to calm down."

"I'll take the Chief Deputy and everyone else down to Torture," Deputy Grant volunteered. His dark crimson curls were slicked back, and his uniform was splattered with mud. "That way you can take your time."

Timmy Grant was one of the youngest deputies who worked for the Wyatt County Sheriff's Department. He was also the most incompetent. Since the beginning of the year, Timmy had pepper-sprayed and tased himself and others on multiple occasions—me included. Timmy had also accidently discharged his weapon seven times, lost his handcuffs so many times that we had lost count, broke over a thousand dollars' worth of equipment, wrongfully arrested two people, and wrecked three sheriff's department cruisers. He damaged two of the cruisers when he backed into light poles. He totaled the third one earlier in October when he swerved to avoid a squirrel. The squirrel was already dead, but Timmy hadn't wanted to run over the carcass. I could only assume that Timmy or his mother had blackmail on Uncle Murph, and that the blackmail was the only reason Uncle Murph had for having not fired Timmy yet.

When he wasn't on duty, Timmy worked at the Body Farm. This season, he popped out of a hole in the wall in the hayride's haunted mine and threatened the customers with a foam pickaxe. At least once a night, he accidentally bonked a costumer on the head with the pickaxe. He'd also fallen out of the hole and into the wagon several times.

After Timmy had led Quaranta and the rest of the deputies towards the Body Farm entrance, I sagged against the side of the wagon and took a few deep breaths to calm down. I then dug my cell phone out of my jacket pocket and called Alberto.

"We've got a problem."

"I should say we do," Alberto said. "This trailer I'm renting from your uncles is a piece of crap. During the storm, the roof leaked right over the bed. My mattress is ruined."

"My problem is a whole lot bigger than that," I said before I filled him in on what was going on out at the Body Farm. "What should I do?"

"Jesus, Mary, and Joseph . . ." Alberto muttered. I could picture him crossing himself as he said it. "Process the scene. I'll call Lieutenant Schmitt and let him know what's going on. If he can, I'll have him send a forensics unit to help you guys out."

By the time I slogged down the muddy path to Torture, the deputies had roped off the barn with caution tape. Quaranta was inside taking video of what was left of the crime scene.

"Are you sure you're up for this, Carrie?" Quaranta asked as I peered inside the barn. "I can handle processing the scene if you want to go to the hospital or deal with your family."

"I can handle it," I said even though I wasn't sure if I could. I learned years ago—back when I was in Nashville and made a living out of processing crime scenes that were far worse than this one—to turn off my emotions and view everything objectively through the camera's lens. I had to force myself not to think about what Wesley, Waylon, and Hank had suffered through during the night. "This is where I need to be."

I snatched a digital camera, notebook, and pen out of Quaranta's crime scene kit. I tossed the notebook and pen to Timmy and instructed him to jot down notes for me while I took photos. The extensive number of notes I had to take while photographing a crime scene would drag out the process. Having Timmy take the notes for me would help speed things up a little bit. I started out with taking long shots, and then I moved in for closeups.

As I took pictures, I looked around for possible evidence. I knew that there would be fingerprints on nearly every solid surface. A nameless, red shirt wearing ensign on "Star Trek: The Original Series" had a better chance of surviving to the first commercial break than we did of finding the attackers' fingerprints among the millions of other ones in the barn.

I did find plenty of hairs and fibers—but they could have come from any one of the actors or even the customers. Same with the random blood drops I found. Working on the hayride was dangerous, and we actors frequently suffered bumps, bruises, and small lacerations.

A couple hours after we had started processing the scene, I was straddling the top of a twelve-foot-high ladder while taking pictures of the rafters when someone shouted, "Everyone stop what you're doing!" I twisted around to look over my shoulder and probably would have knocked the ladder off balance had Timmy not been holding it steady for me.

Standing in the doorway of the barn were two people. They were backlit by the sun, and I couldn't tell who they were until they ducked under the crime scene tape and entered the barn. Right away, I recognized Lieutenant Hugh Underwood and Sergeant Arthur Boleyn of the Texas Rangers. Both were part of the Ranger's B Division, and they were stationed out of Tyler, Texas.

Hugh Underwood resembled a stereotypical mob boss, and he had the presence of one, too. I wasn't intimidated by all that many people—it's hard to find people intimidating when you're related to a bunch of criminals—but Underwood was one of the very few people that did scare me. Underwood and I had recently come to an understanding, and he was working with me, Lieutenant Schmitt, and Alberto to build the case against my family.

I'd only had a few encounters with Sergeant Boleyn in the past four years that I had worked for the sheriff's department. None of those encounters had been pleasant. Boleyn was a strait-laced, arrogant man, and he was not a big fan of the Shatners.

"What are y'all doing here?" I asked Underwood and Boleyn as I climbed down the ladder. "Because if you're here to help, we could certainly use it."

"We're here to take over," Boleyn said. He ripped the digital camera out of my hands and removed the memory card. He then tossed the camera back to me. "This is my crime scene now. I'll be confiscating all of your photos, notes, and video. As well as any evidence you've collected. I will then request that all of you leave because you're now trespassing."

"Now hold on a minute." I stepped closer to Boleyn and glared at him. "Y'all are not kicking me out of my crime scene. Two of my cousins and a family friend were assaulted in here last night. This is my case. Y'all can help, but you're not taking over."

"Lieutenant, please explain to Miss Shatner that she has no choice but to surrender the crime scene. Let her know that if she doesn't, she'll be arrested for obstruction of justice and interference in a police investigation. And I will personally take her to jail and see that she remains there," Sergeant Boleyn said as he shouldered past me. He wrenched the notebook out of Timmy's hands and then demanded that Quaranta hand over his notes and video camera. "You should also let everyone at the Wyatt County Sheriff's Department know that I will not stand for any of them interfering in my investigation."

"Are you really kicking me out of my crime scene, Lieutenant Underwood?" I asked the stern-faced older man. "I can help."

"I don't need your help," Boleyn snapped.

"It's for the best, Detective Shatner." Lieutenant Underwood lowered his voice and said, "I discussed this with Lieutenant Schmitt. We both agree that having the Department of Public Safety take over the investigation into what happened to your cousins is for the best. It will help us build the case against your family. This way we can come in through the front door to obtain evidence opposed to using you to sneak through the back door."

I groaned, but didn't bother arguing with Underwood.

"Have you heard any updates from the hospital?" I asked. I had purposely turned off my cell phone because my family members had been calling and texting me almost nonstop.

"I just got word that the Garrett kid didn't make it," Underwood said. "According to the doctor that I talked to, Hank suffered a skull fracture that ruptured a blood vessel and caused an extradural hematoma. The doctor was trying to stop the bleeding around his brain, but it was too extensive. He died on the operating table."

"Shit . . . Poor Hank . . ." I sank down onto the bottom step of the ladder and rubbed my hands over my face. This was now a murder investigation. "What about Wes and Waylon?"

"Wes is stable. The doctors patched him up. Later they are going to amputate what's left of his pinkie," Underwood said. "And Waylon is in surgery. That's all I know."

Boleyn wrapped his hand around my forearm and yanked me to my feet. "Before you go, Miss Shatner, I'd appreciate it if you told us about what happened here and let us know what all you've done so far to contaminate my crime scene."

I reluctantly gave Underwood and Boleyn a tour of the Torture barn. Boleyn kept making barbed comments about how Wesley had most likely done something to instigate the attack, and that Quaranta and I had probably destroyed evidence in our haste to process the crime scene. Underwood did his best to keep the peace between us.

"I'll need you to provide a written statement, Miss Shatner. Tomorrow morning will be soon enough," Sergeant Boleyn said as he held up the crime scene tape for me. He all but shoved me out of the Torture barn. "What the hell is Jerrod Hardy doing here? Get him out of here."

Jerrod.

The name slammed into me and almost knocked me over backwards.

Sergeant Jerrod Hardy was also a Texas Ranger with the Company B Division, and he was stationed out of Tyler, Texas. He had taken over the post last fall, but I didn't meet him until the wee hours of New Year's Day. I had just found a dead body in the dumpster following my family's big party at the Wyatt County Fairgrounds. Knowing I couldn't investigate a homicide that I was a suspect in—no, I hadn't been involved in how the guy wound up dead in a dumpster, but I had been at the fairgrounds all night and the body had clearly been stuffed into the dumpster sometime during the party—I called in the Department of Public Safety to take over the investigation. The DPS sent me Sergeant Hardy.

The attraction between me and Hardy had been almost immediate. It had started out as a physical attraction, but it had rapidly developed into something more. Despite driving him nuts, interfering with his investigation, and almost getting him killed, Hardy was still interested in me by the time we wrapped up the case. We had dated for around four months, but Hardy finally called an end to it when he realized that he could not deal with my family or the role I played in helping cover up their crimes.

In the months since we had broken up, Hardy had helped me investigate two other murders. Both times Hardy had come to town, we had gotten back together. We knew our relationship had a slow-moving armadillo's chance of making it across the road unscathed, but that didn't stop us from trying.

I had only seen Hardy once since accepting the deal with the DPS and taking over as the head of my family's criminal operation. Three weeks ago, Hardy had come through on the Hayride of Nightmares and I spotted him sitting in the back of the wagon. Billy Bob hadn't even come out of the shack when Hardy and I made eye contact. It wasn't time for me to hit the wagon yet, but I was already up and moving towards Hardy. I couldn't really talk to him—not when he was crammed into the wagon between two other customers. But I had been able to look at him and to touch him for a few seconds.

But that was it. Other than those two minutes in which he had been in Moonshiners' Grove, I had not seen or talked to Hardy since mid-August. We hadn't even texted or emailed each other. There had been zero communication.

I had no idea where we were in our relationship. I didn't know if we even had a relationship anymore. But a possible future with Hardy was the only thing that kept me going as I turned over evidence against the Shatners. He was the light at the end of a long, dark tunnel.

If I was my family's lifeboat, Hardy was my lifejacket. He was keeping me afloat while my family tried to drag me under.

I hadn't said anything to him—heck, I could barely admit it to myself—but I was in love with Hardy. Or, at least, I thought I was. Once things with my family were taken care of and I didn't have to deal with the DPS anymore, I could get my feelings sorted out.

For the time being, I was just glad he was here.

"Jerrod!"

I took off running. My boots slid in the mud as I sprinted towards him. Hardy met me halfway and scooped me off my feet in a tight embrace. In his arms, all the anxiety and stress of the past two months melted away. For a few seconds, I felt peaceful and weightless.

"Hey, darlin'," Hardy whispered against the top of my head. "You've got no idea how much I've missed you."

"Probably nowhere near as much as I've missed you," I said. Pressing my face against Hardy's chest, I could feel his heart pounding beneath my cheek. "What are you doing here?"

"I heard about what happened, so I came to help," Hardy said. "Besides, this is where I should have been all along. I never should have left you to face this on your own."

"You didn't leave," I said. "I forced you to go away."

"Yeah, well, I should never have listened to you."

I leaned back and looked up at Hardy. His face was leaner than it had been two months earlier, and his cheekbones were more pronounced. There were dark purple half-circles under his brown eyes that resembled bruises. Black stubble covered his cheeks, and he was in desperate need of a haircut. I reached up and brushed a stray lock of black hair away from his forehead. As I did so, I noticed silver hairs along his temples that had not been there before.

"I hate to break up this reunion."

Groaning, I let go of Hardy and then spun around to face his lieutenant. I doubted that Underwood felt any regret over interrupting Hardy's and my reunion. If anything, Underwood was probably secretly thrilled. From the moment that he found out that Hardy and I were dating back in January, Underwood had been trying to break us up. He had confronted me multiple times—accusing me of attempting to use Hardy to protect my family and demanding that I end the relationship. Underwood made it clear that he thought our relationship would wind up being detrimental to Hardy both personally and professionally.

"What do you want me to do, Lieutenant?" Hardy asked.

"For now . . . get out of here before Boleyn blows a gasket," Underwood patted me on the back. "Take Detective Shatner home. Or to the hospital. Just get away from the crime scene."

CHAPTER SEVEN

"**Y**OU ASK ME, THEY KILLED THE WRONG ONE. Should have been Wesley that got killed. Not that Hank kid. Would have done the two of you a favor."

"Go to Hell, Dad! If Wes dies, I'll just die, too. I can't live without him."

"Wesley ruined your life, Roxanne. And your brother's life. After them Shatners got me sent to prison, I told you and told you to stay away from them. But neither of you listened and look what happened."

"Knock it off, Dad. You got yourself in trouble. And it's not like it was all Wes's fault. He didn't force us to do nothing. Roxanne and I made our own choices."

"And most of those choices wound up being mistakes."

After leaving the Body Farm, Hardy tried to talk me into making a quick stop at my house so that I could clean up and change into clothes that weren't covered in mud. I refused to go home, and, instead, insisted that Hardy take me directly to Wyatt County General Hospital so that I could check on my cousins. The hospital, which was in the south-western part of Holler, was about a twenty-minute drive away from the Body Farm.

Hardy and I were walking up to the Emergency Room entrance when we overheard the argument. Following the sound of angry voices and the acrid smell of cigarette smoke around the side of the building, we came across a wooden gazebo tucked into an alcove. Inside the gazebo were Pork Chop Devereux and his two kids. Judging by the pile of cigarette butts amassed at Pork Chop's feet, he had been there for a while.

Pork Chop was Catfish Devereux's fifth child overall, and the first child he had with his third wife. Pork Chop had received the most laughable and unfortunate of the nicknames that Catfish had bequeathed on his children. The story was that Catfish's third wife was in the middle of making Sunday dinner when she went into labor. Catfish, who was apparently angry that he had to skip dinner to take his wife to the hospital, nicknamed his new son after the meal that he missed. Unfortunately for Pork Chop, the nickname stuck.

Years ago, Pork Chop had been heavily involved in the Shatners' moonshine business. He not only helped make the moonshine, he also transported it around East Texas to our customers. Pork Chop's involvement came to an unexpected end roughly ten years ago when he got pulled over by a State Trooper for having an expired registration. The Trooper searched the car and found three dozen mason jars full of moonshine hidden in the trunk. Pork Chop was arrested and charged with a slew of crimes. The prosecutor tried his damnedest to get Pork Chop to turn over evidence against the Shatners, but he kept his mouth shut.

While Pork Chop was serving his concurrent sentence, his first wife left him. It was also during this time that Wesley got Roxanne pregnant with their older daughter, and Jason got busted selling marijuana to their classmates at Big Pine Senior High School. Everyone knew that he was selling the marijuana along with Wesley, but Jason refused to turn in his best friend. For punishment, Jason was expelled from school and sent to a juvenile detention center until he turned eighteen.

Since being released from prison, Pork Chop has had nothing to do with the Shatners or our many criminal endeavors. He doesn't associate with his father or any of his siblings all that much either. The same goes for Jason.

"You ask me, Wesley had it coming," Pork Chop said.

"Just because he had it coming doesn't mean he deserved it," I said as Hardy and I joined them in the gazebo. I shot Pork Chop an icy glare. "Are there any updates on Wes or Waylon?"

"Waylon is still in surgery. Sounds like he's pretty messed up," Roxanne said. She then explained that Wesley had a badly sprained left wrist. Bones in his left hand were broken, as was his nose. He also had three cracked ribs and a bruised kidney. "The doc let Woody, Deidra, and Wynonna see Wes. But they won't let me see him."

"Woody and Deidra are his parents. And Wynonna is his sister," Pork Chop pointed out. He ground out what was left of his cigarette and lit another one. "You're nothing more than one of Wesley's baby mamas."

"I'm his fiancée!" Roxanne held up her left hand and showed off the thin band that encircled her ring finger. "We're getting married next year."

I grasped Roxanne's hand so that I could get a closer look at the ring. It was hard to tell if the microscopic stone was a diamond chip or a cubic zirconia. Considering how much money Wesley allegedly made selling drugs, he could have afforded a fancier ring than one that looked like it came out of a quarter gumball machine. No wonder I hadn't noticed it earlier.

Pork Chop snorted. "Quit fooling yourself, Roxanne. Wes ain't gonna marry you. Just like he didn't marry you all those other times he promised."

"He is, too, gonna marry me!" Roxanne jumped up from the bench so that she could shout in her father's face. I stepped between them and tried to push them apart. "Wes promised we'll get married after the baby is born."

"Hold on . . . Roxanne, are you pregnant?" I asked.

Roxanne grinned at me. "Five months along. Wes and I found out about two months ago, but we haven't told many people yet. It's a boy, and we're gonna name him Wesley Junior."

"And Wesley will do the same thing with this kid that he did with the other two," Pork Chop said. "He's gonna deny he's the daddy, break up with you, and then knock up some other girl. And, when he finally comes crawling back to you, you will be dumb enough to forgive him and take him back. He's a bad boyfriend, and an even worse father. He's a criminal, and he don't give a damn about anyone but himself. You and the girls would be better off without him."

"Shut up!" Roxanne screamed at Pork Chop. She pulled back her arm to slap her father, but I stopped her from following through. "I hate you! I hate you! I hate you!"

"Yeah, Dad, you're really one to talk," Jason said. He pushed his twin sister aside so that he could confront their father. "You sure as hell weren't around all that much for me and Roxanne when we were growing up. And that was before you got sent to prison. Let's be honest, you make Wes look like Father of the Year."

"Why are you defending Wesley all of a sudden?" Pork Chop asked Jason. "You were ready to kill him just the other month when Roxanne told us she was pregnant."

"Yeah, well . . . Wes and I talked. We're good now," Jason said.

"Good my ass." Pork Chop tossed his half-smoked cigarette onto the ground and stomped on it. "I'm leaving. If you two want a ride home, y'all better get your butts in the car."

"Give us a minute, Pork Chop," I said as I guided Roxanne out of the gazebo and over towards the Emergency Room entrance. Roxanne had resumed crying, and her entire body trembled. "You've got to calm down. It can't be good for the baby."

"I know. I know." Roxanne wrapped her arms around me and pressed her tear-stained face against my shoulder. It was one of the few parts of my jacket that wasn't splattered with dried mud. "I've been listening to Dad criticize Wes for years. I'm sick of it. He and Bambi won't let Wes in the house, and they talk trash on him in front of the girls. I don't think I can take it any longer."

Bambi was Pork Chop's second wife. She wasn't all that much older that Roxanne and Jason—in fact, Bambi graduated from high school two years after me. It seemed that Bambi's sole purpose in life was to antagonize her stepchildren. Roxanne had been living with her father since her mother kicked her and Summer out of the house on Roxanne's eighteenth birthday.

"Roxanne, did you . . . uhh . . . did you take care of the Code Red situation?" I asked.

"Yeah, I handled it," Roxanne said. She stepped away from me and brushed her long brown hair out of her eyes. "Jason and I went over to the townhouse and got everything cleaned up. Not that Wes and Waylon had all that much illegal stuff there. They ain't *that* stupid."

"Good. The Texas Rangers have taken over the case, and it won't be long before they search the townhouse. We need to clean up after Wes and Waylon the best that we can."

"Then we gotta do something about Wes's car. It's probably still at the Body Farm," Roxanne said. "And there's something else that needs cleaned up, but Jason and I need help. It's not at the townhouse. It's—"

"Move it or lose it, Roxanne!" Pork Chop shouted. He was sitting in his car and honking the horn at her. "You know I'll leave without you."

"Later, Roxanne. We'll take care of it later." I gave Roxanne a gentle shove towards her dad's car. "Go home to your girls. I'll call you sometime tonight."

After watching Roxanne jump into the backseat just as Pork Chop pulled out of the parking space, Hardy turned to me and said, "We should probably check if Pork Chop has an alibi for early this morning."

"Not necessary. Trust me, if Pork Chop had been involved, Wes would be missing a body part other than his pinkie."

"He would have done the rest of us a favor," Hardy said. "We don't need any more versions of Wesley running around. There's too many as it is."

"Maybe I can talk the doctor into giving Wes a vasectomy when they amputate his pinkie," I joked before I turned around and opened the Emergency Room doors.

Inside, Hardy and I found that the waiting room had been taken over by a small horde of Shatners. My family was putting on what appeared to be an amateur, one-ring circus. Wherever the Shatners went, chaos was sure to follow—and this was no exception.

My uncles Woodrow and Murph were over by the front desk. Uncle Woody was leaning across the counter and screaming incoherently at one of the nurses. Uncle Murph had wrapped his arms around his younger brother's thick waist and was unsuccessfully attempting to drag Uncle Woody away from the counter before he physically assaulted the nurse. Nearby, my great-uncles Houston and Bowie were huddled behind a potted plant. They were having what looked like a heated conversation.

Uncle Woody's wife, Deidra, lay sprawled out on a row of padded chairs. She was sobbing and tearing out pieces of her cinnamon-colored hair. If she kept it up, she would be bald by morning. Perched on a chair next to Aunt Deidra was an older, red-headed woman. With one hand, she clung to her oversized purse. With her other hand, she absentmindedly patted Aunt Deidra on the shoulder. At first glance, I mistook the woman for a bystander who had the misfortune of getting caught up in the Shatners' drama. Then I realized the woman was Aunt Deidra's mother.

Seated on the other side of Aunt Deidra was her mother-in-law. My great-aunt-Imogen had her wrinkled hands clasped together under her chin, and she was in the middle of a loud conversation with God about how He needed to spare her grandchildren and take her instead. If Aunt Imogen was to be believed, Wesley and Waylon were good boys who had never done a bad thing in their young lives.

Lying on the floor nearby were Uncle Woody's and Aunt Deidra's two youngest kids. Twelve-year-old Wade and ten-year-old Willow had their handheld video game consoles hooked together and were playing some sort of game against each other. I assumed it was either a violent game or a pro wrestling game considering Wade and Willow were screaming "die!" and "kill him!" at each other. Wade and Willow had always disturbed me. Neither of them really showed any type of emotion, and they barely had a grasp on the difference between right and wrong.

Aside from me, there wasn't a sane Shatner to be seen in the waiting room—and, somedays, I wasn't too sure about my level of sanity.

"You think I could get them involuntarily committed?" I asked.

"In a heartbeat," Hardy said.

"What are you doing here, Carrie?" Uncle Murph shouted. He let go of Uncle Woody and charged across the waiting room towards where Hardy and I were standing by the entrance. "Shouldn't you still be processing the crime scene?"

"I got kicked out of the crime scene. The whole sheriff's department did when the DPS showed up and took over."

Uncle Murph jabbed Hardy in the chest and asked, "If the DPS took over, what are you doing here?"

"It's not my case," Hardy said. "I got kicked out, too. Sergeant Arthur Boleyn is in charge of the investigation."

"Son of a bitch . . ." Uncle Murph muttered. "This ain't good. Ain't good at all."

"Sergeant Boleyn is good at his job. He'll do everything he can to find the people who did this to Wesley, Waylon, and Hank," Hardy said.

"I know Boleyn's good at his job. That's what I'm worried about. Yeah, I want the bastards who did this caught. But I don't want Boleyn looking too closely at the family. Once he starts digging, he's bound to find something. And the more he finds, the more he'll dig." Uncle Murph swiped at the beads of sweat cascading down his forehead. "Why can't you be in charge, Sergeant Hardy? Like you were back in January. You focused on the case and didn't waste much time investigating the family."

"I also had a certain someone keeping me distracted so that I didn't dig up evidence against y'all," Hardy said as he gave me a pointed look. "And the reason I'm not part of this investigation is because I'm too close to your family."

"This ain't gonna end well." Uncle Murph pulled a handful of change out of his pants pocket and then practically sprinted over to the vending machines that were tucked away in the back corner of the waiting room. Uncle Murph selected a candy bar, and he inhaled it in three or four bites. A euphoric look came over his pudgy face.

"About time you got here."

Finally, a sane Shatner aside from myself!

My sixteen-year-old cousin Wynonna Shatner materialized next to me. Wynonna reminded me a lot of myself at that age. She had never gotten into any serious trouble, and she stayed as far away as she possibly could from the family's crimes. She was my sole shining hope for the younger generation of Shatners.

"I tried to get them to stop," Wynonna said. "I kept telling them that something really bad was gonna happen sooner or later. And now it has. Maybe if I had tried harder . . ."

"Don't blame yourself, Wynonna. Your brothers are responsible for their own actions," I said. I put my arm around her slender shoulders and hugged her against my side. "They wouldn't listen to you. They wouldn't listen to me—"

"Wesley won't listen to nobody," Uncle Houston said as he and Uncle Bowie joined us. "Thinks he's the smartest sumbitch in the room."

"The boy just has an independent streak," Uncle Bowie said. He had been making excuses for his grandson since the day Wesley was born.

"No. What the boy's got is an incurable case of stupidity." Uncle Houston took me by the arm and guided me a few feet away from the others. He lowered his voice and said, "Murph told us Wes met up with some Honduran about getting cocaine. Just when I thought Wes couldn't get any dumber . . . Who the heck is this Honduran? Where did Wes meet him at? And why'd this guy and his buddies do this to the boys?"

I shrugged. "I don't think there is any Honduran. It sounds like what happened to the boys last night was a setup to get info on the family. Wes said that's all these people seemed interested in—our family and our current crimes."

"Shit . . . You better find the sumbitches responsible. You gotta catch 'em before they come after the rest of us." Uncle Houston leaned closer to me and whispered, "I don't think I need to explain to you how bad it could turn out if this Sergeant Boleyn comes after our family. It ain't just the family that'll go down. The Devereuxs and Palmers will, too."

"And so will at least a third of the sheriff's department," I said.

"And the officers I have on the payroll with the Holler, Wilder, and Mooresville police departments," Uncle Houston added. "Plus, all the judges in Wyatt County, a bunch of State Troopers, a handful of federal agents, a congressman—"

"You're bribing a congressman?"

"And a senator," Uncle Houston said. "Not to mention El Lobo. He's been callin' me all afternoon askin' for updates and threatenin' me. I need you to nip this in the bud. You gotta find the people who did this to the boys before Boleyn starts lookin' too closely at the family."

"That's what I'm planning to do," I said.

"If you need help hidin' any bodies, you just give your favorite uncle a call." Uncle Houston clapped me on the shoulder and winked.

"Do me a favor, Uncle Houston," I called after him as he headed out the door. "Set up a family meeting for tomorrow around noon. Have all of the Shatners, Palmers, and Devereuxs meet up somewhere private so we can figure out what to do next."

"I hope you got a plan, missy," Uncle Houston called back to me just before the doors slammed shut behind him.

"No, I don't have a plan . . . Not yet at least."

Hardy walked over to where I was standing. "Carrie, the shit has well and truly hit the fan. What is it that you think you can do?"

"No, Jerrod, the shit hit the fan a long time ago. This time it was the whole septic tank." Leaving Hardy by the door, I headed across the waiting room to the vending machines and pushed Uncle Murph out of the way. After consuming the candy bar, he had eaten a bag of artificially-flavored buttered popcorn. He was now rapidly working his way through a bag of pretzels. "Aren't you supposed to be on a diet?"

"Yeah . . . Lydia's got me on another one of them darn fad diets. This time it's creamed corn." Uncle Murph pulled a packet of snack cakes out of his jacket pocket and ripped open the cellophane. As he shoved a cake into his mouth, he mumbled, "Don't tell her about this."

"Your secret is safe with me."

Personally, I agreed with Aunt Lydia—Uncle Murph had a bad habit of consuming unhealthy snacks almost nonstop throughout the day, and he needed to lose weight. I just didn't think force feeding the man cans of creamed corn was going to help him shed some pounds. I was also against the dieting because Uncle Murph was typically meaner than a sack full of rattlesnakes whenever Aunt Lydia attempted to deprive him of his sugary or salty snacks.

"I heard Uncle Houston took you on a field trip earlier," Uncle

Murph said as he moved over to a soda machine and got a Diet Coke. "How'd that go?"

"It was educational. And much more interesting than any of the field trips I went on when I was in school."

"You're in up to your eyebrows now, Carrie," Uncle Murph said. Chocolate cake crumbs spewed out of his mouth as he chewed and talked at the same time. "I voted against Uncle Houston showing you where the grow houses and the stills are. But he said it was time you knew, and my dad and Uncle Crockett agreed with him."

"If Uncle Houston hadn't shown me the stills and grow houses this morning, I wouldn't have gone back to the Body Farm when I had," I pointed out. "It could have been another couple of hours before the boys were found. Waylon could have been dead by then."

"Yeah, well . . ." Uncle Murph sputtered. "Either way I don't care what Uncle Houston says. I'm not going to answer to you. I don't answer to nobody."

"Whatever, Murph." I turned my back to him and dropped some change into the closest vending machine. "You're just upset Uncle Houston didn't put you in charge."

Before Uncle Murph emptied the vending machines, I selected a packet of peanut butter crackers, a Snickers, and a Coke. It was the first food I had eaten since the cheeseburger at the Pumpkin Patch, and that was hours ago.

After eating, I joined the rest of the family in anxiously waiting for an update on Waylon. Every time a door opened or someone on the hospital's medical staff walked into the waiting room, we collectively jumped up and demanded answers. Uncle Woody paced back and forth across the room. Aunt Deidra kept crying. Aunt Imogen kept praying. Wade and Willow played video games until the batteries in their hand-held consoles died. They then switched over to playing games on their phones. Uncle Murph, Hardy, and I also paid a visit to the morgue so that we could see Hank before he was sent off to the medical examiner to be autopsied.

The three of us had just come back from the hospital's morgue when a nurse pulled me aside and asked if I was related to Keaton Mount. After confirming that he was my cousin, the nurse led me to where a doctor was stitching up the inch-long gash on the back of my younger cousin's head.

"What happened to you?" I asked Keaton.

Keaton looked up at me through the curtain of long, blonde hair that fell in front of his face. The doctor had shaved off a patch of hair around the gash.

"I was coming out of the gym," Keaton mumbled. His voice was a bit slurred, and his eyes couldn't seem to focus on my face. "Some big dude jumped me and bashed my head with something hard. Said our family's time is up and that I was next. He seemed to know all about my . . . my . . . you know."

"Extracurricular activities?" I asked.

"Yeah. Those." Keaton winked at me. "I fought the guy off and he ran away. He yelled something about how this ain't gonna be the end of it."

Keaton was an electrician by day, and a professional wrestler at night. While a lot of people would argue that professional wrestling is fake, they couldn't deny that Keaton had better self-defense skills that the average person. I was confident that his attacker had not walked away unscathed.

"Did you get a look at the guy?" I asked.

Keaton shook his head. "Nah. Dude was big. But he had some cheap Devil mask on."

A cheap Devil mask? Like the ones that Wesley's attackers had worn?

After being reassured by the doctor that Keaton would be all right—the head wound was superficial—I rejoined my family in the waiting room and resumed my vigil for Waylon. While waiting for an update, I sent off a group text message to all my family members to be careful. Someone had declared open season on the Shatners, and Keaton had just proved that any one of them could be next.

It was just before nine o'clock when the doors into the Emergency Room opened and a tired looking, middle-aged doctor emerged followed by Sergeant Boleyn and Lieutenant Underwood. Boleyn and Underwood must have come into the hospital through a different entrance since we hadn't seen them come through the Emergency Room's waiting room.

"How's Waylon?" Uncle Woody charged at the doctor and grabbed him by the upper arms. "How's my son?"

"Waylon is out of surgery and is being moved to a recovery room in the Intensive Care Unit as we speak," the doctor said as he tried to pull away from Uncle Woody. I shoved my way to the front of the group and pried Uncle Woody's fingers off the doctor's arms. "My team got

Waylon stabilized, but he is in critical condition. We placed him in a medically induced coma for the time being."

"Thank God he's alive," Aunt Deidra murmured before she fainted. She collapsed on the floor between Wade and Willow, but they were so engrossed with their phones that they didn't seem to notice. The only person who moved to help Aunt Deidra was her mother. She waved a packet of smelling salts under Aunt Deidra's nose, and it brought her back around.

The doctor rattled off a long list of Waylon's injuries that included a small skull fracture, a broken occipital bone, a sprained wrist, a broken wrist, two dislocated shoulders, three broken ribs, two cracked ribs, a collapsed lung, a ruptured spleen, and a number of minor internal and external injuries and contusions. From the waist up, Waylon was a mess. From the waist down—aside from a testicular rupture—he had barely been touched. The doctor said he was cautiously optimistic that Waylon would survive his injuries.

"Can we see Waylon?" Uncle Woody asked. "And Wesley. We want to see him again."

"Of course, you can see your sons," the doctor said. "A nurse can—"

"No. They can't," Boleyn said, cutting off the doctor. "Ain't no one other than doctors or nurses going in to see those boys until after I've had a chance to talk to them. They shouldn't have been allowed in to see Wesley earlier."

"Waylon's in a coma," I pointed out to Boleyn. "He's not going to be doing any talking."

"I still don't want anyone seeing Waylon until after I talk to him," Boleyn insisted.

"The boy could be in a coma for days," the doctor said. "There is a possibility that he may never wake up."

Aunt Deidra screamed and collapsed a second time.

"Oh, let the parents see their boy," Underwood said to Boleyn.

"I'm going, too," I said.

"And me," Wynonna said. "I want to see my brother."

Boleyn sighed. "Fine. Y'all can see Waylon. But not Wesley. Mr. and Mrs. Shatner already saw him, and I don't want anyone talking to him until I get a chance to interview him about last night. I plan to do that in the morning before they amputate what's left of his finger."

The doctor waved over one of the nurses that was seated behind the front desk and instructed her to take me, Wynonna, Uncle Woody, and Aunt Deidra to the ICU so that we could see Waylon. Hardy, Boleyn, and Underwood brought up the rear of our small group. As we followed the nurse through the maze of hallways, I drew Hardy and Wynonna back.

I let two orderlies pushing an elderly man on a gurney get between us and the rest of our group. I then whispered, "I have to see Wes. I want to talk to him again before Sergeant Boleyn does. Once we're in Waylon's room, Wynonna, I'll need you to create a diversion to get us out of there. Fake a panic attack or something."

Wynonna gave me a thumbs up. "One diversion coming up."

"Do you think you can find your way back to Wes's room?" I asked. After Wynonna nodded, I turned to Hardy and said, "And, Jerrod, I'll need you to prevent Boleyn from following me and Wynonna. Can you handle that?"

"I'll do my best," Hardy said.

"Here we are," the nurse announced as she led us around the State Trooper who had been posted outside of Waylon's room. "Remember, the patient is in a medically induced coma."

We crowded into the small room and gathered around Waylon's bed. Because of all the machinery taking up space, we were forced to practically stand on top of each other. Waylon was hooked up to an IV, a breathing machine, and a heart monitor. His entire midsection and both shoulders were wrapped in bandages. He had a cast around one wrist, and a brace around another. There was also a bandage wrapped around his head.

"Oh, Waylon!" Aunt Deidra shrieked as she attempted to embrace her unconscious son. Sergeant Boleyn and the nurse stepped in to stop her from injuring Waylon even more. "My baby. My poor baby."

I nudged Wynonna in the side and gestured for her to head for the door. On cue, Wynonna began hyperventilating and burst into tears. She hurled herself into my arms and almost knocked me over.

"I'm going to take Wynonna back to the waiting room. This is too much for her," I announced as I hustled her out the door and past the State Trooper. I encouraged Wynonna to keep up the act until we had rounded a corner and were safe from the prying eyes of the State Trooper. "We're good. You can knock it off."

"It wasn't all an act," Wynonna said as used her sleeve to wipe away her tears. She led me over to a bank of elevators and punched the "up" button. We took the elevator up to the third floor and got off in the pediatric unit. Wynonna then led the way towards the private recovery rooms. "Wes's room should be down this hallway."

"Whoa. Hold up," I said as we rounded a corner and I spotted a State Trooper. I grabbed Wynonna's arm and yanked her back around the corner. "I'm guessing Wes is in the room that's being guarded by the Trooper."

Wynonna peeked around the corner. "Yeah. The Trooper wasn't there when Mom, Dad, and I came up earlier."

"This could be a problem," I mumbled as I leaned around Wynonna and eyed up the Trooper. He was at least six-feet-tall and built like a brick shithouse. "I don't think he's going to let me into Wes's room no matter how nicely I ask."

"I got this." Wynonna took off sprinting down the hallway. She crashed into the State Trooper and screamed, "I need to see my brother."

"Oh, no, you don't, little lady. No one is allowed in to see the patient until Sergeant Boleyn says so." The State Trooper took Wynonna by the arm and abandoned his post when he guided her down the hallway in the opposite direction. "Let's get you back downstairs."

I waited until Wynonna and the State Trooper were out of sight before I dashed down the deserted hallway and ducked into Wesley's room

"Psst . . . Wesley . . ."

"Carrie?" Because of the neck brace that held his head stationary, Wesley had to roll onto his side to look at me. His smashed nose was covered in bandages. "Yo, were you mud wrestling at the Dancing Cowgirl?"

"No, I was not mud wrestling at a strip club. I was processing the crime scene. You know . . . where you, Waylon, and Hank were assaulted."

"Oh, yeah." Wesley then held up his heavily bandaged left hand and asked, "Did you find my pinkie?"

"No, I did not."

"Damn . . . I'm gonna be a freak. At least those bastards took a . . . a kinda useless finger. Woulda been worse had they chopped off my thumb or middle finger. I use those all the time." Wesley stared at his hand and giggled. "Carrie, you have got to find out what kind of drugs they've got me on. This stuff is freaking amazing."

"They have you on painkillers."

"Get the name of 'em. And tell Aunt Pris to start writing up 'scripts. I could make mad cash selling this stuff."

Our Aunt Priscilla stole prescription pads from her various doctors and used them to write out fake prescriptions. Some of those prescriptions—mainly anxiety medications—were for her personal use. The rest of the fake prescriptions were obtained by various Shatners at pharmacies located in the counties surrounding Wyatt County. The drugs were then resold to our extensive list of buyers.

"Just don't get addicted to the painkillers." I pulled up a guest chair and had a seat next to Wesley. "Waylon is out of surgery."

Some of the fog faded from Wesley's eyes. "Is he okay?"

"He's in critical condition. But the doctor thinks he'll recover."

"Is Hank really dead?"

I nodded. "Wes, do you remember anything else? Anything that could help me figure out who did this to you?"

"I've been thinking . . ." Wes gestured for me to lean in closer and then whispered, "At least one of those three guys had to be a Shatner. Or a Devereux or a Palmer."

I slumped back in the chair. "You think it was one of us . . ."

"It had to have been. They knew too much about our family."

"If it was one of us, why grill you for info on the family."

"I dunno. But I'm telling you at least one of them was one of us."

"Any idea who?" I asked.

"Yeah, I think it was Randy."

"Cousin Randy?" I asked. Randall Mount was one of Aunt Emily Morgan's grandkids. His parents are my Uncle Sterling and Aunt Priscilla. "What does he have against you?"

"It's kinda my fault he spent the past few years in prison," Wesley said. "And this Facundo guy started contacting me a couple weeks after Randy got out of prison."

"How's it your—"

"What are you doing in here?" The hulking State Trooper asked. He stomped across the small room and yanked me out of the chair. "Hey, I know you . . . You're Detective Shatner. You're not supposed to be in here."

As the State Trooper hauled me out of the room, I looked back at Wesley, held a finger to my lips, and then mouthed, "I'll be back."

CHAPTER EIGHT

"Is there a party going on that we weren't invited to?" Hardy asked as he pulled into my driveway and parked his truck.

"Sure looks like it," I said as I craned my neck to inspect the two cars that were parked in front of my house. A green van had ramped the curb and taken out part of the fence around my faux graveyard. The lights were on inside the house, and I could see people moving around through the front windows. "At least whoever's taken over my house had the decency to put my Halloween decorations back outside."

Because Halloween was my favorite holiday, I had gone overboard on decorating the exterior of my house. I had a mausoleum made from plywood and Styrofoam in the front yard. Scattered around the mausoleum were Styrofoam tombstones and plastic bones. I even had a plywood coffin propped up against the side of the mausoleum. A plastic fence—or at least what was left of it—surrounded the graveyard scene.

"You recognize the cars?" Hardy asked.

"Nope," I said.

"I do," Wynonna said. She was seated in the backseat of the truck.

Uncle Woody and Aunt Deidra had remained at the hospital to be near Wesley and Waylon in case something happened. Aunt Deidra's mother took Wade and Willow home with her, but Wynonna refused to tag along with her siblings. She begged me to let her spend the night at my house, and I reluctantly agreed.

"Who's the inconsiderate person who ran over my decorations?" I asked.

"Roxanne," Wynonna said. "And I'm pretty that's Courtney's car."

Courtney Devereux was one of Wynonna's and my many cousins. Her mother, Suzette, was Aunt Emily Morgan's only daughter, and her father was Butch Devereux—Catfish's second oldest son. Courtney, who was in her early twenties, was somewhat involved in helping the family break the law. She was one of the Shatners who filled the fake prescriptions that Aunt Priscilla wrote out on the stolen pads.

"What would Courtney be doing here?" I asked.

"Duh . . . She's been dating Hank for the past few months. They got together right after Courtney graduated from college," Wynonna said. "How did you not know that?"

"No one tells me anything."

I plodded up the sidewalk to my front door. As I passed in front of him, I set off the motion detector attached to my life-size Grim Reaper animatronic. His right arm jerkily moved up to point at me and his eyes glowed red. The Grim Reaper cackled, "It's time for your one-way trip to Hell."

"Already there," I told the Grim Reaper.

It was around eleven-thirty, and I was exhausted. All I wanted to do was get a couple hours of sleep before I set to work figuring out the identities of the three men who had kidnapped and assaulted Wesley, Waylon, and Hank. Instead, I had to deal with more people.

I had barely stepped into my foyer before I was almost knocked over by my dog as she charged out of the living room. Molly barked at me before she took off down the short hallway to the kitchen. Hot on her heels were Autumn and Summer.

After leaving my mud-encrusted boots and jacket in the foyer, I ventured farther into my house. In the dining room I found Veda, Naomi, Roxanne, Jason, and Courtney gathered around the table. They had shoved my Halloween centerpieces to the far end of the table to make room for a short stack of pizza boxes and a pile of take-out containers. I grabbed a slice of pepperoni pizza and took a bite. The pizza was lukewarm and greasy, but I didn't care. It tasted better and was more filling than the vending machine snacks.

When Roxanne saw me, she dropped her slice of pizza, sprang out of her chair, and asked, "How's Wes?"

"He's loopy on painkillers," I said.

"Can I see him?" Roxanne asked.

"The Texas Ranger in charge of the case won't let anyone in to see Wes until after he talks to him," Wynonna said. She picked up the last mozzarella stick, dunked it in marinara sauce, and took a bite. "I helped Carrie sneak into Wes's room. But then a State Trooper caught her and chased her out."

"What about Waylon?" Naomi asked.

"He's out of surgery," Hardy said. "The doctors got him stabilized, but he's in bad shape. They have him in a medically induced coma."

"And Hank's dead," Courtney muttered. Her naturally wavy, dirty blonde hair was disheveled, and her green eyes were bloodshot. Faint black streaks of mascara marred her cheeks that were still chubby with baby fat.

"There's something Roxanne and I need to talk to you about, Carrie," Jason said.

"Can I finish eating first?" I gestured towards my mud-splattered jeans, and asked, "And maybe take a shower and change into something else?"

"Don't bother changing," Jason said. "What we gotta do . . . you're just gonna wind up getting dirty and ruining another set of clothes."

"I don't like the sound of that," I said.

"Umm . . . is it okay to talk in front of him?" Roxanne asked as she pointed at Hardy. "I mean, since he's a Texas Ranger and all."

"I'm on y'alls side," Hardy said. "I'm here to help.

"But this is bad, Carrie. Really bad," Roxanne said.

"Great . . . Why am I not surprised?" I finished eating the slice of pizza, and then tossed the crust to Molly. "Veda and Naomi, can you two keep the kids entertained for a while? The rest of you, follow me."

I grabbed a chocolate-covered donut with rainbow sprinkles and then headed into my living room that was jam-packed with a plethora of Day of the Dead décor. Sugar skulls, Catrina dolls, and candles of various sizes covered almost every flat surface in the room. Life-sized Catrina dolls stood on either side of my entertainment center. I'll admit that the Day of the Dead décor was not simply Halloween decorations—I left it out all year long.

I spread an old blanket out on one of the leather recliners and had a seat. Wynonna sat on the floor by my feet, and Hardy took the other recliner. Jason, Roxanne, and Courtney sat together on the brown and white cowhide leather couch.

"What can you tell us about this morning, Jason?" Hardy asked.

"How am I supposed to know anything?" Jason asked. "It's not like I was there."

"We know you weren't there. Wesley told Carrie that you got called in to work," Hardy said. "But Wesley also told Carrie that you knew about the meeting with this Facundo guy and that you warned the guys not to go."

"How'd you get dragged into Wesley's latest scheme, Jason?" I asked

As far as I knew, Jason had stayed out of trouble since he had been released from the juvenile detention center on his eighteenth birthday. If Jason had broken the law in the four years since then, I was not aware of it.

"I ain't had much to do with Wes since . . . well, since I got out of juvie. I blamed him for getting me in trouble," Jason said. "But we started hanging out again a few weeks ago."

"Yeah, right after you threatened to kill him and tried to beat him up for getting me pregnant again," Roxanne said.

"What? I was pissed," Jason said with a shrug.

"You're not selling drugs again, are you, Jason?" I asked.

"I'd rather not talk about it," Jason said as he shot Hardy a wary look. A deep flush crept up Jason's neck and across his face. "Anyway . . . for the past few weeks, Wes has been talking to different drug dealers. Then this Facundo dude started texting Wes about a week ago. Maybe a week and a half. He said he was part of some Honduran cartel and claimed that he could get Wes better quality cocaine for a cheaper price than what we are getting from the Rio Cartel. Wes thought it sounded like a good idea, but I warned him not to do it. The whole thing seemed shady . . . Like maybe this Facundo dude was an undercover cop or something. Plus, I heard about what happens to people who cross El Lobo."

"I warned him not to do it, too," Roxanne said.

"Wes told me he'd set up a meeting with Facundo for last night. It was only supposed to be Wes that went, but he didn't feel comfortable going alone. He asked me, Waylon, and Hank to go along with him to watch his back. I was gonna go with . . . even though I was worried it might be a setup. But then my manager called and said he needed me to come in and work the first shift. He threatened to fire me if I didn't come in. So, I went home to get a couple hours of sleep." Jason rubbed his hands over his face and groaned. "I should have done something more to stop the guys. Or I should have said something to you, Carrie. If I had, maybe none of this would have happened."

"I wish you had said something." Courtney leaned around Roxanne and punched Jason's upper arm. "If you hadn't kept your mouth shut, maybe Hank would still be alive."

"Had I thought one of them was gonna wind up getting killed, I would have said something," Jason said. "But how was I supposed to know? I can't see into the future."

To diffuse the situation, I pushed myself out of the recliner and then knelt on the floor in front of Courtney. "Did Hank tell you about anything else that was going on, Courtney?"

"He told me some stuff. Like, he told me about this Facundo guy. But not about the meeting," Courtney said. "Hank also told me about Wes's stills."

"What? Did you just say 'stills?' As in moonshine stills?" I asked. I looked back and forth between Courtney, Roxanne, and Jason. They had all taken up an interest in the collection of sugar skulls on my wagon wheel coffee table. None of them would make eye contact with me. "One of y'all better start talking."

"That's . . . uh . . . that's what I've been trying to tell you about since I saw you at the hospital," Roxanne said. She briefly made eye contact with me and then went back to staring at the sugar skulls. "Wes has a couple of stills. He's been making his own moonshine for months."

"And growing his own pot," Jason added.

I opened my mouth to respond, but I was too shocked to form words.

Hardy took over for me. "Any idea where Wesley's stills and the pot plants are located?"

Roxanne shrugged. "He wouldn't tell me."

Jason raised his hand and glanced over at me. "I know where they're at, but I'm not quite sure how to get there. Wes has everything set up in an old single-wide trailer on your family's property. It's where he also stores his drugs and other . . . stuff."

"I don't want to know about the other stuff, do I?" I asked.

Jason shook his head. "Wes said the trailer was your dad's secret spot. I guess your dad stayed there when he and your mom were on the outs."

"Dad probably also took his many girlfriends there," I said. I long ago accepted that my father was not a saint. The less I thought about him, the happier that I was. "But that answers the question of where Dad would disappear to for days at a time."

"You've got to do something about the stills and the other . . . stuff," Roxanne said.

"No kidding. Y'all sit tight. I need to make a phone call."

I stomped through the dining room and into the sunroom. After slamming the sliding door shut, I had a seat at the bar. I briefly eyed up the row of bottles along the back of the bar and debated having a drink. It would certainly help take the edge off. But, because my mom was a recovering alcoholic, I had sworn off drinking alcohol. Aside from a sip of moonshine on my twenty-first birthday, I had never consumed any alcohol—and no matter how bad it got, I was not going to start now.

Turning my back to the bar, I called Uncle Houston. I waited until he finished grumbling at me for waking him up and then asked, "Did you know that Wes has his own stills and was growing pot?"

"That little bastard . . . You know what, I ain't even surprised. If dumb was dirt, Wes's brains would cover a whole acre and then some." Uncle Houston muttered a string of curse words under his breath. "Where's he got these stills at?"

"According to Jason Devereux, they're in a trailer that my dad used when he was hiding out from my mom. I'm hoping you know where it's at."

"Yeah, I know where it's at." Uncle Houston sighed. "Meet me at my house in an hour . . . Make it two. We've gotta destroy it tonight. Who knows if Wes told his kidnappers about the trailer?"

"I hope you got a plan," I said, repeating what Uncle Houston had said to me earlier. "Because I sure don't."

I hung up on Uncle Houston and then slammed my phone down onto the bar in frustration. Within seconds, my phone rang. Thinking it was Uncle Houston calling me back, I didn't bother to check the caller ID before I answered.

"What now?"

"*Hola, Mamacita*," a man with a thick Spanish accent crooned. "Why you ignore all my other calls today?"

"Who is this?" I asked. For a second, I thought it was Alberto Ramos, but the voice was too deep and nasally, and the Spanish accent too thick to be Alberto.

"*Es tu amigo El Lobo*," the man said. "You forget about me already, *Mamacita*? Did El Lobo not make a good enough impression? You and me. We meet alone. I'll impress you."

"I'll pass," I snapped. "What do you want?"

"Heard you got some serious *problemas* up in Wyatt County."

"Oh yeah? What have you heard?" I asked.

"I've got sources, *Mamacita*. And my sources say that *mi dos amigos pelirrojos* got their asses beat. And their *gordito amigo es muerto*. I also hear that *mi amigos* were talking with some Hondurans about *la cocaína*. Is there something wrong with *la cocaína* I get you? Or are *mi amigos estúpido* and trying to piss me off? Because El Lobo don't like to be pissed off. I'd hate to see something even worse happen to *mi dos amigos pelirrojos*."

"Your redheaded friends were being *estúpido*," I said.

Even though I didn't think El Lobo deserved an explanation, I told him about the alleged Honduran drug dealer. I also told El Lobo that I suspected the whole thing had been a setup to get information on my family.

"*No está bien, Mamacita. No es bueno en absoluto*." El Lobo clucked his tongue in disapproval. "I do not tolerate snitches. If Wesley snitched on me, the beating he received from these mystery people is nothing compared to what I'll do to the boy."

"Wesley's not a snitch," I said even though I had no idea what Wesley had told his kidnappers about our family and our crimes.

"Let us hope not. Because it won't end well for Wesley if he did talk. I have ways to stop Wesley from talking ever again. And I hate to see that happen to *mi amigo*." El Lobo chuckled. "Regardless, I'm worried, *Mamacita*. I want to check on *la familia* in Wyatt County. Make sure everything is as it should be. I'll be paying you a visit on Friday, *Mamacita*. Look for me at the high school football game."

"Yeah, all right. I'll see you there."

My hands were trembling and slick with cold sweat. I had to jab at the phone four or five times before I managed to hit the right spot on the touch screen to end the call. It was bad enough that El Lobo had my cell phone number—I certainly hadn't given it to him—but now I had to meet with him in a few days. Considering what a few of the Palmers had told me, meetings with El Lobo usually did not end well.

Trudging back to the living room, I found that Veda, Naomi, and the kids had joined the group. Hardy was filling Veda and Naomi in on what they had missed.

"Is there anything else the three of you need to tell me?" I asked Jason, Roxanne, and Courtney. "Or do you know of anyone outside the family who might have some information?"

Roxanne and Courtney shook their heads.

"You might wanna talk to Lynnette and Shawna," Jason said. "Wes could've told them something."

"He better not be talking to those skanks." Roxanne hurled one of my Texas flag throw pillows onto the floor. "I'll kill him."

"Roxanne . . ." I picked up the pillow and tossed it at her. "Lynnette and Shawna are the mothers of Wes's other kids. He has to talk to them for the sake of the kids."

"No, he doesn't." Roxanne crossed her arms over her chest and stuck out her lower lip. "Shawna's parents have custody of Blake. And Wes signed away his parental rights for Branden. He's got no reason to talk to either of them unless one of the boys needs a kidney."

"Doesn't mean Wes didn't tell them something," I said.

"Lynnette has three or four brothers," Wynonna said. She had picked up Manny, and was cradling my squirming, irritated cat as if he were a baby. "One of them is in my grade, and he's made a bunch of comments to me about how he and his brothers are gonna make Wes pay for what he did to their sister. Maybe they're behind it."

"Or Shawna's new boyfriend," Jason said. "Wes, Roxanne, and I went to school with the guy. He's totally psycho and he worships the Devil. Ever since he got together with Shawna, he's had it out for Wes. He even threatened to kill him a few months ago."

"You threatened to kill Wes a few weeks ago." Roxanne smacked her brother on the leg. "You know, right after I told you I was pregnant."

"Yeah, well, I was pissed. But that doesn't mean I setup Wes and helped beat him up this morning," Jason said. "Remember, had I not gotten called in to work, I probably would have been with Wes, Waylon, and Hank."

"Yeah, I know. You got lucky," Roxanne said. "I don't know what I'd have done if you'd been with them and gotten hurt or killed. Aside from Wes and my daughters, you're all I've really got."

Jason wrapped his arm around his twin sister's shoulders and pulled her against his side. "I hate to say it . . . but Dad has threatened to kill Wes a whole bunch of times over the past five years. Maybe he finally snapped."

Roxanne shook her head. "Dad was at home this morning. Autumn was afraid of the storm and wouldn't sleep. Dad and I sat up with her and watched TV. Plus, Dad wouldn't have worn some stupid mask. He'd have wanted Wes to know it was him."

"My daddy has had about all he can take of Wes and has said a bunch of times that someone needs to do something about him," Courtney said. "Maybe he was involved. Daddy wasn't home last night or this morning. He stayed at the ranch in case the storm caused any problems and Uncle Elvin needed help. Maybe he . . . you know . . . Plus he hates Hank. He threatened to cut off Hank's . . . well, let's just say he threatened Hank a bunch of times . . ."

"You really think your dad could be behind it?" I asked Courtney.

Courtney nodded as she blinked back tears. "Remember what Daddy did to Mitch when he and Robin first started dating? Not only did he answer the door with a shotgun in hand, he fired the gun into the bushes next to the porch to scare Mitch. And Mitch isn't related to our former enemies. Just think of what my daddy could be capable of doing to Hank."

Uncle Butch had been heavily involved in the longstanding feud between the Shatners and the Palmers. Like some of my other uncles, it had been hard for Butch to accept that the feud was over and that the two families were now working together. Knowing his youngest daughter was in bed with the former enemy must have driven him crazy.

"Anything's possible . . ." I said. I added Uncle Butch and Uncle Elvin to the top of the list of people I needed to talk to since they had both been near the Body Farm this morning and because they both had reasons to assault Wesley, Waylon, and Hank. Heck, Uncle Elvin had told me he was tempted to give Wesley a beating just last night.

"What about Wes's customers?" Hardy asked. "Do you know who they are? And if he made any of them mad recently? Or a rival dealer? Maybe one of them was looking for payback."

"Or anyone else who might have had it out for Wesley?" I asked. Roxanne, Jason, and Courtney mentioned a few names, and I jotted them down in a notebook. I then stood up and headed for the front door. "Come on, Jerrod and Jason, let's go clean up the rest of Wes's mess."

"Can I come, too?" Roxanne asked as she followed me into the foyer.

"No, Roxanne. You need to take your girls home."

"Oh, no. I ain't going home. I'm liable to kill Dad or Bambi if they start talking bad about Wes."

"Then you can stay here," I said to Roxanne. I leaned into the living room. "Sorry, Wynonna, but you're gonna have to sleep on the couch. And I've got an inflatable mattress if you want it, Courtney."

After putting my mud-splattered jacket and boots back on, I opened the door and almost ran into Red and Bubba as they walked up to the front door. They were covered in mud from head to toe.

Veda leaned in to give Bubba a kiss. "How are things at the Body Farm?"

Bubba yawned and then said, "Seems like the State Troopers and crime scene guys went over every square inch of the hayride. Far as I could tell, they didn't find nothing outside of the Torture barn."

"They also failed to find Wes's car," Red added. "It's still parked in the staff lot, but none of them noticed it."

"Seriously?" Naomi asked. "How did they miss the pineapple?"

"Because I hid it in plain sight." Bubba chuckled. "Since Sergeant Boleyn allowed us to keep the Pumpkin Patch open, I had some of the volunteers who were working there park their cars around Wes's to block it. Then, when my parking lot attendants showed up to turn people away from the Body Farm, I had them do the same thing. The State Troopers never even bothered to look around the staff lot. Makes me wonder how good they are at their jobs."

"Me, too," Hardy said.

"I'm guessing you had a lot of angry customers," I said.

"Some." Bubba shrugged. "Most people saw the announcement on the website or Facebook that we would be closed tonight. A few people who showed up got belligerent, but I handled them."

"I don't know why Sergeant Boleyn had to shut down the entire Body Farm," Veda said. "He could have let you have run the other three attractions."

"Not when he considers the entire Body Farm to be a possible crime scene," Bubba said.

"Except for the staff parking lot," I said.

"Except for that. But I'm not sure he realized that the Body Farm and Pumpkin Patch share the staff parking lot," Bubba said. "Sergeant Boleyn was real interested in the still down at Moonshiners—"

Interrupting, Red said, "Good thing we dismantled it this afternoon."

"Oh yeah," Bubba continued. "But Sergeant Boleyn swears the Body Farm is still a crime scene and he needs to hold on to it for a few more days. I'm talking the entire Body Farm. Not just the Torture barn. That I could understand. How am I supposed to get the place ready for Fright Night on Saturday if the Ranger won't let me onto my own property?"

Fright Night was always held the Saturday after Halloween. It was an amped up version of the Body Farm. All four attractions stepped up their intensity and scares. Customers had to be over the age of eighteen, and tickets were sold in advance.

"You can't have Fright Night!" Courtney said. She shoved her way past me and got into Bubba's face. "Hank died at the Body Farm. It's disrespectful."

"I can't cancel it, Courtney," Bubba said. "Tickets are sold out. And have been for almost two weeks now."

Courtney screamed at Bubba. She then shoved him aside and ran outside. Before any of us could stop her, she got into her car and sped off.

"Maybe I should just cancel it," Bubba muttered. "If Courtney is that worked up about it, imagine how the Palmers will react."

"Don't cancel. I'll talk to the Palmers about it," I said. "And don't worry about Sergeant Boleyn holding the Body Farm hostage. Jerrod and I will take care of it in the morning. There's something a little more important that we need to tend to at the moment."

CHAPTER NINE

"I DON'T KNOW HOW MY COLLEAGUES MISSED seeing this monstrosity of a car," Hardy said as he used a slim jim to pop the lock on the driver's side door so that we could look inside Wesley's car. Once he had the door open, Hardy shone his flashlight around inside and then pulled a sandwich bag full of marijuana out from underneath the driver's seat. "Check out what I found. There's got to be a couple hundred dollars' worth of marijuana in here."

"That's nothing," Jason said. He flipped up the backseat and revealed a hidden compartment underneath. Inside the compartment was more marijuana along with baggies of prescription pills and a white powder that was either cocaine or heroin. Maybe both. "Wes also has two cases of water bottles full of moonshine in the trunk. This is the rest of the stuff he was planning to sell at the Body Farm before Bubba caught on and put a stop to it."

Hardy whistled. "That could get Wesley sent to prison for a long time."

"And that's why we're taking it with us," I said. I snatched the bag of marijuana out of Hardy's hand. "We can't leave it in the car. It's a smoking gun. Sergeant Boleyn will use it to come after the rest of the family. And we can't have that."

"This will be the first time I've tampered with evidence in the fifteen years since I became a State Trooper," Hardy said.

"There's always a first for everything," Jason said.

I looked over at Hardy and noticed his slumped shoulders and bowed head. When Hardy and I had met at the beginning of the year, it was obvious that he only saw things in black and white. There was no gray area for him. As for the Shatners, we lived and worked in the murky gray areas. We'd taken it over and made it our home. Thanks to me, not only had Hardy been introduced to the gray areas, but I had dragged him down into the gray areas with us.

"I'm sorry, Jerrod. I shouldn't have brought you along. I promised you I would never ask you to help me clean up one of my family member's messes. And now look at us." I held up the bag of marijuana. "I didn't want to you get caught up in my family's mess. That's why I—"

"That's why we broke up," Hardy said. He shot me a warning look and then gestured towards where Jason was digging through the trunk of Wesley's car. "Remember, Carrie, we broke up because I didn't want to be associated with your family's criminal activities."

"Yeah, that's right. That's why we broke up. And there's no reason you should continue being associated with my family." I took a step closer to Hardy and whispered. "You should get out of here. Drop me and Jason off at Uncle Houston's and then go. Things are about to get really ugly, and I don't want you to be involved."

"I've been involved since that night in January when I showed up at the Wyatt County Fairgrounds and met you. I'm not going anywhere, Carrie."

"Jerrod . . . please, get out of here. I don't want you to get hurt. Or lose your job."

"I don't want you to get hurt either." Jerrod cupped my chin in his palm and kissed me. "Remember back in January? When I said that I'm either crazy about you, or just plain crazy—"

"Yeah, and I've since determined that you're crazy. I could probably have you committed along with most of my relatives."

"Carrie . . ." Hardy leaned forward and pressed his forehead against mine. "I'm crazy about you. I wouldn't be here if I wasn't. And I can find another job if I have to. What I can't find is another you. I'm not leaving."

I wrapped my arms around Hardy's waist and hugged him. I knew he would be too stubborn to leave. I appreciated that he was staying to help me—I honestly didn't know how I would get through this without him. But now that he had cast in his lot with my family, I had to do whatever I could to protect him.

"Hey, guys." Jason tapped me on the shoulder. "Hate to break up your moment. But someone is coming over from the motel."

Hardy and I pulled apart and then turned to face the chain link fence that ran along the edge of the property and separated it from the backside of the Roadhouse Motel. A lanky older man slipped between a break in the fence and shuffled across the parking lot towards us.

"Whatcha doing back here?" the man demanded as he spat a glob of salvia onto the ground near my foot.

"What's it to you?" I asked.

"I'm the owner of this fine establishment." The man gestured over his shoulder to the Roadhouse Motel. The name tag pinned to his plaid pajama top said "Abner—Manager." "I looked out my window and saw y'all messing 'round with that there car. Now I know it ain't none of my business, but I'm about to call the police on y'all for trespassing. And for breaking into that car that I don't think is yours."

"We are the police." I held up my sheriff's department badge. "You see anything suspicious early this morning, Abner?"

"I see all sorts of suspicious stuff 'round here. Specially this time of year with that haunted house nonsense. But it ain't none of my business."

"Did you see some young men get assaulted and kidnapped from your motel around four o'clock this morning?" Hardy asked.

"I ain't seen nothing like that," Abner said as he scratched his head and unleashed an avalanche of dandruff. "But, like I said . . . Ain't none of my business."

At the front end of the building, a second story window screeched as an elderly woman shoved it open. The woman then stuck her head out the window and yelled, "What's going on, Abner? Who are those people? Should I call the police?"

"It ain't nothing, Ma. Put your teeth in and go back to bed," Abner yelled at the woman. He shot me and Hardy another dirty look before he ducked back through the hole in the fence and trudged towards the front of the motel. "I ain't seen nothing."

"You hear that, Carrie?" Hardy asked. "Abner ain't seen nothing."

"I kind of want to know why that woman needs to put her teeth in to go to bed . . ." I turned back to the car. "Let's make sure Wes isn't hiding anything else in the car before Abner does decide to call the police."

I leaned over the passenger seat and flipped open the center console. Inside were two cell phones—both of which had less than twenty percent battery life left. One had a picture of Roxanne, Summer, and Autumn as the background. The other had a Texas flag.

"Jason, do you know if this is Waylon's or Hank's phone?" I asked as

I held up the phone with the Texas flag background. There were almost a hundred unread text messages and three dozen missed calls.

"It's Wes's other phone. You know . . . the one he conducts 'business' on," Jason said.

"You mean it's his burner phone that he uses to talk to his clients?" Hardy asked.

Jason nodded. "I got it for him at Walmart. It can't be traced."

I tossed Wesley's regular phone back into the car. I didn't think it would be any use to me. Plus, I had to leave something for Sergeant Boleyn to find when he eventually located Wesley's car.

"Any idea on the passcode?" I asked Jason.

"Try Roxanne's and my birthdate." Jason gave me the month, day, and year that he and his twin sister had been born. "If it's not Roxanne's birthday, it'll be one of the girls. It's the only way Wes can remember their birthdays."

The passcode was Autumn's birthday.

While Hardy and Jason searched the interior of Wesley's car for any other illegal items, I scrolled through the text messages in Wesley's "business" phone. Wesley had all his contacts listed under nicknames—most of which were unflattering. I thought it was strange that one of the contacts was named "Tegucigalpa" until I remembered that Tegucigalpa was the capital of Honduras. I skimmed through the recent text messages from Tegucigalpa and determined that he was most likely the mysterious person who had pretended to be a Honduran drug dealer as a trick to setup Wesley.

Without giving myself a chance to really consider what I was doing—or what I would say if someone answered—I hit the call button. Instead of ringing, the phone dinged in my ear and an automated voice informed me that the phone was no longer in service.

"Let's get out of here," I said as I climbed into the passenger seat of Hardy's truck. "Uncle Houston is waiting for us."

Hardy pulled out of the Body Farm's staff parking lot and a few minutes later we arrived at Uncle Houston's farmhouse.

"Is that a tank?" Hardy asked when he pulled into the clearing. "And does it work?"

"Yes, it's a Soviet tank," I said. "And don't ask questions that you don't want to know the answer to."

I climbed out of the truck and then walked over to where Uncle Houston was leaning against the side of the tank.

"So Wesley has his own stills. If I'd known that, I'd have cancelled that boy's birth certificate a long time ago. You were right all along, Carrie. That boy is a problem." Uncle Houston blew a cloud of cigar smoke in my face. He then looked over my shoulder at Jason and said, "I didn't think you and Wes was friends since high school. In fact, last I heard, you was threatening to kill him for putting another bun in Roxanne's oven."

"We worked things out," Jason mumbled.

"What else was that sumbitch up to that we need to know about?" Uncle Houston asked.

"Aside from that Wes has been using the old trailer to hide his stills, the drugs, and other stuff . . . I don't know nothing." Jason's shoulders almost touched the bottom of his earlobes when he shrugged. "Wes didn't share all of his secrets with me."

Stepping between Uncle Houston and Jason, I asked, "Do you have a plan to get rid of the stills and marijuana, Uncle Houston?"

"I do." Uncle Houston flicked the ash off the end of his cigar and then ground it out. "Where you at, Butch?"

"Right here!" Butch Devereux came loping around the side of the tank while pulling up the zipper on the front of his camouflage pants. The floodlights reflected off his bald head.

"Uncle Butch is your plan?" I asked.

"Best I could come up with on short notice. You got a better one, I wanna hear it, missy." Uncle Houston waited a few seconds, and, when I didn't respond, he said. "Way I see it, we gotta get rid of all traces of this trailer. What is it you always say, Butch?"

"Fire is final," Uncle Butch said. He held up a lighter and almost lit his scraggly gray beard on fire. "I'll burn that trailer to the ground."

"Is this really a good idea?" Hardy asked.

"Yeah . . . The last time Uncle Butch burned down a building, he botched it and got sent to prison," I said.

Uncle Butch was a former volunteer firefighter and a convicted arsonist. When I was a kid, he burned down the bowling alley that he owned so he could get the insurance money. Since the bowling alley was within the Holler city limits, the Holler police and fire departments investigated the blaze and determined that it was arson. Uncle Butch pled guilty to second degree arson and was sentenced to seven years in jail. He served five of those years and then was released for good behavior.

"I didn't botch burning down the bowling alley. There wasn't much left by the time the fire department put out the blaze. What I botched was covering my tracks." Uncle Butch took a step closer to me and lowered his voice. "And who said that was the last building I burned down? I've gotten away with plenty of arsons before and after the bowling alley fiasco. That vegan restaurant that burned down a few years ago . . . That was me. And the convenience store in Mooresville last summer . . . Also me."

"Remember that mansion by the lake your Uncle Vernon built a few years back? The one he couldn't sell because it wasn't up to code?" Uncle Houston asked.

"I made it look like an accidental electrical fire," Uncle Butch said proudly.

"What are you? An arsonist for hire?" Hardy asked Uncle Butch.

"Something like that. Hey . . . you better not be repeating what I just said to anybody, Mr. Lawman." Uncle Butch glared at Hardy. He then tugged the end of my ponytail and said, "Don't worry, Carrie. I'll take care of the trailer. You can count on me to get the job done."

"I'm more worried about the fire spreading than anything else," I said.

"The trees and ground are still saturated from the storm. We should be good," Uncle Butch said. "But to be safe, we're bringing a water pump and a fire hose. Houston says there's a creek that runs by the trailer that we can use if we have to."

Uncle Houston clapped his hands together. "Let's get this show on the road."

The five of us piled into Uncle Houston's all-terrain vehicle—Uncle Houston and Uncle Butch sat up front while me, Hardy, and Jason squeezed into the back—and drove off into the woods. Numerous paths crisscrossed through the collectively held Shatner land, and I quickly got turned around. The path we were on split and then split again. It also seemed to double back and loop around. It didn't help that it was dark out and there was fog drifting through the trees. We finally came to an overgrown dirt road. The tire tracks and crushed underbrush revealed that the old road had been used recently.

After about ten minutes of driving around, I leaned between the front seats and said, "Hey, Uncle Butch . . . I heard you weren't happy that Courtney was dating Hank the Third."

"You mean Hank the Turd?" Uncle Butch asked. He chuckled at his own joke. "Yeah, I was none too pleased about it, to be honest. But

Courtney was happy, and Hank was treating her all right. I made sure of that."

"Where were you at early this morning?" I asked. "Between three and eight?"

"What's that got to do with anything?" Uncle Butch asked.

Uncle Houston slammed on the brakes and brought the ATV to a stop. He then turned around to face me. "There a reason you're askin' Butch what he was doing this morning'?"

"I snuck into Wes's room at the hospital earlier," I said. I knew that I'd wind up regretting it, but I decided to pass along what Wesley had told me. "Now, this stays between the five of us, but Wes told me that he thinks that at least one of the people who assaulted him was a Shatner. Or maybe a Palmer or Devereux. He said that at least one of the assailants knew too much about us not to be one of us."

"For real?" Jason asked. "Man, I was half-joking when I accused my dad. And I don't know how serious Courtney was when she accused Uncle Butch."

"You kiddin' me, Carrie?" Uncle Houston asked. "You sure Wes didn't get knocked in the head a few too many times and his got brains all scrambled?"

"Wes doesn't have enough brains to scramble," I said.

"Well, shit," Uncle Butch muttered. "I wasn't killing Hank or beating up my nephews, I can tell you that. You talk to Elvin. I was with him in the alpaca barn during the storm."

"At the hospital, you told me that Wes said that the people who attacked 'em wanted info on our family," Uncle Houston said. "Now you're tellin' me Wes thinks the people are our family? That don't make no sense. If it was family, why would they have interrogated Wes?"

"I didn't say it made sense," I snapped. "I'm just repeating what Wes said."

"If that's the case, I'm more inclined to believe a Palmer was behind it," Uncle Houston said. He hit the gas and we jerked forward. "Them Palmers always were lower than a snake's belly in a wagon rut. And they ain't never had the same sense of family loyalty that us Shatners got. I just never thought them capable of murderin' one of their own."

"We don't know if the assailants meant to kill Hank or if his death was accidental," Hardy pointed out. "The boys were left in a place where they could be found fairly quickly. Had Hank been found sooner, he might have survived his head injury."

"If it was family behind this, they probably did it to send a message to Wes to knock it off. A bit of an extreme message considering they cut off his finger. But our family has done worse over the years," I said, voicing the opinion I had formed over the past few hours.

"And if the assailants weren't y'alls family, it seems to me they just wanted to send a message by kidnapping and assaulting the boys," Hardy said. "Stop breaking the law and tell your families to knock it off as well. Either things got out of hand or went too far, and one of them delivered a blow to Hank that eventually proved fatal."

"Any idea why Cousin Randy blames Wes for him going to prison?" I asked. "And what would he have against Keaton? He got attacked by a Devil mask wearing individual, too."

"I don't know if Randy's got anythin' against Keaton. They're 'bout the same age though. Randy could have spent those five years in the joint stewin' on an old grudge from when they was kids," Uncle Houston said. "And Randy blames Wes for him gettin' busted because Wes was in the car with him when the Louisiana State Troopers pulled him over."

"That I did not know," I said.

I had been living in Nashville when Randy was arrested for transporting moonshine across the state line into Louisiana. All I knew was that he had gotten pulled over by a Louisiana State Trooper, and that the trooper had found jars of moonshine hidden under a blanket in the trunk. Randy had spent five years in prison. About six weeks ago, he was released from prison and came home to Wyatt County.

"Randy is about as reckless and brainless as Wesley," Uncle Houston said. "First, he took a fifteen-year-old kid with him on a moonshine run into another state. And then he decided to see how fast his car could go. The Trooper clocked him goin' over a hundred-and-thirty in a fifty-five mile-an-hour zone."

"So, it's basically his own fault he got caught," Hardy said.

Uncle Houston shook his head. "Randy swears that the State Trooper wouldn't have checked the car if Wes hadn't started actin' all squirrely."

"You think Randy is the one behind what happened to the boys?" Uncle Butch asked.

"He's got a motive," I said. "I'll have to find out if he has an alibi."

I leaned back in my seat and held on as the ATV bounced over the rough road.

A few minutes later, Uncle Houston brought the ATV to a stop in a small clearing. He flipped on a searchlight mounted to the top of the

ATV and lit up the dilapidated single-wide trailer that took up most of the clearing. "That's Elliott's trailer."

"So this is where my dad would disappear to," I said.

I climbed out of the ATV and walked over to the trailer. The roof over the tiny porch had collapsed, at least one window was broken, and most of the siding had fallen off. All the windows had been boarded up, and there was a new padlock on the door.

"I guess we won't be getting inside," I said.

"Nothing stopping us from looking in the windows," Hardy said as he grabbed a loose board and pulled it away from the window that was next to the door.

Uncle Butch and Jason helped Hardy remove the rest of the boards covering the window. Hardy then used one of the boards to shatter the glass so that we could see inside without the flashlight reflecting back at us.

"Wes has two stills in there. Look like hundred-and-fifty-gallon ones to me," I said as I swept the flashlight beam across the small living room. A moonshine still sat on either side of the room. There were barrels of fermenting mash lined up against the wall, and the room smelled like a frat house after a hard night of partying. "He's got something cooking."

"What's that chemical smell?" Uncle Houston asked. "That don't smell like no mash I've ever made."

"Let me see," Hardy said as he crowded in between me and Uncle Houston. "Hold on. What's that over there?"

Hardy grabbed my arm and directed the flashlight beam across the living room to the tiny kitchen area. The flashlight illuminated a jumble of glass cookware and pans spread out over the kitchen counters and the stove. I spotted empty rolls of duct tape, antifreeze containers, and small mounds of batteries scattered on the floor near the kitchen.

"It's a meth lab," Hardy and I said at the same time.

"Meth lab?" Uncle Houston asked. "Am I hearing you right? Or do I gotta turn up the sound on my hearing aid?"

"No, we said meth lab," I said. I turned around and smacked Jason upside the head. "Why didn't you mention that Wes also had a meth lab?"

"Because I didn't know. I swear." Jason wrapped his arms around his head to protect himself from another blow. "None of that was there the last time Wes brought me out here."

"How the hell did Wes not accidentally blow himself up?" Uncle Houston asked. "Or die from breathin' in the fumes?"

"Wes always was a lucky one," I said. The chemical-smell was starting to make me feel lightheaded. I walked over to the edge of the clearing and drew in a deep breath. "It's a good thing Wes is so lucky, because he's about the dumbest person I've ever met."

"What was Wes using to run the equipment? I can't believe this place still has electricity," Hardy said.

"I took a look around back," Uncle Butch said as he joined us. "Wes has got a big ol' generator set up back there. It's a pretty nice one. We should take it with us. I could use I to . . . uh . . . well, let's just say I could use it."

"Then load it up," I told Uncle Butch. I then asked Jason, "You said Wes was growing pot, right? Where's it at?"

"In the trailer's bedroom," Jason said.

While Uncle Houston and I poked around the outside of the trailer and peered in other windows, Jason and Hardy helped Uncle Butch load the generator into the back of the ATV. Once the generator had been taken care of and I had determined that there wasn't anything else of value inside or around the trailer, I asked Uncle Butch how he planned to destroy the trailer.

"Hold on. I'll show you." Uncle Butch scurried over to the ATV and picked up a bottle full of a gold-hued liquid. He stuffed the end of a handkerchief into the bottle's open top. "Molotov cocktail, anyone?"

"That would work if it was just pot," Hardy said. "But you can't burn up a still."

"Why not? Moonshine is flammable," Uncle Butch pointed out.

"And so is the meth lab. You can't blow that up. You'll kill us all," Hardy said. "We have to properly dispose of the meth lab."

"Well, we didn't know it was a meth lab 'til now," Uncle Butch said. "Otherwise, I would have planned accordingly."

"And we ain't got time to do things the 'proper way,'" Uncle Houston added. "We're gonna do it the Shatner way."

"Which means we're going to do it half-assed," I muttered.

"Like I said, fire is final." Uncle Butch manically grinned as he held up a lighter.

"Come on." Hardy grabbed my arm and yanked me behind a cottonwood tree. The tree's trunk was at least five feet across in diameter. Hardy wrapped his arms around me and tucked my head under his chin. "This better not be how we die."

"Here we go!" Uncle Butch yelled.

Seconds later, there was the tinkling sound of breaking glass. It was followed by a whoosh and then a deafening explosion. The temperature in the clearing flared up as a massive fireball shot skyward. Debris whizzed through the air—embedding into the tree trunks and slicing through the heavy underbrush. A few feet away, a pine tree went up in flames.

"Holy shit!"

"I told you that wasn't the right way to get rid of a meth lab."

"YOU ALL RIGHT, CARRIE?"

"No, Jerrod. I am about as far away from being 'all right' as I have ever been. My family is under attack, and I just helped blow up a meth lab," I said as I crawled in bed next to him. Molly was curled up at the foot of the bed, and Manny was stretched out on my pillow. It was almost four in the morning. I could barely keep my eyes open, and my hair continued to faintly smell of smoke despite washing it three times. "But I'm better now that you're here."

"I never should have left." Hardy pulled me into his arms and held me tightly against his chest. "You shouldn't have had to face this alone."

"This was something I had to do on my own, Jerrod. I didn't want you involved."

"I know. But I should have figured out a way to support you." Hardy kissed my forehead. "You do know that I'm insanely in love with you, right?"

I lifted my head and looked at Hardy. I could just barely make out his features in the soft glow of my alarm clock. Had he really just said that he loved me? Or was I so exhausted that I was hallucinating the conversation? Heck, maybe I'd fallen asleep in the shower and this conversation was a dream.

"Do I know you're insane? Yes. I figured that out months ago," I said after a few awkward seconds. "Did I know you were in love with me . . . No. But I kinda suspected you were. I can't come up with any other reason why you would put up with me and my family."

"You do come with a whole lot of interesting baggage."

"Some of which is about to get shipped off to prison in the near future."

"It'll all work out in the end, Carrie."

"I hope so. I really do."

I wanted to tell Hardy that I was in love with him as well. I wanted to tell him that he was the only thing that was keeping me sane and getting me through this. The thought of him had gotten me through the past two months when I'd thought I was losing my mind and wanted to throw in the towel. Not only was Hardy the lifejacket keeping me afloat, he was also the light at the end of the tunnel. I had to keep going forward if I was ever going to reach him.

"I love you, too, Jerrod."

Hardy's response was a soft snore.

CHAPTER TEN

JUST AFTER SEVEN O'CLOCK ON MONDAY MORNING, two State Troopers pounded on my front door and demanded that I come with them to the Holler Police Department. Without giving me a chance to brush my teeth or fix my hair, the Troopers hustled me out to their cruiser and drove me to the Holler Police Department. It was a good thing I had already changed clothes or else I would have had to suffer the indignity of being perp walked into the police station in my pajamas. Luckily there hadn't been too many people outside the police department when I was brought in.

One of the Troopers stayed with me while I wrote out my multi-page, overly detailed statement concerning the events that I had witnessed between arriving at the Body Farm yesterday afternoon and eventually getting kicked off the property by Sergeant Boleyn after he hijacked my investigation in the early evening. I left out the part about dismantling the moonshine still on the haunted hayride.

Once I completed writing out the statement, I was left in the interrogation room to cool my heels and twiddle my thumbs. I quickly got sick of staring at my reflection in the one-way mirror, but there wasn't much else for me to do other than examine my surroundings. The Holler police department's interrogation room was almost identical to the one at the Wyatt County Sheriff's Department. Their interrogation table didn't wobble, and their flooring was nicer. But their metal folding chairs were just as uncomfortable.

One hour passed . . . and then another. Soon it was ten o'clock and

I was starting to get angry . . . and hungry. I couldn't believe that they'd forgotten about me. But maybe something exciting was going on and it had slipped everyone's minds that I was wasting away in the interrogation room. I was debating if I should pound on the one-way mirror and make a scene—it might finally prompt someone to come check on me—when the door into the interrogation room swung open.

"About time. I was beginning to think . . ." I trailed off when I realized who was standing in the doorway. "What are you doing here, Ethan?"

Ethan Yates—an officer with the Holler Police Department—leaned nonchalantly against the doorjamb and smirked. Ethan and I had been sworn enemies since high school, and our mutual dislike for each other overwhelmed the small space. The interrogation room wasn't much larger than a handicap bathroom stall. There was just enough room for the table and four chairs. Ethan's bulk—not to mention his body odor—took up a considerable amount of the remaining real estate

"I figured you would appreciate some company," Ethan said as he stepped into the room and shut the door behind him.

"Stay back!" As I stood up, I grabbed ahold of the folding chair that was next to me. I held it out in front of me and jabbed it in Ethan's direction. "Don't come any closer."

"Put the chair down, Carrie. You look like a deranged lion tamer," Ethan said as he pulled out a chair and had a seat at the table. "What do you think I'm going to do to you? The cameras are rolling, and a State Trooper has been watching you this whole time."

"Don't make any sudden moves. And keep your hands where I can see them." Tentatively, I put the chair down and perched on the edge of my seat. "Nice shiner."

Ethan gently touched the swollen, purple bruise beneath his right eye. "I hate working third shift. Last night I got called over to the one bar to arrest a drunk guy. He took a swing at me before I could get the cuffs on him."

"What do you want?" I asked. "Did you come in here to gloat?"

"No, I came in here to talk." Ethan clasped his hands together and propped them on the edge of the table. "There's something we need to discuss."

"Ethan, I don't know how many times I need to go over this with you," I said as I got the proverbial ball rolling and confronted Ethan about what I assumed he was there to talk about. "But it was self-defense.

Your dad had me in a kill-or-be-killed situation. Had I not found that shotgun and used it to defend myself, your dad would have shot me. I'd be dead."

"Yeah, but now my dad's dead thanks to you," Ethan said, stating the obvious.

"It was a justifiable homicide," I hissed through clenched teeth.

"I know. I came to accept all that months ago. My dad was nuts, and his obsession with your family is what got him killed." Ethan waved his hand around, dismissing the matter. "You just happened to pull the trigger."

My family's history with the Yateses was long and complicated. I preferred not to think about it, but Ethan's presence forced me on an unpleasant trip down memory lane.

Ethan's father, Isaac Yates, had started working for the Wyatt County Sheriff's Department around the same time that my granddaddy had been elected sheriff. This was before Ethan and I were born. It took him a few years, but Ike eventually figured out that Granddaddy—along with my dad and Uncle Murph—was using his position with the sheriff's department to cover up the Shatner family's crimes. Ike made it is his personal mission to expose the coverups, and he went about obtaining damning evidence against some of the Shatners. My dad and Ike had been partners, and Dad had quickly caught on to Ike's scheme. Dad told Granddaddy what Ike was up to, and Granddaddy fired Ike.

After his dismissal from the sheriff's department, Ike Yates walked over to the Holler Police Department and got a job as an officer. He then worked his way up to chief—though I have no idea how he managed to do that, considering he had been the poster boy of incompetence.

I had only been three or four when Ike had gotten fired from the sheriff's department. I knew nothing about it until years later. By the time I met Ethan at Big Pine Senior High, I still had no clue about the animosity between the Shatners and Ike Yates. Ethan clearly hadn't known about it either, otherwise he probably wouldn't have asked me to be his date for my freshman Homecoming Dance. I turned Ethan down, and he's held a grudge against me ever since. His dad had further inflated Ethan's grudge by filling his head full of lies about the Shatners.

To make matters worse between the Shatners and the Yateses, during my sophomore year of high school, my dad had an affair with Ethan's mother. The affair became public knowledge, and the last couple months of the school year were hellacious for both of us. Ethan had been a loner in high school. He hadn't had many friends, and he got made fun of a lot. The other students had brutally picked on Ethan once word of the affair made it through the high school's grapevine. I'd fared better than Ethan had simply because I was a Shatner and, thanks to my family's infamous reputation, the rest of the student body was smart enough not to mess with us. No one had directly said anything to my face about Dad's affair, but I knew that everyone was talking about it behind my back. By the fall of my junior year, the scandal had blown over and there were new topics to gossip about.

As for Ike Yates, he never got past his desire to bring down the Shatner family—and my dad's affair with Ike's wife only made it worse. For over thirty years, Ike went about trying to obtain evidence of my family's illegal activities. In the past few years, his hobby had turned into an obsession, and the obsession drove him to an early grave.

"If you're not here to talk about your dad, what are you here to talk about?" I asked.

"I want to talk about what's going on with your family," Ethan said. He leaned across the table and lowered his voice. He also used his hands to block his mouth. If the security cameras in the interrogation room were like the ones at the sheriff's department, they didn't record audio. "What happened to your cousins and that other kid is awful. No matter how I feel about y'all, I wouldn't wish that kind of beating on anyone. And I don't think it's fair that Sergeant Boleyn swooped in and stole the investigation from you."

"You're not telling me anything I don't already know."

Ethan huffed. "Stop acting like a bitch. I'm offering to help you. The least you can do is be civil to me."

"Why would you help me?" I asked, sounding more intrigued than I wanted to.

"Because . . . Look, I ain't happy that my dad is dead. But he made his choices. And his obsession with your family drove him crazy. For a long time, I blamed your family for making my dad nuts. But the therapist I went to after my dad died helped me see that y'all aren't responsible for my dad's actions. I mean, indirectly y'all kinda are since y'all are criminals. But the only person responsible for my dad getting killed is himself. As far as I'm concerned, as long as your family keeps their crimes out of Holler, it's . . . well, it's none of my business," Ethan said. When I started to respond, he motioned for me to stop. "I know what you're thinking . . . I should be on Boleyn's side. Helping him investigate your family and bring y'all down. Do it in honor of my dad since that's what he always wanted. But what happened to your cousins and that other kid ain't right. And, like I said, it ain't fair that Boleyn kicked you off the case."

"Ethan, I haven't really slept in the past few days and I'm really stressed out. You're going to have to stop beating around the bush, and just tell me about whatever it is you're offering to do."

"Look . . . Sergeant Boleyn has taken over our conference room for the time being. No one is allowed in there other than DPS personnel. But I can hear everything they're talking about from the room next door."

"How's that possible?" I asked.

"Through the building's old ventilation system." Ethan winked at me. "It's how my dad used to listen in on his officers' conversations. Dad also planted recording devices all over the building. Most of them are still in place. There was nothing that went on in the police department that my dad didn't know about."

"Sounds kind of illegal."

"That's the pot calling the kettle black," Ethan snapped. "Only reason I'm telling you is because I can spy on Sergeant Boleyn for you. I can keep you up-to-date on the investigation. And give you a heads up if anything is about to happen. So, whaddya say? Do you want my help or not?"

"Yeah, I want your help," I said. I felt like I was making a deal with the Devil. "You got any useful info for me?"

"In fact, I do. Sergeant Boleyn sent a crime scene unit out to Wesley's and Waylon's townhouse this morning. It sounds like they tore the place apart, but they didn't find anything. No drugs. No moonshine. Nothing illegal at all. You—or whoever you had do it—did a good job cleaning up after them. Boleyn is upset and he's kicking himself for not sending a State Trooper over to the townhouse yesterday to guard the place."

"Maybe there never was anything illegal in the townhouse to begin with," I said as I fought back my grin. I would have to thank Roxanne and Jason for cleaning up the townhouse and helping keep us one step ahead of Sergeant Boleyn. "Anything else?"

"Yeah. Another crime scene unit went through Wesley's car and the motel room where the initial assault took place."

"They find anything in the car?"

Ethan shook his head. "Just Wesley's cell phone. They didn't find anything illegal."

"What about the motel?"

"The Roadhouse doesn't have security cameras other than inside the office. And the motel room was useless."

"Did the cleaning staff already get to the room?"

Ethan snorted. "What cleaning staff? It doesn't sound like that place has been cleaned in months. Like the Torture barn, every hard surface in the motel room was covered in fingerprints. And the crime scene unit found a whole heck of a lot of DNA samples and pieces of trace evidence. They might have found the attackers' prints or DNA, but it will take months for the lab to sort it all out. They also found bed bugs."

"Gross . . ."

"I'll let you know when I hear something else." Ethan stood up and stepped over to the door. "And, just so you know, I ain't doing this for nothing. You owe me, Carrie. I want a date . . . and maybe something more. And I want it tonight."

Ewwww! He wanted a date? A date! I couldn't believe that Ethan was still hanging onto the past and had yet to get over his high school crush on me. You'd think that my shooting and killing his father would be a major turn off. Apparently not . . .

"You know, Ethan, we shouldn't be seen together if you're going to be helping me."

"When this is all over with then."

Before I had to give Ethan some sort of answer, the door swung open and Sergeant Boleyn stepped into the interrogation room. He was followed by Lieutenant Hugh Underwood. Underwood leaned against the wall and scowled. I wasn't sure if the scowl was directed at me, Ethan, Boleyn, the world in general, or nothing at all since it was Underwood's typical facial expression.

"What are you doing in here, Officer Yates?" Boleyn asked.

"Just wanted to tell Carrie how I hope this turns out to be the downfall of her family," Ethan said before he slipped out of the room.

"Don't we all," Sergeant Arthur Boleyn muttered to himself. He then gave me a tight lipped, insincere smile as he had a seat across from me at the table. "Thank you for coming in to give your statement this morning, Miss Shatner. I appreciate your cooperation in this matter."

"It's not like you gave me much choice." I returned Boleyn's fake smile with one of my own. "And I'd appreciate it if you stopped wasting my time."

"I do apologize for keeping you waiting," Boleyn said. He laid a sheaf of papers and a cell phone down on the table. "I was at the hospital visiting with your cousins."

I perked up a little. At least Boleyn had been doing something productive while I was stuck in the interrogation room. I'd suspected that he had spent the past few hours watching me from the other side of the one-way mirror and laughing as I got more and more annoyed.

"How's Wesley doing?" I asked. "And Waylon? Is he awake?"

"Waylon remains in the medically induced coma," Boleyn said. "And Wesley seems to have contracted a convenient case of amnesia. The doctors found no evidence of him having suffered any type of head injury, but Wesley swears he was hit in the head. All he has been able to tell me was that he was supposed to meet with his friend Benjamin Dover at the motel sometime after the Body Farm closed for the night. I have a couple State Troopers attempting to track down this Mr. Dover."

"Good luck," I said. "Let me know if you ever locate Ben Dover."

Underwood snorted.

Boleyn ducked his head and cleared his throat as his cheeks turned a bright shade of red. "As I was saying . . . Wesley claims he has amnesia and that he can't remember anything that happened after he arrived at the motel. He can't even tell me how many perpetrators there were."

"Wesley did go through a traumatic experience. It's no wonder he can't remember what happened to him. His subconscious probably doesn't want to remember and is blocking out any memories that he has of what happened," I said.

"Mhmmm." Boleyn didn't roll his eyes, but his tone implied that he wanted to. "I'm sure Wesley remembers a lot about what happened to him. He just does not want to talk to me about it. It's almost like someone told him to . . . I don't know . . . keep his mouth shut. Miss Shatner, you were one of the few people who got to speak to Wesley before he was taken to the hospital. And I know you snuck into his hospital room last night after I made it clear that no one aside from medical personnel could see him until after I had interviewed him. You didn't, by chance, tell him to hinder my investigation by withholding information?"

"You really think I'd do that?" I asked, trying to sound offended.

"Yes. I do."

"I want to catch the people who hurt my cousins and killed Hank just as badly as you do. If not more so."

"Exactly." Boleyn snapped his fingers and pointed at me. "*You* want to catch the people responsible. *You* also want to protect your family because *you* know what Wesley was really doing at that motel. And *you* don't want me to figure it out because it involved Wesley breaking the law and *you're* trying to cover for him. Therefore, *you* told Wesley not to talk to me."

"Arthur . . ." Underwood growled.

"Whether Wesley is faking the amnesia or not, the longer he goes without talking, the longer it will be until any of his family members—including you, Miss Shatner—will be allowed to see him." Boleyn picked up the sheaf of papers and tapped the edges against the tabletop to straighten them. "Miss Shatner, this is the typed version of your written statement. I'll have you initial each page and sign at the bottom of the last page."

I snatched the papers out of Boleyn's hands and spread them out on the table. I took my time reading over my statement. Boleyn was an ethical man, and I didn't think he would tamper with my statement—either by adding something incriminating or leaving out an important detail. But Boleyn probably wasn't the person who had gone over my written statement and typed it up. That person might have a hidden agenda against me or my family. I didn't have my handwritten notes to compare to, but everything seemed to be in order. I initialed each of the pages and then signed the last page with a flourish.

I shoved the papers back at Boleyn. "When do you plan to release the Body Farm? My cousin Bubba and his crew need to get in there and start cleaning up so that we're ready to go on Saturday night."

"As I'm sure you're aware, Miss Shatner, the Body Farm is a crime scene," Boleyn said in a condescending tone. "And, as such, it needs to be searched for evidence that may be linked to the crimes that took place there. You wouldn't want us to release the crime scene without thoroughly searching it, would you?"

"Any trace evidence outside of the Torture barn would have been washed away or destroyed by the storm." I placed my hands on the metal tabletop and leaned towards Boleyn. "And, from what I've heard, the crime scene unit and the State Troopers went over the haunted hayride quite thoroughly yesterday."

"It doesn't hurt to look twice. Like I said, I want to be thorough." Boleyn leaned towards me until we were almost nose to nose. "I might need to hold on to the Body Farm through the weekend. I hope that won't be a problem."

"You know it will be."

"Arthur . . ." Lieutenant Underwood had a seat next to Boleyn. "If there are areas of the Body Farm that still need to be searched for evidence, why didn't you send the crime scene unit out there this morning?"

"Because . . . well, because there were other crime scenes that needed to be searched this morning," Boleyn sputtered. "Wesley's and Waylon's townhouse . . . The motel room where the initial assault took place."

"You have until the end of the day to finish up at the Body Farm. You may continue holding on to the building in which the assault took place until Saturday morning," Underwood told Boleyn. He then turned to me and said, "I'm sure Detective Shatner understands why we may need to go over the Torture barn again. But the rest of the Body Farm will be released by the end of the day. Your family can get in there tomorrow morning to do whatever needs done so you can operate as scheduled on Saturday night."

"Thank you, Lieutenant Underwood." I rewarded Underwood with a genuine smile and then stood up. "If we're done here—"

"We're not," Boleyn said, cutting me off. He gestured for me to sit back down. "I have a few more questions for you, Miss Shatner. Then we'll see if you're free to go."

"You want to ask me to help you with the investigation?" I asked. "I figured you'd realize you needed my help sooner or later. And the answer is yes."

Boleyn scoffed. "Miss Shatner, you've made a career out of destroying evidence and covering up your family's crimes. Do you really think I'm dumb enough to let you assist me in investigating a case in which your family is involved?"

"Do I think you're dumb? Yes. I do."

"Let me make myself clear, Miss Shatner . . . I do not want nor do I need your assistance. Unlike Sergeant Hardy, I am not fooled by you. Nor am I overcome by your apparent charms."

Boleyn picked up the cell phone that he had laid on the table alongside my statement. I had assumed that it was Boleyn's phone, but, when he turned it on, a picture of Roxanne, Summer, and Autumn stared back at me. Boleyn played around on Wesley's phone for a few seconds, and then slid it across the table to me. On the screen was the text message that I had sent Wesley on Saturday night.

"*WTF Wes?!?!? R u kidding me? Selling f'n drugs from the game stand? What the hell is wrong with u? I've had about all I can take of ur BS. If u don't knock this shit off, I'm gonna make u stop. And ur not gonna like what I do to u."*

Boleyn leered at me. "I'd like to hear you try to explain this, Miss Shatner."

"What's there to explain?" I asked. I leaned back in the chair and crossed my arms over my chest. "I knew Wesley committed a crime, and I called him out on it."

Boleyn stood up and circled the interrogation table so that he was standing behind me. "What really interests me is when you say, 'If you don't knock this shit off, I'm going to make you stop. And you're not going to like what I do to you.' Tell me, Miss Shatner, what exactly did you mean by that?"

I shifted around in the chair so that I could face Boleyn. "It was an empty threat."

"Was it?" Boleyn asked. "You're sure it wasn't a real threat? One that you might have seen through on Sunday morning at the Body Farm?"

"Hold on." I moved to stand up, but Boleyn stepped closer and crowded me back into the chair. "Are you accusing me of assaulting Wesley, Waylon, and Hank?"

"Arthur, I advise you rethink what you're doing before you fully insert your foot into your mouth," Underwood warned Boleyn.

Boleyn waved off his lieutenant's warning. He then said to me, "Isn't it your job to deal with your family's problems? And the people who cause those problems?"

"Abducting my cousins and beating them like piñatas is not how I deal with family problems."

"Where were you early Sunday morning?"

"At home asleep until around six," I said. "Then I was with my Granddaddy and uncles Houston and Bowie from about seven until noon."

"Your family members . . . Hardly a solid alibi. I'm sure they would lie for you. Maybe they even helped you take care of your little problem known as Wesley. I heard a rumor that he is involved in some terrible things, and that he gets in trouble quite often." Boleyn leaned closer to me and whispered, "I'll make you a deal. Now that I'm investigating what happened to your cousins and that Garrett boy, you know I'm going to come across incriminating evidence against your family. And, if I don't find it, one of the agents with the DPS's Drug Unit will . . . Oh, yes, Miss Shatner, I placed a call to the Drug Unit this morning. It won't be long before Wyatt County is swarming with agents. And it wouldn't surprise me if the Drug Unit calls in agents from the DEA and the ATF to help them out. So, do us both a favor . . . Turn over evidence against your family, and I'll give you a free pass. Help me, and I'll help you stay out of prison."

"No, thanks. I'll take my chances." I stood up, forcing Boleyn to take a step back. "And I'll see myself out."

CHAPTER ELEVEN

"**I**DIOT!" I SAID AS I SHOVED OPEN THE FRONT DOOR of the Holler Police Department and stepped outside. I sucked in a deep breath of crisp, fall air and forced myself to calm down. "You really messed up this time, Carrie."

I had completely forgotten about the text message I had sent Wesley on Saturday night. Had I remembered, I never would have left Wesley's phone in his car for Boleyn to find. Now Boleyn had solid evidence of me concealing a crime. He could come after me with charges of accessory to a crime and concealing evidence of a crime. And there was no doubt in my mind that he would come after me. I had my doubts that he would be able to make any of the charges stick—he didn't have any evidence aside from my text message—but it was just one more thing for me to worry about.

Shaking off the sense of foreboding, I cut through the town square as I made my way over to the sheriff's department. The town square—which served as a small park—was decorated for fall with strategically placed pumpkins, smiling scarecrows, and haybales.

The Holler Police Department was located on the east side of the town square, and the Wyatt County Sheriff's Department took up the entire block on the west side. The old red brick building housing the sheriff's department used to be a general store. After the store closed in the 1950s, the county acquired the building and converted it into the sheriff's department. The exterior of the building was in the process of being refurbished, and there was talk that the interior would be getting fixed up as well.

The other buildings located around the town square—including the Holler Police Department, the fire department, the county courthouse, city hall, a Baptist church, and the Wyatt County Historical Museum— were also housed in the original buildings that had been constructed during the early 1900s.

"What took so long?" Hardy asked as he jumped down the front steps outside the sheriff's department and joined me on the sidewalk. "I was starting to worry. I thought the Troopers were just taking you in so that you could make your statement. That shouldn't have taken four hours."

"Boleyn had them keep me locked up in the interrogation room until he came back from talking to Wes at the hospital," I said. "And you know what else Boleyn did? He accused me of being behind the assault on the boys. He also offered me a deal to turn on my family."

"Whoa . . . What did you tell him?"

"I turned him down," I said. "Your lieutenant was in the room and he heard everything."

"That's good," Hardy said as he moved out of the way of a woman with a stroller. "Speaking of my lieutenant, he just sent me a text and asked us to meet him, Lieutenant Schmitt, and Agent Ramos at the Roadhouse Motel tonight at midnight. He wants to discuss the case."

"No, he probably just wants to pick my brain and find out what I held back from telling Boleyn," I muttered. I glanced up and down the sidewalk to make sure there wasn't anyone around. I then leaned closer to Hardy and said, "You'll never guess who decided to keep me company while I was stuck in the interrogation room."

"Probably not," Hardy said. "Who was it?"

"Ethan Yates."

I explained to Hardy about my conversation with Ethan and how he offered to help me by passing along any information that he overheard.

"Do you trust him?" Hardy asked.

"Not at all," I said. Despite not trusting him, I fully planned on taking advantage of his willingness to help—even if I took everything he said with a grain of salt. "But I can use him."

"Be careful, Carrie. Ethan might be using you, too. Or Boleyn could have put him up to it to see if Ethan could get any info from you."

"I wouldn't put it past either of them . . ." I glanced down at my watch and saw that it was a quarter after eleven. I had forty-five minutes until I needed to be at the family meeting that I had asked Uncle

Houston to set up. "Let's see if we can track down my cousin Randy. He should be at work right now."

After being released from prison six weeks earlier, Randy moved home to Wyatt County and immediately went to work as a mechanic at the You Wreck 'Em, We Fix 'Em Paint and Body Shop. Our cousin Dale worked there, and he had helped Randy get the job.

"Do you want me to tag along?" Hardy asked. "Or do you think Randy will be more forthcoming if I'm not there."

"Randy doesn't exactly like me. I think you better come along to mediate."

Randy's twin sisters were a year younger than me, and—mainly because they had lived in the same neighborhood—we had spent a lot of time together when we were kids. Taryn, Tawny, and I used to dress Randy up in frilly princess costumes and parade him around the neighborhood. It was one of the least humiliating things we had done to him during our childhood, but I don't think Randy has forgiven us for it.

Randy and Taryn had followed their parents into the family business. Aside from running moonshine, Randy had also sold marijuana and other drugs to people throughout the area. Taryn had been one of the many Shatners who used fake IDs and the forged prescriptions to get various medications that other family members—including her brother—would then resell. Taryn and her husband, Stewart Devereux, had gotten out of the family's illegal business when their daughter was born.

You Wreck 'Em, We Fix 'Em was located one block to the west of the sheriff's department. I led the way around the side of the sheriff's department and across the street. The auto repair shop was a Mom-and-Pop operation, but it was the best garage in the county. Unbeknownst to me, my cousin Dale had been running a chop shop out of the garage for years. It was Dale's brother, Dickie, who finally let the clichéd cat-out-of-the-bag and told me about the chop shop. I then had a heart-to-heart with Dale and convinced him to relocate the chop shop to an old barn on the Shatners' collective property.

Dale and Dickie had been stealing cars off and on for the past few years, and they had yet to get caught. As far as I knew, they had never stolen a car within Wyatt County. But they had stolen cars from all the counties surrounding Wyatt County. Dale and Dickie specialized in jacking vehicles that had been abandoned on the side of the road. Dale would just load the vehicle up on his tow truck and drive away with it.

The tow truck was unmarked, and the license plate on it was kept purposely obscured so that any witnesses wouldn't be able to read it.

At the edge of the lot, Hardy and I passed a row of damaged cars. We then entered the garage through one of the open bay doors. The exterior of the T-shaped building had recently been painted a garish shade of basketball orange, but the inside remained a dingy gray. Despite all the garage bays being open, the combined scent of motor oil, gasoline, and burnt rubber was overpowering and immediately gave me a headache.

After letting my eyes adjust to the dim interior, I glanced around the garage. I didn't see Randy, but I spotted Dale standing under a car lift with four of his coworkers—all of whom wore matching dark blue work shirts and pants. The five of them had their heads tilted back and were examining the undercarriage of the sedan that was on the car lift.

Where Uncle Murph was bordering on the obese, his oldest son looked like he hadn't had a solid meal in months. Dale, who took after his mother, had always been lanky. Between his plain features and washed-out, shaggy blonde hair, Dale would be considered homely looking at best. The dark grease stains that coated his hands and his arms up to his elbows did nothing to improve his looks.

Dale was a couple years younger than me, but we had never been all that close. Sure, he was a likable enough guy. But I had just never bonded with him like I had with some of my other cousins. It probably didn't help that I had always been under the impression that Dale's IQ level wasn't all that much higher than plant life. He wasn't the smartest Shatner on the family tree, but he did have the mentality of a criminal mastermind.

"What's so interesting?" I asked, as I walked up to Dale and pointed up at the undercarriage of the car. Clumps of gooey pumpkin, dirt, and grass coated the undercarriage, and there were other pieces of detritus wrapped around the axle, the control arm, and the sway bar. I batted at an electrical cord dangling from the undercarriage. "What happened?"

"Some mom got mad that her daughter was booted off the Big Pine High School's volleyball team for smoking pot. The mom did donuts on the coach's front lawn and took out the Halloween decorations," Dale said.

Dale grabbed an extension cord and plugged the tail end of the electrical cord into it. Small, multicolored skull-shaped lights lit up throughout the undercarriage. Dale tugged at the cord, but it didn't budge from where it was threaded through and wrapped around the car's parts.

"That's going to be a pain in the butt to clean up," Hardy said.

"Yeah, it is." Dale took me by the hand and pulled me away from his coworkers. He led me and Hardy into the empty front office. "I gotta talk to you about Beto."

"Who's Beto?" Hardy asked, playing dumb. He leaned against the front desk and crossed his arms over his chest. "Is he a Shatner I haven't met yet?"

"He's uhh . . . he's Carrie's . . ." Dale gave me a desperate look as he trailed off.

"Beto is a friend," I said.

"More like boyfriend." Dale looked back and forth between me and Hardy. "Yo, so what does this mean for Beto? Are you getting back together with Ranger Hardy?"

"First of all, Dale, my love life is none of your business." Deciding to put a stop to the ruse, I said, "And, second of all, Beto and I are not and have never been in a relationship."

"So, it's just casual. Gotcha." Dale winked at me. "But that's not how Beto makes it sound. Remember, Carrie, I act in the same scene as him on the hayride. He talks about you nonstop between the wagons. And he makes it sound like things are pretty hot and heavy between you two."

"There is nothing going on between me and Beto," I reiterated.

"Well, you should have said that a while ago, Carrie." Dale picked up an oil filter and tossed it back and forth between his grease-stained hands. "Only reason any of us put up with Beto hanging around was because we thought he was your boyfriend."

"Could one of you please explain who Beto is?" Hardy asked.

"He's a smalltime criminal," I said.

"He showed up in Wyatt County about two months ago. Carrie said she trusted him, so the rest of us let him hang around. Now I'm thinking it was a mistake," Dale said.

"Why is that?" I asked.

"You know how he claims he used to steal cars and work in a chop shop?" Dale asked. "Well . . . I don't believe it. And neither does Dickie."

"I looked into Beto, and he's got a rap sheet," I said. A rap sheet that I had helped create. "Last year he was busted working at a chop shop in Houston."

"Then he must have been in the wrong place at the wrong time." Dale slammed the oil filter down on top of the desk. "You can't work for a chop shop unless you know something 'bout cars. And Beto don't know the difference between an alternator and a spark plug."

I mentally cursed Alberto for not telling me or his lieutenant that he didn't know the first thing about cars. We wouldn't have given him a fake criminal history with a chop shop otherwise.

"Just because he doesn't know much about cars doesn't mean he hasn't stolen them in the past," I said.

"You may be right, Carrie," Dale said. "But Dickie and I have been talking. At first, we thought maybe Beto worked for El Lobo, and that he sent Beto to spy on us. But now we think Beto is an undercover cop."

"That's just crazy, Dale," I said. Out of all the Shatners to figure it out . . . I never would have placed my money on Dale or Dickie. I guess the old saying is true—a blind squirrel does occasionally find a nut. "You and your brother always did have wild imaginations. Have you guys told anyone else that you think Beto is an undercover cop?"

"Just our dad. And I think Dad said something to Uncle Houston." Dale shrugged. "Maybe you're right, and Dickie and I are crazy. Just be careful, okay?"

"Yeah, I will." Changing the subject, I asked, "Is Cousin Randy working today? I need to ask him something."

"Randy should be around here somewhere." Dale walked over to the windows that looked out into the garage bays. He pointed to the far bay and said, "He's down there changing the brake pads on the Mustang."

"Thanks for the help Dale," I said.

I hustled back into the garage with Hardy on my heels. Weaving our way around the scattered tools and car parts, we made our way down to the last garage bay where Randy was struggling to replace a brake pad. A baseball cap covered his brown hair, and he had streaks of grease through his patchy beard. A gray and brown, shaggy-haired Lhasa Apso lay on the floor next to my cousin.

"Cute dog," Hardy said.

"Her name is Selena," Randy said. The dog lapped at his face with her little pink tongue, and he shoved her to the side. "She's my therapy dog. She's helping me get used to being back on the outside."

"She looks like she's a big help," I said. I extended my hand to Randy and pulled him to his feet. "You got a minute?"

"Taking a break," Randy shouted to no one in particular. He then walked outside and around the side of the building. The dog loyally followed him. Leaning up against the side of a dumpster, Randy lit a cigarette and pointed at Hardy. "Who's he? And whatcha want?"

"Sergeant Jerrod Hardy with the Texas Rangers." Hardy held out his hand, but Randy didn't shake it. "I'm in town looking into what happened to your cousins."

Randy took a long drag on the cigarette and then blew out a perfect smoke ring. "You ask me, that little shithead Wesley finally got what he had coming to him. Someone should have beat the snot out of him years ago."

"I heard you think it's Wes's fault that you got caught running moonshine by the Louisiana State Troopers," I said.

"I don't *think* it's Wes's fault. I *know* it's his fault," Randy snapped at me. He tossed the cigarette on the ground and stomped on it. "When the po-po pulled us over, I told Wes to stay cool. Instead, he started acting all shifty. He had sweat pouring down his face and could barely remember his own name. Then, when the po-po asked us what we were doing, Wes was all like 'we ain't doing anything illegal, officer.' Of course, the po-po is going to search the car after he said that. Had Wes just acted cool, all we would have gotten was a speeding ticket."

"Randy, had you not been speeding, you wouldn't have gotten pulled over in the first place," I pointed out.

"What the hell you want with me, Carrie?"

"Just checking in," I said. "I haven't really seen you since you got out of prison."

"Cut the crap," Randy said as he lit a second cigarette. "If you gave a damn about me, you would have checked up on me six weeks ago. What is it you really want?"

"What happened to the boys was a set up. Wesley thinks at least one of the people behind it is a Shatner, and he's fairly sure it was you," I said. "Where were you on Sunday morning?"

Randy yanked up his right pant leg and revealed an ankle monitor. "Does this answer your question?"

"You're the one who needs to cut the crap," I said. I tapped the toe of my boot against the ankle monitor. "I know that's a fake monitor. The real one is on Selena's collar."

Hardy knelt and brushed Selena's shaggy hair away from her neck to reveal the ankle monitor. "How'd you know the dog was wearing the ankle monitor?"

"It's my aunt Priscilla's dog. She claims it's her therapy animal, but the silly thing is more neurotic than she is. There's no way Randy would willingly bring the dog to work with him unless he had an exceptionally good reason," I said. "Plus, my Uncle Vernon did something similar when he had to wear an ankle bracelet after his last DUI."

Randy blew a cloud of smoke out of his nostrils. "I'm supposed to wear that damn thing for the next three years. It's part of my probation. I can't go anywhere other than my parents' house, work, or a couple stores. I gotta be home by a certain time. Plus, I gotta waste two hours of my day charging the damn battery. I can't live like that. Not after spending five years trapped in that little jail cell. Uncle Murph put the real monitor on the dog and he gave me a fake monitor to wear in case my parole officer makes a surprise visit. Mom lets me bring the dog to work with me so that it looks like I'm where I'm supposed to be."

"That explains how you've been able to work at the Body Farm. I was wondering how you talked your parole officer into allowing it," I said.

Randy was one of the chainsaw-wielding "animals" in Slaughterhouse. During the show, he wore a sheep mask along with his butcher's apron and blood-splattered costume. The other actors in Slaughterhouse wore similar costumes along with their horse, pig, and cow masks.

"You ain't gonna tell anyone, are you, Carrie?" Randy asked.

"Just tell me where you were on Sunday morning, and I'll forget about the whole thing."

Randy breathed out a sigh of relief. "I was at the Dancing Cowgirl."

"The strip club was open that early in the morning?" Hardy asked.

"They had a hurricane party," Randy said. "Dollar drafts and two-dollar hurricanes. I went straight there after leaving the Body Farm. Got there around three probably. I stayed until they closed at six. Then I hung out for a while and helped them clean up. Figured it was better than going home and dealing with Mom. Ask the Palmer who tends bar. He'll tell you I was there. And talk to that Levi Palmer kid. He ain't a big fan of Wes's either. He told me why, but I was, uh, heavily intoxicated at the time so I don't really remember what he said."

"Hey, you guys," Dale shouted as he shuffled around the side of the building and joined us by the dumpster. "That family meeting is gonna start in, like, ten minutes. If we don't leave now, we're gonna be late. Randy, stick that hairball in her crate and let's go."

"Come on, Jerrod," I said as I headed across the street to the parking lot behind the sheriff's department. "Time to go deal with my family."

Hardy and I were climbing into his truck when my phone rang. "Hello?"

"Carrie . . . it's Ethan . . . Ethan Yates."

"You got an update for me already?" I asked.

"I, uh, I just wanted to let you know that Sergeant Boleyn is looking for some of your family members. He wants to talk to them about Wesley. But the State Troopers he sent out can't find any of 'em," Ethan said. "He also really wants to talk to Roxanne Devereux. He knows that she's Wesley's girlfriend, and he thinks she might know something."

"I'll let everyone know that Boleyn is looking for them," I said. "And Roxanne can decide if she wants to cooperate with Boleyn or not. Is there anything else?"

"Yeah, Boleyn wants to arrest Wesley as soon as he is released from the hospital. But, thanks to you cleaning up after Wesley, Boleyn doesn't have anything to charge him with yet," Ethan said. "Boleyn is also planning on getting an arrest warrant for you. He just needs to find a judge to sign it."

"I guess it's a good thing that all of the local judges are on Uncle Houston's payroll."

CHAPTER TWELVE

"**Y**OU EVER ON TIME ANYMORE, CARRIE? And why are you bringin' a lawman to the family meetin'?" Uncle Houston asked as he pushed open the door to the Arm Bar and stepped out onto the concrete pad that served as a front stoop. Without giving me a chance to respond, Uncle Houston brandished the lit end of his smelly cigar under my nose and said, "This family meetin' was your idea, missy. Yet you're the last one to show up. We've got over a hundred people in there. And they're getting restless waitin' for you to make an appearance."

Uncle Murph followed Uncle Houston outside. He had a basket of tortilla chips clutched to his chest, and he was shoving the chips into his mouth by the handful. Broken and half-chewed pieces of tortilla chips fell out of his mouth as he asked, "Why would you pick a bar for the family meeting? Especially when the owner of the bar will serve only beer? And he's limiting us to just one."

The Arm Bar—formerly known as Catfish's Cantina—was located on the southern edge of Holler. A few months ago, Catfish gave up ownership of the bar when he sold it to Red. Aside from changing the name of the bar, Red had also renovated both the interior and the exterior of the shabby, wooden structure. The place now resembled a respectable sports bar with a professional wrestling theme opposed to a rundown biker bar.

"I didn't pick the meeting place," I said as I waved cigar smoke away from my face.

"I wasn't talking to you, Carrie." Uncle Murph used the plastic basket to gesture towards Uncle Houston. "I'm talking to him."

"How was I supposed to know Red was gonna limit the number of beers he'd give us?" Uncle Houston asked. He pulled a dented metal flask out of his jacket pocket and held it up. "You gotta start carryin' one of these around, Murph."

I waited while Uncle Houston passed the flask to Uncle Murph so that he could take a swig. I then cleared my throat and said, "And it's not my fault I'm fashionably late. I've been stuck in an interrogation room for most of the morning. On the wrong side of the table."

"Dang." A fine mist of moonshine spewed out of Uncle Murph's mouth. "Sergeant Boleyn was interrogating you all morning?"

"Not all morning. Probably not even for half an hour," I said as I dabbed at the sheen of moonshine that covered my forehead. "But he thinks I'm behind the assault on the boys. And he has evidence that I knew the Three Stooges were selling drugs at the Body Farm. Boleyn is planning to get an arrest warrant for me."

"None of the local judges will sign it. I pay them not to," Uncle Houston said.

"I know." I reached around Uncle Murph and grabbed the door handle. "Let's not keep the family waiting any longer."

Uncle Murph leaned back against the door and prevented me from opening it. "I oughta warn you, Carrie . . . you're 'bout to walk into a powder keg."

"If you haven't heard, we had an actual explosion last night when Uncle Butch blew up the trailer that Wes was making moonshine and meth in," I said. Between the explosion and the fire, the single-wide trailer and everything in it had been destroyed. We also managed to incinerate a few of the nearby trees. That we somehow didn't start a forest fire is a miracle. "We don't need a figurative explosion today."

"Everyone is angry and scared." Uncle Houston puffed on his cigar. "Doesn't help that a bunch of them received threatening notes this morning."

"Threatening notes?" I asked. Having been stuck in the interrogation room all morning, I hadn't been able to keep up to date with what all was going on. "What kind of threatening notes?"

"Bunch of your uncles and cousins had notes taped to their front doors or stuck under their windshield wipers this morning," Uncle Murph said. He held open his jacket and pointed at a manila envelope that was tucked into an oversized inner pocket. "I collected the notes for you. They all got about the same message—knock off your crimes and turn yourselves in before we come after you. Said more than Hank will die if we don't follow their instructions. Keaton got one that said next time he won't be so lucky to get away. The notes are all signed 'your friend, Facundo.'"

"I didn't get no note," Uncle Houston said.

"I got one. Found it in my mailbox. It listed a lot of my . . . indiscretions. And my boys' crimes. Whoever this Facundo guy is, he knows all about us," Uncle Murph said. "Facundo also threw eggs at my house. And he slashed some of your cousins' tires. He keyed a couple cars, broke a few windows, and did some other types of petty vandalism around our properties. I got pictures on my phone I can send you."

"Sounds like Facundo thinks he is some sort of vigilante," Hardy said.

"That's the general consensus," Uncle Murph said. "While we were waiting for you to show up, I tried to set everyone straight on what we know happened. Now the family is split over whether to stand behind Wes or condemn him for getting the rest of us caught up in his mess. And the Palmers all blame Wes and the rest of us for Hank getting killed. No one is happy that Wes shared family secrets with the assailants, and they're all worried about what he said. And who he said it to."

"Your granddaddy is in there trying to keep the peace, so the feud don't get started up again," Uncle Houston said.

"We definitely don't want that to happen," I said.

Off to my left, one of the Arm Bar's brand-new picture windows shattered as a barstool slammed into it. Shards of glass flew out into the parking lot and rained down on the vehicles parked closest to the building. The barstool was followed by the sounds of multiple people screaming and the thuds and slaps of fists and other hard objects connecting with soft flesh.

"Sounds like the feud just got started back up," Hardy said.

I shoved my uncles out of my way and wrenched open the door. After racing into the dimly lit bar, I scrambled up onto the nearest table so that I could see over top of the chaos.

The small barroom was crammed full of family, friends, and—when it came to the Palmers—frenemies. Most of the women in the room had fallen back and were pressed against the walls or hiding behind the overturned tables. Some of the braver—or dumber, depending on how you judged them—women had jumped into the middle of the fray and were trying to get the men calmed down. MeMaw Devereux, Catfish's one-hundred-and-two-year-old mother, was walloping people left and right with her cane.

Across the room from me, Red was spraying the people closest to the bar with whatever beer he had on tap. And over by the pool table, a handful of my cousins were exchanging blows with a group of similar aged Palmers. Ralph Walker—who was married to my cousin Julianna—had ripped a WWE WrestleMania commemorative folding chair off the wall and was indiscriminately hitting people with it. Merle Devereux, Gopher's oldest son, had grabbed a replica title belt and was swinging it around by the end of the leather strap. Heath Palmer had randomly ripped his shirt down the middle in an impersonation of Hulk Hogan.

Some of the older men had shoved the tables and chairs out of the middle of the room and were gathered around two armed combatants. My Uncle Woody clasped the neck of a broken beer bottle in his hand, and Hank Garrett the Second brandished a switchblade. They cautiously circled each other, exchanging words and slashing at each other with their weapons.

"Carrie!"

I looked around the room for the person who had shouted my name and spotted Hank the Third's older sister Amelia charging at me from across the room. Amelia and I had gone to high school together. We had not been friends.

"It's your fault my brother got killed!" Amelia screeched at me as she hurdled over a fallen chair. "You were supposed to protect him!"

Amelia wove her way around the people, tables, and chairs as she charged across the room at me. I was debating whether it was a good idea to take a flying leap off the table and land on top of Amelia when Veda came out of nowhere and tackled her.

"Knock it off!" I screamed as loudly as I could. I grabbed an empty beer bottle off a nearby table and hurled it to the floor. The glass smashed on impact. One by one, the Shatners, Devereuxs, and Palmers lowered their weapons. Conversations and accusations drifted off as all eyes—including the eyes of the pro wrestling action figures, autographed photos, and cardboard standees that decorated the walls—turned to look at me. "Y'all are acting like a bunch of lunatics. What is it y'all are fighting about now?"

"Yo, Carrie," Chris Palmer shouted at me. "Is it true that Wes thinks one of us was behind the attack on him, Hank, and Waylon?"

I groaned in frustration. "Who said that?"

At least two dozen people pointed towards where Uncle Butch was leaning up against the vintage pro wrestling arcade game.

"Oh, was that supposed to be a secret, Carrie?" Uncle Butch asked me.

"What part of 'this is between us' did you think meant 'go tell everyone'?" I asked.

Uncle Butch sneered at me. "Maybe next time you'll think twice before accusing me of committing a crime . . . that I had nothing to do with."

"Maybe next time, don't seem like you might be guilty of committing said crime."

This morning—just before the State Troopers hauled me off to the Holler Police Department—I had talked to a couple of the ranch hands at the alpaca farm. They confirmed that Butch and Elvin had been with them in one of the barns throughout the storm. There was no way that either of my two uncles could have been involved in the assault on the boys.

"So that's a yes?" Chris Palmer asked. "Wes thinks one of us was involved?"

"Yes, Wes thinks that. He doesn't know for certain," I said.

"How do we know you ain't behind it?" Uncle Delmar asked.

"Yeah, you've been trying to shut us down for years," Aunt Bunny added.

Others began voicing their opinions and accusations that I was behind the assault on Wesley, Waylon, and Hank—as well as the assault on Keaton. They also blamed me for the threatening notes. Within seconds, they switched from accusing me to accusing each other.

I grabbed another empty beer bottle and hurled it against the wall. "That's enough! Y'all need to calm down before you do something stupid that we'll all regret."

Reluctantly, and with a lot of bellyaching and angry glances cast about, everyone worked together to straighten up the tables and chairs before they returned to their seats.

"I thought we were going to have another murder on our hands," Hardy muttered to me.

"We still might before all this is over."

Once everyone was seated, I strode to the middle of the room and looked around. The bar was a mess. Broken glass and spilled drinks covered the floor. Two wooden chairs had been smashed, and the pieces lay strewn across the floor. A stuffed toy that was supposed to resemble Stone Cold Steve Austin had been disemboweled.

"Y'all should be ashamed of yourselves," I said. "We've got enough problems right now. Y'all don't need to be causing any more."

As I surveyed the room, I noticed that the Shatners and the majority of the Devereuxs—those that had married into my family or were part of my family's extensive criminal operations—had taken over the tables and chairs. My grandparents, Uncle Bowie, and my great-aunts were at a table with Catfish and his current wife. My aunts, uncles, and cousins were scattered about the rest of the tables. There were only a few Shatners—not counting the school age kids—who were not present.

None of my sisters were here. My older sisters, Holly and Rosie, had never taken part in any of the Shatners' criminal endeavors, and they rarely visited Wyatt County. My half-sister Piper lived in Las Vegas with her mom, and they had no ties to the Shatner family's crimes. My twin half-sisters Melody and Brooklyn . . . well, I wasn't quite sure where in the world they were. I just knew it was in a country without extradition.

Also not present was Uncle Murph's daughter. Luanne was attending Texas A&M in College Station, and she had been instructed to stay away from home for the time being. And the four members of the Flaming Outhouses were in Nashville.

The rest of the Devereuxs—including Pork Chop and his wife—were seated off by themselves at tables near the double doors that opened onto the bar's new deck area. Out of Catfish's eleven children, only two of them had never been involved with the Shatners' crimes. Toad and Dinker sat on either side of Pork Chop, and, judging by the disgusted looks on their faces, they wanted to be anywhere but here.

The Palmers, who were gathered around the bar, were descended from the union between Otto Palmer and his wife. Like my great-grandfather Shooter, Otto Palmer was the only one of his many siblings who survived the family feud and federal agents long enough to reproduce. Otto and his wife had had three children—Oscar, Omar, and Ophelia.

Oscar—who had spent roughly a third of his eighty-four years behind bars—had been running his family's illegal operations up until January of this year when he was arrested for accessory to murder. During a recent pre-trial hearing, the judge had taken into consideration Oscar's early onset dementia and the court-appointed doctors deemed him mentally incompetent to stand trial. As a result, the charges against Oscar had been dropped, and he was free to resume breaking the law.

All three of Oscar's sons had rap sheets, and one of them was currently in prison. Seven out of Oscar's nine grandchildren had been arrested at least once, and two of them were awaiting trial for murder. Unless she had gotten lucky and never been caught, Oscar's daughter was the only one of his descendants to have never broken the law.

Ophelia Garrett was seated at the bar next to Oscar. She and her late-husband, Hank the First, had never had anything to do with the Palmers' wrongdoings. That didn't stop either of their sons or their grandsons from getting mixed up in the family's crimes.

Omar had also been heavily involved in the Palmers' crimes up until he died while in prison a few years ago. Omar's son and one of his two daughters had rap sheets, as did three out of his five grandchildren.

"'Bout time you got here, little lady," Oscar said to me, breaking the awkward silence. He slid off his barstool and shuffled across the room towards me. He shot me an indignant glare before leaning around me to jab his cane into Hardy's chest. "None of this would have happened had my family not teamed up with the Shatners and Devereuxs. I never should have listened to you when you said we needed to 'put the past in the past' and quit the feuding."

Hardy shoved the tip of Oscar's cane away from his chest. "All I said was to knock off the stupid feud. The pranks y'all were playing on each other were dangerous and senseless. I never suggested that y'all become best friends and combine your criminal operations. In fact, I specifically asked y'all not to do that."

"That ain't how I remember it," Oscar said.

"You're also senile, ya old coot," Uncle Houston said. "I bet you can't remember what you ate for breakfast."

"And you!" Oscar swung his cane in front of my face and pointed it at Uncle Houston. "I put you in charge of my family. And what do you do? You hand it off to some no-good woman who ain't got no business being in charge of nothing. Carrie can't handle running the family. 'Bout all she can handle is heading to the kitchen and making me a dang sandwich."

"Excuse me?" I asked, bristling at the insult. "Aunt Emily Morgan ran the Shatner family for almost sixty-five years, and she was a woman.

She also did a whole hell of a lot better running my family than you ever did running yours."

"Yeah, but Emily Morgan knew what she was doing. You ain't got no clue," Oscar said. "Besides, we ain't never had no one in law enforcement covering our butts like y'all do."

"Oscar's right," Ophelia said. She had followed her brother to the center of the room. Nudging Oscar out of the way, Ophelia pushed herself up onto the tiptoes of her thick soled, white orthopedic shoes so that she could look me in the eye. "My grandson would still be alive if it wasn't for you and your kin. Hanky was a good boy until he took up with Wesley."

"In case you forgot, Ophelia, 'Hanky' had a rap sheet longer than my arm. And that was from before he started hanging out with Wesley. Hank's lucky he wasn't in jail. Truthfully, he would have been better off in jail. He'd probably still be alive." Gesturing to all of the Palmers, I said, "Most of y'alls kids and grandkids were criminals long before our families combined our operations. And I have binders full of the y'all's arrests records and court transcripts to prove it."

"Why I never . . ." Ophelia huffed.

Hardy stepped between me and Ophelia. "Everyone . . . let's all take a few deep breaths and calm down. Now is not the time for y'all to be turning against each other."

"I'll gladly turn against them sumbitches. I never should have teamed up with them in the first place," Oscar said as he waved his cane around. "I'll tell you whatever you want to know Mr. Ranger, and then you can put them Shatners behind bars where they belong."

Uncle Houston shoved Oscar aside. "And I'll tell you everything you need to know about the Palmers so you can lock them up."

"If y'all don't watch it, I'll tell Jerrod everything I know about all y'all," I said. I had already told Lieutenant Schmitt and Agent Ramos everything. But no one needed to know that. "Then I won't have to deal with any of you!"

"Carrie . . ." Hardy hissed at me. He walked to the far side of the room and climbed up onto the pool table. "Does everyone remember what Abe Lincoln said? About how a house divided against itself cannot stand? Well, y'all are now a house. And if you keep fighting with each other, your house is going to fall apart. And I can guarantee that things will be worse for y'all if you start stabbing each other in the back. Is that what y'all want? Or do you want to stick together and try to make the best of it?"

I joined Hardy on top of the pool table. Since Uncle Murph had already set the record straight on what had happened to the boys, I decided to get right to the point.

"I know a lot of you . . . make that almost all of you . . . have been against me taking charge from the start. And you can go ahead and keep feeling that way. But now is the time that y'all better start listening to me," I said. Lieutenant Schmitt was right—I might not *want* to be in charge, but I *needed* to be in control. Now was the time to take charge. "And I'm not going to sugar coat it, y'all . . . We're fucked."

"What in tarnation is that supposed to mean?" Catfish asked. He tipped his chair back and clasped his hands over his immense beer belly.

"Do I really need to spell it out for y'all?" I asked. I looked around the room and saw a few bewildered faces. "Roxanne, Jason, and I did our best to clean up after Wes, Waylon, and Hank. A . . . well, let's call him a confidential informant . . . told me that the DPS's crime scene unit didn't find any illegal substances at their townhouse or in Wes's car. But Sergeant Boleyn is bound to dig up something against them. And he will use that to come after the rest of us. The first domino has fallen, and the rest of us are about to fall with it."

"Y'all heard of the ripple effect?" Hardy asked. When he received a lot of blank stares, he explained, "It's like when you drop a rock in a pond. It causes ripples that affects the water in the area around where you dropped the rock. Those ripples can be far reaching."

"Look at it this way . . . what happened to the boys is a boulder," I said. "And it was heaved into our pond. Now the ripples that it caused are coming for the rest of us."

"Ain't like you gotta be worried 'bout it," Uncle Sterling shouted at me. "Ranger Hardy is going to take care of you. It's the rest of us that have got to be worried."

"You're right. I probably have a better chance of coming out of this unscathed than a lot of you do," I said. I didn't confirm or deny that Hardy would protect me. He'd already done what he could by setting up the deal I had with the DPS. "But do I have to remind you that a bunch of y'all broke the law? You had to know that at some point it would catch up to you."

"Carrie's right. It's time to accept the consequences of our actions," Uncle Houston said. "What I want to know is if there's something you can do to stop Sergeant Boleyn."

"What do you think I can possibly do?" I asked.

"I ain't talkin' to you." Uncle Houston pointed at Hardy. "I'm talkin' to the Ranger. Is there anything you can do to help us out, Jerrod? Can you sabotage Boleyn's case? Or get Boleyn kicked off the case so that you can take over?"

"The only thing I can do is help Carrie find the people who did this to the boys," Hardy said. He jumped off the pool table and then had a seat on the edge. "Sabotaging the case will only make things worse for y'all and cost me my job. And, while there is a slim possibility that I could get Boleyn kicked off the case, there is no way I'd ever be put in charge due to my relationship with Carrie. I'm sorry, but there isn't much I can do to help all y'all."

"Can you at least stop Boleyn from investigating our family?" Uncle Bowie asked.

Hardy shook his head. "Like Carrie said, the first domino has fallen. Sergeant Boleyn is going to take whatever he can figure out from looking into Wesley, Waylon, and Hank, and he's going to use that to come after the rest of y'all."

"The only thing we can do is try to prevent any more dominos from falling," I said as I paced back and forth across the pool table. "And the only way to do that is to destroy everything illegal that we've got. That way there won't be anything for Sergeant Boleyn to find."

Hardy looked up at me and whispered, "What are you doing, Carrie?"

"My job," I whispered back. "I'm doing what I should have done over two months ago when you told me that the Drug Unit was looking into us. I'm cleaning up after my family."

"If you have them destroy everything, there won't be anything for the DPS to find."

"Exactly. I'm sorry, Jerrod. But I have to protect my family."

"I can't be part of this, Carrie," Hardy said. "I won't stop you from destroying or hiding evidence. But I can't know what you do with it."

I waited until Hardy walked across the room and disappeared through the door into the bar's storage room. I then said, "Y'all need to get rid of anything illegal that you have. That includes any moonshine that's sitting around. And all the stills. The marijuana. Everything in the grow houses—"

"Wait one cotton pickin' minute!" Uncle Ted shoved back his chair and stood up. "You're asking some of us to destroy our livelihoods, but you don't even know for sure that this Ranger is going to come after us."

"Sergeant Boleyn made it crystal clear to me this morning that he's coming after all of us. He told me that he called in the DPS's Drug Unit to help him investigate," I said. "Once they show up, it won't be long before the feds start sniffing around."

An investigation conducted by the Drug Enforcement Administration or the Bureau of Alcohol, Tobacco, Firearms and Explosives was my family's worst nightmare. We had somehow managed to stay off their radar for this long. But I had a feeling that they would jump onto the DPS's investigation at the first opportunity.

"Well I ain't getting rid of any of my plants or tearing down my grow houses on your say so. I'm drying out the Purple Kush that I just harvested. And I've got some Acapulco Gold that's about ready," Uncle Ted said. "I'll take the risk."

"Think of all of the other people who you are putting in jeopardy, Uncle Ted." I had to shout so that I could be heard over the rising din of protests being voiced by the others. If I didn't make them see reason, I would have a mutiny on my hands. "You won't be the only one going to prison if the agents find the grow house under your garage. Aunt Eileen will most likely wind up going to prison, too. Is that a risk you're willing to take? And what about the grow house on Rooster's and Becky's property. What do you think will happen to them? And their kids?"

"CPS already took my kids once," Becky said, referring to the time that the local Child Protective Services briefly took custody of her three kids after Rooster was arrested in Tyler, Texas, for possession of marijuana with intent to sell. "I ain't losing my kids again."

"And I don't want to go back to prison," Rooster said.

"You always were as yellow as mustard, but without the bite," Uncle Ted said. He ducked to avoid being hit in the head by the metal napkin dispenser that Rooster lobbed at him. "But I'll tear out the grow house under your blacksmith shop if it'll make you feel better."

"You'll tear them all out," I said. I grabbed a pool cue that was leaning against the table and used it to point at Uncle Ted. "What do you think will happen if the agents find the grow house under Ellie May's greenhouse? They'll get a warrant to search the rest of the property, and then they'll find Billy Bob's moonshine still. Same with the grow house under Aunt Bunny's goat barn. And the one under Uncle Leroy's taxidermy shop. If the agents find those, they will then find the stills. Most of our crimes are connected, and that's why the grow houses and stills have to go."

"Carrie's right," Uncle Houston said. "We've had a good run. A damn good run. And it's lasted a lot longer than I ever thought it would. But our time is up. For the sake of our kids and grandkids, we have got to clean up our mess."

"All right, all right." Uncle Ted waved his arm in a dismissive gesture. "I'll tear out the grow houses."

Oscar Palmer pounded the tip of his cane on the floor. "It pains me to admit it, but the little lady is right. But what puzzles me, Carrie, is how are we supposed to get rid of all this stuff? Ain't like we can put it out on the curb and have the trash man haul it away."

"That is the million-dollar question," I admitted. Coming up with the plan to get rid of everything illegal had been spur of the moment. I hadn't thought it all the way through, and I had no idea how to dispose of the evidence. There was just so much of it. "The marijuana, prescription pads, and some other stuff can be burnt. And the pills can be flushed."

"Do not flush any pills down the toilet," my cousin Tawny Mount said. She worked as a pediatric nurse at the Wyatt County General Hospital. "The wastewater treatment plant won't remove the pills, so it will just wind up contaminating our food and water supplies. We have a bin in the main lobby at the hospital where you can dispose of unused medications. Please bring the pills in to the hospital to get rid of them properly."

"Y'all are gonna need a bigger bin," Aunt Priscilla said.

"So, we take the pills to the hospital, and we torch anythin' that's flammable," Uncle Bowie said. "But what 'bout the big stuff? Like the stills and the lights in the grow houses?"

At the far end of the room, Uncle Vernon's hand shot up in the air and he waved his arm around like a kid desperate to get his teacher's attention because he had to go to the bathroom. Uncle Vernon was one of Aunt Emily Morgan's kids, and he helped the rest of the family by laundering some of our dirty money through his construction company.

"You have an idea, Uncle Vernon?" I asked.

Uncle Vernon jumped to his feet. I could almost see his sleazy mustache quivering in excitement. "We can bury everything else under the new museum at Old Town Texas . . . That is, if Elvin and Bubba are okay with it. I've got the stone base laid out for the foundation, but we can move that out of the way and then dig a hole or two or three to bury everything tonight. Then I can put the stone base back and pour the concrete as planned in the morning."

At a nearby table, Uncle Elvin and Bubba were engaged in a heated conversation. I didn't have to hear what they were saying to know that Bubba was against the plan. Uncle Elvin also looked a bit reluctant, but it appeared that he was in favor of it. The argument went on for another minute or two before Uncle Elvin and Bubba agreed to Uncle Vernon's plan.

"Everything illegal needs to be disposed of by dawn tomorrow morning. And that is an order," I said. I jumped down from the pool table. "Are there any questions."

"I got one," Naomi's mom, Glenda, said. "Considering what happened to Wes, Waylon, and Hank. Then Keaton getting jumped, and now the threatening notes that some of us received . . . Do you think we are seriously in danger?"

"Yeah, do you think this Facundo guy is going to try to come after more of us?" Aunt Margaret asked. "Should we take precautions?"

"I think we should definitely be on alert," I said. I had to choose my words carefully or else I could start up a mass hysteria among my family. Last time they thought they were in danger, most of them had converged at Uncle Houston's house and put a sizable dent in his stockpile of toilet paper and emergency meals. "I have no idea if Facundo will attack again. But it sounds like he's planning to. I suggest not going around by yourselves if you can help it. Lock your doors. And just keep an eye out for anyone suspicious."

"So you're saying to shoot first and ask questions later?" Uncle Sterling asked.

"Let's try not to shoot anyone unless you absolutely have to. I don't need any of you calling me saying you accidentally shot the mailman or a Jehovah's Witness who was knocking on your door. Just be aware of your surroundings and stay safe," I said. I could only hope that none of them got trigger-happy and shot an innocent person by mistake. "Now, we also need to figure out the identities of the three people who assaulted Wesley, Waylon, and Hank. And the person who attacked Keaton. Even if one or more of those assailants is in this room."

There was an eruption of accusations and finger pointing.

"This isn't a witch hunt, and I'm not going to let it turn into one," I shouted. "If any of you have any information or suspicions, come and see me and Jerrod privately. We'll be back in Red's office. Or you can call me later today."

I headed through the double doors that led into the bar's storage area. Red had recently put up some plywood partitions to make a small office in the back corner. Inside the cramped, chilly area was a beat-up metal desk and a couple folding chairs.

I had barely had a chance to sit down or say anything to Hardy before Granddaddy walked into the overcrowded office. It was my first face-to-face encounter with him since the "field trip." While I understood that Granddaddy had been trying to protect me, I hadn't yet gotten over being angry at him for keeping so many secrets from me.

Skipping over the niceties, I asked, "What's up?"

"I was afraid something like this would happen someday." Granddaddy unfolded a metal chair and had a seat. "Carrie, it's 'bout time I told you about my brother Ben."

Benjamin Milam Shatner was my Granddaddy's youngest brother. All I knew about Uncle Ben was that he had died while taking part in some sort of criminal activity when he was nineteen. That's all anyone in my generation knew. My cousins and I had always wondered about what happened to our great-uncle, but our parents either didn't know or wouldn't tell us. Our grandparents wouldn't talk about their youngest brother. It was considered taboo for anyone to even mention his name.

"We don't have time for story time right now, Granddaddy," I said. I wasn't intentionally trying to be difficult. I just was not having a good day, and I didn't want to waste any more time.

"Knowing what happened to Ben might help you find the people responsible for what happened to the boys." Granddaddy rubbed his hands over his wrinkled face and back through what little hair he had left. "Ben was the baby of the family. He was eight years younger than Bowie. And he was just a tyke when our pappy got sent to prison. Without Pappy around to raise him with a firm hand, Mama and us kids coddled him. Ben grew up spoiled. He also grew up watching the rest of us break the law. The poor kid never had a chance."

To speed things up, I asked, "And all this has to do with Wesley how?"

"What you have to know 'bout Ben is that he was a lot like Wesley," Granddaddy said.

"Reckless and stupid?" I asked.

"I was going to say Ben was too big for his britches . . . but reckless and stupid is a fairly accurate description." Granddaddy said. He gave me a sad smile. "Ben was going to mess up and get us all in trouble. It was just a matter of time, and we all knew it."

"But Uncle Ben wound up getting killed first."

"Emmy sent Ben on a moonshine run by himself," Granddaddy said. "I told her it was a bad idea. But she wouldn't listen to me. And neither would anyone else. Ben left on the run, and he never came back. The next day some people found him shot to death on a backroad in the southern part of the county. I was working as a deputy for the sheriff's department, and the sheriff and I kept it quiet about the shooting. The sheriff let everyone believe that Ben died in a car accident while running moonshine."

"I'm guessing the shooter was never caught," Hardy said.

Granddaddy shook his head. "I always suspected that Emmy or Houston set Ben up."

"Did I hear you right?" I asked. "Did you just say that you think Uncle Houston and Aunt Emily Morgan killed y'all's little brother?"

"I said there's a damn good possibility that Emmy or Houston set Ben up. They might have worked together, or it could have been just one of them. I want to believe that Emmy had nothing to do with it. She loved Ben. But I'm sure Houston was part of it. He's said some things over the years . . ." Granddaddy shook his head. "Either way, if Houston or Emmy was behind it, then it was most definitely Catfish who pulled the trigger. You know that Catfish has always helped Houston take care of 'problems.' What you don't know is that, back in the day, there wasn't anything Catfish wouldn't have done for my sister. He was in love with her, but she wasn't ever goin' to leave Hayworth for him. Emmy might not have returned Catfish's affections, but she toyed with them and kept him at her beck and call. It's why none of Catfish's first five marriages lasted. His wives all got sick and tired of playing second fiddle to Emmy."

Interrupting, I said, "Since Aunt Emily Morgan is no longer alive, there's no way she could have setup Wesley and the boys. Can I assume you think it was Uncle Houston? Maybe with some help from Catfish?"

"It's something I can see them doing," Granddaddy said.

"Uncle Houston told me on Sunday that the boys wouldn't be a problem for much longer." I kicked the side of the desk. "Fuck!"

"This is an extremely serious accusation, Crockett," Hardy said.

"And I hate to accuse my own brother, but I think he's been setting the whole family up to take a fall." Granddaddy sucked in a deep breath and then shakily exhaled. "Carrie, I've suspected that Houston was up to something ever since he asked you to take over the family—"

"Why me? That's what I still can't figure out," I said. I tried to pace back and forth across the office, but there wasn't all that much room to maneuver. "Why not Uncle Delmar? Or Uncle Murph? Anyone but me."

"Because Emmy really did want you to take over for her. You were her handpicked successor," Granddaddy said. "At least, Emmy wanted you to take over up until she realized that you've got a moral compass."

"Or at least more of one than anyone else in this family does," I said. "That still doesn't explain why Uncle Houston put me in charge. He's never seemed to like me all that much."

"Houston doesn't really like anybody," Granddaddy said. "And he would make a deal with the Devil—"

Interrupting, I said, "I can guarantee he's already done that. And he didn't have much of a soul to bargain with."

"Houston would sell us all upriver if it meant saving his own sorry behind," Granddaddy said. "Mark my word, Houston is up to something. And I bet it won't end well for the rest of us."

"There's no honor among thieves anymore," I muttered.

CHAPTER THIRTEEN

"I GOT FAITH IN YOU, CARRIE." Uncle Houston leaned back in his chair and winked at me. He might have also grinned, but it was hard to tell since his bushy, white mustache covered most of his mouth. "Darn near everyone else thought I was a couple sandwiches short of a picnic when I handed over the reins to you. They was all questionin' my sanity and accusin' me of comin' down with a bad case of dementia. Why, just a few days ago, some of our kin was telling me I'd made a huge mistake by puttin' you in charge."

"They're not the only ones who can't figure out why you put me in charge," I said as I shifted uncomfortably on the hard metal seat that I had been stuck sitting on all afternoon. As I moved, I accidently bumped my knee against Hardy's leg. Because of the close confines of Red's office, I was practically sitting on Hardy's lap. "I'm still trying to figure out why you made me the new head of the family."

"You were the right person for the job." Uncle Houston's blue eyes quickly cut over to Hardy and then back to me. I noticed that his left eyelid was rapidly fluttering. "I put you in charge of our family for a reason, Carrie. I knew you'd take care of us better than any of your uncles or aunts could."

My great-uncle had a nearly flawless poker face. If lying was an Olympic sport, he would most certainly take home a medal. Maybe not the gold, but definitely the silver or bronze. Uncle Houston's only tell was the twitching eyelid that he couldn't control. The tic was barely noticeable to someone who didn't know to look for it. Sitting across from him and watching his eyelid twitch, I instinctively knew that he was either lying or nervous about something.

"I'll do what I can," I assured him. "But I'm not a miracle worker. And, after what happened, and the scrutiny it's going to bring down on us, we might need a miracle."

"Like, I said, Carrie . . . I got faith in you."

Uncle Houston was the last in a long line of people who had cycled through Red's makeshift office at some point in the afternoon to speak with me and Hardy. He had spent the past four hours sipping moonshine and playing pool out in the barroom while waiting to talk to us. Exhibiting patience was out of character for Uncle Houston. Whether it was a line to the buffet or the receiving line at a funeral, Uncle Houston usually forced his way to the front. I suspected that he had stuck around the Arm Bar so that he could keep an eye on things. Whether or not he was behind what happened to the boys, he would want to know who had come in to talk to me and Hardy. He'd also want to know what those people had said. It wouldn't surprise me at all if Uncle Houston had interrogated every single person before allowing him or her to leave the bar. There was also a probability that some of the Shatners and Devereuxs—and maybe even a couple of Palmers— had been more candid with Uncle Houston than they had been with me and Hardy. Chances were, Uncle Houston had learned more than Hardy and I had, and I could only hope that he had the decency to share whatever information he might have—unless, of course, Uncle Houston didn't want us to find out certain information because he had played a part in what happened.

Throughout the past four hours, Red's office had served as a conference room, an interrogation room, and a confessional for various Shatners and Devereuxs. Not too many Palmers had stuck around to talk to me and Hardy. Most of them scattered like cockroaches as soon as I headed back to the office.

One of the few Palmers who had stuck around was Oscar. He'd charged into Red's office as Granddaddy was leaving. I didn't have a chance to recover from the shock of Granddaddy's revelation about his youngest brother's murder or the accusations he had lobbed at his older brother and only sister before Oscar started in on his long-winded lecture. Between blaming me for being at least partially responsible for what happened to Hank, bad-mouthing my entire family, and cursing himself for allowing his family to team up with mine, Oscar went over everything that he personally thought I had done wrong or mishandled since taking over as head of the family two months earlier. I had no idea how Oscar knew about what all I had been up to since I certainly had not consulted him about any of it—and, apparently, that was another one of my many recent mistakes. In Oscar's esteemed opinion, none of this would have happened had I just asked for his input and guidance.

After running out of steam for the lecture, Oscar denied having any involvement in the attack on the boys. He also denied any involvement for his entire family. Oscar stated that none of the Palmers could have possibly been involved because they're "more civilized than that." When I asked if he was implying that the Shatners and Devereuxs were uncivilized, Oscar waved his cane at my head, muttered a few curse words, and then shuffled out of the office.

The only other Palmers who had come in to speak with me and Hardy had been Hank Garrett the Third's parents and two sisters. Amelia had calmed down considerably since her attempt to attack me earlier—though she did call me every nasty name that she could come up with. She might have even invented a few new ones. The other sister, Harriett, didn't have anything to say to me or Hardy. She also seemed like the kind of person who would make a Voodoo doll to represent me and then stab it with a few dozen pins before running it over with her car.

Hank Garrett the Second had done all the talking for his immediate family. By the time he was finished berating me and criticizing Wesley, he had blamed the two of us for everything from the mass extinction of the dinosaurs to the fall of the Alamo to General Antonio López de Santa Anna's troops during the Texas Revolution.

While most of the Palmers had skedaddled from the Arm Bar so that they didn't have to talk to me, nearly every single adult Shatner and Devereux had stuck around for the opportunity to run their mouths. They came into Red's office singly, in pairs, and in small groups. Some of them accused me of being indirectly responsible for what happened, others pointed the finger at each other, and a few of them confessed to me about crimes that I knew nothing about. Hardy and I also learned a lot about their personal lives—most of which we did not need to know. Almost everyone wanted to play "armchair detective" and share their theories—some of which were plausible, but the majority of which were downright insane. Unlike Gopher Devereux, I was not convinced that extra-terrestrials were responsible for the assault on the boys.

I can't say that the four hours Hardy and I spent talking to various Shatners and Devereuxs were overly productive or informative, but we did whittle down our list of possible suspects to a manageable number as we gathered up a slew of alibis. Almost all the Shatners and Devereuxs had willingly told us where they had been early Sunday morning, as well as who they had been with. There were a few holdouts who refused to provide an alibi, but that didn't necessarily mean that he or she was one of the three people who had assaulted the boys. It could simply mean that they had been up to no good elsewhere and didn't want to admit to it in front of Hardy. At least I had been able to rule out several of my uncles, aunts, and cousins before I was forced to add them to my suspect list.

Uncle Butch and Pork Chop Devereux seemed to be at the top of every armchair detective's suspect list. No matter how many times Hardy or I stated that Butch and Pork Chop had alibis, we had to listen to stories about how Pork Chop had threatened to kill Wesley on at least four-hundred-and thirty-seven separate occasions in the past five years and about how Uncle Butch had taken a shot at Hank when he caught Hank sneaking in Courtney's bedroom window last month.

Hardy and I were also told countless "he said" and "she said" stories—a lot of which sounded extremely farfetched and unbelievable. And we listened to enough "I heard from so-and-so who heard from someone else who's brother's barber's stepsister's dog walker that . . ." stories to last us a lifetime.

Cousin Billy Bob—who had taken their complaints about Wesley on Saturday night a little too seriously—had roughly escorted Festus and Cletus into the office and accused them of being part of the assault on the boys. Neither Festus or Cletus had a solid alibi—Festus claimed he had been at home with his wife and daughter on Sunday morning, while Cletus admitted that he had been so drunk and high that he had been nearly incapacitated—but I had serious doubts that either of them had been involved. When gauging my family members by their violent tendencies, Festus and Cletus both fell towards the "least violent" end of the spectrum.

Billy Bob wasn't the only person who pointed the finger at Cletus. Because Wesley and Cletus were about the same age, they had spent a lot of time together growing up. While Cletus was no saint, it seemed like most of the trouble he had gotten into while a juvenile was on account of Wesley. I had also been reminded of the time that Wesley "borrowed" Cletus's brand-new dirt bike and then crashed it in an Evel Knievel-style stunt gone wrong.

Dickie was another one of my cousins who had been accused by more than one person. At least five of our cousins recapped how Wesley had yanked down Dickie's swim trunks in front of a bunch of other kids at summer camp back when they had been in elementary school. Thanks to that, Dickie had become the laughingstock of camp, and Uncle Murph and Aunt Lydia had to pick him up halfway through the first week. Dickie swore that he had long ago gotten over the embarrassment, but a few of our cousins seemed to think he was still mad about it.

Tadpole Devereux—Toad Devereux's only son—had made it clear to me that he and his father were still angry at Wesley for almost getting him expelled from high school a few years earlier. According to Tadpole, Wesley had gotten word that the principal was going to search his backpack and locker for illegal substances. To protect himself, Wesley relocated a few ounces of marijuana from his backpack to Tadpole's gym locker. Unaware the marijuana was there, Tadpole accidently dumped it all over the locker room floor before football practice later that day. Tadpole's fast talking saved him from expulsion, but he wound up serving a week of in-school-suspension and had gotten kicked off the football team. Fortunately for Tadpole, he had an alibi. Toad, on the other hand, did not—and that landed him on my suspect list.

Levi Palmer also made his way onto my suspect list. It was common knowledge that Hank had been Levi's lackey for several years. Hank had sold drugs for Levi, and he had also taken the fall for him numerous times. Without Hank, Levi was now forced to sell the drugs himself—and suffer the consequences when he got caught. Word was that Levi was furious with Hank for deserting him and had even threatened to kill both him and Wesley on at least five separate occasions.

Hardy and I had also been subjected to at least a dozen conflicting stories concerning the physical altercation that had taken place between Jason and Wesley about two months earlier. It had happened at a preseason get-together for the actors and crew at the Body Farm. I hadn't attended the meeting, so I missed out on witnessing the showdown. But, depending on who I believed, the fight had been everything from a minor scuffle to an all-out brawl. The only consistency between the various stories was that Jason took a swing at Wesley because he was mad at him for getting Roxanne pregnant for a third time.

By the time that Uncle Houston had strolled into Red's office late in the afternoon, I had confirmed my theory that Wesley was probably the least liked Shatner among the family. From the sound of it, it was an exceedingly small minority of Shatners who not only tolerated Wesley, but actually liked him. That's not to say that everyone who disliked him had a reason to use him, Waylon, or Hank as punching bags.

"You know, Uncle Houston," I said after a lengthy pause, "I'm surprised you stuck around all afternoon."

"It ain't like I had anythin' else to do today."

That could have been the truth, but I was betting it was another lie. For being retired, Uncle Houston sure kept busy.

"You learn anything while you were sitting out there?" Hardy asked.

"You mean did anyone confess to me?" Uncle Houston ran his fingers through his scraggly beard and hummed to himself for a few seconds. "Nope. Can't say anyone did. Carrie knows how hard it is gettin' our family to admit to anythin'. And I, for one, refuse to believe that any of them did this. Ain't none of them had a reason to do it."

"You really have lost your mind." I chuckled without humor. "You know as well as I do that most of our family can't stand Wes. Or Waylon and Hank."

"I never said whether they liked or disliked the boys," Uncle Houston said. "I just said none of 'em had a reason to kidnap the boys, assault 'em, and leave 'em for dead. I mean, I could see a few of them teaching the boys a lesson. Lord knows they needed one. But what happened the other night . . . that's just too extreme for us."

"You've done far worse than cut off someone's finger," I pointed out. I had firsthand knowledge of the extents to which Uncle Houston would go. Just a few months ago, I had to stop him from shocking Nate Palmer with a car battery. "And you know as well as I do that just about everyone was getting sick and tired of Wes's shenanigans. You remember on Sunday when you told me that the boys wouldn't be a problem—"

Uncle Houston's chair skidded backwards on the rough concrete floor as he stood up. "You're nuttier than a portapotty at a peanut festival if you think I'm behind what happened to the boys. I might have done some rotten things back in the day, but I ain't never done nothin' that bad. And to my own brother's grandkids . . ."

"Sit down, Uncle Houston." I walked around the desk and shoved the metal folding chair towards him. "I wasn't accusing you of anything.

I was just making a general statement about how you said the boys wouldn't be a problem for much longer."

"You was accusin' me, and you know it. No reason to lie about it." Uncle Houston slumped down in the chair and crossed his arms over his chest. "And I darn well know what I said. But that ain't what I meant by it."

"Then what did you mean?" I asked.

"I just meant that I was fixin' to take care of the problem."

Knowing from experience that Uncle Houston wouldn't elaborate, I abruptly changed the subject. "What do you know about your brother Ben getting shot up while delivering moonshine back in the day?"

Uncle Houston lurched forward and nearly toppled out of the chair. "Crockett was runnin' his mouth, I see. He always had a notion that Emmy, Catfish, and me was the ones who setup Benny and killed him before he could bring us to ruin. You tell your granddaddy—"

"Tell him yourself," I snapped. "At the moment, I'm not concerned about figuring out who killed your brother all those years ago. All I'm concerned about is finding out who killed Hank, and left Wes and Waylon for dead."

"You're barking up the wrong tree interrogatin' me. I ain't had nothin' to do with it." Uncle Houston pushed his chair back and stood up. He took two steps towards the door before he glanced over his shoulder at me and said, "Carrie, if it turns out a Shatner done it . . . . I suggest we handle it among the family and keep the law out of it."

"You know I can't allow that, Houston," Hardy said.

"I wasn't talkin' to you." After shooting Hardy a disgusted look, Uncle Houston slipped out the door and slammed it shut behind him.

"That man is so full of crap, his eyes should be brown."

Hardy turned to me and asked, "You really suspect that Houston could be involved in what happened to the boys?"

"That man is definitely up to something . . . or he's lost his mind. I could count on one hand the number of times Uncle Houston has agreed with me during the past four years. But earlier today he backed up everything I said, and he was going on about how we need to protect the kids and grandkids. He's never been all that worried about them before now."

"Maybe Houston finally had a come-to-Jesus moment and decided it was time to change his ways," Hardy said.

"Ha! That I highly doubt. Uncle Houston would need to have even a fraction of a conscious or a soul to be capable of having a come-to-Jesus moment." I stood up and stretched my aching back. "I didn't trust Uncle Houston before this. And I trust him even less now. My gut tells me that he is not one of the three assailants. He's gotten too old to take part in something like that. But I think he could be behind it. He knows that a bunch of Shatners were mad at Wes, and he could have easily talked them into setting up and assaulting the boys. If he is behind it, he must have thought that I wouldn't be smart enough to figure it out. But I'm on to him . . ."

Exiting the office, I headed across the storage room and out into the barroom. It was late in the afternoon, and only a few of the barstools were occupied. During the time that Hardy and I were in his office, Red had cleaned up the mess and covered the broken picture window with a piece of plywood. Red waved at us from behind the bar, but I wasn't in the mood to chat. Instead, I headed across the room and walked out into the parking lot.

"What I just don't understand is why you are so protective of your family," Hardy said to me as we walked across the gravel lot to his truck. "You don't seem to like most of them all that much. And, considering what I heard this afternoon, half of your family seems to be more than willing to sell out the other half."

"No, you wouldn't understand, Jerrod." I leaned my hip against the tailgate of Hardy's big black truck. "From birth, us Shatners are taught that family is everything. And loyalty to the family is required. It's beat into our brains. We're practically brainwashed. If you haven't noticed, we Shatners have a clan mentality about us. Before she died, Aunt Emily Morgan was to my family what David Koresh was to the Branch Davidians. Then Uncle Houston assumed that role. And now it's my turn. All I can do is try to prevent things from going as badly as they did at Mount Carmel."

And that's how incidents like the sieges at Mount Carmel and Ruby Ridge, and the mass suicides/murders by cyanide-laced punch orchestrated by James Warren Jones happen—a "leader" uses a mixture of brainwashing, gullibility, unquestioned loyalty, and fear to keep his or her followers under control.

"On a positive note, your family's clan mentality is starting to fall apart," Hardy pointed out. "Like I said, we saw a lot of backstabbing between your relatives this afternoon."

"I'm aware that the family is falling apart. It has been for a while now. And, yeah, they may have sounded willing to stab each other in the back, but, if push comes to shove, they will have each other's backs in the end. And that includes Wesley's back," I said. I kicked at a clump of weeds that had sprouted amongst the gravel. "What makes things harder for me is that I grew up watching my dad and granddaddy clean up after the rest of the family. I just followed in their footsteps. I know that about half of my family members aren't worth protecting. But I have to do it if I'm going to protect the ones that are worth saving."

"You're right, Carrie. I don't understand," Hardy said. "I had a vastly different upbringing than you did. My parents abandoned me and Josh for the first few years of our lives. Our mom's parents raised us, but it wasn't out of love. They did it because they felt obligated to. Even as little kids, Josh and I knew we were unwanted. We were just two more mouths to feed on top of their own horde of children. That's probably why our grandparents didn't put up a fight when our mom and stepfather came to get us. Most likely they were glad to see us go. And it's not like Mom wanted us either. She just wanted to use us. So, while I can understand family loyalty, I can't wrap my head around your loyalty to your entire family."

"Let me put it this way . . . when you look at my family, all you see is the crazy. I see the crazy too, but I have the benefit of knowing why they're crazy. It makes sense to me," I said. I pushed away from the tailgate and walked around to the passenger side of the truck. "Come on. Let's get something for dinner. I haven't had much to eat since breakfast, and you know how I get when I'm hungry."

"Yeah . . . Hangry." Hardy unlocked the truck and we climbed inside. "After we eat, do you want to start tracking down some of the people on our list of suspects? We heard some pretty serious allegations today, and we need to confirm if they're true."

"We can get started on the list tomorrow. Or Uncle Murph can," I said as I buckled my seatbelt. "For now, I want to eat and then go home and sort through all my notes. I've got to get them into some sort of order if I'm going to make sense of what we were told this afternoon."

After grabbing food from Whataburger, Hardy and I headed back to my house. My Grim Reaper mannequin greeted me with an ominous "I'm coming for you next" as I scooped up a small package off my welcome mat. Inside, I dumped the package and my keys on the table in the foyer, and then tended to Molly and Manny. Once they were fed and loved upon, Hardy and I ate. We then spread out our lists of case notes as well as the threatening letters that several of my family members had received earlier.

I was reading over the threatening note that had been stuck under cousin' Festus's windshield wiper when my vision blurred, and my eyelids slowly closed. Hardy woke me with a gentle nudge.

"Go take a nap, Carrie."

"I can't." I gave myself a shake to rid myself of the fatigue. "I don't have time to sleep. My family needs me."

"And I need you at one hundred percent. You're no use to me if you can't keep your eyes open," Hardy said as he pulled my chair away from the table. He then helped me stand up and guided me into the living room. "I can organize the notes while you rest."

"All right," I said as I sprawled out on the leather couch. "But don't let me sleep for more than an hour. Two hours tops."

CHAPTER FOURTEEN

"**W**HY DID YOU LET ME SLEEP SO LONG?" I asked as I stomped into my home office and confronted Hardy. He was seated at my desk and was typing away on my laptop. "I told you to let me sleep for no more than two hours. It's been over five hours."

Hardy spun the office chair around to face me. "I let you sleep because you needed it."

He made a good point. I hadn't gotten much sleep over the past couple of days thanks to the late night at the Body Farm on Saturday, yesterday's "field trip" and the following fiascos, and everything that had happened today. After the few hours of sleep, I now felt rested and mostly human.

"Did I miss anything?"

"Right after you fell asleep, Sergeant Boleyn hauled Bubba in for questioning," Hardy said. "I talked to Lieutenant Underwood and he said that someone called in an anonymous tip about how Bubba caught the Three Stooges selling drugs at the game stand on Saturday night. I guess he threatened them with bodily harm if he caught them at it again."

"Bubba's not under arrest, is he?"

"No, he's not," Hardy said. "And Boleyn released Bubba almost four hours ago, so there is no need for you to rush down to the police department to rescue him."

"Well . . . At least you were productive." I stepped closer to the wall on which Hardy had hung up what looked to be about two hundred notecards. The notecards were in various colors. From past experiences—like when I was a kid and had covered this very same wall in posters of George Strait—I knew that the tape would leave a sticky residue on the pale purple wall. It looked like I would be painting in the near future. "What is all this?"

"This is what I came up with to keep everything organized." Hardy stood up and joined me. "I found a stack of colored paper in here, so I cut them down to notecard size. I then wrote out a card for everyone who could possibly be involved in the assault. The Shatners and Devereuxs are on the yellow cards. I figured y'all are too intermarried to bother separating you into two families. The Palmers are on pink cards. Wesley's drug connections are the green cards. And everyone else is on blue cards."

I glanced over the rainbow of cards and plucked a yellow one off the wall at random. It was Cousin Dale's card. Written on the front of the card was Dale's name, his motives for possibly wanting to harm any of the Three Stooges, and his alleged alibi. Hardy had jotted down the names of the two people who had accused Dale. On the back of the card, Hardy documented that Dale had received a threatening note from Facundo.

I grabbed another card off the wall and looked it over. This one was Jason Devereuxs'. The front of the card was packed with notes about Jason's motive and who had accused him. At the bottom of the card, Hardy wrote that Jason had been either at home sleeping or working at Walmart when the assault took place. The back of Jason's card was blank. Unlike Dale, Jason had not received any threatening notes or suffered any vandalism.

I flicked the red "X" drawn in the upper right corner of the card. "What's this for?"

"That means Jason has an alibi," Hardy said. "I drew X's on the cards of everyone who has a solid alibi. And I drew a slash mark on those who claim they have an alibi, but they can't prove it. Or we haven't looked into it and confirmed it yet."

"It's a good way to keep track of everyone," I said as I taped the two cards back to the wall. "Just looks very tedious."

"Oh, it was," Hardy confirmed. "Especially Wes's drug connections. He has them all listed under nicknames in his phone. Roxanne and Jason gave us some of their actual names. But I have no way of knowing which of them are the same people. Plus, one of us has to read through all of the text messages to see if there are any threatening ones."

"I'll get Deputy Grant to read through the messages tomorrow," I said. Timmy might not be good at much, but he could handle reading through text messages and taking notes. "For now, we can just focus on the Shatners, Devereuxs, and Palmers. We find the one who was involved, and he or she can then give us the names of the other two people."

"I have been able to eliminate a few of y'all. But it's just a small dent." Hardy gestured towards the short row of cards that all featured red X's. That row was dwarfed by all the other cards. "There are a lot of y'all that have motives. And not many with solid alibis."

"What about the threatening notes? What happened to them? And who received them?"

Hardy spun me around so that I was facing a different wall. Taped to the closet door were copies of the threatening notes along with pictures of the various acts of vandalism.

I moved closer to the closet so that I could skim over the notes and look at the pictures. Uncle Murph was right—whoever had written the notes knew a lot about my family member's individual crimes. Heck, it looked like he knew more than I did. Then again, it seemed like just about everyone knew more than I did—except for Hardy. As for the vandalism, it appeared that most of it was minor.

"Whoever is involved would be smart to leave himself a note or cause a little damage to his personal property," I said as I read over the list of names Hardy had made up to keep track of who had received the notes and who had been targeted with vandalism. "But . . . considering who we are dealing with . . . that person might not be smart enough to think of that."

"No, but the ringleader could be."

THE ROADHOUSE MOTEL'S SIGN ADVERTISED ROOMS by the hour, day, week, and month. The sign also boasted that the motel had air conditioning and color TVs. The word "pool" had been partially covered with a streak of black spray paint.

As for the motel itself—it would take a complete transformation to make the rundown, two-story building appear even halfway hospitable. The faux adobe walls were crumbling away to reveal the cinderblocks underneath, ribbons of paint had peeled away from the doors and window trim, and a section of railing along the second story walkway was held together by duct tape and a prayer. At the back end of the parking lot, two or three feet of scummy water filled up the bottom part of the pool's deep end, and a small tree grew out of a crack in the concrete in the empty shallow end. Next to the pool was a rusting, broken-down jungle gym and swing set. A person would need a tetanus shot and a death wish to go anywhere near it.

"Welcome to the honeymoon suite," Lieutenant Underwood said as he ushered me and Hardy into the first-floor motel room for our midnight meeting.

I stepped inside and kicked the door shut behind me. "I hope you're being sarcastic calling this the honeymoon suite."

I glanced around the dingy, cramped room, and tried not to gag. The room's walls were covered in faded and water damaged faux-wood paneling. The carpet, which had started out as either beige or light brown, was now nearly colorless. It was also threadbare in spots. As for the mismatched furniture, I'd seen nicer stuff sitting on the side of the road on trash day. In fact, the rusting metal patio set that Alberto was seated at looked suspiciously like the set that I had thrown away last fall.

"Is there a reason you two drove separate vehicles?" Alberto asked as he peeked around the tattered curtains.

"Because I have another meeting after this," I said.

I had decided that it would be in my best interest to go over to Old Town Texas and check on my family. And it would be in Hardy's best interest not to tag along.

"Don't touch anything in the bathroom. There's mold everywhere. Even the towels are moldy," Lieutenant Schmitt said as he walked out of the bathroom that was at the back part of the room. There wasn't a lot of space to maneuver, and he had to turn sideways to scoot through the narrow passage between the foot of the bed and the lopsided dresser. As he passed the antique cathode ray tube television, he patted the top of the box and said, "Don't bother trying the TV either. The sign out front might advertise color TVs, but the darn thing don't work."

"I'm not planning to touch anything in this place," I said as I took up a stance in front of the nightstand. It was bad enough that the soles of my boots were touching the carpet. I didn't want to accidently touch anything else. "Is there a reason why we're meeting here?"

"I figured you would want to see where the initial assault took place," Underwood said.

"Oh, gross." I pulled up my right leg and posed like a flamingo. "I heard the crime scene unit found bedbugs in here."

"They found one bedbug," Underwood said. "And it was dead."

"Dead or alive, that's one bedbug too many," I said.

"Wesley told Carrie that he rented the room for the meeting," Hardy said. "Did you figure out how the assailants got into the room before the boys did?"

"Boleyn is trying to figure that out," Underwood said. "The owner and operator of this place is an elderly man named Abner—"

Interrupting, Hardy said, "Carrie and I made his acquaintance last night."

"Abner is also the handyman around here," Underwood said. "When he's off taking care of his handyman duties, his semi-senile mother-in-law handles the front desk. This place hasn't caught up to the twenty-first century yet, and they're still using actual keys for the rooms. It's possible the assailants picked the lock. Or stole a key. In the past week or two, Abner noticed that some keys have gone missing. He figured his mother-in-law had misplaced them. It's possible this Facundo guy snuck in and stole the keys while she was at the front desk. Heck, the woman is so batty she might have handed over the keys if someone asked nicely enough. There's also Abner's daughter. She's the housekeeper—"

"Clearly she's not very good at her job," Schmitt said.

"Last week, the daughter apparently lost her skeleton key that opens all the doors," Underwood continued.

"Sounds like Wes set up this meeting a few days ago," I said. "Facundo had plenty of time to get his hands on a key to this room."

"Are there any security cameras?" Lieutenant Schmitt asked as he turned on the TV and began to fiddle with the cables that were hooked up to it.

Underwood laughed. "Does this place look like it has security cameras? They don't even have a computer at the front desk."

"What about witnesses?" Alberto asked. "Did anyone see anything?"

"Abner, his mother-in-law, and daughter all live on site. They swear they didn't see anything because they were asleep," Underwood said. "And Boleyn has a couple State Troopers tracking down the handful of people who stayed here that night. So far, no one has admitted to seeing anything."

"Has Boleyn made *any* progress in his investigation?" I asked.

"Some," Underwood said. "But he keeps getting sidetracked looking into your family. I've had to remind him multiple times that we are investigating who killed Hank and assaulted your cousins. It doesn't help that Wesley was being difficult this morning and sent Boleyn on a wild goose chase after 'Ben Dover.' When it comes to Sunday night, I'm sure you know more about what happened than Boleyn does. And, like your cousin, you don't seem all that willing to share what you know."

Ignoring the barb, I asked, "Did Boleyn really call the Drug Unit?"

"Yeah, he called me this morning and suggested that I send some of my agents to Wyatt County," Schmitt said. He switched around two of the cables and the TV went from static to porn. The image was upside down, and the colors were psychedelic. "I asked Sergeant Boleyn to send me whatever evidence he's got and to keep me in the loop. When he started giving me a hard time about not jumping on this, I told him that I don't want to move too soon and interfere with his investigation. But what happened to the boys might force me to move faster than I had initially intended. Agents from the ATF and the DEA have been calling me all day, and they are champing at the bit to start investigating."

"That's not what I want to hear," I said. The Shatner family's day of reckoning was coming sooner than I had anticipated. Hopefully, it wouldn't turn out as badly as I had originally predicted considering my family was disposing of all physical items that were illegal or linked them to a crime. "Will you warn me before they swoop in?"

"Yeah, I'll give you whatever warning I can," Schmitt said.

"Did you tell Boleyn or anyone else that you have an agent under-cover?" Alberto asked.

"The DEA and ATF, yes, I told them," Schmitt said. "But, unless Boleyn pulls you in for questioning, I don't see any reason why he has to know that you're in Wyatt County."

I cleared my throat and then said, "My cousin Dale said something to me earlier today about how he and his brother suspect 'Beto' might be an undercover cop. And I'm not the only Shatner they voiced their suspicions to."

"Dale and Dickie?" Alberto spewed soda out of his nose when he laughed. "You for real? Those two don't have a fully functioning brain between them. But they're the ones who guessed I'm an undercover cop? What makes them think that?"

"My cousins might not be all that bright, but they've got enough common sense to know that a person who claims he used to work in a chop shop should have more than a basic understanding of cars . . . Which you apparently don't."

"Damn it, Alberto . . . If I'd known that you knew jack about cars, I would not have made that part of your background story," Lieutenant

Schmitt grumbled. "Maybe we should pull you out. According to Sergeant Hardy, the Shatners, Palmers, and Devereuxs are in a tizzy as it is."

"I ain't worried," Alberto said.

"You should be." I jabbed my finger into Alberto's chest. "As I'm sure you've discovered in the past few weeks, my family members are always armed and at least somewhat dangerous. Between the assault on the boys and Keaton getting jumped, they're even more on edge than usual. The safeties are off, and their fingers are on the trigger. If anything happens, they're going to shoot first and ask questions later. At this point, Facundo and his cronies are more in danger from us than we are of them."

"In your opinion," Alberto said.

"Alberto, we can't risk having one of them decide you're Facundo and turn on you," Schmitt said. "I don't want you to wind up in a shallow grave on Houston's property."

"Pulling me out now would just confirm that I was undercover," Alberto said.

"Not if you say you're skipping town because there's a Texas Ranger sniffing around," I said. "Just tell a couple of my relatives that you've got an active warrant and that you're afraid of getting picked up. They'll understand and probably won't think anything of it."

"I agree with Detective Shatner," Schmitt said. "It's time you got out of Wyatt County."

"Aw, come on, Lieutenant," Alberto whined. "I've made good progress in this case. Give me a couple more days. I can lie low while we see how this plays out."

Schmitt sighed. "Let's step outside and discuss this. I'm sure Lieutenant Underwood, Sergeant Hardy, and Detective Shatner have some things to discuss that don't concern us."

Underwood waited until Schmitt and Alberto had gone outside before he turned to me and said, "Jerrod has filled me in on what's been going on earlier. I knew about your cousin Keaton getting jumped outside the gym. I didn't know about all of the threats your family members have received or the vandalism to their property. And it's those threats that have got me concerned—"

Interrupting, I said, "They've got me concerned, too."

"And for good reason." Underwood said as he tossed me a USB drive. "That's got all of Sergeant Boleyn's notes and crime scene photos on it. Including the crime scene photos that you took. Hank Palmer's autopsy report is also on it."

I tucked the USB drive into my jacket pocket. "Why are you helping me?"

"For the record, helping you goes against everything I believe in," Underwood gruffly said. "I'd prefer if you stayed out of it and left it up to Sergeant Boleyn. But, short of locking you up, I know nothing is going to stop you from looking into this threat against your family. Least I can do is provide you with everything I know and help keep you safe."

"I appreciate it," I said, and I meant it. Every little bit of assistance and whatever scraps of information that I could get would help me to track down Facundo and expose him. "Since you're helping me, is there any way you can get me into Wesley's hospital room? I need to talk to him."

Underwood shook his head. "Sergeant Boleyn has State Troopers guarding the door around the clock. Only hospital personnel are allowed into the room. If I tell the Troopers to let you in, Boleyn will find out that I'm helping you."

"No problem. I'll find my own way in."

IT WAS JUST AFTER ONE IN THE MORNING when I pulled into the gravel parking lot at Old Town Texas and parked alongside the handful of vehicles near the entrance to the living history museum. None of the parking lot lights were on, nor were any of the lights in the town. My family didn't want to draw attention to themselves by having the lights around the replica old west town on in the middle of the night. But the third quarter moon provided only so much light, and the darkness and shifting shadows made me uncomfortable. If Facundo or one of his cronies really was a Shatner, Palmer, or Devereux, he or she knew what the rest of us would be up to tonight. And that person could be lurking around the town waiting for a prime opportunity to attack several of us at one time.

Climbing out of the Jeep, I dashed over to the train depot that marked the entrance and ducked into the shadows cast by the building. The brick depot was an authentic building from the late eighteen-hundreds that Uncle Elvin had torn down, hauled to the property, and then rebuilt. The depot's old ticket booth continued to serve its intended purpose, and the interior of the building had been converted into a gift shop, snack bar, and restrooms.

Uncle Elvin—who had watched a few too many westerns while growing up—had developed an unhealthy obsession with the American West. Not long after he married my Aunt Loretta, he took that obsession to the extreme when he set to work constructing Old Town Texas. It took him a couple of years to erect the small, replica Wild West town, and he continued to add to and make improvements on a regular basis.

By the time I was born, Old Town Texas was the top tourist attraction in Wyatt County—not that it had all that much competition. The living history museum was open year-round, and actors of dubious talent put on fake gunfights, can-can shows, and other forms of Wild West entertainments. As a kid, I'd gone on a field trip to Old Town Texas every year from kindergarten through twelfth grade. I had also worked at the attraction during the summer when I was a teenager.

Uncle Elvin claimed that all the buildings on the property were authentic, but I knew that was a lie. Yes, a couple of the buildings aside from the depot did date back to the late-1800s, but most of them did not. Uncle Vernon had built a few of the larger buildings—including the saloon, brothel, and mercantile—and Uncle Elvin had purchased the rest from an old Wild West tourist attraction in Oklahoma that had closed in the early 1980s. Like the depot, Uncle Elvin had the buildings dismantled, shipped to Texas, and then rebuilt.

Nearly all the buildings that made up Old Town Texas were located along the wide main street. The first building to my right was the original museum. The one-story building was crammed full of antiques and Wild West artifacts that were part of a collection or didn't really belong in any of the other buildings. The museum was chaotic, and most of the display cases were overflowing with random items. The new museum was meant to provide more space and structure for Uncle Elvin's collection. Once the new, two-story building was complete and all the displays moved into it, the old museum would become the new home for Uncle Bowie's model train display.

Next to the original museum was the Soiled Dove brothel. Beyond that was the combined doctor's and dentist's office, the undertaker, the sheriff's office and jail, and the barbershop. On the other side of the street was the general store, saloon, land office, casino, and post office. On a side street that ran parallel to the main street there was a small church, a one-room schoolhouse, the livery stable, and a blacksmith. There were also a few shanties, cabins, and houses that depicted the various ways in which early settlers had lived across the American West.

Facundo or his cronies could be hiding in any one of them.

I was debating whether I wanted to hang a target on my back by walking up the middle of the wide street or if I wanted to slink along the buildings on either side and risk getting grabbed by someone in the shadows when the sound of tires crunching over gravel drew my attention to the parking lot.

I walked over to the edge of the platform and watched as a golf cart rattled over the train tracks between the depot platform and the Baldwin steam locomotive that Uncle Elvin had spent a small fortune on. The train—which towed around two passenger cars—ran on a narrow-gauge track that ran for a mile-and-a-half loop around Old Town Texas and through part of the ranch.

"I want you to know that I'm doing this under protest," Uncle Ted yelled at me as he parked the golf cart in front of the depot. Hitched to the back of the cart was a utility trailer. "I'm doing it because Crockett and Houston are forcing me do it. Not because you said I have to."

I jumped off the platform and walked over to the golf cart. I tried to peek under the tarp that Uncle Ted had stretched over the top of the utility trailer, but he had it tied down tight.

"You get rid of everything?"

"Just 'bout."

"What's that supposed to mean?"

"Means I'm meeting up with one of my usual buyers tomorrow night." Uncle Ted held up his hand and waved off my protests before I could voice them. "Bad enough I gotta watch everything else go up in flames. I ain't gonna burn up the Purple Kush. Or the Acapulco Gold. Rooster, Becky, and I spent all afternoon harvesting it. My buyer agreed to take it even though it ain't dried out yet."

"Uncle Ted . . ." I wanted to scream at him, but I knew it wouldn't accomplish anything. "If you get busted, I can't help you."

"I've been doing this since before you was born, and I ain't been caught yet. Tomorrow ain't gonna be the day it happens."

"You better be right."

I climbed into the golf cart and Uncle Ted floored it. We flew down the dirt road through the town to where the new museum was being built next to the two-story dancehall. The building would be constructed out of brick and would resemble an old courthouse.

Leaving Uncle Ted to unload the utility cart, I walked over to where Granddaddy and Uncle Houston were huddled together at the edge of the construction fence that had been erected around the area. Since I didn't trust Uncle Houston, I had put Granddaddy in charge of making sure that the family followed through with my directive.

"I was wonderin' when you'd show up to stick your nose in things, missy," Uncle Houston sneered at me. I took the hint that he was still upset that I had accused him of being involved in the assault on the boys. "Didn't you think we could handle things without you breathin' down our necks?"

Ignoring Uncle Houston's comments, I asked, "How's it going?"

"Better than I expected. Other than Ted having a conniption, ain't no one else caused a problem or complained too much." Granddaddy pointed over to where Uncle Vernon was operating a backhoe. "Vernon's digging out a second hole. We filled up the first one with the moonshine stills."

"What about the burnable stuff?" I asked.

"Butch is takin' care of that," Uncle Houston said. "He and Bowie hauled it all out to Wes's trailer. Figure it can't do no harm to incinerate the little bit of rubble that's left."

"And Grandma told me she dropped all the pills and other medications off at the hospital," I said as I fought back a yawn. "Anything else I need to know about?"

"A couple of your cousins and uncles received additional threating notes this afternoon. 'Bout the same as the other ones. I collected them for you." Granddaddy handed me an envelope. "We got things covered here. Why don't you head home and get some sleep?"

"Sounds like a good idea."

I made a quick lap around the construction area to make sure everything was okay before I had Uncle Ted give me a ride back to the parking lot. I had just pulled out of my parking spot when my phone rang. Without checking the caller ID, I answered.

"What?"

"Carrie? It's Jason Devereux. Sorry if I woke you . . . but . . . but . . ."

"But what, Jason?"

"I'm at work. At Walmart. I went out back for a smoke break and some dude in a Devil mask jumped me."

I slammed on the brakes. "Are you okay?"

"Yeah. I mean, the dude split my lip. And he chipped my one tooth. But otherwise, I'm okay. One of my coworkers came out and the dude ran off before he did any real damage."

"Did the guy say anything?"

"Yeah . . . he told me to tell Wes that they're not done with him," Jason said. "And to tell you to back off."

CHAPTER FIFTEEN

"Does Sergeant Hardy know what you're doing?"

"Jerrod is waiting outside in the getaway car."

"The Ranger is either in love with you or he needs to get his head checked."

"I think it's a little bit of both."

"You are a horrible influence, Carrie," my cousin Tawny Mount said as she held out her hospital badge. "If you get caught, I'm going to say that you stole my badge and the scrubs. I'm not going to lose my job over your crazy stunt."

Tawny was a registered nurse, and she worked first shift in the pediatric unit at the Wyatt County General Hospital. She had just arrived at work when I accosted her in the parking lot and forced her into being my accomplice.

I needed to get into the room where both Wesley and Waylon were recovering. With the State Trooper guarding the door, I knew that I wouldn't get into the room unless I was wearing scrubs or a doctor's lab coat. It would also help to have a hospital badge so that I looked official. As the lone medical professional in the family, Tawny was the only one who could help me.

"Don't worry." I snatched the badge out of Tawny's hand before she could change her mind. I pinned the badge to the front of the hot pink scrubs that I had also borrowed from her. "I don't plan to get caught."

"I can't believe I let you talk me into this," Tawny mumbled under her breath as she helped me tuck my hair up under a dark blonde wig.

"It has to be illegal. And I've never done anything illegal in my life."

I snorted. "Oh really? Because I seem to remember back when we were teenagers—"

"All right, all right . . . I haven't done anything illegal since high school."

Tawny grabbed a couple towels from the metal rack that took up the entire back wall of the supply closet that we were hiding in. To help me look the part, she had decided to load up a cart with supplies for a sponge bath.

"You know the only reason I'm helping you is because my parents and sister were threatened." Tawny grabbed a metal basin and clonked it down on top of the cart. "And because that Facundo guy tipped off Randy's parole officer about the ankle monitor being on Selena's collar. I'm not saying Randy should have done that, but now he's going back to prison."

Randy had gotten picked up late last night. His ankle monitor had indicated that he was at his parents' house—which is where the dog was and where he should have been. Instead, a couple of State Troopers found him at the Dancing Cowgirl strip club. I had just gotten home from Old Town Texas when Aunt Priscilla called and told me that Randy had been arrested. Facundo—or one of his accomplices—had left a note stuck under Randy's windshield wiper to take credit for his arrest. Because Hardy and I had to deal with that, we didn't get to bed until almost three-thirty.

As for Tawny's parents, yesterday afternoon they had each received a gift-wrapped box from a courier service. The box that was addressed to Uncle Sterling was full of illegal steroids—the same illegal steroids that he sold to a handful of the pro wrestlers who competed for the Shatner Wrestling Association of Texas. The box for Aunt Priscilla was full of empty prescription bottles. Tawny's twin sister Taryn and her husband, Stewart Devereaux, had been on the receiving end of some minor vandalism.

"I just don't want anyone else to get hurt," Tawny said as she finished loading the cart with supplies and pushed it over towards the door. "Wesley is doing a lot better, and Waylon is improving. Keaton and Jason will be fine. But Dickie has a bad concussion. And I heard John Garrett's arm is broken in two places."

"Too many people have already gotten hurt," I said. "And that's why I'm doing this, Tawny. To try to prevent anyone else from getting hurt. Or killed."

Around four in the morning, Cousin Dickie had accidently injured himself while in pursuit of someone he thought was Facundo. He'd taken his dog out to the bathroom and caught someone messing around with his car. When Dickie went to confront the person, he tripped over his dog and slammed the back of his head against the curb.

And, while we weren't sure if Facundo was behind it or not, John and Peter Garrett—Ophelia Palmer-Garrett's other two grandsons—had been run off the road while driving home from work at a local dairy. Whether it was Facundo or a drunk driver behind the wheel didn't change the fact that Peter's truck was totaled, and John had suffered a broken arm.

Facundo and his cronies had to be stopped. As the head of my family—and a law enforcement officer—it was my job to stop them.

I put on a pair of fake glasses and asked, "How do I look?"

"You're missing something." Tawny pulled a stethoscope out of her pocket and looped it around my neck. "Now you look like you could be my twin."

"Don't you mean triplet?"

"I'm being sarcastic. But you look enough like me to pass if the Trooper examines the badge." Tawny opened the door and pushed the cart out into the hallway. "And, even if the Trooper knows you, I don't think he'll recognize you with that wig."

"Wish me luck." I took the cart and headed down the hallway. "I'll meet you by the pediatric nurse's station when I'm done."

The State Trooper guarding the door to Wesley's and Waylon's room was not the same one as Tuesday night. This one was older, and he looked like he was struggling to stay awake. He barely even glanced at me as I rolled the cart past him and entered the room. He only spoke up when I tried to shut the door behind me.

"Door's gotta stay open, ma'am."

"I'm here to give the patient a sponge bath." I pointed at Waylon who was lying in the bed closest to the door. Like Sunday night, Waylon was hooked up to an IV, a breathing machine, and a heart monitor. There were a few other pieces of medical equipment surrounding his bed that I didn't recognize. "Don't you think that poor boy has suffered enough? At least let him have some privacy and a little dignity."

"I ain't supposed to . . . But, all right."

As the door shut behind me, I breathed out a sigh of relief. I had gotten into the room without being stopped or recognized.

"Hello, nurse!" The curtain separating the two beds was flung back to reveal Wesley's grinning face. From what I could see around the bandage covering his nose, the bruises on his face were fading from purple to green. "Can I get a sponge bath, too?"

"Don't make me tell Roxanne that you're flirting with the nurses," I hissed.

"Carrie?"

"Shhh! Not so loud."

"Holy crap . . . It is you. I've got two black eyes. I'm on drugs. I didn't recognize you with the wig and glasses," Wesley whispered. "Please don't tell Roxanne. She'll finish me off."

"Are you really planning on marrying her after Wesley Junior is born?"

"Yeah, I guess so."

"Wes, one thing this family hasn't had in a long time is a shotgun wedding. But if you don't do it willingly, I will march you down the aisle at gunpoint and force you to marry her. And then I'm going to use the shotgun to murder you. A meth lab! Really, Wesley?"

"I guess you discovered my dirty little secret."

"Yeah, and then I had Uncle Butch blow it up." I pushed the cart into the bathroom and ran some water into the basin. I then went back into the room and started messing around with the towels and other items so that it looked like I had used them to give Waylon a sponge bath. "How are you feeling, Wes?"

"Awful. The doc cut back on my pain meds. Now everything hurts, and I ain't had any more funky dreams." Wesley held up his bandaged left hand. "And what's left of my pinkie is throbbing. You got any morphine on that cart?"

"No, I don't."

Wesley muttered a curse word under his breath. "Are you at least here to bust me out? Sergeant Boleyn keeps coming by and threatening to arrest me as soon as the doc releases me. He also offered me a deal to turn over evidence against the family. But I won't do it. I already talked once and look what happened. I ain't doing it again."

"Next time Boleyn comes by to see you, tell him about Facundo and send him on a wild goose chase." I dunked a washcloth in the basin and then wrung it out. "With Boleyn wasting time chasing down that lead, it'll buy me more time to find the people who did this to you."

"Be careful, Carrie. This Facundo guy and his buddies are dangerous. I don't want you to get hurt. You can see what he's capable of."

Wesley gestured towards himself and then over to Waylon. "Besides, I already told you that Randy is one of the three guys. Why don't you, I don't know, torture him and make him confess or something."

"I talked to Randy. Yeah, he hates you. But he's got an alibi." I hadn't confirmed that Randy had spent Sunday morning at the strip club, but I believed him. "The family really isn't happy with you right now, Wes. And they're even less happy that you're accusing one of them. Are you absolutely sure one of your attackers is a Shatner?"

"The family is never happy with me," Wes snapped. "And, no, I'm not absolutely sure. It could have been a Palmer or a Devereux. But I'm telling you one of the attackers is family. They knew way too much about us and our crimes."

"And I'm telling you it's not Randy," I said. "So, who else could it be? Who hates you, but also hates Waylon and Hank? Aside from Uncle Butch. And Uncle Elvin. Because neither of them was involved."

"I don't know . . . Maybe Dickie. Or Cletus. Bubba threatened to kick my ass on Saturday night. And recently so has Uncle Delmar. And Uncle Sterling."

"And just about everyone else in our family," I said. "What about the Palmers?"

Wesley shrugged. "Well . . . Levi Palmer has never liked me. And now he's pissed at me for 'stealing' Hank away from him. I didn't steal nobody. Hank was tired of taking the fall for Levi, so he came to me. And Nate and Dylan Palmer have never like me. Lately they've accused me of stealing some of their customers. And they've accused Hank of betraying Levi. Plus, they ain't happy that Waylon was hooking up with their sister."

"Waylon's been dating Tina?"

"I said hooking up. Not dating. Wasn't anything official about their relationship."

Tina Palmer was Nate and Dylan's younger half-sister. They were overly protective of her, and I couldn't imagine they would be too happy about her "hooking up" with Waylon. I doubted they would be any less upset if the relationship had been official.

"Who else, Wes?" I asked. "Who are some non-family members that hate you?"

"El Lobo. He told me he'd kill me if I ever double crossed him."

"He tells everyone that. He even threatened me."

"Umm . . . Maybe that Beto guy. I ain't had any problems with him. But there is something fishy about him. It's weird that he showed up in

Wyatt County and just started hanging out with us. And then, a few weeks later, this Facundo guy starts contacting me."

"Could just be a coincidence."

"I don't believe in coincidences," Wesley said. "Maybe Beto works for El Lobo."

"That's ridiculous. El Lobo works alone."

"Well, there is definitely something suspicious about Beto."

"Dale and Dickie think Beto is an undercover cop," I said. I wasn't sure why I said it. But the words were already out of my mouth and it was too late to take them back. "It seems like a pretty crazy theory to me."

"No way that dude is a cop." Wes snickered. "Yo, maybe it was Lynnette and her brothers. She might look all sweet and innocent, but, trust me, that girl is pure evil. She's spiteful enough to have pretended to be Facundo to lure me into the trap. And the three attackers could have been Lynnette's brothers. They all threatened to kill me after I got her pregnant. And I kinda remember one of the attackers saying something about how I need to treat my baby mamas better. Yo . . . Shawna's new man—"

"It wasn't Lynnette or her brothers. Uncle Murph talked to them and they all have alibis. Same for Shawna and her new boyfriend," I assured him. "Besides you're the one they hate. Far as I know, they don't have anything against Waylon or Hank. And they're the ones who got the worst of the beating. Not you."

"You think I don't know that?" Wesley used the bandages on his hand to wipe away his tears. "I ain't got nothing to do other than stare at my brother and mentally kick myself for getting Hank killed. If I hadn't dragged them along with me, Hank would be alive. And Waylon would be fine. This is all my fault."

"Calm down, Wes."

I glanced at the clock on the wall and realized that I had been in the hospital room for fifteen minutes. I considered myself lucky that the State Trooper hadn't stuck his head in to see how things were going. Or that a doctor or real nurse hadn't come in.

"Let's look at things in a different way," I said. "What did the three attackers look like?"

"Uhhh . . . They were wearing masks. I never saw their faces."

"I'm not talking about their faces. I mean their height and weight. Was there anything distinctive about them? Having a general idea could help me narrow down the suspects."

"Well . . . The guy claiming to be Facundo was definitely the one in charge. He wasn't much taller than you. He also did most of the talking. The other two guys didn't say all that much."

"Good." I grabbed a notepad off Wesley's bedside table and began jotting down notes. "What else?"

"Umm . . . Facundo was doing something to disguise his voice. He sounded kinda like a robot. And he knew all about our family. Like I said the other day, he knew things that I don't know about. I doubt you know about some of it." Wesley leaned back against the pillows and closed his eyes. "Facundo didn't get too physical. He smacked me around a few times when I wouldn't cooperate, but that was it. I don't remember him hitting Waylon or Hank."

"What about the other two?"

"The one was big. Not fat. Just big. You know, bulky. I'm almost six-foot, and I was looking him in the eye when they had me hanging from the ceiling. He's gotta be close to six-and-a-half feet. And probably weighs about two-fifty." Wes opened his eyes and looked up at me. "He's the one who did most of the roughing up. And it was obvious that he was pissed. Like, he was doing this out of hate. Facundo and the other guy had to hold him back a few times."

"Is he the one who cut off your finger?"

Wesley shook his head. "Naw, that was the third guy. The skinny one. I'd say he's about the same size as me. He was angry too. But his anger was directed towards me. He never laid a hand on Waylon or Hank. And he was trying to stop the big guy from hurting them too bad. Yeah, the skinny guy definitely had it out for just me. The big guy seemed to hate all of us. And Facundo . . . man, I don't know what to say about him. It's like he was detached from the whole thing. Like he was orchestrating it but was also outside of it."

"Which one of them do you think is one of us?"

"Honestly . . . The more that I think about it . . . All three of them could be one of us."

The sound of the doorknob rattling nearly gave me a heart attack. I had just enough time to shove the notepad and pen into my pocket and step over to Waylon's bed. I grabbed a towel off the cart and started patting it against his exposed lower legs as Sergeant Boleyn walked into the hospital room.

"Yo, Sergeant Boleyn, my man," Wesley said. "You find my friend Ben Dover yet?"

"You ready to tell the truth yet?" Boleyn asked. "Because some of your family members are talking. And they told me that you were assaulted by a Honduran drug dealer. And others told me that you think it was a setup perpetrated by one of your own family members."

I had to bite down hard on my bottom lip to keep from asking Boleyn who he had talked to. I thought we had all agreed not to rat each other out to Boleyn. In fact, I had explicitly told my family not to talk to Boleyn. That someone had cooperated with a law enforcement officer was just further proof that certain family members did not take me seriously and refused to accept that I was now in charge. The only one I could forgive for talking was Bubba. If Boleyn had been putting the pressure on him last night, it was possible Bubba would have said something to direct suspicion away from him.

"Yo, whichever one of my kin said that musta been smoking some of that wacky weed. Ain't none of my kin involved," Wesley said. "But they're right about one thing. It was a drug dealer that set me up. He's part of some Honduran cartel, but I ain't sure which one."

"I don't believe a word you say, Wesley." Sergeant Boleyn stepped between the beds, trapping me between him and the hospital machinery. "How's the patient doing today, nurse?"

"Improving," I said in a falsetto.

I ducked my head so that the wig and glasses hid the side of my face. I then pushed past Boleyn, grabbed the cart, and headed for the door. In my haste to flee the room, I almost ran over a doctor who was standing in the hallway. The doctor said something to me about helping him examine the site of Wesley's amputation, but I was already halfway down the hall.

I found Tawny sitting at the nurse's station in the pediatric unit. I tossed her the stethoscope and her badge.

"Where's the closest exit?" I asked.

"There's a stairwell around the corner." Tawny came around the desk and took the cart. "You got caught, didn't you?"

"Almost." I said as I headed for the stairwell. "But you know what they say, almost only counts in horseshoes and hand grenades."

I raced down the two flights of steps and then out the door into the parking lot. I wasn't sure where I came out of the hospital at, but I knew it wasn't where I had entered. I hadn't planned on having to flee the hospital through a different exit and I had left my phone in Hardy's truck, so I was unable to call him and tell him where I was and ask him to come get me.

With no idea where I was—or where Hardy was at in relation to me—I decided to take a lap around the building in search of Hardy's truck. I had just passed the entrance to the morgue when someone honked their car horn. I spun around and spotted Hardy's big black truck as he drove across the parking lot towards me.

I jumped into the passenger seat and asked, "How'd you know?"

"Tawny called me," Hardy said as he gunned the engine and headed for an exit. "She said I would find you wandering around the parking lot. She also said you almost got caught."

"Boleyn came in the room as I was talking to Wes." I pulled the wig off my head and tossed it into the back seat along with the fake glasses. "He didn't recognize me."

"Good." Hardy handed me my cell phone. "Your family has been blowing up your phone while you were in the hospital. Hope you don't mind that I talked to a few of them. I also read the messages and looked at the pictures they sent."

"It's cool," I said. I could only hope that Hardy hadn't scrolled back too far in the messages. "What did they have to say?"

"Well, it sounds like Facundo and his buddies were busy overnight. They left more threatening notes and committed some more acts of vandalism. They also left some 'gifts' for a few of your family members. Not only is Facundo getting bolder, he's also getting creative," Hardy said before he summed up what he had learned between the calls and messages.

Uncle Houston had found a plastic skull stuffed into his mailbox along with a summons for federal jury service. Scrawled across the top of the skull was the message "I know where the bodies are buried." According to Hardy, Uncle Houston seemed more upset about the jury summons than the skull.

Cousin Dale had been on the receiving end of vandalism. He had been getting ready to leave for work when he went outside and saw that his blue 1977 Pontiac Firebird was up on cinderblocks. All four tires were gone, as were some crucial parts—including the battery.

Billy Bob had found the coil for a moonshine still at the end of his driveway along with a note that stated Facundo knew what Billy Bob had done with his still. Granddaddy and Uncle Vernon had been at Old Town Texas all night, and they said that no one had snuck in and dug up the ground underneath the new museum's gravel foundation. The coil couldn't possibly have come from there. Uncle Vernon had also left a message assuring me that the concrete foundation was being poured as planned this morning. It wouldn't be long until the family's contraband and illegal items were completely covered in a thick layer of concrete. Once the concrete was set, Uncle Vernon promised to get his crew started on framing the building.

It was Uncle Leroy who had received the most unusual of Facundo's many "gifts." He and Uncle Delmar had gone into Guns 'n Stuff earlier than usual to take inventory, and they'd found a taxidermized raccoon sitting in the middle of the outdoor gun range. Uncle Leroy had recognized the raccoon as one of his pieces. Tucked into the raccoon's mouth was a note stating that Facundo knew that Uncle Leroy smuggled drugs inside some of his taxidermy. It really bothered me that Facundo had known about Uncle Leroy's drug smuggling while I had no clue.

"Facundo and his buddies weren't the only ones who were busy last night," Hardy said as he pulled into the parking lot at the sheriff's department. "Pastor Kemp or one of his congregants left advertisements for the Hell House at a bunch of your family member's houses. Same with the Devereuxs and the Palmers."

"Pastor Kemp didn't leave one for me. And he knows where I live," I said as I climbed out of the truck. "I'm not sure if I should feel offended or not."

"Actually . . . He did leave one for you," Hardy said as he opened the back door of the sheriff's department. "I found it tucked under the corner of your welcome mat this morning when I went out to get the newspaper. I wasn't going to tell you since I figured it would upset you."

"You've got that right. As if I don't have enough going on at the moment . . . Now I have the Kemps harassing me. Given they've been harassing me since I was a teenager . . ."

After changing out of Tawny's pair of hot pink hospital scrubs, I walked down the hallway to Uncle Murph's office to let him know that I was back. Aside from Hardy, Uncle Murph was the only other person who knew of my plan to sneak into Wesley's and Waylon's hospital room this morning.

As usual, Uncle Murph's office resembled a disaster zone. There were piles of junk scattered about the floor, and on his desk was a mountain range of paperwork. Last week—while Uncle Murph had been at an all-day meeting for county planning—I had cleaned up his office. I had organized the paperwork and thrown out the trash. I had straightened out everything on his bookcases and alphabetized the files in the filing cabinet. By noon the next day, it looked like a tornado had gone through the room.

Uncle Murph was seated behind his desk. Between the computer monitor and the piles of paperwork, he was almost hidden from view. Seated across from Uncle Murph was Mutt Devereux. They were working their way through a dozen mini cupcakes. Like Uncle Murph, Mutt was overweight and had a bad habit of overindulging in unhealthy snacks.

Mutt—who was the same age as Wesley, Roxanne, and Jason— had always been five-and-a-half beers short of a six pack. But he had destroyed what few brain cells he had by huffing spray paint while in high school.

"I managed to see Wes. He gave me some new information." I leaned against the edge of Uncle Murph's desk and then grabbed the last chocolate cupcake. The flaming orange icing tasted faintly of peanut butter. "What are you doing here, Mutt?"

"I have some information concerning the assault of Wesley, Waylon, and Hank," Mutt announced in the formal way he had of speaking. "I know the identity of the three assailants."

"Is Larry one of them?" I asked.

"Larry" had been Mutt's imaginary friend since he was a kid. It hadn't seemed weird when Mutt was a child. Afterall, I had a couple imaginary friends of my own when I was a kid. As had almost everyone else I knew. What was concerning about Mutt was that, as he got older, he continued talking to his imaginary friend. "Larry" was now a mainstay in Mutt's life. Mutt was also one of the many Devereuxs who volunteered at the Body Farm. He worked in the Psych Ward skit on the Hayride of Nightmares. Mutt wore a straitjacket and spent the entire night talking to "Larry" or mumbling "ears and eyeballs" repeatedly.

"Had Larry not been with me all Sunday morning, yes, I would think he might have done it," Mutt said. He popped one of the vanilla cupcakes in his mouth. "As you know, Larry is very vindictive. And he has held a grudge against Wesley for many years. He blames Wesley for my former addiction to huffing spray paint. But Larry was with me. And we were at home. But who was not home was my father."

"You think Gopher is one of the people involved?" I asked.

Mutt's father, Gopher Devereux, was Catfish's oldest child. Like "Larry," Gopher blamed Wesley for getting Mutt addicted to huffing spray paint and causing him to fry his brain.

"Initially, yes, I believed that my father was involved. He has threatened Wesley on numerous occasions," Mutt said. "But I have since determined that it was impossible for my father to have done it. Unlike Larry, my father cannot be in two places at the same time."

I wasn't aware that "Larry" could be in two places at once.

"Where was Gopher on Sunday morning?" Murph asked.

"At the Billy Club."

The Billy Club was Wyatt County's only country club. It featured an eighteen-hole golf course, a clubhouse, a swimming pool, tennis courts, and a fishing hole that was kept stocked with bass and other fish. Gopher was the owner of the Billy Club as well as the head greenskeeper.

"You're sure of this?" I asked.

Mutt nodded. "The Billy Club hosted a charity golf tournament on Sunday. My father and a couple of his landscapers all arrived around five in the morning to check the greens. The landscapers confirmed that my father was there all morning. It is impossible for him to have also been at the Body Farm."

"If Larry and Gopher aren't two of the assailants, who is?" Uncle Murph asked.

"I believe the other people involved are my uncles Toad, Cooter, and Rooster. They all resent Wesley for various reasons."

Toad and his older brother Pork Chop were the two children that Catfish had with his third wife. And Cooter and Rooster were the byproducts of his fourth failed marriage. Rooster was married to my cousin Becky—Aunt Eileen's and Uncle Ted's oldest daughter. Neither Toad nor Cooter had followed their half-siblings' trend and married into the Shatner family.

"I know why Toad hates Wes," I said. "It's Wes's fault for getting Tadpole kicked off the high school football team thanks to him hiding all that marijuana in Tadpole's gym locker."

"It also cost Tadpole a couple of scholarships," Uncle Murph reminded me. "Remember he had two or three offers to play football at Division One schools."

"Instead, Tadpole wound up going to community college," I said. "But, Mutt, what do Cooter and Rooster have against Wes?"

"They are both upset because they have recently discovered that Wesley had Cooter Junior and Douglas working for him. They are selling marijuana and other drugs to their classmates at the high school."

A white-hot bolt of rage ripped through me. Earlier, when I had threatened to shoot Wesley following his shotgun wedding to Roxanne, I had been joking. Now I was tempted to follow through with it. Wesley was out of control.

"How do you know this and I don't?" I asked Mutt.

"Because no one trusts you," Mutt said. "And people say all sorts of things in front of me because they do not think I understand. But I understand far more than everyone assumes."

CHAPTER SIXTEEN

"I FORGOT YOUR FAMILY OWNS AN ADULT STORE," Hardy said as he parked in front of the one-story building that housed the Den of Depravity.

"Sometimes I do, too."

Uncle Houston had purchased the building about a year ago, and the Den of Depravity had its grand opening back in February. Because all the business conducted in the Den was of the legal variety—at least I hoped it was all legal—I rarely thought about the adult store. During my lone visit to the store, I hadn't made it past the front door. That night, Uncle Houston had been hanging out in the foyer to greet the customers while handing out raffle tickets and mini bottles of sample lubricants. As we so often did, Uncle Houston and I had gotten into an argument and I stormed off before I could go inside the store and take advantage of the family discount.

Stepping through the doors, my feet sank into the thick pile of the blood red carpeting.

"I wasn't sure what to expect," I said as I looked around the store. The walls were painted a pale gray, and the merchandise had been separated into sections for toys, lingerie, and videos. There were a couple of customers perusing the merchandise, and one of the younger Devereuxs was behind the cash register. "But it's nowhere near as trashy as I thought it would be."

"You're right," Hardy said. "It's almost classy, considering what it is."

Hardy and I had spent the afternoon tracking down the Shatners and Devereuxs who we had not spoken to the day before. We had motives for many of them, but we needed to see if they had alibis. If any of them did have a solid alibi, they were promptly removed from the suspect list. Unfortunately, not many of them had alibis.

We confirmed that Gopher Devereux had spent early Sunday morning at the Billy Club. In fact, he had been there throughout the entire day on Sunday because of the charity golf tournament.

Since we had talked to Toad yesterday, we didn't bother speaking to him today since we had already discussed his resentment of Wesley. We knew that Toad had a motive and no alibi.

We also tracked down Rooster for a chat. Hardy and I had talked to him yesterday while at the Arm Bar, but Rooster had failed to mention that Wesley had fifteen-year-old Dougie doing his dirty work. Getting a straight answer out of Rooster had been like pulling teeth. Luckily, my cousin Becky had no problem talking about it—and threatening to skin Wesley alive should he ever come near her son again.

Before leaving Rooster's and Becky's house, I had a heart-to-heart chat with Dougie. When it became clear that he did not take me seriously, I handed him a brochure for a reform school that was in the middle of nowhere in North Dakota. I warned Dougie that if he didn't get his act together immediately, he'd be spending the next few years away from home. Rooster and Becky both backed my play, and Dougie suddenly decided to listen to what I had to say and promise me that he would stop breaking the law.

Cooter was the last Devereux on the list of those that I needed to talk to. We had saved him for last because I knew we could catch him at work. Cooter managed the Den of Depravity, and he usually worked during the store's later hours.

"Carrie. Sergeant Hardy." Cooter greeted us as he came around a trio of mannequins that were dressed in skimpy outfits. Cooter, who was about ten years older than I, was about my height. He'd gone gray early—probably thanks to his only child's antics—and recently all of his hair had fallen out. He'd grown a bushy beard to draw attention away from his bald head. "If you're looking to spice up your love life, you've come to the right place. We have just about everything that you could possibly want."

"We're here for business. Not for . . . err . . . pleasure," I said. "We've got a couple of questions for you."

"I'm guessing it's about CJ," Cooter said as he gestured for us to followed him into the backroom that served as an office, breakroom, and storage room. "Rooster called me earlier and let me you know that you'd found out that Wes had our boys dealing for him."

"Why didn't you tell me what was going on? As the head of the family—"

"Spare me the lecture, Carrie," Cooter said as he interrupted me. "I get that you're supposed to be the head of the family now. I'm one of the few people who actually supports you. But you've proven that you have no control over Wes. Neither does Houston. Or Woody. That's why Rooster and I decided to handle things on our own."

"Did 'handling things' involve kidnapping Wes, Waylon, and Hank?" Hardy asked. "Are you and Rooster two of the assailants?"

Rooster's alibi for Sunday morning was weak. He claimed to have been at home with his wife and kids. Becky swore he was at the house the entire time, but I was not about to take her word for it. She had proven herself to be a pathological liar a long time ago.

"I swear to you, Rooster and I were not involved," Cooter said. He grasped me by the upper arms and leaned closer so that he could look me in the eye. "We have nothing against Waylon or Hank. Just Wes. We might have hurt Wes. I'll admit we both wanted to kick his ass. But we wouldn't have brutalized Waylon or Hank. Heck, we wouldn't have even done that to Wes. Yeah, we were pissed. But we're not cruel."

"Do you have an alibi for Sunday morning?" Hardy asked.

"I was at home. You can ask my wife and kid. They'll tell you. After working at the Body Farm until two in the morning, I didn't get out of bed until almost noon."

"I will ask your wife," I said. "I would also like to talk to CJ."

"Of course. Of course. The boy needs a good talking to. I've tried to put the fear of God into him, but he's a teenager and doesn't take his old man seriously anymore. You can probably scare him straight if you talk to him like Emily Morgan used to talk to us. He'll be back on the straight and narrow in no time."

"I'll swing by your place sometime," I said as walked back out into the store. "Let me know if you discover any additional information."

As Hardy and I passed the checkout counter on our way to the front door, Newt Devereux stepped in front of us and blocked our path. Newt was another one of Toad's sons, and he was younger than Tadpole by a year or two. His bugged-out eyes reminded me of the amphibian he was named after.

"My dad didn't do it," Newt said.

"And you know this how?" I asked.

"Because I do," Newt said. "Wes has a talent for making enemies. He uses people. He's been using his brother pretty much since the day Waylon was born. He used me and my brother. He used my cousins Jason, CJ, Dougie and Mutt. And he's still using Roxanne. He used your cousin Cletus. And, because he used Hank, Wes got him killed. Give me half-an-hour, and I can probably give you a list of about a hundred people who Wes has either used, humiliated, or pissed off in the past few years. Any one of them might want him dead."

"How did Wesley use you?" Hardy asked.

"Explaining that would take all night," Newt said. "You ask me, what happened to Wesley on Sunday morning was karma. It finally caught up to him and he was punished for all the horrible things he has done to people. I'm just sorry that Waylon and Hank got caught up in Wesley's mess. They didn't deserve what happened to them."

"Seems to me that it was more like payback instead of karma," I said. "Someone finally had all they could take of Wesley, and they got their revenge."

"Call it whatever you want," Newt snapped. "Either way, Wesley got what he deserved. He's screwed over and hurt so many people in the past few years . . . It doesn't surprise me one bit that someone finally turned it around on him."

"I gotta ask, Newt . . . but where were you on Sunday morning?"

"I was here. Restocking the merchandise."

"Can anyone confirm that?" Hardy asked.

Newt turned around and pointed at the security camera mounted above the door. "That can. Security footage don't lie."

"I believe you," I said as I pushed by Newt on my way to the door. "And I'd appreciate it if you made up that list of names for me."

Hardy followed me outside to the parking lot. "Do you believe Cooter when he says he wasn't involved?"

"I'm not sure yet," I admitted.

"Well, Cooter was the last Devereaux on the list. Should we move on to the Palmers?"

"The Palmers can wait until tomorrow," I said as I headed to the far side of the parking lot where Hardy had parked his truck. As I got closer, a gust of wind caused a sheet of paper to flutter against the windshield. "Oh, look, you got a flyer. Probably from someone protesting the adult store."

Hardy plucked the sheet of paper out from under the windshield wiper. "It's from your new friend Facundo."

"Are you serious?" I leaned closer to Hardy so that I could peer over his shoulder at the note. "It is for me?"

"No, it's addressed to me." Hardy cleared his throat and then read the note aloud. "It says, 'Sergeant Hardy, now is not the time to play Detective Shatner's Prince Charming. There is no happily-ever-after in your future. May I suggest leaving town on your own? Otherwise, I will escort you out of Wyatt County in a body bag.' And it's signed 'Facundo.'"

I glanced up and down the road, searching for someone who might have left the note. Hardy and I had only been inside the Den of Depravity for fifteen minutes. Whoever had left the note might still be nearby. The only people I saw were a couple of older men who were congregating in the strip club's parking lot across the street while they smoked. The only other cars on the road were a beat-up truck, a vintage Cadillac, and a police cruiser. The cruiser was too far away and it was too dark out for me to be able to tell if it belonged to the sheriff's department or the Holler police.

I was debating running across the street to talk to the strip club patrons when my phone rang. I pulled the phone out of my pocket and checked the caller ID. The area code was local.

"Hello."

"Detective Shatner . . ." The voice sounded garbled and robotic. Whoever was calling must have been using a voice altering device. "I see you and Sergeant Hardy found my note."

I jabbed at the touch screen and put the call on speaker. "Who is this?"

"My name is Facundo. I believe you know who I am."

"I also know that you're not really named Facundo. You're not a drug dealer. And you're not part of any Honduran cartel. How about you tell me who you *really* are."

Facundo chuckled. "You may know who I am not, Detective Shatner. But I am not going to tell you who I am. For now, you may refer to me as Facundo."

"What do you want?" I asked.

"For starters, I want Sergeant Hardy to leave town."

"Not going to happen," Hardy said. "Your little love note doesn't scare me."

"It appears you don't put too much value on your life, Sergeant Hardy."

"Why did you setup my cousins and their friend?" I asked.

"Detective Shatner . . . you don't need me to explain to you that Wesley is the weak link in your family. Misleading him was like taking candy from a baby . . . Easy and oddly satisfying. Waylon and Hank were collateral damage. I can assure you that my associates and I did not mean for Hank to die. Had Wesley come alone like I requested, Hank would still be alive."

"If you hadn't intended to kill Hank, you or one of your associates shouldn't have cracked him over the head," I said.

"I assure you that was unintentional. Our intentions were to gather information on your family. I knew that once I had Wesley in my control, I could make him talk. He held out longer than I thought he would, and I admire that. I also admire that he was willing to share the Shatner family secrets to save his brother. Saving Waylon's pathetic life might be the only admirable thing Wesley has ever done. And the information he provided will help my mission."

"What exactly is that mission?" I asked.

"You mean you haven't figured that out already? I thought you were smarter than that, Detective Shatner," Facundo said. "The Shatner family's time is up. You all must be stopped. And it is my mission to stop you. As someone who has spent the past four years trying to shut down your family's illegal operations, I assume you can appreciate what I am doing."

"I'll admit that my family needs to be stopped. I'm also aware that either you or one of you lackeys is a Shatner. Or maybe a Devereux or a Palmer. I'm going to find out who it is, and I'm going to make that person talk."

"I don't suggest doing that, Detective Shatner," Facundo said. "It would be better for you to heed my warning and leave it well enough alone."

"What warning is that?" I asked. "The note you left for Jerrod? Or all the notes you left for my relatives? Those are hardly messages directed at me."

"As for my direct message for you . . . I know you got my package, Detective Shatner. I watched you pick it up off your doormat when you got home last night. If the note wasn't enough of a warning, the contents should have been. My associates and I are not playing around.

And, personally, I would hate to see you get hurt."

The line went dead.

I looked up at Hardy and said, "I think I know where Wesley's finger is."

CHAPTER SEVENTEEN

"**D**O YOU REALLY THINK WESLEY'S FINGER IS IN THE BOX?" Hardy asked as he blew through a four-way stop sign down the road from the Den of Depravity. He had a red, rotating warning light mounted on his dashboard, and he was honking the horn to warn other drivers to get out of our way. "For all you know, the package is something that you ordered online."

"Even if it turns out to be something that I ordered online, Facundo claims he saw me pick it up off my doormat last night. That means he was watching me."

"Seems like he's still watching you. How else would he have known that my truck was parked at the adult store?" After repeatedly honking his horn at a slow-moving driver, Hardy finally blew past in the other lane. "Do any of your neighbors have it out for Wesley? Or have a grudge against him?"

"Not that I know of." I clutched the grab bar above the passenger side door while Hardy took a sharp turn at a high rate of speed. "But you heard what Newt Devereux said. The list of people who don't like Wes could reach from here to Austin."

"What about you? Any neighborhood squabbles that you're involved in?"

"I don't even know most of my neighbors."

There were between thirty-five and forty houses in my small neighborhood. Back when I was a kid, I had known most of the neighbors—if not by name, at least by sight. Most of the people who had lived in my neighborhood back then had since moved away or died. The turnover rate had been high in my neighborhood in the past fifteen years, and people had moved in and out of the area in rapid succession. When it came to the current residents, I had no idea who most of them were. The house across the street from me had changed hands three times in the past ten years—with my cousin Naomi being the most recent owner. While I might recognize some of my current neighbors because I'd seen them walk or drive past my house, I had no idea what their names were or which house they lived in. It was entirely possible any one of them could have a problem with Wesley. But I couldn't think of anyone who had a problem with me—unless, of course, one of the neighbors had developed homicidal sentiments against me for my excessive Halloween decorations.

"It doesn't necessarily have to be a neighbor," I said. "Facundo could have been parked down the street or in someone's driveway. He also could have been hiding behind a tree or a bush in someone's yard. It was almost dark when we got back to my place last night."

"It doesn't help that your neighborhood doesn't have streetlights," Hardy added. "You're right, Facundo or one of his cronies could have been lurking in one of your neighbor's yards. Heck, they could have been inside that damn mausoleum in your front yard."

"Don't say that!" I reached across the center console and smacked Hardy on the bicep. "This Facundo guy has me freaked out enough as it is. Don't make it worse."

We fell silent as we came to the outskirts of Holler. Hardy mashed the pedal to the floor, and we raced along the backroads going almost twice the speed limit. On a typical day and going the speed limit, it took me ten to fifteen minutes to get from the center of town to my house. Hardy nearly cut that time in half, but, to me, the drive felt like it took an eternity.

Hardy almost missed the turnoff into my neighborhood, and the back end of his truck fishtailed when he slammed on the brakes. After getting his truck under control, he turned down my street and cruised past the houses.

"Whose car is in your driveway?"

"I don't know."

The motion-activated light above my garage door illuminated the red mid-sized sedan that was parked in my driveway. When Hardy pulled into my driveway—parking diagonally behind the sedan to block it in—his headlights flashed across the car's bumper. The license plate was from Tennessee.

I unbuckled my seatbelt and shoved open the passenger side door. Hardy hadn't quite brough the truck to a complete stop before I hit the ground running. My knees trembled, and I had to force one foot in front of the other. Hardy shut off the truck's engine and yelled at me to wait for him. While it would have been the smart thing to do, I didn't think that stopping to assess the situation was an option. There was a strange car parked in my driveway, and my defenseless pets were home alone. I could hear Molly barking inside the house. It didn't sound like a scared or ferocious bark, but she was still barking at something or someone.

My heart rate—which had doubled when Facundo called a few minutes earlier—doubled again. Black dots swam in front of my eyes and my lungs felt like there was a vice grip tightening around them. I couldn't seem to draw in a complete breath. The anxiety attack that I had been holding at bay since late yesterday morning came crashing over me.

Sprinting across my front yard, I hurdled the plastic cemetery fence and Styrofoam headstones. As I ran, I wrestled my handgun out of the holster on my right hip and my keys out of my jacket pocket.

"Time's up," the Grim Reaper cackled as I set off his motion detector. The red bulbs in his eye sockets glowed ominously in the shadows. "You're next."

"Not tonight." I flailed at the Grim Reaper with my left arm, knocking him backwards over the porch railing. He landed upside down in a barberry shrub.

As I yanked open the storm door, I saw that my front door was slightly ajar. A thin strip of light escaped between the edge of the door and the jamb. My keys slipped out of my left hand as I brought it up to help steady the gun that I clenched in my shaking right hand. I didn't waste a millisecond considering what to do. Acting on instincts alone, I raised my leg and kicked the front door the rest of the way open.

As I stepped through the doorway and into the foyer, I swung the gun up and pointed it at the person who had knelt to pet Molly.

"Freeze motherfu—" I shrieked, cutting myself off when I recognized the person in my foyer. "Andrew?"

"Not quite the 'welcome home' that I was expecting," my cousin Andrew Bohannan said. He stood up and took a giant step to the side.

He then gently pulled the gun out of my sweaty, trembling hands and flipped on the safety. "Is the gun really necessary?"

"An . . . Andrew . . ." I stammered. My arms fell limply to my sides, and I patted Molly on the head as she rubbed against my legs.

Andrew Bohannon was my cousin, though we were frequently mistaken for siblings because we so strongly resembled each other. Once, when Andrew had grown out his hair, he had been misidentified as me without makeup. Neither of us had been all that flattered by the comparison. Andrew, who was a couple of months older than me, was Uncle Ted's and Aunt Eileen's only son. We had grown up together, and he was one of my closest friends. He was also one of the few Shatners who I knew was in no way involved in the family's criminal endeavors. Sure, he smoked the marijuana and drank the moonshine, but he didn't participate in the manufacture or sale of either. As the lead singer and main guitarist for the Flaming Outhouses, Andrew spent most of his time in Nashville or on the road. When he did come home to Wyatt County, he almost always stayed with me.

"Andrew?" I asked for the third time as it finally began to sink in that there was not an intruder in my house. At least, there wasn't a dangerous or vengeful intruder.

"Hands in the—Andrew?" Hardy yelled as he rushed inside the foyer. He swung the gun back and forth between me and Andrew before quickly lowering it. Hardy stuck the gun in his holster and then wrapped a steadying arm around my shoulders. "What are you doing here?"

"I could ask you the same thing, lawman," Andrew said as he glared at Hardy. "But the guys and I heard about what happened to Wes, Waylon, and Hank. We don't have any gigs for the next week, so we decided to come home and offer . . . I don't know . . . moral support, I guess."

"And that's your car in the driveway?" Hardy asked.

Andrew nodded. "Yeah. It's new. I got it a couple weeks ago."

"You about gave me a heart attack," I said.

"Likewise." Andrew held up my gun. "My testicles are up by my nipples."

My knees gave out and I sank down to the floor. Molly, who had been desperately trying to get my attention, nearly knocked me over as she alternated between licking my face and sniffing my clothes. I wrapped my arms around her neck and buried my face in her fluffy, blonde fur. Holding her, the anxiety attack began to subside, and my heart rate returned to normal.

Molly was okay.

And, if the scuffling and meowing sounds coming from my living room were any indication, Manny was also okay.

"You should have told me you were coming home," I said to Andrew.

"Check your phone," Andrew said. "I texted you and left a couple voicemails."

I pulled my cell phone out of my jacket pocket and glanced at the screen. I had almost a hundred unread text messages and nearly two dozen voicemails. Andrew had called me three times in the past twenty-four hours, but I hadn't answered. He had also sent me several text messages—including ones where he said that he and the guys were coming home from Nashville. He had sent the most recent text message less than fifteen minutes earlier. The text had been to let me know that he had just gotten to my house.

"Uhh, Carrie, I don't want to be rude or nothing," Andrew said, distracting me from my phone. "But it kinda smells like something died in here. Did you forget to take out the trash?"

"The package!"

I pushed Molly aside and then scrambled across the foyer on my hands and knees to where I had a narrow table sitting against the wall. I used the table as a dumping ground for my keys, mail, and Molly's leash. Last night, after bringing the small, cardboard box inside, I had tossed it onto the table and subsequently forgotten about it. I shuffled through the stacks of unopened junk mail and a collection of odds and ends that had wound up getting discarded on the table. After knocking nearly everything onto the floor, I came to the realization that the box was missing.

"Where the hell is it?" I asked.

"Calm down, Carrie," Hardy said as he pulled me to my feet. "There were a lot of people here last night and this morning. Any one of them could have moved the package."

"You talking about this package?" Andrew asked as he held up a familiar looking cardboard box. My name had been scrawled across the one side in black marker. "Manny was batting it around the living room. Looks like he chewed a hole in the one corner."

"Give it to me." I snatched the box out of Andrew's hands and then tossed it to Hardy. I was beyond caring about preserving evidence. Besides, my fingerprints were already all over the box from last night. "Get it out of my house, Jerrod."

Hardy caught the box in one hand. He then hustled outside with it.

"What's with the box?" Andrew asked. "Y'all are acting like there's a bomb in it."

"It's Wes's finger," I said.

"What?" Andrew's eyes bugged out, and the blood drained from his face. "For real?"

"It's definitely a severed finger," Hardy yelled from the front porch. "And the sick son of a bitch wrapped a big bow around it like it's a present or something."

"Oh my God." I flapped my hands at my face to dry the cold sweat on my forehead. Turning to Andrew, I said, "That's why it smells like something died in here. That box has been in my house since last night. And the finger is decomposing."

"I think I'm going to be sick."

Andrew bolted into the kitchen. He barely made it to the sink before throwing up.

"Molly, come." I grabbed my dog by the collar and pulled her into the living room. I then scooped up Manny and tucked him under my arm. "Let's get you guys out of here."

I took Molly and Manny into my sunroom and shut the door behind us. The nauseating smell of rotting meat had penetrated the small room, but it was faint. I opened all the windows, and the smell began to dissipate.

Leaving my pets in the sunroom, I headed back into my dining room. Bypassing the kitchen where Andrew was dry heaving at the sink, I headed for the tiny bathroom that was off the foyer. I grabbed a bottle of air freshener from the sink cabinet and sprayed it liberally as I walked around the foyer and living room. After opening the windows in the living room, I made my way throughout the rest of the house, opening windows and spraying the air freshener. The air freshener didn't quite eliminate the smell of decomposition, and my house soon smelled like artificial lavender scented death.

By the time I emptied the bottle of air freshener, Andrew had gotten over being sick. I found him and Hardy sitting in the shadows at the far end of my porch. They had moved the skeleton bride and groom out of the Adirondack chairs and unceremoniously dumped them in the driveway. The cardboard box containing Wesley's severed finger was on the table between them.

"You want to see it?" Hardy asked me as he gestured towards the box.

"No. I don't."

"Good choice," Andrew said. "It's the most disgusting thing I've ever seen. And I have seen some pretty sick stuff on the internet."

And I had seen far worse back when I had worked for the Nashville Crime Scene Investigation Section. Dismembered limbs and decomposing bodies had been part of the job, and I had almost grown desensitized to it. A severed finger shouldn't affect me at all—it wouldn't have if the finger had belonged to someone other than a family member.

"Was there anything else in the box?" I asked. "I mean, aside from the bow?"

"There was a note from Facundo," Hardy said. "He basically tells you to back off or you'll be next. This is just the beginning, and he's not going to stop until he shuts down your family's criminal operation."

"Not very original," I said. "Your threatening note was much more interesting."

"I called Sergeant Boleyn. There's no way I could keep this from him. He and my lieutenant were at the Holler Police Department. They're on their way over here."

"Jerrod, if you hadn't called Boleyn, I would have. You're right, we have to let him know that Facundo sent me Wes's finger."

"You going to tell Boleyn that Facundo called you?"

"Not yet. I'm going to tell him that Andrew got here, smelled something funky, and called me. We came home, opened the box, and discovered the finger." I nudged Andrew with my elbow. "You okay with that story?"

"I'll say whatever you want me to," Andrew said.

"What about you, Jerrod? You okay with altering our story."

"Whatever you want to do, Carrie."

The three of us sat in silence while we waited for Sergeant Boleyn and Lieutenant Underwood to arrive. Not even ten minutes had passed before a truck that was nearly identical to Hardy's pulled up to the curb in front of my house. Sergeant Boleyn was behind the wheel, and Lieutenant Underwood was in the passenger seat.

"Heard someone gave you the finger, Miss Shatner," Boleyn said as he walked across my front yard and knocked over one of the Styrofoam tombstones.

"People give me the finger on a frequent basis," I said sarcastically. "But this is the first time that someone has given me an actual finger."

Hardy, Andrew, and I moved towards the other end of the porch and stood under the light that was mounted next to the front door. I glanced at the box Hardy held, and saw the tip of Wesley's shriveled, green-tinted finger poking up out of a tangle of bright purple ribbon. Did Facundo somehow know that purple was my favorite color? Or had he just grabbed whatever ribbon he had on hand?

"No addresses, stamps, or post office markings. Looks like this was personally delivered," Boleyn said as he pulled on a pair of latex gloves and then took the box from Hardy. "Did you just get it?"

I shook my head. "It was on my porch when I got home last night. With all the excitement going on, I tossed it on the table and forgot about it. Andrew got home about half-an-hour ago, smelled something bad, and called me. Jerrod and I rushed over here to see what was causing the smell."

"I'll have the finger tested to make sure it matches Wesley's blood type," Boleyn said.

"Which one of you nibbled a hole in the box?" Underwood asked.

"That would have been my cat," I said.

"Cats are nasty little beasts. Yours probably would have eaten the finger had he been able to get to it," Boleyn said. He pulled a wrinkled, bloodstained piece of paper out of the box and looked it over. "If you won't heed my warning from yesterday, I strongly suggest you pay attention to this one, Miss Shatner. You are not part of any official investigation, and you need to stop snooping around."

"Who said I was snooping around?" I asked.

"I know you've been going around talking to your family members as well as the Devereuxs and Palmers. And I'm sure you're telling them not to talk to me," Boleyn said. "I also know all about your little family get-together that took place yesterday afternoon."

"Aside from knowing that it took place, I highly doubt you know anything about it."

"I stand corrected, Miss Shatner." Boleyn reached up and tipped his white Stetson in my direction. "I don't know anything about what happened at your family's secret meeting. I just know that it took place. And I sure wish I could have been a fly on the wall."

"You and just about every lawman in the state," I said.

"I know one lawman who was in attendance." Boleyn turned to Hardy and asked, "Learn anything interesting, Sergeant Hardy?"

"Plenty," Hardy said. "None of which I'm willing to share with you."

"Tsk tsk. You're a disgrace to the badge, Sergeant Hardy." Boleyn took a step closer to me and said, "I'm going to give you one more chance to save your sorry behind, Miss Shatner. I am willing to offer you a deal. You know I'm going to find evidence against your family. Evidence that is going to send quite a few of you to prison for a long time. Help me out by turning over evidence, and I'll make sure you don't get charged with any crimes."

I cut my eyes over to Underwood, looking for some sort of sign. He jerked his chin back and forth just enough for me to know he was shaking his head.

"No thanks, Sergeant Boleyn. I'll take my chances."

Boleyn huffed, and his vinegary breath tickled my nose.

"Well, I can't say I didn't try." Boleyn backed up and stepped off my porch. "Stay out of my way, Miss Shatner. And you, too, Sergeant Hardy."

Sergeant Boleyn headed back across my front yard to his truck. He knocked over part of my plastic cemetery fence and chipped a chunk of Styrofoam off a tombstone when he kicked it. Underwood trailed after him.

Boleyn's taillights were still in sight when my cell phone rang. I recognized the number from earlier.

"What?"

"I see you finally opened my present, Detective Shatner," Facundo said in his robotic voice. "Did you like it? I picked out the purple ribbon especially for you."

"You're a sick bastard."

"There's really no need for name calling, Detective Shatner," Facundo chided me. "And why did you give the finger to the Texas Ranger? It was meant for you."

I walked out into my front yard and looked around. I didn't see any strange cars parked along the street or in any of the nearby driveways. But there were several trees and bushes that Facundo could have been hiding behind. At least I knew he wasn't in my mausoleum.

"I know you're around here somewhere, Facundo. Why don't you come over here and we can talk face-to-face?"

"Why not meet in the middle of the street at high noon and shoot it out like we're in some cheesy western? How fast is your draw, Detective Shatner?"

"Fast enough to put a bullet between your eyes."

Facundo chuckled. "I hope you take my warning seriously, Detective Shatner. Let me and my associates do our job, and we will leave you alone."

"What if I don't heed your warning?"

"Then we will come after you."

"You came after my family," I said. "That means you already came after me."

"If you're not smart enough to take your own well-being into consideration, what about the well-being of your pets? I know you have a dog and a cat, Detective Shatner. I'm sure you wouldn't want anything to happen to Molly or Manny."

I froze. Until that very moment, I had never quite understood the old saying about having ice-water in my veins. Facundo and his cronies coming after my family members was one thing. Most of them could defend themselves. But to threaten my pets . . . That reached a whole new low. There would be no more anxiety attacks. Until this was over—and I had every intention of ending it—I would keep myself under control.

"Let me make something crystal clear to you, Facundo," I said between clenched teeth. "If you hurt my pets, I will move heaven and earth to get to you. I will walk through hell and shake hands with the Devil—No! You hurt my pets, and I will become the Devil. In fact, I'll be much worse. Nothing will stop me from getting to you. And, by the time I'm done with you and mercifully end your worthless, pathetic existence, you will regret that your ancestors didn't die in some medieval plague."

"Medieval plague . . . You are quite creative, Detective Shatner," Facundo said. "Get Sergeant Hardy to leave town, and your pets will be safe."

"Deal."

After hanging up, I stuck my arm in the hair and raised my middle finger. If Facundo was watching me, he would get the message. I then turned around and walked up onto the porch. Hardy and Andrew were standing at the railing, and they were both giving me a wide-eyed look.

"Remind me to never piss you off," Hardy said.

"Shoot, lawman . . . If you think this is Carrie pissed off, you ain't seen nothing yet." Andrew said. He stepped inside and then reemerged with the shotgun that I kept stashed in the foyer closet. "Don't worry, Carrie, I'll guard the house while you go find this nutcase. All I need to know is what you want me to do with this Facundo guy if he tries something. You want him dead or alive?"

"Preferably alive so that I can question him," I said. "But, if someone is trying to hurt Molly or Manny, you better shoot to kill. Just don't hit one of my pets by mistake."

"Of course not." Andrew looked over the gun and then nodded in satisfaction. "I'll call the guys and get them over here to help."

I waited until Andrew had gone inside before I turned to Hardy. "You better get out of here. Before things get any uglier than they already are. I don't want to find out if Facundo is willing to follow through on his threat of sending you out of Wyatt County in a body bag."

"I'm not going anywhere, Carrie. Facundo's little love note doesn't scare me."

"Well, it scares me. I don't know who this guy is, but he's nuts. I have enough to worry about right now. I can't be worried about you getting killed. Plus, Facundo said if you leave, he won't come after my pets."

"And you trust him to keep his word?"

"No. But I'm also not willing to take any chances."

"All right, I'll go. But only if you come with me."

I shook my head. "I need to see this through to the bitter end."

"Even if it ends in you getting killed?"

I laughed. "That's not going to happen, Jerrod. Facundo may have gotten the jump on us, but he has no idea who he's messing with. My family is like a pack of wild dogs. We'll hunt our prey down, and we won't leave any trace of him behind."

"Oh, Carrie . . . I'd give you a lecture about letting law enforcement handle this, but I know you won't listen. Just promise me that you won't investigate by yourself." Hardy took my hands in his and pleaded with me. "Take Murph with you. Or Quaranta. Or any of the deputies. Heck, take one of your uncles or cousins that you trust with you."

"The question is who can I trust?" I asked as I pulled my hands away from him. "But I promise I will have someone with me to watch my back. And I'll try not to do anything stupid."

Jerrod pulled me into his arms and kissed me. "I'll leave for now, Carrie. But I'm just a phone call away if you need me."

I walked Hardy over to his truck and then watched him drive away. He had just turned out of my neighborhood when I heard the squeak of a storm door's pneumatic closer. My hand went to my hip and clutched at my empty holster. My handgun was inside the house.

I was about to dive behind Andrew's car for cover when I heard someone shouting my name. I glanced around and spotted Uncle Leroy standing in Naomi's driveway. He waved at me before climbing into his truck and driving away. While Uncle Leroy frequently came by to fix things around Naomi's house, it seemed like too much of a coincidence that he was there now—especially because it didn't look like either Naomi or Red was home.

"Not Uncle Leroy . . . It'll destroy Naomi if her dad is involved in this."

I stepped out into the street and watched Uncle Leroy's taillights disappear as he turned out of my neighborhood. There was no way he could be Facundo, but he did fit the physical description of the crony who was tall and slender. Uncle Leroy also didn't have an alibi for Sunday morning. And he had made his dislike of Wesley known on several occasions.

Knowing that at least one of my family members might have been involved was killing me. Yes, I knew that several of them were criminals, but I couldn't bring myself to believe that any of them could be capable of being involved in the assault on the Three Stooges. But, if I wanted to protect myself, I had to believe it. And I couldn't trust anybody.

CHAPTER EIGHTEEN

MY WEDNESDAY MORNING GOT OFF TO AN EARLY AND JOLTING START when someone rang my doorbell just after three-thirty. As I scrambled to get up, I remembered that I had fallen asleep on one of the recliners in my living room. Unfortunately, I remembered this too late. Halfway to my feet, I got caught on the arm of the chair and wound up faceplanting on the floor. Molly and Manny trampled over me as they raced out of the room. Molly ran over to the front door to bark at my nocturnal visitor, and Manny made a beeline for my bedroom so that he could hide.

"It's Wynonna," Andrew said as he set down the shotgun and helped me up from the floor. "Ethan Yates is with her."

Wynonna knocking on my door in the middle of the night was nothing new. It happened at least once or twice a month. She didn't get along very well with her siblings, and her mother drove her nuts. Whenever she needed a break, Uncle Woody would drop her off at an unsuspecting relatives' house. I was usually that unsuspecting relative.

To have Wynonna show up accompanied by Ethan Yates was concerning.

I grabbed Molly by the collar and yanked open the front door.

"What the hell is going on?"

Ethan pointed at Wynonna and asked, "Is she one of yours?"

"Yes, she's one of mine." I handed Molly off to Andrew so that I could open the storm door and pull Wynonna inside. I then stepped out onto the porch and pulled the door shut behind me. "What's going on? Why do you have my cousin?"

"I was out on patrol when I got a call that the fire alarm had been activated at Calvary Baptist. I was one street over, so it didn't take me long to get there. As I was driving up, I saw three people fleeing the scene. You cousin tripped and fell, so I grabbed her."

I mumbled a string of swear words under my breath. "Was the church on fire?"

"No, it wasn't," Ethan assured me. "But I heard over the radio that someone broke in and destroyed the Hell House scenery and props. I'm guessing that your cousin and the other two people I saw with her are the ones responsible."

I sighed. "How much?"

"How much what?"

"Money." It was my first time bribing someone, and I wasn't sure if I was doing it right. Was there a right way to bribe someone? "How much money to keep your mouth shut?"

"I'm not looking for a bribe." Ethan towered over me. "And I won't take one if you're offering it."

"Then what exactly are you doing here?" I asked. Ethan had me so confused and frustrated that I was ready to strangle him. "You caught my cousin fleeing from what sounds like the scene of a crime. Instead of detaining her, you brought her here. Why?"

"I didn't exactly see her fleeing the scene," Ethan said. "I saw her near the scene. For all I know, she's on the track team and was out training. I saw her fall down. I was concerned that she was hurt, so I offered her a ride. She asked me to bring her here."

I shot Ethan a wary look. I didn't trust him at all, and I knew to take this conversation at more than face value. Ethan was up to something.

"Why are you doing this?"

"Because I hate Hell House," Ethan said with contempt. "You know, my parents and I attended Calvary Baptist. Dad made me take part in the Hell House when I was a teenager. Because I was chunky, Pastor Kemp made me the star of the gluttony scene four years in a row. I'd have to sit there all night pretending to stuff my face with food and refuse to share with the skinny kids who were pretending that they were starving to death. It was awful."

"So what you're saying is that you're willing to look the other way because my cousin and her accomplices destroyed something that you hate?"

"Basically." Ethan nudged me in the arm with his elbow and

smirked. "I know y'all are paying the new Holler police chief to look the other way. But this is one case where I know he won't. He attends Calvary Baptist, and he's madder than a wet hen about what happened. If we find some evidence proving that your cousin vandalized the church, my chief won't sweep it under the rug. So, you better hope that your cousin and whoever helped her didn't leave behind any incriminating evidence."

Ethan's radio crackled and then someone demanded that he hurry up and get over to the church. His help was needed at the crime scene. Without a word, Ethan spun around and walked across my yard to his police cruiser.

I waited until Ethan drove off before I went inside to confront Wynonna. I found her seated on my couch looking petulant. I'm sure I had looked similar when I had been her age. I hadn't been a saint when I was a teenager. I had just gotten lucky and never been caught.

"You want to tell me what happened?"

"I destroyed Hell House." Wynonna jutted her chin out and glared at me. "And don't you dare start lecturing me. I know you did the exact same thing when you were my age."

The girl had a point.

"Fine. I won't deny it." I gestured towards the other room where Andrew, Junior, Luke, and Skeeter were seated around my dining room table. "They were with me that night. They'll also tell you that I had a darn good reason to destroy Hell House."

Not that having a reason made it right.

The summer before eleventh grade, my best friend Paige Kemp ran away while she was on vacation in California with me, Veda, and Veda's parents. Veda and I had no idea what Paige had been planning to do, but that didn't stop Ambrose and his wife from accusing us of helping her. Ambrose had harassed me and Veda for weeks straight despite our protests of innocence. In response to Ambrose Kemp's accusations, Veda and I—along with a several of my cousins—vandalized Hell House the night before it was set to open. We destroyed all of the props and costumes, causing Hell House to be cancelled not only for that year but indefinitely.

After Ambrose Kemp retired last year, his son, Thaddeus, took over as the pastor. Thaddeus was the one responsible for resurrecting Hell House.

"We had a reason, too," Wynonna said.

"First off, who is 'we'? Who helped you?"

"Roxanne and Jason."

"That doesn't surprise me." I had a seat next to Wynonna. "All right, let's hear your reason for destroying Hell House."

"Pastor Kemp . . . the young one . . . he was at my house when I got home from school yesterday. He was talking to Mom and both of my grandmas. He was going on and on about Wesley's and Waylon's sins and how they need to be saved. And you know how my mom is . . ."

"Yeah, I do," I said.

Aunt Deidra was gullible. She would have believed anything that Thaddeus Kemp told her even if he was talking badly about her sons.

"When I got home from school, Pastor Kemp started in on me. He was telling me that I need to come to Hell House and that I can be saved from following my brothers 'down the path of sin.' I told him to . . . well, what I told him wasn't nice. But it was nowhere near as bad as what Roxanne said to him when she came by a few minutes later to pick up Autumn. Pastor Kemp started calling her a whore and . . . and . . ."

"So whose idea was it to destroy Hell House?"

"Roxanne's. But I went along with it."

"And you almost got busted." I put my arm around Wynonna and hugged her. "In the future, do as I say and not as I do. I know you look up to me. But just because I did something stupid in the past doesn't mean you should do it, too."

Before I could come up with a way to punish Wynonna for her stupidity, my cell phone rang. The area code was local, but the number didn't match Facundo's. Either he had gotten a new phone or someone else from Wyatt County was calling me. I answered with caution.

"Detective Shatner? It's Chief Wollard with the Holler Police. Sorry to wake you at this ungodly hour, but I've got a crime scene and no one to process it. I've got one officer with training in forensics, and he's on vacation. I talked to the sheriff, and he said it's okay if I borrow you for the day to help process the scene over at Calvary Baptist. Some punks broke in and destroyed the Hell House."

I sighed. "I'll be there in half an hour."

Considering Facundo's threat to myself and my pets, I was reluctant to leave my house. Above all else, I wanted the three of us to remain safe. But, the way I saw it, I had two choices. I could stay at home with Molly and Manny, and huddle in the bathroom in fear until this was all over. But I had never been the type of woman who stayed at home when there was work to be done. Especially when it was work that only I could handle. Unfortunately, I would have to deal with the mess at Calvary Baptist before I could get back to my investigation.

My sole comfort was knowing that I was leaving Molly and Manny in capable hands. Andrew had called in the troops, and my half-brother Luke and cousins Skeeter and Junior had come over to help guard my pets and my house. Though I had my doubts that my house would survive their invasion unscathed.

"Please tell me that y'all wore gloves," I said to Wynonna.

"And masks," Wynonna said. "Don't worry, Carrie. You won't find any evidence."

"I better not." I stood up and walked into the kitchen. I needed to eat something. "Which one of you three dummies pulled the fire alarm?"

"Roxanne. She thought it would set off the sprinkler system. Jason and I tried to tell her that's not how it works . . ."

"But Roxanne didn't listen."

I grabbed a couple breakfast bars and poured myself a glass of orange juice. While eating, I texted Roxanne.

"Thanks Rox. I was gonna spend the day talking 2 the Palmers. Now I have to clean up ur mess at the church. Do u want me 2 find the people who assaulted Wes or not?"

"WHAT IS SHE DOING AT MY CHURCH?" Ambrose Kemp, the former pastor of Calvary Baptist, shouted as he broke away from the small group of people who were huddled together under one of the church's parking lot lights. He shuffled towards me—leaning heavily on his cane and shaking a gnarled fist in what I assumed was supposed to be a threatening manner. The light reflected off his bald head, highlighting the tufts of white hair that dotted his liver spotted scalp. "I don't want that degenerate woman on my church's property."

"Now, now, Pastor Kemp. Please, calm down," Fred Wollard said as he rushed after Ambrose. "I told you I was going to have Detective Shatner come take a look at the crime scene. You knew she was going to be here."

Fred Wollard was the current chief of the Holler Police Department. Prior to his promotion, he had been the department's captain. It hadn't been hard for Uncle Houston to bribe Wollard into looking the other way when a Shatner was caught committing a crime within the Holler city limits—not when Wollard had already been on the take for years already. But, like Ethan had pointed out, the destruction of Hell House might be the one crime that Chief Wollard would not overlook.

"This woman is responsible for my granddaughter's murder, Chief Wollard," Ambrose shouted as he jabbed me in the chest with the head of his cane.

I shoved Ambrose's cane away from me. "I had nothing to do with Paige's death. Why do you keep blaming me?"

"Because it is your fault. Had Paige never met you, she would not be dead." Ambrose slammed the tip of his cane onto the pavement, narrowly missing the pointed toe of my cowboy boot. "Had Paige not met you, she would not have turned her back on me and her grandmother. She would not have strayed from the Lord's path. And she most certainly would not have run away from home to seek out her jezebel of a mother—"

"And if Paige hadn't found Trixie, she never would have found out that my dad was also her dad," I said, interrupting Ambrose to finish the story for him. "And if Paige hadn't found that out, she would have kept running. Instead, she came home to confront my dad and wound up getting killed. I know what happened, Ambrose. Remember, I'm the one who figured it out. I just don't understand how any of it is my fault."

Just over a year before I was born, Dad had what would be the first of many affairs. The other woman was Ambrose Kemp's eighteen-year-old daughter. Dad had apparently been planning to leave Mom for Trixie when Mom found out that she was pregnant with me. To complicate matters even more, Trixie was already pregnant with Paige.

Dad wound up staying with Mom while Trixie left her daughter with her parents and took off for the West Coast. Dad, Mom, and Trixie were the only ones who knew who Paige's father was. I hadn't known that Paige was my half-sister until a few months ago—after Paige's remains were discovered buried in a shallow grave near Wyatt Lake and I began investigating what had happened to her.

"You may think you are innocent, but I hold you solely responsible for what happened to my granddaughter. And the Lord holds you responsible as well." Ambrose used his cane to gesture towards my Jeep. "Normally, I would welcome sinners and ne'er-do-wells into my church. But you—and your whole family—are not welcome. I demand that you leave."

"Father," Pastor Thaddeus Kemp said as he materialized next to Ambrose. Not a hair of his perfectly coiffed dirty blonde hair was out of place, and I couldn't find even one wrinkle on his dress shirt or pants. "Detective Shatner is here to help gather evidence against the trespassers who destroyed Hell House. And need I remind you that Calvary Baptist is no longer *your* church? Calvary Baptist is *my* church."

"And look what you've done to it," Ambrose said as he shook his fist under Thaddeus's nose. "Almost half of the congregation has either transferred to other churches or stopped attending services altogether."

"That's why I brought back Hell House," Thaddeus said, sounding exceptionally arrogant. He fairly oozed with all the charm of a stereotypical used car salesman. "To remind people of the Lord's path, bring them back to the church, and save their souls. I am working to rebuild our congregation. And I will succeed."

"You might have succeeded had you brought back my Hell House—"

"What I created is even better," Thaddeus said. "My Hell House portrays modern day sins. The sins that are a danger to our children."

Ambrose Kemp had based his Hell Houses around the Seven Deadly Sins. Guides would lead visitors through scenes that were set up to depict each of the sins. After viewing the Seven Deadly Sins, the patrons would encounter the Devil who would try to tempt them into sin. The Devil would then be overtaken by God. Ambrose Kemp always played the role of God, and he would preach to the patrons and encourage them to repent their sins and live a more Christian lifestyle so that they could eventually go to Heaven.

Starting when I was thirteen—the minimum age required to tour the Hell House—my mom had forced me to go through the production at least once a year until Ambrose Kemp shut down the operation after I helped trash it when I was sixteen.

But the main reason I hated Hell House was because Ambrose Kemp would single out the Shatners and tell us that we were beyond saving and that we were destined for Hell even if we did repent and change our ways. The Shatners were Baptists, but we were not part of the Calvary Baptist Church's congregation. Ambrose had made it clear that he thought us Shatners were irredeemable sinners and that we were not welcome in his church. Ambrose would specifically single me out each year because he didn't approve that I was friends with his granddaughter. Ambrose thought that I was a bad influence on Paige, and he was determined to sever the friendship and prevent me from leading her astray.

Shuddering at the rush of bad memories, I asked, "Do you have any idea who might have done this?"

"Aside from a Godless and soulless individual or group of individuals?" Thaddeus asked.

"It could be any one of the heathens who've been protesting Hell House," Ambrose said. "We've received threatening letters from all over Texas, Louisiana, and Arkansas. We've received more threatening letters from people than we have received letters of encouragement. People want us to shut down the Hell House. It's one of *those* people who did this."

"We'll need those threatening letters," Chief Wollard said to Thaddeus. He then took Ambrose by the elbow and guided him away from us. "Pastor Kemp, why don't you let me walk you home? You've had too much excitement for one night, and it's not good for your heart."

Ambrose mumbled something, but allowed Chief Wollard to help him up the hill towards his old, two-story Victorian house that was surrounded by well-tended flower gardens.

"I'm sorry about that, Detective Shatner. Father has become quite excitable in his old age. He knows you are not responsible for what happened to Paige," Thaddeus said. He ran his fingers over his handlebar mustache and then gestured for me to follow him over to the doors that led into the church's gymnasium.

"Let me grab my crime scene kit, and then you can show me around," I said to Thaddeus. Ethan fell into step with me as I walked back over to my car. "Did you get a look inside? How bad is the damage?"

"Oh, it's completely destroyed. There isn't going to be a Hell House this year."

Ethan handed me his phone. On the screen was a picture of a cheap metal altar that had been decorated with rainbow-colored streamers. The altar had been bent and twisted out of shape. Spray painted on the backdrop behind the altar were the words "LOVE IS LOVE." I flipped through the rest of the pictures, but, since I didn't know what the Hell House scenes had looked like before the vandalism, I didn't have anything to reference Ethan's pictures against. It was safe to assume that none of the scenes were meant to be covered in graffiti or smashed.

"Yeah, I'd say that Hell House is destroyed," I said after looking through all of the pictures. I handed the phone back to Ethan.

"The damage to Hell House is way worse than the time it was vandalized when we were teenagers." Ethan winked at me. "But you'd know more about that than me."

"I plead the fifth," I said as I walked back towards the church. Ethan carried my crime scene kit. "Any idea how the vandals got in?"

"When the firefighters got here, they realized that one set of doors leading into the gym was unlocked. We're not sure if someone forgot to lock up or if the vandals had a key," Ethan said as we walked through the double doors into the gym. "The fire alarm that was activated is in the gym. That much we do know."

At the far end of the gym, a Halloween-style arch framed a doorway. As we got closer, I could see that the arch was made out of painted plywood and Styrofoam. Cheap, plastic skeletons were attached to the arch. It looked like someone had taken a baseball bat to it.

"My wife is distraught over what happened," Thaddeus said. He reached out and pulled a loose piece of Styrofoam away from the arch. "Faith has a degree in Art Education, and she created the majority of the scenery and props for Hell House. She came by to look at the destruction earlier, but seeing it made her physically ill."

The seed of guilt that had been germinating inside of me ever since Ethan dropped Wynonna off at my house abruptly bloomed. I might not be a fan of Hell House—or agree with its purpose—but it clearly meant a lot to Thaddeus and the other people who attended Calvary Baptist. They had worked very hard and spent a lot of time creating Hell House, only to have it destroyed in a matter of minutes.

Thaddeus led us out of the gymnasium and into the hallway. A portable room divider cordoned off the end of the hallway and blocked us from going any farther.

"This section of the hallway is where the patrons would have met their guides. My plan had been to send through groups of fifteen-to-twenty people at ten-minute intervals," Thaddeus said. "Teenagers—including my son—were going to guide the people through the Hell House. They were going to wear devil masks and black robes. The guides would have then taken the patrons into the first scene of the Hell House which is in the Fellowship Hall."

Thaddeus led me and Ethan through the open doorway into the Fellowship Hall. When I was a kid, my Girl Scout troop used to meet in Calvary's Fellowship Hall every Wednesday night during the school year. Not much had changed in the room in the twenty-or-so years since I had last been there. The walls had probably been repainted, but that appeared to be it.

Set up along the far wall were four hospital beds that were separated by privacy screens. The screens had been slashed, and the beds turned upside down. Everything had at least one streak of red or black spray paint on it.

"As you can see, this was supposed to be our hospital scene," Thaddeus said, continuing the tour. "The first bed was going to have a teenage boy overdosing after taking a single puff of marijuana. In the second bed—"

Interrupting to point out what I felt should be obvious, I said, "Uhhh . . . it's impossible to overdose on marijuana. Sure, you can have a bad reaction. But you can't overdose on it."

"I would not know," Thaddeus said. "I have never consumed the Devil's Lettuce."

"Neither have I," I said.

"But you are related to many sinners who have." Thaddeus glared at me. "In fact, your family helps other sinners indulge in the sin of marijuana. And many other sins. Including devil worshipping at that immoral haunted attraction your family operates."

Thaddeus took me and Ethan through the rest of the Hell House. He thoroughly explained each scene and the beliefs behind it. There were scenes that depicted drinking and drug use, the fatal aftermath of driving while intoxicated, gay marriage, domestic abuse, pornography, and participation in the occult. The second-to-last scene was based on the torments of Hell, and the final scene—which was in the church's original sanctuary—depicted Heaven. Thaddeus had taken over his father's role of God.

After Thaddeus had given us the extended tour, he turned to me and asked, "Do you think you'll find any evidence of the delinquents who desecrated my church and destroyed Hell House? Will the Holler Police be able to charge them with a crime? Will they be punished in this life as they so rightly deserve to be? Or will they have to wait for punishment in the Afterlife?"

I shrugged noncommittedly. "It's hard to say. I'm sure there are just way too many fingerprints on everything. And it's not like y'all have any security cameras around here. Chances are we'll never know who did this. But I'll be here all day searching for evidence."

I silently cursed Wynonna, Roxanne, and Jason. I had a murderer to find. And, thanks to them, I'd wind up wasting the entire day cleaning up their mess.

CHAPTER NINETEEN

I PARKED IN THE HANDICAP SPOT CLOSEST TO THE STRIP CLUB'S DOOR and then turned to face Deputy Timmy Grant. "Thanks for volunteering to come with me."

"You're welcome, Carrie. I know I wasn't your first choice."

Timmy hadn't been my last choice either. He wasn't even on my list of choices. But he was the one who had stepped up to help me. Not that I expected Timmy to be much help. From past experiences—including the times when Timmy had accidentally pepper sprayed and tased me—I knew that he did not hold up well in high pressure situations. He barely kept it together in low pressure situations. In all honesty, having Timmy come along had probably placed me into an even more dangerous situation than coming alone would have.

"I hate this place," I said as I eyed up the front of the long, low bunker-style building that housed Wyatt County's only strip club. "Come on, Timmy. Let's get this over with."

I climbed out of the Jeep and then trudged the few feet to the front door of the club.

"Need to see your ID, folks."

"You know who I am," I said to Heath Palmer. He was seated on a wobbly barstool in the club's cramped foyer area. "And you know I'm over eighteen."

"Yeah, but I don't know how old he is," Heath pointed at Timmy. "Boy don't look like he's old enough to be out of high school."

"We went to high school together, Heath. I was your chemistry partner in tenth grade."

"Timmy Grant?" Heath leaned forward and peered at Timmy. "Shoot boy, who was dumb enough to give a spaz like you a gun?"

"That's what I'm still trying to figure out," I whispered.

"Hey, Carrie." Heath stuck his arm out and prevented me from passing him. "Your personal life ain't none of my business, but I heard you've been hooking up with that Beto guy. And I don't know if you care. But he's here. Again. Guy practically lives here."

"Beto is not my boyfriend."

Heath lowered his arm. "Well, that's good . . . I guess."

I pushed past Heath and entered the main room of the strip club that had been shabbily decorated for Halloween. On the left side of the room was a small stage, and the bar was on the right. Scattered about on the mismatched plastic lawn furniture were a handful of customers. Alberto was not among them. From what I could see in the dim light, the customers seemed to be more interested in the all-you-can-eat hot wings buffet than in the young woman dressed in a skimpy witch costume who clumsily swung around the pole.

Turning away from the stage, I crashed into Zeke Palmer. Zeke, who had the expansive forehead of a Neanderthal, was the club's main bartender.

"What are you doing here, Carrie?"

"I need to talk to you and your brothers. Are they here?"

"They're here." Zeke sighed before turning and plodding across the room. "Follow me."

I took Timmy by the arm and guided him through the strip club and then down the narrow hallway to the small office. There we found Milo and Levi Palmer. I got the distressed Timmy settled in a chair before confronting the Palmer brothers.

"Was my cousin Randy here during the storm on Sunday morning?" I asked.

"Yeah, he was here," Zeke said. He patted the top of an old VCR that was sitting on a table next to him. "If his bar tab doesn't prove it, the security tapes will."

"I'll take your word for it, Zeke," I said. Confirming Randy's alibi took a small weight off my shoulders. I stepped closer to Levi and nudged him in the arm. "A little birdie told me that you've been selling cocaine and other drugs to the strip club patrons. Is that true?"

"What?" Levi scurried away from me. "No way. I ain't been doing that? Who said I was? Because that person is a bloody liar."

"The lady asked you a question. And I don't think you answered her honestly." Milo grabbed his brother by his disheveled blonde hair and slammed his forehead onto the desktop. "Have you been selling drugs in my club again, Levi? After I told you not to?"

"No," Levi said. His voice was muffled by a red feather boa that lay curled up on the corner of the desk. Milo increased the pressure on the back of his neck causing Levi to yelp. "I swear, Milo, I ain't been selling it in the strip club. I was selling it out in the parking lot. But I ain't doing it no more. Not since Grandpa told us we gotta stop breaking the law the other day."

"You idiot!" Zeke shoved Milo away from Levi. He then grabbed Levi and threw him against the wall. "If you weren't my brother I would—"

"Now, boys. Let's all calm down." I pushed my way in between Zeke and Levi. I then forced Levi to have a seat in the chair next to Timmy. "Do you even pay attention to who you sell drugs to? How do you know one or more of them isn't an undercover agent?"

Levi shrugged. "I ain't gotten caught yet. Unlike your uncle Ted."

"If he'd just burnt up the marijuana like I told him to . . ."

Uncle Ted had done the one thing that he assured me he would not do—get caught with his precious Purple Kush and Acapulco Gold. I didn't have the whole story yet, but, going off the few details that Uncle Ted had been able to share with Aunt Eileen, his buyer had set him up. Deputies with the Smith County Sheriff's Department were waiting for Uncle Ted last night when he had arrived at the designated meeting place outside of Tyler, Texas. A couple of the DPS's Drug Unit agents were there as well as a DEA agent. Uncle Ted had led the law enforcement officers on a high-speed chase that soon ended when he ran over a set of spike strips and popped all four tires. He was now sitting in a jail cell somewhere in Smith County.

"I'm not here to talk about my uncle Ted," I said to Levi. "I'm here to talk about you. And I heard that you threatened to kill Wesley and Hank on a few occasions. You don't happen to be one of the people who attacked them on Sunday morning, are you?"

"Heck no!" Levi said. "Yeah, I was mad. And I'll admit I threatened Wes and Hank a few times. But Hank was my partner—"

"Hank was your fall guy," Milo, Zeke, and I said almost simultaneously.

"He was my partner," Levi insisted. "And he wanted to ditch Wes and come back to working with me again. A few weeks ago, Hank told me about how Wes was making him nervous. He was afraid that El

Lobo would find out that Wes was talking to those other drug dealers about getting cocaine. I told Hank not to worry about El Lobo. I talked to him—"

Cutting Levi off, I asked, "You told El Lobo that Wes was talking to other cocaine suppliers? When was this?"

"Umm . . . three or four weeks ago, I think. El Lobo laughed and said that he wasn't worried about it. He also said something about how one of these days Wes would learn his lesson." The color drained from Levi's face. "Oh my God . . . Do you think El Lobo attacked Hank and your cousins? Is what happened my fault? Did I cause it to happen? Because I didn't mean to. I swear. Just because I was mad at Wes and Hank doesn't mean I wanted anything bad to happen to them."

"It's something El Lobo would do. The guy is insane," Zeke said. "And he wasn't too happy back at the beginning of the year when our two families started working together."

"Last time I talked to El Lobo, he said something to me about how he didn't trust Wesley," Milo said. "And that was about two months ago."

I groaned. "I'm meeting with El Lobo Friday night."

"Alone?" Zeke asked, sounding alarmed.

I shook my head. "I'm meeting him at the high school football game."

"Take my advice, Carrie," Milo said. "I've dealt with El Lobo a lot in the past. He is a dangerous man. Don't go anywhere alone with him. Stay near people and in a well-lit area. And, beforehand, let us or someone else know exactly where you're meeting him at so that we can keep an eye on you. Even if El Lobo isn't pretending to be this Facundo guy, he could be setting you up. And none of us want to see you get hurt."

"I was already planning to be careful. But I'll be sure to take extra precautions now," I assured Milo. I then looked over at Levi and said, "Where were you at on Sunday morning?"

"I was here," Levi said.

"No. You weren't." Milo smacked Levi upside the head. "Boy, if you don't tell Detective Shatner the truth, I will open the biggest can of whoop ass that you've ever seen."

"All right, all right." Levi wrapped his arms around his head to ward off any more blows. "I was with Babette."

"As in my cousin Babette?"

Babette was Festus' and Cletus' sister. I couldn't imagine they would be any more pleased to find out that their sister was dating a Palmer than Nate and Dylan were when they found out that Tina was hooking up with Waylon. Actually, my cousins would probably be more upset. Despite his many faults, Waylon was a nice guy. Levi, on the other hand, was scum. And that had nothing to do with his Palmer DNA.

"I didn't know you and Babette were dating," I said.

"We ain't told anyone," Levi said.

"Probably because you don't want your side piece to find out." Milo smacked Levi upside the head. He then turned to me and said, "You should warn Babette that Levi has been hooking up with one of my dancers for the past few months."

"I will tell her," I said. I picked up the red feather boa and looped it around Levi's neck. "After I'm done killing Levi."

It took the combined efforts of Milo, Zeke, and Timmy to wrestle me away from Levi. Once they had freed Levi from the boa, Milo dragged me behind his desk and shoved me into his well-padded desk chair.

"Cool it, Carrie," Milo admonished. "What's gotten into you lately?"

"Yeah, Detective Shatner, you've been acting crazier and crazier for the past couple months," Timmy said. "And, to be honest, you never were totally sane to begin with."

"Is it any wonder I've been acting crazy?" I asked as I fought back the urge to scream. Instead, I ran my hands over my face and back through my hair while I got myself under control. "Two months ago, Uncle Houston asked me to take over the family's entire criminal enterprise. That added a whole lot more pressure to my already stressful life. And now I've got some lunatic coming after the family. He's already killed one person and injured a few more. He's threatened just about everyone else. He even threatened my pets. To answer your question, Milo . . . that is what has gotten into me lately. Timmy, that is the reason I've been acting crazy. Except it's not an act. I really am going crazy."

"Carrie, I think it's time you threw in the towel," Zeke said. He knelt next to the chair so that we were nearly at eye level with each other. "Clearly this is getting to you. And it can't be healthy. Stop driving yourself nuts and wearing yourself out. Let the Texas Ranger handle the case. If some of our family members wind up getting arrested because of his investigation . . . well, that ain't your fault."

"Hey . . ." Levi jumped up and leaned over the desk. "What if I wind up being one of those people who gets sent to prison? That ain't fair to me."

"You should have thought about that before you broke the law," Milo said.

I took a few deep breaths to help clear my head. "El Lobo is now at the top of my suspect list. But whether he's involved or not, Wes is convinced that at least one of the three assailants is either a Shatner, Palmer, or Devereux. I've ruled a lot of them out by confirming their alibis. Levi, I will have to talk to Babette to confirm yours. Zeke and Milo, I assume you were both here on Sunday morning?"

"I was helping Zeke tend bar Saturday night. After we closed, we stuck around and restocked the bar. We had to be here till at least eleven," Milo said. "Ask your cousin Randy. He was sitting at the bar talking to us most of the morning."

"What about your cousin Nate?" I asked. "I heard he hates Wes for some reason."

"Nate blames Wes for stealing away customers," Levi said.

"And he and Dylan are both upset that their sister has been hooking up with Waylon," Zeke added. "You know Nate's reputation, Carrie. And I'm sure you've seen his arrest record. Nate is not a nice guy, and he's got a violent streak. Dylan is a lot more easygoing than his brother. But he's equally protective of Tina. I can see Nate setting up Wes. Dylan, not so much."

"But I can definitely see both of them beating the crap out of Waylon," Levi said.

"Nate works for me as a bouncer. But he wasn't here on Saturday night," Milo said. "Well, he was here. But he wasn't working. He was in the backroom playing poker with some of our other cousins."

"Can anyone who isn't one of your cousins confirm that?"

Milo shrugged. "Nate's girlfriend can. She was back there with them during all of her breaks. Levi, go get Jane. Tell her that I need to talk to her."

Levi jumped up and rushed out of the room. He came back a few minutes later with a scantily clad woman. Nearly every part of her exposed skin was covered in a layer of glitter.

"Sparkles . . . Long time, no see," I said. I had first encountered Jane—previously known to me only by her stripper name of Sparkles—back in January.

"What do you want?" Sparkles nodded at me. Her rat's nest of teased out, bleached blonde hair barely moved, and the fumes from her hairspray gave me a headache. "And where is that sexy Texas Ranger who was with you back in January?"

Ignoring the question, I said, "I heard you're dating Nate Palmer."

"Yeah. And someday he's gonna marry me. What's it to you?" Sparkles crossed her arms over her chest and tried to glare me. She couldn't quite pull off the glare because a facelift had drawn her eyebrows halfway up her forehead. She looked more surprised than angry. "What does my relationship with Nate got to do with anything?"

"Nothing," I said. "Was he here all Saturday night and Sunday morning."

"Far as I know. He was back there every time I took a break. And we went home together around four," Sparkles said. She then turned around and left the office, slamming the door behind her.

"All right, Timmy," I said as I stood up. "Let's go track down Nate and Dylan."

Leaving the three Palmer brothers arguing in the office, Timmy and I headed down the hallway and into the strip club's main room. As we crossed the room, Alberto approached me.

"Can we talk?"

"I'm a little busy right now, Beto," I said.

"It'll only take a minute," Alberto said as he followed me and Timmy into the small lobby where Heath Palmer was flirting with one of the dancers. "It's important."

"All right," I said to Alberto as I shoved open the door and stepped outside.

Glancing over to where my Jeep was parked near the door, I instinctively knew that something was not right. The right side of the bumper was resting on the concrete parking stop. I ran around to the passenger side and screamed in rage when I saw the handle of a screwdriver protruding from the right front tire. The screwdriver held a note pinned to the side of the flat tire. The note read, "I doubt you're here to change professions. Back off!"

"Son of a bitch!" I yelled. "I know you're around here somewhere, Facundo. And you just crossed the line. No one messes with my Jeep."

I kicked the flat tire in frustration.

"You want me to help you change that?" Alberto asked.

"Yeah. And then I'm going home."

"What about Nate and Dylan Palmer?" Timmy asked.

"Hank's funeral is on Friday. I'll talk to Nate and Dylan there," I said. "Right now, I'm tired and I'm fed up with Facundo."

"Then maybe you should listen to him and back off," Alberto said.

"He's the one who needs to back off."

I leaned against the wall and read through my backlog of text messages as Alberto and Timmy worked together to change my tire. They had just removed the flat tire when a hunk of junk car pulled into the space next to me. Ethan slid out from behind the wheel.

"What are you doing here?" Ethan asked.

"Running down a lead," I said as I gestured over my shoulder. "While I was inside, the asshole tormenting my family sliced my tire."

"Speaking of the asshole . . ." Ethan stepped closer to me and dropped his voice to a whisper. "I overheard Sergeant Boleyn talking to someone on the phone earlier. He's convinced that you created this Facundo guy and had Wesley lie to him about what really happened on Sunday morning."

"What does Boleyn think I'm hiding?"

"He thinks you know exactly who assaulted the boys and that you're covering for them," Boleyn said. "He's also convinced that one of the three assailants is Bubba. Multiple people overheard Bubba threaten Wesley on Saturday night at the Body Farm. Boleyn believes Bubba is behind the whole thing and he's trying to get an arrest warrant."

"First me and now Bubba. And obviously Wes," I said. "Who else is Boleyn going to try to get an arrest warrant for?"

"If he has his way . . . your entire family."

"DETECTIVE SHATNER!" DEPUTY TIMMY GRANT SHOUTED as he burst out of the back door of the sheriff's department and raced across the parking lot to where I had parked my Jeep. "The sheriff needs you in his office right now. Before it gets any uglier."

"What's going on?"

I grabbed my purse off the passenger seat and then hurried across the parking lot. I had spent the morning getting stonewalled by various Palmers. Despite Hank getting killed, most of them were reluctant to provide me with any information that could help me find his killer. Giving up on the Palmers, I grabbed a quick lunch and then swung by the sheriff's department.

"Chief Wollard is here." Timmy herded me towards the building. "Officer Yates is with him. And so is Pastor Kemp. The old one and the young one. They all want to know where you are. And they're yelling at the sheriff because he won't tell them."

"Got to be about Hell House." I tossed my purse to Timmy and took off running towards Uncle Murph's office. When my high-speed entry into the room went unnoticed, I asked, "Heard y'all are looking for me."

Thaddeus Kemp—his face red with rage—pointed at me and screamed, "Arrest that wicked woman!"

Taken aback by the venom in his voice, I asked, "What did I do?"

"Aside from causing my granddaughter to get murdered?" Ambrose muttered.

"You darn well know what you've done, young lady," Chief Wollard said. "And this time you've gone too far. Sergeant Boleyn informed me this morning that you were aware that it was Roxanne Devereux who destroyed Calvary Baptist's Hell House prior to you processing the crime scene for evidence."

"Whoa. Whoa. Whoa," I said as I gestured for Wollard to calm down. "What evidence does Boleyn have?"

"Sergeant Boleyn spoke with Miss Devereux yesterday," Wollard explained. "He had a warrant to look at her phone. While searching her phone, he found a text message from you chastising Miss Devereux and saying that you're going to have to clean up the mess she made at the church."

"There are over two dozen churches in Wyatt County," I pointed out. "How does Boleyn know I was talking about Calvary Baptist?"

Wollard sputtered. "This is inexcusable, Detective Shatner. You're out of control. And so is your entire family. You Shatners and Devereuxs have been running amok in this county for far too long, and, as of now, I'm going to bring an end to it."

"Does this mean you won't be taking our money anymore?" I had a seat on the corner of Uncle Murph's desk and smirked at Wollard. "Because for the past ten years or so, you didn't seem to have much of a problem with getting bribed to look the other way. As I recall, you even asked for a raise once you were promoted to chief."

"Why . . . why . . . this is . . . it's outrageous, I tell you!" Wollard stammered. "How dare you accuse me of taking a bribe?"

"Doesn't sound like Carrie is accusing you of anything," Uncle Murph said. "Sounds to me like she's stating a fact. One that we can very easily prove."

"My dad's probably spinning in his grave knowing you took over his job," Ethan said.

"Frederick . . . Is she speaking the truth?" Ambrose asked, his deep voice rumbling.

"I . . . I . . . I . . ."

"Fred, you are no longer welcome in my church," Thaddeus said. He looked wildly around the room before focusing on Ethan. "Officer Yates, something must be done about this. The Hell House was destroyed. You used to be part of Calvary's youth group. I remember that you were the star of the gluttony scene for several years. You understand the importance of Hell House and its message. You know how many souls we used to save each year. I was bringing that back. I was going to save more souls. But Roxanne Devereux destroyed all of that in a matter of minutes. She and her accomplices need to be punished for their crime."

"I couldn't agree more," Ethan said.

I glanced over at Ethan who was giving me a pleading look. I could easily drag him under the bus with me. And a small part of me wanted to do it. The rest of me didn't want to betray him. Not because I felt any loyalty to him. No, the reason I wouldn't expose him for the time being was because he was still useful to me. If Ethan kept passing along information that he overheard about Boleyn's case, I'd refrain from sticking the knife in his back.

"Let's take a minute and discuss why Roxanne might have been driven to destroy Hell House." I slid off the edge of the desk and paced across the narrow room. "I am not saying that Roxanne destroyed it. But I am saying she never would have done it had you not insulted her, her fiancé, and their daughters on Sunday afternoon at the Pumpkin Patch—"

"What were you doing at the Pumpkin Patch?" Wollard asked Thaddeus.

"Faith and I were leading a group of congregants in protest of the devil worshipping activities being held there," Thaddeus said. "We were handing out Biblical tracts and inviting people to come to Hell House. I merely extended the invitation to Miss Devereux to come through the Hell House so that she can see the error of her ways, repent for her sins, and be saved. I never insulted her."

"You called Roxanne a whore. And you called her daughters bastards," I said. "And you did so again on Tuesday night while at my Uncle Woody's house."

"Sounds like insults to me." Uncle Murph stood up and came around to the front of his desk. "Also sounds like you provoked Roxanne, Pastor Kemp."

"I was speaking the truth. It is not my fault that certain people cannot handle the truth." Thaddeus twirled the ends of his mustache.

"I've heard countless tales of Roxanne's debaucheries from her brother and—"

"Hold on," I said, cutting Thaddeus off. "How do you know Jason?"

"After Jason was released from the juvenile detention center, he came to Calvary Baptist seeking counseling and salvation. I took him under my wing and helped guide him back to the Lord's path. I also got him involved with the youth group. He started out speaking with our younger parishioners about obeying the law and God's commandments. When my father retired as pastor and I took over his duties, Jason stepped up and took over running the youth group. He played a major role in helping me bring back Hell House. I can only imagine how devasted he will be when he finds out that his sister is the one who destroyed it."

That would explain how the three of them got into the church. As the head of the youth group, Jason would have a key to the church. And, if that was the case, they technically couldn't be charged with breaking and entering.

"Yeah, but I'm also sure that Jason didn't appreciate you insulting his only sister."

"Jason is aware of what kind of woman his sister is." Thaddeus snatched a pair of handcuffs off Uncle Murph's desk and held them out to Ethan. "Please arrest Detective Shatner for . . . for accessory to a crime or concealing evidence or something. Just arrest her."

Ethan took the handcuffs from Thaddeus. He then took a step towards me.

"Now hold on there," I said as I moved around to the other side of Uncle Murph's desk. "You can't arrest me because of a text message. A good criminal defense lawyer would get that text stricken from evidence. I would know, my brother-in-law is one of the best criminal defense lawyers in the state. And he would laugh you out of the courtroom if you tried to arrest me on something so flimsy. That text does not prove anything. For all you know, it's an accusation. Not confirmation."

Thaddeus turned to Chief Wollard and asked, "Is she right?"

"Well, she's not wrong," Wollard said. "We don't have any direct evidence that proves Roxanne Devereux was ever in your church. You don't have any security cameras in the building or around the property. There is no physical evidence that can prove Roxanne was there—"

"That's because Detective Shatner destroyed it," Thaddeus said.

"You were hanging over my shoulder almost the entire time I was processing the church for evidence," I said to Thaddeus. "Did you see me tamper with any evidence?"

"Well, no. But—"

Cutting Thaddeus off, I turned to Ethan and asked, "Officer Yates, did you see me destroy or tamper with evidence while in the church?"

"Nope," Ethan said. "And I don't know how you could have. Everything you collected was immediately turned over to me."

Spittle flew out of Thaddeus's mouth as he shouted, "Carrie, you and that no-good family of yours should be behind bars. Whoever this person is that is targeting your family is doing Wyatt County a favor. And I will not let the reckless destruction of my Hell House deter me from saving souls. I can do that without the Hell House."

Ambrose, Ethan, and Wollard followed Thaddeus out of Uncle Murph's office.

Before Wollard slammed the door, he looked back at me and said, "You went too far this time, Carrie. And you probably just cost me my job. You need to learn to keep your mouth shut."

Once we were alone, I turned to Uncle Murph and said, "That was interesting."

"Sure was." Uncle Murph grabbed a box of chocolate chip cookies out of his top desk drawer. "Where the heck were you all morning?"

"Talking to a few Palmers." I grabbed a cookie before Uncle Murph inhaled them. "Do you have any new information for me?"

"I narrowed down your suspect list by a few people." Uncle Murph handed me the list of names that I had given him the day before. Only a couple of the names had been crossed off. "Then Wollard and the Kemps stormed in here looking for you and I got sidetracked."

"Keep looking into these people." I handed the list back to Uncle Murph and headed for the door. "I'm going to meet Quaranta out at the Body Farm to go over the Torture Barn for anything the crime scene unit might have missed. Then I'm going home to update my notes and go over all of the threatening messages and gifts that our family members received between yesterday and today."

If I had time, I would also swing by the hospital to talk to my cousin Kermit. Like his younger brother, Keaton, Kermit had been jumped while leaving the gym. A Devil masking wearing individual had hit him from behind with a baseball bat or similar weapon. Keaton had hit the ground hard and broken his jaw. He also had suffered two cracked ribs.

"Are you any closer to solving this. Carrie."

"I don't know. But Facundo keeps threatening me, so I'll take that as I sign that I'm getting closer," I said. "I just feel like I'm missing something that is staring me right in the face."

CHAPTER TWENTY

"**T**RICK OR TREAT!"

I held the plastic candy dish tightly against my chest as I eyed up the three costumed kids crowding my porch. The little girl was dressed as a unicorn. The younger of the two boys was a pirate, and the older boy was a zombie football player.

Andrew prodded me in the back. "They're kids, Carrie. Give 'em some candy."

I pushed open the storm door and then dropped candy bars in the kids' treat bags. Once they had their treats, they raced back to where their dad was waiting for them at the end of the driveway. The dad—who was wearing a wizard hat and cape—raised his arm and waved at me. I tentatively waved back. The man looked familiar. I assumed he was one of my neighbors.

"Carrie, you have got to stop eyeing up everyone. You're starting to creep people out," Andrew said. He was wearing an orange t-shirt that had "here for the boos" written across the chest. "Do you really think this Facundo guy is going to come trick or treating? Where would he get the kids?"

"It's not implausible that Facundo has his own kids. Especially if Facundo is a Shatner, Devereux, or Palmer," I said. "One of his cronies could also have kids and he could have borrowed them for the evening."

"I think you're starting to lose it, Carrie."

Ignoring Andrew, I stepped out onto the porch and handed candy bars to two kids who looked a couple years too old to be trick or treating.

I wasn't going to say anything. I'd rather have them going door to door collecting treats than coming out later and playing tricks.

There was a lull after the two teenagers ran off. Back when I was a kid, the neighborhood had been full of trick or treaters. My parents would go through bags of candy each Halloween. These days there weren't as many kids in the neighborhood, and I was lucky if I had twelve to fifteen kids come by on Halloween.

I was debating turning off the front lights and calling it a night when my cell phone rang. Instinctively, I knew who it was.

"Nice wig, Carrie," Facundo said in his robotic voice. "You should wear your hair like that more often."

Subconsciously, I reached up and patted the black beehive wig. Two white steaks stretched from the temples to the top of the beehive. Bride of Frankenstein had been my go-to costume for the past few years.

I walked out into the middle of my front yard and looked around. "I've got plenty of candy left over, Facundo. You're welcome to come over and get some."

"Who says I haven't already?" Facundo asked. "You know, you're the only person in your neighborhood handing out full size candy bars. A couple of your other neighbors handed out some decent stuff. But the rest weren't worth it."

"Is the woman on the corner still handing out toothbrushes and mini toothpastes?"

"She's also handing out floss now."

I continued to peer into the shadows, hoping to catch sight of Facundo. There were still a few kids running around, and I spotted a few of my neighbors sitting out on their porches. Facundo could be any one of them.

"What do you want, Facundo?"

"For you to stay out of this and to let me finish my mission," Facundo said. "I would really hate for something to happen to you, Carrie. Don't sacrifice yourself for people who aren't worth saving."

Before I could respond, the line went dead.

"WHOSE TRUCK ARE YOU DRIVING?" Alberto asked as he pulled up next to me. It was midnight, and we were meeting at a defunct gas station outside of Holler. "And why are you driving it?"

"It's my neighbor's truck," I said. "Facundo is watching me. I didn't want to risk having him follow me here, so I borrowed Floyd's truck."

"Does Floyd know you borrowed his truck?"

"Yes. I said I borrowed it. Not stole it."

While I would gladly have led Facundo away from my house, I couldn't risk having him follow me to the late-night meeting. To hopefully prevent Facundo from seeing me leave, I had climbed out of the guest room window. The window was partially obscured by an overgrown lilac bush, and my hair and clothes had gotten snagged on several branches. After extricating myself from the bush, I crept along the fence line until it butted up against the decaying shed. I then climbed over the fence and dropped down into my neighbor's backyard.

My overly nosy neighbors, Floyd and Margie, lived diagonally across the street from me. Unable to take the direct route to their house, I meandered around as I did my best to stick to the shadows as I cut through the yards and climbed over fences. I also had to circumvent pools, flower gardens, and other obstacles. It reminded me of the times when I had snuck out of the house as a teenager. Except, back then, the only homicidal maniac that I had to worry about was my mother.

Floyd and Margie were waiting for me by the back door when I got to their house. I had called them to let them know what was going on and ask if I could borrow their truck. Floyd had been more than willing to hand over the keys, but he wanted information in return. I shared what I could about my investigation—wetting their curiosity more than satiating it. I also informed them that I had a stalker who was lurking around the neighborhood. Neither Floyd nor Margie had noticed any strangers hanging around in recent days, but they promised to keep an eye out. Floyd also volunteered to patrol the streets, but I told him that wasn't necessary.

When Floyd and Margie finally let me leave, I wasted another half-an-hour driving around Wyatt County to make sure no one was following me. It would have been easy to pick up a tail since there was hardly anyone driving around on the backroads at midnight.

"What's this meeting about?" I asked. "And where's Schmitt?"

"Lieutenant Schmitt couldn't make it."

That seemed odd—especially since Schmitt was the one who had called for the meeting. At least, that's what Alberto had told me.

"Then why are we meeting?" I asked.

"Figured we may as well catch up," Alberto said. He propped his elbow on his car's windowsill and looked up at me. The truck was sitting about two feet higher than his car. "Have Dale or Dickie said anything else about me being an undercover cop?"

I shrugged even though Alberto couldn't really see me in the moonlight. "If they have, they didn't say it to me."

"That's good. It's been getting boring hanging out around the trailer all day. I'm thinking of putting in an appearance at Hank's funeral tomorrow. I'll see how your family reacts to me publicly before I see any of them privately."

"Maybe you should just go home. This is almost over. There's no point in you hanging around and getting caught up in the middle of it."

"And miss all the fun?" Alberto chuckled. "Besides, I'm not like Sergeant Hardy. Unlike your knight in shining armor—that is what Facundo called Sergeant Hardy, right?"

"Prince Charming."

"Yeah, Prince Charming . . . unlike him, I ain't leaving town with my tail between my legs just because some nutcase made some lame threat against me."

"Excuse me?" I leaned out the window and glared at Alberto. "Did you just call Jerrod a coward?"

"If he really cared about you, he wouldn't have abandoned you," Alberto said. "But what was he doing here anyway? I thought y'all broke up."

"We pretended to break up. And I don't see how it's any of your business anyway."

"How is it not my business? I thought we had something going on."

"Seriously?" I asked, wondering if Alberto had hit his head while acting at the Body Farm and was suffering from a concussion. I had assumed he was developing some actual feelings for me, but I had no idea that he was viewed our fake relationship as the beginning of a real one. "Whatever we pretended to have going on is just that. Pretend."

"I know it's pretend," Alberto said. "But I was hoping it might turn into something real."

"Yeah, well, it's not going to," I said before I turned the key and fired the engine. "Now, if you'll excuse me, I need to get back to searching for the people threatening my family."

"HEARD YOU HAD SOME EXCITEMENT over at your place this morning," Uncle Murph said when he joined me in the condolence line at the End of the Line Funeral Home on Friday morning. "Are Floyd and Margie okay?"

"Shaken. And they have a couple bumps and bruises. But they'll be all right."

Just before six o'clock this morning, Andrew had burst into my bedroom and rudely awoken me as he waved around a bouquet of yellow roses. Cousin Skeeter had found the bouquet on the front porch a few minutes earlier when he had gone outside to get the newspaper. Written on the back of the attached card were the words "From: Your Secret Admirer." The flowers had to be from Facundo. It creeped me out that not only did he know that my favorite color was purple, he also knew my favorite flower was yellow roses.

What creeped me out even more was that Facundo or one of his cronies had been able to place the bouquet on my well-lit front porch without any of my "armed guards" noticing. It made me question how qualified they were at their jobs. Andrew, Skeeter, Luke, and Junior might be doing a good job watching my pets. But it didn't seem like any of the guys thought to keep an eye on what might be going on outside.

Fortunately, Floyd had been watching the front of my house with night vison goggles, and he had seen a person wearing a Devil mask creeping through my faux cemetery.

Unfortunately, Floyd decided to take matters into his own hands and tried to sneak up on the prowler. Floyd swore he got in at least one punch before the prowler hit him with a taser. When Margie attempted to come to her husband's rescue, she got tased as well.

Not long after finding the bouquet of yellow roses on the front porch, Skeeter had come across Floyd and Margie in the mausoleum. The prowler had used the sashes from their bathrobes to hogtie them, and he'd stuffed their socks in their mouths to gag them.

After helping free Floyd and Margie from their confines, I got dressed in my most somber but professional looking outfit and then headed over to the funeral home.

"Boy, do I hate funerals," Uncle Murph muttered.

"I know," I said as I handed him a copy of Hank Garrett the Third's funeral program. "You remind me of how much you hate funerals every time we go to one."

I stood on my tiptoes and tried to see over the heads of the fifty or so people who packed the stylishly decorated lobby at the End of the Line Funeral Home. Hank Garrett the Third's casket was on display at the far end of the room, and the lengthy line of mourners was gradually snaking its way past. Hank's parents and sisters stood at the head of the casket to greet the mourners and accept their condolences. The line of mourners stretched out into the funeral home's parking lot, and late-comers were forced to park in the grass or across the street at the VFW Hall. If too many more people showed up, the funeral would be standing room only.

I had been stuck in line for almost half an hour and had only just made it inside the building when Uncle Murph joined me. I could have used my badge to jump to the front of the line, but that seemed rude.

Uncle Murph held his arm in front of his face and sneezed into this elbow. He then wiped his nose on the cuff of his suit jacket.

"Gesundheit." I pulled a tissue out of my purse and handed it to Uncle Murph. "You're an adult. Don't use your sleeve."

"It's these damn flowers." Uncle Murph gestured towards one of the nearby floral sprays. "I've got pollen allergies."

"Same here," I said. The combined scent of various flowers—not to mention the different perfumes and body odors—was overpowering, and I was getting a headache. I plucked the card off the plastic holder to see who had sent the potent floral arrangement. "It's from El Lobo."

"The Palmers have been loyal customers of his for years," Uncle Murph pointed out.

"Still a little weird that a drug dealer is sending funerary flowers. Definitely not what I would expect from a guy like El Lobo."

"What would you expect him to send? A brick of cocaine?" Uncle Murph chuckled. "Besides, it's not like El Lobo can show up at the funeral home to pay his respects in person."

"Why not? There are plenty of other criminals in attendance," I said. And not all those criminals belonged to either the Palmer, Shatner, or Devereux families. I recognized at least half a dozen people who I had arrested over the past four years. I leaned closer to Uncle Murph and whispered, "You think El Lobo could be behind what happened to the boys?"

"It's crossed my mind." Uncle Murph shuffled forward two steps as the line moved. "Are you really meeting with him tonight at the football game?"

"Yeah, I am."

El Lobo had called me late last night to remind me of our scheduled meeting. We also discussed when and where we would meet up with each other at the football stadium.

Across the room, Hank's mother let out an ear-piercing wail as she threw herself across the foot of the casket. Hank Garrett the Second, along with the aid of his daughters, wrestled his wife away from the casket and into a highbacked chair that was lined in gold velvet. Hank's mother continued to keen as the mourners who were waiting outside pushed into the overcrowded lobby for a closer look at the hysterics. The Wyatt County deputies and Holler police officers who had been enlisted to help maintain crowd control and direct traffic worked together to herd some of the people back outside.

"Funerals should be private affairs. I bet at least a third of the people here didn't even know Hank. They're just being nosy because he was murdered." Uncle Murph pointed at a short, plump man with thick glasses and bushy eyebrows who stood in line a few feet in front of us and said, "Like that guy . . . I think he's a reporter for one of the news stations up in Tyler."

"No, he's not. That's Omar Palmer's son Magnus."

"You sure about that?" Uncle Murph asked as he pulled a packet of salted peanuts out of his jacket pocket. "I ain't seen Magnus for a while. Not since you arrested him a few summers ago. What was he allegedly doing?"

"Selling homemade fireworks. And there was nothing alleged about it. I caught him in the act." I took a few steps forward as the line shifted. "And you saw Magnus the other day at the Arm Bar. You're the one who broke up the fist fight between him and Uncle Delmar."

"Oh yeah . . . I forgot about that." Uncle Murph popped a handful of peanuts in his mouth. "Hey, Carrie, what do you think the odds are that one of Hank's killers is here for the funeral?"

"Well, considering Wes thinks that either a Shatner, Palmer, or Devereaux is involved . . . and almost all of them are here . . . I'd say the odds are pretty high that one of the assailants is in attendance," I said.

As we moved past the set of double doors that opened up into the chapel, I glanced inside at the rows of seats that were beginning to fill up. Standing towards the front of the spacious room were a group of Palmers—including Nate and Dylan. Set out on the low stage behind them were five gigantic floral arrangements made up entirely of orange chrysanthemums. The flowers had been positioned on mesh screens to spell out "Hank 3." On either side of the flowers were poster-sized pictures of Hank at various ages.

"I'll be back," I said as I moved towards the chapel. "I need to talk to someone."

"I'll be here," Uncle Murph called after me. "This line in moving slower than an asthmatic snail."

I headed up the chapel's center aisle. Nate and Dylan were not the only Palmers who I didn't have alibis for early Sunday morning. Nor were they the only Palmers who fit the description that Wesley had given me of two out of the three assailants. But, as far as I knew, Nate and Dylan were the only two who had a motive to assault Wesley, Waylon, and Hank.

Nate was at least six feet tall, and it looked like he weighed over two hundred pounds. He also had a reputation for being violent. Nate had been a year ahead of me in school, and I had experienced his excessive bullying firsthand. After all, his favorite targets were Shatners. Nate had gotten suspended at least a dozen times for starting fights and beating up other kids. He was finally expelled during his junior year of high school. Nate then did a brief stint at military school, before winding up in a juvenile detention center. He had been in and out of prison since then. In fact, if Nate's trial for aggravated assault hadn't kept getting delayed, he would be sitting in a jail cell right now.

I didn't know Dylan very well—he had been a couple of years behind me in school and we had never really interacted. As far as I knew, he didn't have any assault charges on his record. What I did know was that he was tall and skinny like the person Wesley claimed had cut off his finger. But what reason would Dylan have had to do that?

"I need to talk to you two," I said to Nate and Dylan.

"'Bout what?" Nate asked.

"Probably 'bout how you threatened to kick Waylon's ass because you didn't approve of our relationship."

I glanced over to where Tina Palmer was perched on a chair at the end of the second row. She was using the rear-facing camera on her phone to check her makeup.

"I heard there wasn't anything serious between you and Waylon," I said to Tina.

"There wasn't. It was causal," Tina said as she rummaged around in her purse and pulled out a tube of deep purple lipstick. "And that's mainly what Nate was mad about."

"You deserve better than some casual fling, Tina," Nate said. "Especially with some good-for-nothing criminal like Waylon Shatner."

"First of all, you're one to talk. You're a 'good-for-nothing crimi-nal' too," Tina said. "And second, doesn't your lady friend with the excessive glitter deserve more than . . . whatever it is that you two got going on?"

"That's different."

"No, it ain't."

"What is going on between you and Sparkles?" I asked Nate.

"Nothing much. We just hook up sometimes."

"She told me that y'all are gonna get married someday."

Nate snorted. "Not in this lifetime."

Dylan stepped closer to me and asked, "You really think my brother and I were involved in what happened to Hank and your cousins?"

"I don't know," I said. "Were you?"

"No," Nate and Dylan said at the same time.

"Sure, we weren't happy that Waylon was hooking up with our sister," Dylan continued. "And we were mad at Wes for stealing some of our customers."

"But we wouldn't set them up like that," Nate said. "You know how I operate . . . I want my victims to see me coming."

"And we definitely wouldn't have killed our own flesh and blood," Dylan said.

"Even if he did betray our family by teaming up with Wes," Nate added.

"Where were you two on Sunday night after you left the Body Farm?" I asked.

"Poker game in the back room of the strip club," Nate said.

"With all of them," Dylan gestured towards where some of their cousins were huddled together. "Our cousins Peter, John, Heath, and Chris were all there. And so were Amelia's, Harriet's, and Ramona's husbands. We were there all night. You can ask any of 'em."

"Hank was supposed to be there, too," Nate said. "Instead . . ."

"Anyone there who isn't related to you?" I asked.

Nate and Dylan both shook their heads, and Dylan said, "You'll just have to take our word for it."

"And y'alls word is about as good as gold," I said. "Fool's gold."

I turned around and headed back up the aisle towards the lobby. I had to pause every few feet to wave at someone or say hi. The Shatners and Devereuxes were starting to take over the chairs directly behind where the Palmers would be sitting. Lieutenant Underwood and Sergeant Boleyn were on the far end of a middle row. Alberto had claimed a seat in the back. And there were other people scattered throughout the chapel who I knew or, at least, had a passing acquaintance with. Naturally, they all wanted an update on my investigation.

"I see you got far," I said to Uncle Murph when I rejoined him in the lobby a few minutes later. "I don't think you've moved ten feet."

"This line would be moving a lot faster if they'd just kept the dang casket closed," Uncle Murph grumbled as he shuffled forward a couple steps. "That's what I hate most about funerals. Putting the corpse on display. When I die, I don't want people lining up to gawk at me."

"I'll make a note of that."

"Considering how bad Hank looked, I'm surprised this ain't a closed casket funeral."

"It was going to be closed casket, but Naomi worked her magic."

Cousin Naomi was the mortuary makeup artist at the End of the Line Funeral Home. Not long after graduating from high school, Naomi's fiancé practically left her at the altar when he got cold feet and called off the wedding two days before the event. A week later, Naomi packed up her things and headed north to Nashville. Without asking if I was okay with it or not, Naomi moved into my apartment. She spent two weeks crying her eyes out and declaring that her life was over before she pulled herself together and enrolled in cosmetology school. After a brief stint working at a high-end salon in Nashville, Naomi decided she would much rather work with the dead, opposed to the living. The dead were much less demanding.

Naomi had told me—in far greater detail than I had needed to hear—about how she had reconstructed the damaged part of Hank's skull using molding clay. To cover the heavy bruising on Hank's face, Naomi had used an airbrush to apply a layer of white liquid makeup. She had then added a layer of flesh colored makeup on top. Naomi claimed that her only difficulty had been in reconstructing Hank's broken nose. No matter what she did, she couldn't quite get it to resemble what Hank's nose had looked like prior to the assault. But the Garretts had been pleased with her work, and they had decided to go ahead with an open casket.

Uncle Murph and I inched forward a few more feet and peered down at the casket. Hank's head and upper body were propped up on a white pillow. His lifeless hands were clasped over his chest, and a white sheet covered the lower half of his body. The area around Hank's left eye was a bit swollen, but he otherwise looked good.

"I'm sorry Hank," I murmured as I placed my hand on his shoulder. "I promise I'll find the person who did this."

"Have y'all figured out who killed my brother?" Hank's sister Harriet asked as Uncle Murph and I approached the family.

"I'm working on it," I said. "I might not know who did it yet. But I have a long list of people who I know didn't do it."

"That ain't much help," Amelia snapped. "What's taking so long?"

"This ain't TV, Amelia," Uncle Murph said. "You can't expect Carrie to neatly solve this in an hour time slot."

Amelia looked like she was ready to argue. Maybe even throw punches. I was mentally and physically preparing for the assault when I felt my phone vibrate in my purse.

"Sorry. Gotta take this," I said as I grabbed my phone. Leaving Uncle Murph to deal with the Garretts, I walked a few feet away. "What's up, Tawny?"

"Are you somewhere private?" Tawny whispered into the phone.

"No." I glanced around the funeral home's packed lobby. "I'm at Hank's viewing."

"Well, can you go somewhere private."

"Yeah. Give me a second," I said.

To the right of the chapel was a corridor that led to the back part of the funeral home. Along the corridor were the bathrooms and the casket showroom. Both bathrooms were occupied, but the showroom was empty. I locked the door behind me and then walked through the maze of caskets to the other side of the room where a glass display case was packed full of urns in every conceivable shape and color. The End of the Line was the only funeral home in Wyatt County, and the owner, Oswald Line, liked to joke that he had a monopoly on death.

"Okay, Tawny," I said. "What's going on?"

"I just wanted to let you know that this morning Wes had a septo-rhinoplasty to fix his broken nose and is in the recovery room right now. The doctors plan to release him tomorrow."

"That's good."

"No, it's not," Tawny said. "I mean, it's good for Wes to get his nose fixed. But Sergeant Boleyn has an arrest warrant for him. The hospital's medical staff is required to release Wes to either Boleyn or a State Trooper."

"Oh, yeah, that's definitely not good," I said. Uncle Houston had bribed all the local judges. I wanted to know which one of the judges had broken his word to Uncle Houston and signed the arrest warrant for Wesley. I also wanted to know what the warrant was for. "Is there any way I can bust Wes out before he's released tomorrow?"

"That's why I'm calling. A couple nurses and orderlies are willing to help smuggle Wes out of the hospital—"

"Won't they get in trouble if someone finds out that they helped him escape?"

"The security cameras are all going to mysteriously malfunction at the time of Wes's escape," Tawny said. "I have no idea why these nurses and orderlies are so willing to help. But they insist."

"Even with the security cameras malfunctiojning, how do they plan to get him out of the hospital without anyone noticing?"

"That's the other reason why I'm calling," Tawny said. "They need a plan, and they need it now. Since Wes was under anesthesia, there isn't a State Trooper in the recovery room with him. This might be the only chance you have to get him out of here. Because once he wakes up and they take him back up to his room, the two State Troopers guarding the door have strict instructions to not let anyone in the room that isn't hospital personnel. And Wes isn't allowed out of the room unless he's in cuffs."

"All right." I ran my hand back through my curls while I racked my brain for a plan. "Tell the nurses and orderlies to get Wes down to the morgue and into a body bag. I'll take care of the rest."

CHAPTER TWENTY-ONE

Ignoring the sign that said "Employees Only", I shoved open the door and walked into the funeral home's preparation area. The small room reeked of embalming fluid and disinfectant, and the combined scents added to my pollen-induced headache.

"I need to borrow the hearse."

Ozzie Line—the funeral director's only son and the head mortician at the End of the Line—looked up from where he was scrubbing one of the steel embalming tables. "What the heck could you possibly need the hearse for, Carrie?"

"I'd really rather not say."

"Then I'd really rather not let you borrow it," Ozzie said. His shoulder-length black hair was tucked behind his ears, and I could see the top part of his Grim Reaper tattoo peeking out over the deep V-neck of his t-shirt. Having grown up in the funeral business, Ozzie was creepily obsessed with death. "Besides, we're gonna need the hearse in the next hour or two to transport the casket to the cemetery."

"If you need a hearse that bad, why not borrow Uncle Elvin's hearse?" Naomi asked as she emerged from the supply closet with a cart laden with hair products and makeup supplies.

"Because Uncle Elvin's hearse is hardly inconspicuous," I said. Someone would be sure to notice the Body Farm's hearse parked outside the hospital's morgue—especially since Uncle Elvin had plastered Body Farm logos all over the hood and sides. "What if I promise to have your hearse back before the funeral service is over?"

"I still want to know what you need it for, Carrie," Ozzie said.

"And I would really rather not tell you. The less you know, the better."

"That means Carrie needs it for something illegal," Naomi said.

"Then why didn't you say so? I'm more than willing to help. Remember, Carrie, I went to high school with Dale, Kermit, and Festus. They involved me in their shenanigans when we were kids. This will be like old times." Ozzie tossed the rag into a bucket of sudsy water. "So, are you transporting moonshine or drugs?"

"What?"

"Shhhh . . ." Naomi admonished Ozzie as she slapped a hand over his mouth. "He's just joking, Carrie."

"No, he's not," I said. I wanted to ask Ozzie to expand on his comment, but I didn't have any time to waste. "Look, I need the hearse to smuggle my cousin Wes out of the hospital. A couple orderlies are going to take him down to the morgue and they're going to stick him in a body bag. I need the hearse to pick him up."

"Carrie, we don't . . ." Ozzie's chuckle morphed into a full-blown belly laugh. Within seconds, he was doubled over at the waist with tears streaming down his cheeks. "We don't . . ."

"What he's trying to say is that we don't use the hearse to pick up bodies," Naomi said when I turned to her for an explanation. "We use a van."

"Then can I borrow the van?" I asked.

"Of course." Ozzie used the hem of his t-shirt to wipe away his tears. "It just so happens that I need to go pick up a body at the morgue. An elderly man died this morning. We can head over to the hospital right now and pick up Wes and the corpse."

"I'm coming, too!" Naomi said as she shoved her supply cart into the corner of the room.

I followed Ozzie and Naomi through the funeral home's supply closet and out into the garage. Ozzie opened the back of the van and gestured for me to climb inside. Naomi had already claimed the passenger seat. There weren't any seats in the back, and I had no other option than to sit on the floor. It would be a fun trip back sitting next to a corpse.

During the fifteen-minute drive to Wyatt County General Hospital, I forced Ozzie to tell me about how he occasionally allowed some of my uncles and cousins to use the funeral home's hearse to transport moonshine and drugs throughout East Texas. Since it was highly unlikely that any law enforcement officers would pull over a hearse, it was a rather ingenious way to smuggle contraband—especially since they hid all the illegal products in one of the funeral home's display caskets. After all, even if they did get pulled over, the chances of a law enforcement officer looking in the casket were between slim and none.

At the hospital, Naomi and I stayed in the van while Ozzie and the two orderlies brought first one and then another body bag outside and loaded them into the back of the van. Before slamming the doors shut, one of the orderlies told me that Wesley had come out from under the anesthesia but that he was very loopy. He also explained that one of the nurses was going to make it look like Wesley had escaped under his own power while he was being wheeled upstairs.

"Where to, Carrie?" Ozzie asked as he climbed in behind the wheel and pulled away from the entrance to the morgue. "Or are we taking Wes back to the funeral home with us?"

"No, we can't take Wes back to the funeral home. There's too many people there right now," I said. I wondered how much time we had before Wesley was reported missing. "We need to take him somewhere that no one would ever think to look for him."

"And where's that?" Naomi asked.

"Whispering Pines Trailer Park," I said as I leaned over the body bag closest to me and yanked the zipper partway down. The cloudy brown eyes of an elderly man stared back at me. "Whoops. Wrong one."

I tugged the zipper back up and then moved closer to the other bag. I'd barely pulled the zipper down when Wesley's redhead popped out. A massive white bandage covered his nose. Wesley looked around the back of the van before turning his unfocused eyes towards me.

"You've got two heads." Wesley giggled. "Am I in a sleeping bag? Are we camping?"

"Yep, we're camping," I said as I helped Wesley climb out of the body bag. He then toppled over and landed on top of the corpse. "Someday I'll expect you to thank me for this."

Within minutes, we arrived at the trailer park and Ozzie parked the cargo van in front of Alberto's trailer. It took all three of us to get Wesley out of the van and onto his feet.

"Isn't this where Dale's ex-girlfriend got murdered?" Naomi asked me as she helped Ozzie propel Wesley towards the trailer. "Why are we hiding Wes here?"

"Because Beto lives here now." I walked around the water-stained mattress that lay in Alberto's miniscule front yard and approached the front door. "And Beto owes me a favor."

While undercover, Alberto was renting one of the trailers that my uncles Sterling and Vernon owned. Alberto's trailer was one of the six single-wide trailers on Cedar Lane in the Whispering Pines trailer park. "Lane" was a misnomer considering it was a cul-de-sac. The trailer was infamous because a double murder had taken place there earlier in the year. For that reason, my uncles knocked fifty-bucks a month off the rent to entice Alberto to live there.

"But I saw Beto at the funeral home. How are we going to get in?" Naomi asked.

"With a key." I picked up a small bronze hedgehog outdoor decoration and twisted off the head. Inside the hedgehog was a key.

"You claim Beto ain't your boyfriend, but you know where he hides his house key?"

"I also know where you hide your key," I said as I used the key to unlock the front door.

"Yeah. But I'm your cousin," Naomi said as she abandoned Ozzie and Wesley to follow me inside the single-wide trailer. "It smells like wet dog in here."

"That's because the roof leaked during the storm," I said. I held the door open while Ozzie helped Wesley stumble inside. "Let's put him on the couch."

We got Wesley settled on the lumpy, plaid couch and turned on the TV for him to watch. Wesley immediately struck up a one-sided conversation with the morning talk show hosts.

After getting Wesley settled, I herded Naomi and Ozzie outside. We climbed back in the van and then headed for the funeral home that was on the eastern side of Holler. Leaving Ozzie and Naomi to unload the corpse, I slipped into the chapel and had a seat next to Alberto in the back row. The Methodist minister had handed over the podium to Hank Garrett the Second, and he was in the middle of a speech about his son. I noticed that the number 3 that had been created out of orange chrysanthemums was missing, and that there were orange petals all over the stage.

I leaned closer to Alberto and whispered, "What did I miss?"

"Your uncle Woody and Hank the Second exchanged words before the funeral started. Hank tried to bash your uncle over the head with a flower arrangement, but he hit the funeral director by mistake. Some of your deputies broke things up before it got out of hand."

"Can't the Shatners or Palmers get through one funeral without starting a fight?"

"Apparently not," Alberto said. "Where have you been?"

"I went to see a man about a horse," I whispered to Alberto, "And, just so you know, when you get home, Wesley is in your trailer."

"How the heck did Wes get there? He's supposed to be in the hospital."

"And he was until about half-an-hour ago," I said. "Now he's at your trailer."

"Carrie . . ." Alberto leaned forward and pressed Hank's obituary card against his forehead. "I can't harbor a fugitive that my own department is going to be looking for."

"Lieutenant Schmitt offered to pull you out," I reminded Alberto. "You're the one who insisted on staying undercover."

"And it might be the biggest mistake of my life."

Hank the Second had a seat, and the minister returned to the podium to finish up the funeral service. Afterwards, I headed outside to wait for Uncle Murph so that I could fill him in on the latest developments. I was leaning against the front bumper of Uncle Murph's car while checking my phone for updates when Sergeant Boleyn stomped across the parking lot and knocked the phone out of my hand.

"Where is he?"

"Where's who?" I asked as I knelt to pick up my phone.

"Wesley."

"I'm assuming he's at the hospital."

"He's not." Boleyn leaned closer to me and screamed. "Somehow Wesley managed to get away from the nurse who was taking him back to his room after surgery. I can't believe he did it without help. Not when he was just under anesthesia. The hospital security team and State Troopers are searching the hospital, but they can't find your cousin anywhere. Where is he?"

"How should I know?" I asked. I leaned back as far as I could to get away from Boleyn. "I've been here the whole time. I didn't know he'd gone missing until you just told me."

"Let me talk to Detective Shatner," Lieutenant Underwood said as he roughly pulled Boleyn away from me. After Boleyn had walked out of earshot, Underwood turned to me and asked, "Do you know where your cousin is?"

"Yes. And he's safe."

"Carrie . . . when Lieutenant Schmitt made this deal with you, we agreed to overlook any of your past indiscretions. We weren't giving you a hall pass to commit more."

"Technically you did," I pointed out. "Both you and Lieutenant Schmitt told me to do what I had to do. Which is what I did this morning. I'm not proud of myself. But I have to look out for Wesley's wellbeing. Boleyn isn't going to. How did he get an arrest warrant anyway?"

"Someone approached Boleyn with solid evidence of Wesley selling drugs. I don't have all of the details yet. But, from what I understand, things don't look good for Wesley. He's being charged with trafficking in a prohibited or controlled substance."

"Shoot. That's a felony." I leaned closer to Underwood and said, "Look, I've got a way to make it up to you. So maybe we can overlook my . . . helping Wesley evade arrest."

"This better be good."

"You know who El Lobo is?"

"Carrie, every law enforcement officer in East Texas has heard of El Lobo."

"How would you like to arrest him tonight?"

MY EARPIECE CRACKLED AND LIEUTENANT SCHMITT said, "I don't think El Lobo's coming."

"No, I don't think he's coming either," I said. Absentmindedly, I scratched at the itchy tape that held the wire taped to my chest. The small recording device was hooked to the front of my bra, and the microphone was hidden in the folds around the neck of my hooded sweatshirt. "I can't believe I got stood up by a drug dealer."

Last night, El Lobo and I had agreed to meet near where the food trucks were set up behind the one endzone. The plan had been to meet at the beginning of halftime. Now the third quarter was about to start, and El Lobo had yet to make an appearance.

The area behind the endzone was crowded, and, from all sides, I could feel eyes on me. Lieutenant Underwood had called in Lieutenant Schmitt and some of his agents in the Drug Unit to help bring El Lobo into custody. There were a handful of DEA agents lurking around as well. They had been hunting El Lobo for years and had wanted in on the action.

I had also told a few Shatners, Palmers, and Devereuxs about when and where I would be meeting with El Lobo. The only thing was that none of them knew that I was setting him up.

I watched one of the Big Pine players return the second half kick-off for a touchdown and then asked, "What do you want me to do?"

"You may as well meet us out at the van," Schmitt replied.

Hardy, who had been standing by the funnel cake truck along with Cousin Bubba, Red Devereux, and Chris Palmer, walked over to join me as I weaved my way through the crowd of people. I glanced around, wondering who were undercover DPS or DEA agents and who were innocent bystanders enjoying a mid-game snack.

"Here," Hardy said as he handed me an oily, powdered sugar-encrusted paper plate that held the remains of a funnel cake. "It looks like you could use a pick-me-up."

I tore off a piece of the fried dough and stuffed it into my mouth. A cloud of powdered sugar billowed out of my mouth as I mumbled, "Thanks."

Hardy and I exited the stadium and then walked to the far end of the high schools' parking lot in silence. The DEA had parked their surveillance van under a burnt-out overhead light, leaving the black van in shadows. Decals on the sides of the van advertised a fictitious soft pretzel company.

As Hardy and I approached, the van's door slid open and Lieutenant Schmitt stuck his bald head out. Behind him, computers, monitors, and other electronics lined the one side of the van's interior.

"Don't worry, Carrie," Schmitt said. "I'm not all that surprised El Lobo didn't show up. At best, I figured we had a fifty-fifty shot of arresting him tonight."

"It did seem like a weird place to have a meeting," I said as I stuffed the last bite of funnel cake in my mouth. I then removed the tiny earpiece and tossed it to Schmitt. "Very public place for a private guy like El Lobo."

"Or maybe there was never supposed to be a meeting." The van's door slid the rest of the way open to reveal an agent from the DEA's Houston division. The middle-aged Black man glared at me as he said, "Maybe you were setting us up to look like fools, Detective Shatner."

"Why would Carrie set us up, Foster?" Schmitt asked the agent. "Do I have to remind you of the conversation we had earlier today? You know, when I explained to you about how Carrie has been providing us with information on her family's criminal endeavors."

"I remember the conversation quite vividly," Agent Foster said. "I also remember you forcing me to sign paperwork in which I acknowledge

Detective Shatner's assistance and promised not to hold her accountable for any of her past indiscretions."

"That's the deal," Schmitt said.

"Look, I don't know why El Lobo didn't show up." My phone vibrated and I pulled it out of my sweatshirt pocket to see who was calling. "But here's El Lobo's opportunity to tell us."

"El Lobo's calling?" Schmitt asked. After I nodded in confirmation, he leaned back in the van and instructed someone to trace the call. "Keep him talking as long as you can, Carrie."

I motioned for everyone to be quiet before I answered the call.

"*Hola, Mamacita,*" El Lobo crooned. "I will never understand you *Tejanos* and your obsession with *fútbol americano*. Why call it *foot*ball when they rarely use their feet?"

"Maybe if you had showed up for our meeting, we could have watched the game together and you could have developed a better understanding of the sport."

El Lobo chuckled. "I had every intention of coming to see you, *Mamacita*. That is, until a . . . *cómo se dice en Inglés* . . . a little birdie told me that you were setting me up with *la policia*."

"Well, someone was lying to you. I—"

Cutting me off, El Lobo snapped, "No, *Mamacita*. The only one lying is you. And who said I did not show up? I see you right now. *Te ves hermosa esta noche*. The *azul* of your sweatshirt brings out the *azul* in your eyes."

"How?" I asked as I frantically looked around the parking lot. I didn't see anyone lurking nearby. "Where are you?"

"I see you, *Mamacita*. But you no see me."

"Get in the van," Hardy said.

After shoving me into the van, Hardy climbed in and then slammed the door shut. Meanwhile, Schmitt was on the radio telling the undercover agents that El Lobo was somewhere on the property.

El Lobo chuckled. "You'll never find me, *Mamacita*. And you can tell the agent not to bother tracking my call. *No soy tan estúpido*. I use *teléfono* that cannot be tracked."

I doubted that the agents would find him. There were no known photographs of El Lobo. He had no distinguishing features and was of average weight and height. No one knew how old he was—though the consensus was that he was in his late-thirties or early-forties. All the agents had to work off were some comparable-looking sketches that had been put together over the years. There were a few thousand people packing the high school's football stadium. El Lobo was one unremarkable person lost in a sea of other unremarkable people. I had met El Lobo face-to-face, and I doubted that I would be able to accurately pick him out of a lineup.

"Who told you I set you up?" I asked El Lobo.

"Oh, *Mamacita* . . . how do you think I've managed to get away with it all these years?" El Lobo asked. "Just like your *tío* Houston, I know how to grease a few palms. Your family is not the only one with *policía* on the payroll. And *mi chico*, he's . . . how would you *Tejanos* say it? . . . Dirtier than a toilet seat at a truck stop."

"I should have known," I said. "Oscar Palmer warned me that you're slicker than snot on a doorknob. His words. Not mine."

"*Señor* Oscar *es un hombre inteligente. Mucho más inteligente* than *tu* or any of *tu familia*. Oscar knows not to cross me. I told him I did not want to do business with *tu familia*, but he insisted. I had to remind the Palmers of what happens when El Lobo does not get his way. And now your family does, too. But still you try to stick me in the back."

"Stab you in the back," I corrected him. "Hold on . . . I knew it! You're behind what happened to my cousins and Hank Garrett, aren't you? You're Facundo."

"Yes and no, *Mamacita*," El Lobo said. "I am not Facundo. But the person calling himself Facundo set them up on my say so. You could say that I am the man behind the curtain."

"Who is it? Who's Facundo? Is he your dirty cop? And which one of my family members helped you?"

"Unlike you, *Mamacita*, I do not betray *mi amigos*. But I will punish the people who try to deceive me."

El Lobo laughed and then ended the call.

Hardy, Schmitt, Agent Foster, and I sat around in silence. It was the other agent, tucked in a back corner of the van while he furiously clicked away on his laptop, who broke the silence.

"No luck tracing the call," the agent said.

"Well, we know he's in the general vicinity," Schmitt said. "He saw the van. And he knows Carrie is wearing a blue sweatshirt."

"No, that doesn't necessarily mean he's nearby," Foster said. "You heard El Lobo say that he's got an officer on the take. That person could have been passing along info to him."

"The question is who is El Lobo's guy?" Schmitt asked. "Is he one of yours? Or one of mine? Aside from Lieutenant Schmitt and Sergeant Hardy, the only agents who knew about this are either in my division or yours. And I only told a couple of my guys."

I was about to voice my opinion when my phone rang. "Little busy right now, Andrew."

"Carrie, you need to come home. Now." Andrew said. "We've got . . . well, we've got a couple problems. Major problems."

If Andrew's tone of voice hadn't convinced me of the emergency situation, then the sirens wailing in the background would have.

CHAPTER TWENTY-TWO

A shot of panic ripped through me as I turned down the street and spotted two firetrucks, an ambulance, and a handful of cruisers parked in front of my house. The vehicles' emergency lights illuminated a cloud of dark smoke that was billowing up into the air. I didn't see any flames, but that didn't mean my house wasn't on fire. The firemen had a hose hooked up to the nearest hydrant, and they were spraying a steady stream of water at something.

Leaving my car in the middle of the street, I sprinted towards my property. Hardy, who had come with me from the high school, ran alongside me. I could hear him speaking to me, but, over the ringing in my ears and the engulfing wave of anxiety crashing over me, I couldn't quite make out what he was saying. A handful of my neighbors—ones who hadn't attended the football game—were gathered in Naomi's front yard. They shouted at me, but I ignored them.

"Please be okay," I begged. "Please let them be okay."

Rounding the side of a firetruck, I crashed into Dinker Devereux. He was standing at the end of my driveway and shouting into a radio. Like his older half-brother Butch, Dinker was a volunteer firefighter. Unlike Butch, Dinker was not an arsonist. Or, if he was, he had not yet gotten caught. Also, unlike Butch, Dinker had never been involved in any of the Shatners' or Devereuxs' crimes. Well, as far as I knew, Dinker had never been involved. In the past two months, I had learned that the Shatners, Devereuxes, and Palmers had more secrets than Texas had bluebonnets. Who knew what secrets Dinker was hiding?

"Carrie!" Dinker wrapped his arms around me and lifted me off my feet to prevent me from going any farther. "It's not your house. It's your graveyard building . . . whatever it is."

"It's a mausoleum." I sagged against Dinker. My knees gave out I would have collapsed to the pavement if he hadn't continued to hold me up. I shakily drew in a deep breath and inhaled the acrid smoke. After a fit of coughing, I asked, "My house is okay? What about my pets?"

"Your dog and cat are fine. They're inside with Andrew and Junior," Dinker assured me. "As for your house . . . some of the siding along the front might be singed or even melted. But the structure is fine. I can't say the same for the mausoleum. Or the cottonwood tree."

"What happened here?" Hardy asked.

Dinker shrugged. "We got the call about a structure fire and responded. When we got here, the mausoleum and nearby tree were engulfed in flames. Skeeter and Luke were using garden hoses to keep it contained. You can thank them for saving your house. Had they not acted as quickly as they did, the fire probably would have spread from the tree to the house."

"We figured saving your house was more important than the mausoleum," my half-brother Luke said as he walked over to join us. "It's a good thing we were keeping an eye on the front yard. We saw the mausoleum go up in flames and were able to keep it from spreading."

I went to hug Luke but stopped short after I got a good look at him. His face and blonde hair were streaked with soot, the front of his shirt and jeans were singed and torn, and he was soaking wet. He also had bandages wrapped around both of his hands.

"Are you okay?" I asked.

"First degree burns. The EMTs said I should be all right in a few days," Luke said as he held up his hands and showed off the bandages. "A branch broke off the tree and landed in the bushes along the front of the house. I grabbed the branch and pulled it out of the bushes. Burnt my hands in the process. And broke your bedroom window. But I saved your house."

I walked a few feet up the driveway so that I could see the front of my house around the remains of the mausoleum. Beneath my bedroom window, the barberry shrubs were crushed. Streaks of black soot marred the pale gray siding.

"Thank you." I wrapped my arms around my half-brother and gave him a hug.

I let go of Luke and turned to face my cousin Skeeter who had just walked over to join us. Much like Luke, Skeeter was a soaking wet, sooty mess. His brown hair was nearly black, and his t-shirt was torn from collar to hem.

"There's something you need to see, Carrie," Skeeter said.

Hardy, Luke, Dinker, and I followed Skeeter across my front yard. I paused to look at what was left of the mausoleum. The wooden roof had collapsed, as had two of the four sides. The plywood coffin was burned beyond recognition. The tombstones and fencing were smashed and destroyed. As for the tree, the part of the trunk that was closest to the mausoleum had been blackened by the fire and a section of branches had been burned away. I'd have to get an arborist to look at the tree to see if it could be saved.

Chief Deputy Juan Quaranta knelt in front of the mausoleum alongside two firefighters. They were shining flashlights onto the ground, and the beam caused something in the patch of burnt grass to sparkle.

"Is that glass?" Hardy asked.

Quaranta held up the neck of a glass bottle. "We'll have to send it to the lab for testing, but I smell kerosene. Looks like this fire was set intentionally."

"Molotov cocktail," Dinker said. "My brother Butch's specialty."

"Yes, this was definitely intentional," I said. "Not that I think Uncle Butch did it. Unless he's still mad at me for accusing him of setting up and assaulting the boys . . ."

"Butch can be vindictive . . ." Dinker said.

"The glass bottle isn't the only thing that proves it was arson." Skeeter took me by the arm and led me around to the other side of the tree. He pointed a wooden tombstone that had been stuck in the ground. "Pretty sure that's not one of yours."

The tombstone in question had been crudely cut from a piece of plywood. The curve along the upper edge was uneven and the wood had splintered. Written across the tombstone was "RIP Carrie Shatner." A date had been scrawled underneath.

"That's Sunday's date," Hardy said.

"I guess I should thank El Lobo and Facundo for the warning," I said sarcastically. I used my phone to take a picture of the tombstone. "When Andrew called, he said we had a few problems. What else is going on?"

Skeeter took a step closer to me and whispered, "It—or should I say he—is waiting for you inside."

"If you tell me El Lobo is inside—"

"He's not," Skeeter assured me. "But your favorite pain in the ass is."

"Great . . . Wesley."

After skirting around the still-smoking mausoleum, I headed across the yard to my front door. Someone had rescued my Grim Reaper mannequin from the bushes and set him back up on the porch. As I walked by him, the Grim Reaper shakily raised his arm. In a robotic voice, he said, "I'm coming for you, Carrie Shatner."

"Oh, shut up," I snapped.

It was bad enough that someone had burned down my mausoleum. Manipulating the Grim Reaper's voice box was just rubbing salt in the wound. I grabbed the Grim Reaper, dragged him out into the yard, and tossed him onto what was left of the mausoleum. A hotspot underneath the rubble flared up, igniting the Grim Reaper's black robe.

"Let him burn," I shouted at Dinker when he grabbed a hose and moved to extinguish the flame.

Andrew was waiting for me by the front door. He pushed open the screen door and asked, "Was that necessary?"

"Yes, it was." I stepped inside and looked around the foyer. Aside from reeking of smoke and trails of muddy footprints leading into the living room and back to the kitchen, this section of my house appeared unscathed. "Where are Molly and Manny?"

"Molly is in her favorite hiding spot," Andrew said as he pushed open the door to the half-bathroom. Molly had stuffed herself in the narrow space between the toilet and the wall. "Manny is hiding under your bed."

"And Wesley?"

"Also hiding under your bed."

I spent a few minutes comforting Molly, and then I followed a trail of muddy footprints back the hallway to my bedroom. A light haze hung in the air and the room smelled of smoke and burnt plastic. On the far side of my queen-sized bed, Junior was picking slivers and shards of glass out of the gray carpet.

"How bad is it?" I asked Junior.

"You're gonna need a new window." Junior pulled the sodden curtains aside to reveal the window. The lower pane was shattered, and the screen was mangled. "Water got in. Your curtains are ruined, the carpet is soaked, and the drywall under the window will need patched. I already checked in the garage, and you've got enough leftover purple paint to cover the patch."

"Your bed also got wet," Andrew said. "I stripped the bedding off and stuffed it in the washing machine. It should be okay. But I can't say the same for your mattress."

"Great . . ." I glanced around the room for additional damage. The furniture seemed unharmed, and nothing else appeared to be wet or damaged. It could have been a lot worse than it was. The challenge would be getting rid of the smoke smell that was seeping into every fabric and porous material in my house.

I knelt next to my bed and peeked underneath. Wesley, Manny, and a small army of dust bunnies stared back at me. Wesley still had the large bandage taped over his nose, but he appeared to be much less loopy than he had earlier in the day.

"Hi, Wes. You want to crawl out from under there?" I waited until Wesley slithered out from under my bed and then asked, "What are you doing at my house? How did you get here?"

"I got an Uber." Wesley pulled something out of his sweatshirt pocket and tossed it onto the floor next to me. Manny darted out from under the bed and pounced on it. "Dale and Dickie were right. Beto . . . or should I say Alberto Ramos . . . is an agent with the DPS."

"Shit." I snatched Alberto's badge and identification away from Manny before he could bat it across the room. "Where did you find this?"

"Hidden in the exhaust fan in his bathroom."

"Where was Beto when you were snooping in this bathroom?" I asked.

"He went to the football game."

"Seriously? Beto wasn't supposed to leave you home alone."

Lieutenant Schmitt hadn't said anything to me, but I assumed he had requested Alberto's presence at the football game in case he was needed to help take down El Lobo.

"His name is Alberto. Not Beto," Wesley reminded me. He stood up and paced back and forth along the foot of my bed. "And, yeah, he left me alone. I got bored, so I decided to snoop around to see if Bet— Alberto was hiding any drugs—"

"In his bathroom exhaust fan?" I asked.

"It's where I keep mine. Well, some of them," Wesley said. "Figured it was a good place to look. I didn't find any drugs. But I found his badge and ID. No way was I staying in his trailer after I saw that. So I got an Uber and came over here. But Andrew said it would have to wait until you got back from meeting with El Lobo at the football game."

"I only called when the mausoleum went up in flames," Andrew added. "Did you talk to El Lobo?"

"Nah. He never showed up," I said.

Wesley stuck his bandaged covered nose close to Hardy's face and asked, "Did you know Beto was an undercover cop?"

"No," Hardy and I said at the same time.

Hardy gave me a warning look and then said, "Had I known there was an undercover agent in the area, I would have told Carrie."

I pressed my hands over my forehead and muttered, "Beto had me fooled."

"He had all of us fooled," Wesley said.

"Have you told anyone else?" I asked Wesley.

Wesley nodded. "I told everyone. They're looking for him at the football game, and a few of our cousins are waiting at his trailer in case he comes back."

"Let me make some calls. I'll try to figure out what is going on around here," Hardy said before he disappeared down the hallway. A few seconds later, Hardy yelled, "Hey, Carrie, Sergeant Boleyn and my lieutenant just got here, and they're headed this way."

"Get back under the bed," I said to Wesley as I pushed him to the floor.

"DID YOU REALLY SMUGGLE ME OUT of the hospital in a body bag?" Wesley asked. "Because that's just messed up."

"It worked, didn't it?" I asked. "And you're welcome."

"I never said 'thank you.'"

"No, you didn't. But you should."

Wesley snorted.

It was just after midnight and I was driving Wesley over to Uncle Houston's house. I had to hide my cousin somewhere, and Uncle Houston's secret Man Cave seemed like the best option. I couldn't imagine anyone looking for Wesley there—especially since the majority of the people who knew about Uncle Houston's bomb shelter were under the impression that he used it as a grow house for marijuana plants.

For the past two hours, Wesley had been stuck hiding under my bed while I was interrogated by Sergeant Boleyn and Lieutenant Underwood. From the bedroom, Wesley hadn't been able to hear anything we had said—which was a good thing because Underwood informed Boleyn about the deal I had made with the DPS. Thankfully

Hardy had kept Andrew, Junior, Skeeter, and Luke out of the house throughout the interrogation. I didn't need them knowing about the deal I had made either. The five of them had spent the past two hours tearing down what was left of the mausoleum and cleaning up my front yard.

Boleyn had been left momentarily speechless when he found out that I was helping the DPS's Drug Unit by turning over evidence against my family members. He had wanted to know more about my family's crimes, but Underwood pointed out that Boleyn wasn't part of that investigation and didn't need to know all of the facts. Besides, discussing the long list of crimes would take all night and we had more important things to go over.

Discovering the identity of Facundo and his two goons was crucial. They had to be stopped before they caused any more damage or hurt anyone else. Boleyn and I compared notes on our separate investigations, and it quickly became obvious that he had not made much progress. Boleyn snidely reminded me that the reason he had made such little progress was because Wesley and I had withheld information from him, and the rest of the Shatners, Devereuxs, and Palmers had not cooperated when he questioned them. They might have been willing to point the finger at each other while talking to me and Hardy, but they weren't about to betray the family to any other law enforcement officers.

I handed over my list of suspects—including their motives and alibis—to Boleyn. I also gave him all the threating notes and "gifts" that Facundo had sent to us. Boleyn had wanted to go over everything in detail, but Underwood convinced him that it could wait until morning. After making plans to meet up at the Holler Police Department at eight in the morning, Boleyn and Underwood finally took their leave around midnight.

"I can't believe that Dale and Dickie were right," Wesley muttered.

"About what?"

"Beto. You know . . . That he was an undercover cop. Totally shot my theory to hell."

"What theory was that?"

"That Beto is Facundo. And that he worked for El Lobo." Wesley shifted around in the passenger seat so that he was facing me. "Like I said at the hospital, Beto showed up a couple weeks before Facundo contacted me. Didn't seem like a coincidence to me. Plus, he's been sticking his nose in our business. He's about the same size as 'Facundo.'

He's got a major attitude and control issues. He's also got two phones. I noticed that today. I figured he's like me. He's got one for personal stuff and another phone for business. I guess his other phone was so he could contact his superior officers. But now that I know he's a cop . . . Unless he's a dirty cop."

"You have any other theories?" I asked.

"Yeah. Kinda," Wesley said. "Before your mausoleum went up in flames, Andrew took me in your office, and we went over your case notes. Good idea using the notecards."

"Who do you suspect?" I asked.

Wesley sighed. "I don't know if I suspect anyone specifically. But I narrowed down who matched the physical description of each of the three bad guys. Aside from Beto, Cousins Bubba and Billy Bob . . . Heath Palmer. Cooter Devereux. They're all about the same size as the lead guy. And none of them like me all that much."

"Bubba, Billy Bob, and Heath all have alibis. Though I'm not sure how much I trust Billy Bob's or Heath's alibis," I said. "But Cooter doesn't have one."

"A couple guys I sell drugs to are about the same size, too. I left you some notes."

"I saw them," I said. I had also handed Wesley's notes over to Sergeant Boleyn. "What about the bigger guy?"

"Well, Nate Palmer. He's a big guy," Wesley pointed out. "So is Red. But I know it wasn't him. And Cousin Tate is about the right size. But I can't believe he'd do it."

"No, I can't picture him doing either."

"Some of our uncles are tall and . . . well, chunky."

"Like Uncle Delmar," I said. "And Kinky, Woody, and Butch."

"Pork Chop. But Roxanne swears he was at home with her on Sunday morning."

"If Pork Chop had been involved, you would have lost more than just your pinkie."

"He'd have finally followed through with his threat to chop off something else. Or he would have killed me." Wesley thumped his fist against the dashboard. "This is so frustrating."

"Tell me about it."

"The skinny one is going to be the hardest to figure out. Like, half the men in our family are about six-feet tall. Uncle Elvin. Uncle Leroy. Keaton and Kermit. Festus and Cletus."

"Dale and Dickie," I added.

"Chris Palmer. John and Peter Garrett," Wesley said. "Tadpole and Jason Devereux."

"Except you can't really suspect Jason since he was supposed to go with you."

"Ha. I doubt Jason would have tagged along. He was looking for a way to get out of it from the second I brought up the meeting. I doubt he even got called in to work that morning. He probably made it up as an excuse to get out of going with me. Not that I wish he had been there. I'm glad Jason didn't get hurt. I just wish that Waylon and Hank had listened to him instead of me. It should have just been me that was there. I'm the one who should be dead. Not Hank."

I had just passed the Roadhouse Motel and was nearing Uncle Houston's driveway when I caught sight of the billboard advertising the Body Farm. I slammed on my brakes.

"Did you see that?" I asked.

"See what?"

I put the car in reverse and backed up about a hundred feet so that we could see the billboard. A spotlight illuminated the sign—as well as the damage done to it. Someone had used red paint to write the word "Evil" across the billboard in eight-foot-high letters.

"Calvary Baptist?" Wesley asked.

"I'd put money on those odds. Thaddeus knows Wynonna, Roxanne, and Jason destroyed the Hell House."

"Even if they hadn't, them Kemps have always hated our family. And the Body Farm." Wesley reached across the car and grabbed my arm. "What if Thaddeus is Facundo?"

"That I seriously doubt."

"He's the right size."

"And so are a lot of other people."

I snapped a picture of the billboard before continuing to Uncle Houston's house. I had called ahead and warned him that I was on my way.

"What's so important you gotta come by at this hour?" Uncle Houston asked as I climbed out of my car. He was sitting on the back porch of the farmhouse. The lights were off, but the glowing end of his cigar gave away his location. "You ain't here to accuse me of tryin' to burn down your house, are you? Because I ain't had nothin' to do with that."

"I don't think you did," I said.

"That's what you get for tryin' to set up El Lobo."

"How do you know about that?"

"I've got eyes and ears all over. Nothin' goes on 'round here that I don't know about."

As I walked towards the farmhouse, I set off the motion-activated light above the back door and almost blinded myself. "I'm here because I need a favor."

Wesley popped out of the passenger side of my car and ran over to the porch. "Yo, Uncle Houston, you'll never guess what I found out. That Beto guy . . . He's an undercover cop! I found his badge while I was hiding out in his trailer."

"Is that so?" Uncle Houston ground out the end of his cigar and then tossed the stub into the yard. "What're you doin' here, Wes?"

"That's the favor," I said. "I need you to hide Wes in your Man Cave."

"Walk with me, Carrie." Uncle Houston pushed himself out of the plastic lawn chair and then gestured for me to follow him across the yard to his barn. When Wesley moved to follow us, Uncle Houston told him to sit down on the porch. Once we were out of earshot from Wesley, Uncle Houston said, "Carrie, you know I'd do just 'bout anything to protect our family. But you gotta find somewhere else to stash Wes."

"But—"

"No buts," Uncle Houston said, cutting me off. "In less than eight hours, this place is going to be crawlin' with federal agents."

"What are you talking about?"

"The DEA and ATF have warrants to search my property. All our properties."

I sank down on the woodpile. "Are you serious? How do you know?"

"I've got a DEA agent on the payroll," Uncle Houston said. He had a seat next to me. "Missy, do you really think that anything happens in this county without my knowin' 'bout it? Well, except for the identities of who attacked the boys and is threatenin' the family. That I ain't got no clue about."

"Do you know how they got the warrants? Is it because of Uncle Ted? Did he talk?"

Uncle Houston nodded. "As soon as Ted got arrested, I called up your brother-in-law and asked him to be Ted's lawyer. According to Bradley, Ted sang like a canary. Told the DEA agents everything they wanted to know about the grow houses and the moonshine stills. Just like I knew he would."

"What's that supposed to mean?" I asked. "How did you know Uncle Ted would talk."

"This stays between you and me." Uncle Houston put his arm around my shoulders and drew me closer. He then whispered, "It wasn't Ted's buyer that set him up. It was me."

My jaw dropped. "You did what?"

"I tipped off the Smith County Sheriff's Department and the DEA." Uncle Houston increased the pressure around my neck so that I couldn't pull away. "It was just a matter of time before they came after us. I figured I'd make things easier for 'em."

"But you setup Uncle Ted."

"You think Ted didn't know he was the family's sacrificial lamb? He knew he was gonna get busted. It was all part of the plan."

"What plan?" I swatted Uncle Houston's arm away. "I wasn't aware of any plan."

"The plan that Ted and I came up with. I'd set him up, and he'd talk. Ain't like them DEA agents are gonna find anythin' since we got rid of it." Uncle Houston stood up and then helped me to my feet. "And I don't gotta tell you everythin', missy."

"When the rest of the family finds out about this—"

"They ain't gonna find out 'bout it." Uncle Houston grabbed me by the shoulders and hissed, "You ain't gonna tell anyone 'bout this, Carrie. 'Cause if you do, I'll tell them that you sold us out to that undercover agent . . . Don't look so shocked. Wes's revelation was no surprise. You think I didn't know that your buddy Beto was an undercover agent? Or about the deal that you and Crockett made? Just so happens I approached Beto and made a deal myself."

"Of course, you did."

I should have been stunned that Uncle Houston knew that Alberto was an undercover agent and about the deal I had made with the DPS. But I wasn't.

"Missy, I told you that there ain't nothin' that happens in this county that I don't know 'bout," Uncle Houston said.

"Except for who attacked the boys, right?" I asked. "I'll keep your secret as long as you keep mine. But if I find out you setup the boys—"

"I swear I had nothin' to do with that. And I didn't kill my brother Benny neither."

"I don't know if I believe you."

"You don't have to believe me," Uncle Houston said. "But, for once in your life, I'm gonna need you to trust me. I have a plan."

"Was putting me in charge of the family part of that plan? Was I ever really in charge?"

Uncle Houston shrugged. "You were as in charge as I needed you to be."

"When did you find out that I made a deal? Was that before or after your put me in charge?" I asked. "And how did you find out?"

"Before," Uncle Houston said. "And Crockett told me. We agreed putting you in charge was the right thing to do. We knew you'd be safe."

"Granddaddy was in on this?" I fought back the urge to scream. I had never felt so betrayed in my life. The one person who I had always trusted had set me up. "I'm going to need an honest answer Uncle Houston . . . Are they going to find anything?"

"Not a damn thing."

"What about the stuff we buried under the museum's foundation?"

"Your granddaddy, Vernon, and I moved it before the concrete was poured. Ain't no one ever gonna find that stuff. It's not even in the country anymore."

"Unbelievable." I walked across the yard and yelled for Wesley to get back in the car. I didn't say anything until we reached the road. "Wes, how do you feel about spending the night in a casket?"

"Are you talking 'bout burying me alive?"

"No. I'm talking about the display caskets at the funeral home."

"I guess that would be all right."

CHAPTER TWENTY-THREE

"WOOHOO! IT's MAMA MOONSHINE!" a teenaged customer yelled. "What's for dinner tonight, Mama?"

"You come trespassin' on my land and it'll be you!" I yelled back. I waved at the sizable group of customers who were waiting in line at the Body Farm's ticket booth. "Y'all look like you'll taste good deep fried."

"Would you stop waving at people like you're the bloody Queen of England and hold on?" Bubba asked before accelerating the four-wheeler. We dodged customers and their vehicles as we raced down the paved road that cut through the Body Farm's parking lot. The sun was in the process of setting, and overhead lights helped illuminate the lot. "And pull your hood up. The fewer customers that see you out here—and out of character—the better. I don't need them knowing that Mama Moonshine is a law enforcement officer."

"Why not? It might encourage some of them to behave better if they know I could arrest them. And that I carry around a real gun for my day job."

Bubba may or may not have snorted in response—it was hard to tell over the sound of the four-wheeler's engine.

In compliance to Bubba's request, I tugged my sweatshirt hood up and over my teased-out hair to hide my makeup covered face. Tonight, it looked like I had just barely survived a bar brawl. With one hand, I held the hood in place. With my other hand, I clung to the four-wheeler and tried not to get thrown off due to Bubba's erratic driving.

To keep from kicking up gravel, Bubba slowed when we reached Old Town Texas's parking lot. Ten to twelve government-issued SUVs were parked near the old train depot. Agents from the Department of Public Safety, Drug Enforcement Administration, and Bureau of Alcohol, Tobacco, Firearms and Explosives had showed up at Old Town Texas at dawn with a warrant to tear up the new museum's concrete foundation to search for the illegal items that we had buried underneath. They also had warrants to search the rest of the ranch for evidence of illegal activities. The only section of the ranch that the warrants did not cover was the Body Farm—and that's only because the DPS's crime scene unit had thoroughly searched the area.

As far as I knew, after nearly eleven hours of searching Old Town Texas and the ranch—as well as multiple other Shatner-owned properties—the agents had yet to find anything overly criminal. Sure, they had come across a few jars of moonshine and a little bit of marijuana and other drugs—but it wasn't enough for anyone to be concerned about.

"I about messed my boxers this morning when Dad called and said the agents were raiding the ranch," Bubba said as we both rudely saluted the State Trooper standing guard at the train depot. The agent returned the gesture. "You know, you could have had the decency to tell me that our grandpas had moved all the illegal stuff before Uncle Vernon's crew poured the concrete. Watching them bust up that concrete . . . I've never been so nervous in my life . . . Well, except for that time Veda thought she might've been pregnant. I hope I never have another day as bad as today."

"No matter how bad your day was, I can guarantee that mine was much worse."

"Where were you all day?" Bubba asked. "I figured you'd . . . I don't know . . . make your rounds and provide moral support for our family members who were being raided."

"I would have. Except I was stuck in an interrogation room until about two hours ago."

Actually, I had spent the day stuck in the conference room at the Holler Police Department, but considering the number of questions I had been asked by various law enforcement officers, it felt like an interrogation. I would rather have spent the day with my family—fretting that the agents might find something we had overlooked during our massive cleanup and then arrogantly celebrating when the agents were unsuccessful.

I also could have helped rescue the agents who had gotten caught in the booby traps that Uncle Houston had set up throughout the property. He had warned the agents about the booby traps, but not all of them took him seriously. At last count, six agents had fallen victim. Five of the agents had walked away with only minor injuries, but the sixth had broken his ankle after falling into a well-concealed pit trap.

Instead of supporting my family during this trying time, much of my day had been spent at the police department comparing notes and going over evidence with Sergeant Boleyn. Hardy and Lieutenant Underwood had kept the peace between us. Even after combining everything we had—and narrowing down the list of suspects—neither Boleyn nor I was any closer to figuring out the identity of the three attackers.

Throughout the day, the four of us had frequently been interrupted by Lieutenant Schmitt and the lead DEA and ATF agents. They had popped into the conference room numerous times to demand that I tell them what had happened to the moonshine stills and the grow houses. When Uncle Ted had talked to the DEA agents on Thursday, he had told them the location of each still and grow house. What Uncle Ted had failed to mention was that we had already torn down and disposed of the evidence. With each warrant served, the various law enforcement organizations found only empty bomb shelters, sheds, and garages.

My standard answer to all questions became "I don't know." I'm sure Lieutenant Schmitt and the other agents thought I was lying. Truthfully, I had no idea what Granddaddy and Uncle Houston had done with the illegal items, and, even if I asked them, I doubt they would tell me. No, this was a secret that Granddaddy and Uncle Houston would take to their graves. Just one of what I assumed were many secrets.

Sergeant Boleyn probably would have kept me in the conference room all evening, but Hardy and Underwood convinced him to let me go so that I could go act at the Body Farm.

I had enough time to catch up on everything I had missed throughout the day before I changed into my costume and got my makeup done. I was headed to Moonshiners' Grove when Bubba picked me up on the four-wheeler.

Bubba came to a stop about a hundred feet away from the gate that marked the entrance to the ranch. Blocking the entrance were about three to four dozen people. Some of the protestors stood in the middle of the two-lane highway and waved around their homemade signs. They were impeding traffic in both directions. Other protestors were going car to car and handing out what appeared to be pamphlets. Most of the drivers did not seem happy. They were honking their horns and yelling obscenities at the protestors.

Thaddeus Kemp and his congregants from Calvary Baptist had arrived early in the afternoon to stage their protest at the Body Farm. At first, they had assembled around the staff parking lot and tried to convince the volunteers that they were destined to go to Hell for working at the Body Farm. Bubba and Uncle Elvin had initially ignored the protestors—but, when Thaddeus and his congregants moved en masse over to the ticket booth area and began preaching to the customers, Bubba decided to act.

"I should have just let them protest by the entrance," Bubba muttered. "Yeah, they were a nuisance and they were bothering the customers who were waiting in line. But it was kinda funny watching the customers banter with them. Plus, they weren't preventing people from getting on the property. Dad had to take down a section of fence in the south pasture so that we could get customers into the parking lot. If I have to hear one more person complain about getting alpaca crap on their car . . ."

"I'll take care of them."

I grabbed the megaphone that Bubba had slung over the four-wheeler's handlebars and then approached the group of protestors.

"This is typically our busiest night of the season," Bubba said as he followed me. "And I have a feeling that we're going to be even busier than usual since people are nosy and will want to see the Torture barn where the boys were . . . you know . . ."

"Tortured?"

I crept up behind Thaddeus and then turned on the megaphone's siren. He jumped about five feet in the air, and most of his congregants screamed. Faith Kemp took one look at my makeup covered face and fainted.

"Attention everyone . . ." the megaphone amplified my voice. "I am Detective Carrie Shatner with the Wyatt County Sheriff's Department."

"Carrie?" Thaddeus asked. He took a couple tentative steps towards me and peered at my face. "Are you okay? Do you require medical attention?"

"Yes, it's me. And it's makeup," I said. "What are you doing here, Thaddeus?"

"Saving souls." Thaddeus raised his voice and said, "Since my Hell House was destroyed, I was forced to come up with another way to do the Lord's work. By protesting this work of Satan, I will save the souls of the customers and workers."

"Looks to me like the only thing you are doing is illegally blocking traffic. And you're not really preventing anyone from getting into the Body Farm. We're just bringing them in a different way," I said loud enough for everyone to hear me. I then lowered my voice and whispered to Thaddeus, "You know, I could call the sheriff's department and have some deputies come out and arrest you. I'd really rather not do that—"

"Then we will protest from the side of the road." Thaddeus pushed past me and took up a stance next to the gate. His congregants followed him. "Now we are no longer blocking traffic."

"No. But you are back to trespassing on private property," Bubba said. "My father owns the land that you're standing on."

"Then we will protest on the other side." Thaddeus stomped across the road. "Now we aren't trespassing or blocking traffic."

"Actually, you are trespassing." I held the megaphone up to my mouth and announced, "The land on that side of the road is owned by my family as well. Therefore, you are once against trespassing on private property. If you want to protest from the side of the road, you will have to go about a mile in either direction to get to land that is not owned by the Shatners. That land is also privately owned, and the owners may consider you as trespassers. But that's not my problem. May I suggest leaving and spending a nice, relaxing evening at home?"

"We will leave," Thaddeus said as he began ushering his congregants over to the cars that they had parked along the shoulder. "But I refuse to be thwarted. I will save souls. And I will make sure this place of Satanism and sinfulness is shut down for good."

Bubba and I watched at the protestors drove off in both directions. With them gone, the Body Farm's staff was able to resume bringing the customers through the normal entrance.

"I can't guarantee that's the end of them protesting," I said. "But, at least, they won't be protesting at the entrance."

"I have a feeling that's not the last we'll be seeing of Thaddeus tonight." Bubba fired up the four-wheeler and headed back towards the Body Farm. "I better get you down to Moonshiners and then go send out the first wagon. Thanks to Thaddeus, we're running twenty minutes behind."

Bubba and I arrived at Moonshiners' Grove just in time to break up a brawl between Billy Bob, Festus, and Cletus. According to Elijah—who had been ineffectively whacking at them with a branch—Billy Bob had further accused Festus and Cletus of being involved in what happened to Wesley, Waylon, and Hank. Sick of the accusations, the brothers had jumped Billy Bob. Even though there were two of them, Billy Bob had quickly gotten the upper hand.

Once we had the three of them calmed down, Bubba took off to the loading area to send out the first wagon.

"You got a lot of nerve showing your face around here, Carrie," Billy Bob said. "After what happened to the family today . . . Not to mention that the three people who assaulted Wes and Waylon are still at large. Plus that Beto guy."

Thanks to Hardy tipping him off, Alberto had been able to get out of Wyatt County before any of my relatives tracked him down at the football stadium. I don't want to know what they would have done to Alberto had they gotten their hands on him.

"You've got the worst taste in men, Carrie," Festus said. "First the Texas Ranger. Then an undercover cop. And now you're back with the Ranger. Not that I can blame you. He's gonna keep you out of jail."

"Did you know that Beto was undercover?" Billy Bob asked me.

"Of course not," I said. "And, need I remind you, y'all fell for his lies, too."

"Dale and Dickie had him figured out," Cletus pointed out.

"Are you any closer to figuring out who attacked Wes and Waylon?" Billy Bob asked.

"No. And, now that I know El Lobo and Facundo are working together, I'm not investigating anymore. Not after they came close to burning down my house last night. They also threatened to kill me sometime tomorrow."

"I never pegged you for a quitter, Carrie," Billy Bob said.

"I may not be the smartest person alive, but I know when to throw in the towel."

I climbed up onto the porch and sank down into my rocking chair. I was trying to figure out how I would make it through the night when the first wagon pulled into Moonshiners' Grove. Billy Bob came flying out of the shack threatening the trespassers and waving around the shotgun. After he fired the second shot, a bolt of adrenaline raced through me and I sprang out of the rocking chair and hit the side of the wagon.

I grabbed the customer closest to me, leaned in close to his ear, and whispered, "I'm going to mount your head above my fireplace."

"You look like a raccoon."

Hardy glared at me from where he was stretched out on the backseat of my car. His brown eyes were almost lost in the thick black makeup that covered his face from his eyebrows to halfway down his cheeks. He also had dark makeup around his mouth.

"With your hair like that, it looks like you stuck a fork in a socket."

"Thanks. This might just be my new look." I fluffed my teased out, faux-blood-streaked hair. I then reached into my backpack and pulled out a packet of makeup wipes. I had already used a couple wipes to remove most of my makeup. I tossed the packet to Hardy so he could do the same. "Did you have fun tonight?"

Hardy shrugged. "Don't get me wrong, scaring people was fun. But I couldn't really enjoy it since I was worried about someone attacking you."

Hardy had spent the night acting on the Hayride of Nightmares so that he could be close to me. The threat implied on the plywood tombstone had rattled both of us. I figured I would be safe while acting. But Hardy didn't want to risk it. He had tried to talk me out of acting, but I insisted. Yes, El Lobo or Facundo could have easily ridden through the Hayride of Nightmares as customers. The Body Farm had record-breaking attendance numbers, and they would have been just two people among the thousands. But the odds of them attacking me from the wagon were low. It would have been nearly impossible to get away with it. Packed into the wagon with fifty or so other people, there would have been no means of escape.

Initially, Hardy's plan had been to hide in the woods around Moonshiners' Grove where he would be able to keep an eye on me while remaining out of sight. Instead, Bubba put Hardy to work. To keep his identity a secret, Bubba and I had dressed Hardy in a cheap gorilla costume. As "Bigfoot", Hardy had hung out in the area between Slaughterhouse and Moonshiners' Grove. That kept him within shouting distance of me should I have needed him. But my night had been mostly uneventful. I had some customers yell unflattering comments at me, but that was nothing new. I also had a woman take a swing at me because she didn't appreciate it when I said a skit line to her boyfriend—also, not the first time that happened.

"Let's get out of here."

I fired up the engine and pulled out of the nearly empty staff parking lot. It was almost three in the morning on Sunday. There were twenty-one hours left in the day for El Lobo or Facundo to come after me.

"Do you really think they're going to attack you on the drive home?" Hardy asked.

"That crappy tombstone they left for me had today's date," I said. "If they're going to come after me, now would be the perfect time. As far as they know, I'm alone and vulnerable. And most of my drive home is on winding backroads where few people live. And, at this hour, not many people will be out and about."

"I hope you're right." Hardy sighed. "I also hope you're wrong."

The backroads were dark and the nearly full moon was hidden behind a thick layer of clouds. I was about halfway home when another vehicle seemingly came out of nowhere and pulled up to my bumper. I didn't even know the other car was behind me until the driver turned on the headlights.

"Holy high beams," I said as the car's headlights flashed in my sideview mirror and nearly blinded me. A jolt of adrenaline shot through me. "I think this is it, Jerrod."

I had just enough time to tighten my grip on the steering wheel before the other car rammed into the back of my Jeep and almost turned me sideways. I wasn't too worried about my bumper—my trailer hitch would protect the back end of my car. It would also cause some damage to the other car. But I was worried that if the other driver didn't let up, he would spin me off the road and into the trees on either side.

"Oh, you've definitely crossed the line," I muttered as I fought to keep the car on the road. I pressed the pedal to the floor and shot forward. "No one messes with my Jeep."

"Pull over, Carrie!" Hardy yelled from the backseat. "Before he wrecks us."

"Not a chance." I whipped over into the other lane and slammed on the brakes. Anger overrode my anxiety. My tires squealed in protest as the other car blew past and disappeared around a curve. "I'm going to take this SOB out."

"Are you talking about a PIT maneuver? Do you know how to do that?"

"No. But I've watched a lot of NASCAR in my life." I hit the gas and raced after the other car. "I know how to spin someone out. It's basically the same thing."

I easily caught up to the other car—it was limping along as smoke billowed out from under the hood. As predicted, my trailer hitch had caused serious damage.

I pulled up alongside the other car. When the front end of my car was lined up with the back end of the other car, I eased into the right lane. As my car moved sideways, it forced the other car to turn across my front bumper. I gave it a little gas and sent the other car spinning off the road and into a ditch.

"You did it," Hardy shouted from the backseat.

I breathed a sigh of relief. "We aren't done yet."

I spun around so that my headlights were directed at the wrecked car. It was my first real look at it, and I immediately recognized the hunk of junk. It was the same car that Ethan Yates had been driving the other night when I ran into him at the Dancing Cowgirl.

"Son of a bitch! I knew Ethan was up to something," I muttered as I climbed out of my car and ran down the road. Ethan was big and bulky, and he fit the physical description Wesley had given me of one of the three attackers. Ethan also had a motive to come after me and my family. "I should have suspected he was part of this."

"What are you talking about?" Hardy asked.

"That car belongs to Ethan Yates."

Hardy growled. "I warned you not to trust him."

"I never trusted him. I was using him. You know, keep your friends close and your enemies closer. I just didn't think he was the enemy that was currently after my family." I screamed in frustration as I mentally kicked myself for not suspecting him from the beginning. He had been too nice and helpful. That should have been a massive red flag that something wasn't right. "I should have known he'd keep trying to do what his daddy couldn't."

Hardy and I had just about reached the other car when the driver scrambled out of the front seat and hurriedly limped towards the trees. A Devil mask hid his face. He also appeared to be much too skinny to be Ethan.

Hardy sped up and hit the person with a flying tackle just before he made it to the tree line. While they rolled around in the underbrush exchanging blows, I reached into the fray and grabbed ahold of the Devil mask.

"Jason!" I said when I got a good look at his face. I should have been surprised. But I wasn't. Wesley was right, one of the family was involved. "This is the last time I take someone's word and neglect confirming their alibi."

"Carrie . . . I swear no one was supposed to get hurt," Jason stammered as tears streamed down his cheeks. "I mean, Wes was supposed to get hurt . . . But not Waylon. And Hank wasn't supposed to die . . . And no one else was supposed to be involved. But it got out of hand . . . They made me do it . . ."

Jason fell silent as blue and red lights flashed in the distance.

"Since I don't believe in coincidences, I'm going to assume that's Ethan."

Jason nodded. "I was supposed to run you off the road. And then he was gonna come pick you up and . . . and . . . I swear I didn't want to do any of this to you."

"Get him out of here," I said to Hardy. I slipped my hand into my jacket pocket and wrapped my fingers around my taser. I had been carrying it around all night just in case Facundo or his cronies tried to come after me at the Body Farm. "I'll handle Ethan."

Hardy grabbed Jason by the back of his shirt and hauled him into the woods just as Ethan pulled over to the side of the road and parked.

"Carrie?" Ethan stuck his head out of the driver's side window and looked at me. "Is that you?"

"Fancy seeing you here, Ethan," I said in what sounded like a normal tone of voice. "Aren't you a little outside your jurisdiction?"

"Seemed like a nice night for a drive." Ethan pushed open the car door and stepped out onto the road. "What happened to you."

"Some asshole tried to run me off the road. I spun him out."

"Oh yeah? What happened to the driver?"

"Took off into the woods."

Ethan shook his head and muttered, "He was supposed to wreck you. Not get wrecked by you. Boy can't do anything right. But that plan always was for me to finish you off."

Ethan lunged towards me, but I was ready. I yanked a taser out of my jacket pocket, and, just as Ethan wrapped his hands around my throat, I pressed the taser against his thigh and let it rip. Ethan's hands slipped away from my neck and he collapsed to the ground at my feet.

"This is for being a sleazeball," I shouted as I kicked him in the ribs. A surge of anger ripped through me, and I kicked him a second time. "And that's for killing Hank. And this—"

"That's enough, Carrie." Hardy wrapped his arms around my waist and yanked me away from Ethan. "We need him alive if you want a confession."

"I want to take him out to the middle of nowhere and leave him for dead."

"Fuck you," Ethan mumbled.

While I fought to get my rage under control, Hardy grabbed Ethan's twitching arms and secured them behind his back with a zip tie. He cinched another zip tie around Ethan's ankles. Hardy then stuffed a rag in Ethan's mouth to gag him. At some point, I would like to hear what Ethan had to say—but not now. Not when I was feeling moderately homicidal.

I turned towards the trees and spotted Jason peeking at me around a bush.

"You want to come out and clue me in to what's going on, Jason?" I asked. "Where were you and Ethan supposed to take me?"

"To the Body Farm," Jason said as crept out of the woods. He had a seat on the ground next to Ethan. Ethan glared at him and tried to say something around the gag. "El Lobo and Facundo are waiting for us there."

"And who exactly is Facundo?" Hardy asked.

I pressed my hand over Jason's mouth to keep him from answering. "Have you really not figured it out yet, Jerrod?"

"No," Hardy said. "When did you figure it out?"

"Well, I'm not positive. But I've got a theory." At some point between recognizing Ethan's junker and unmasking Jason, the pieces had abruptly come together. I looked down at Jason and asked. "It's Alberto . . . I mean . . . Beto, isn't it?"

Jason nodded. "I had no idea he was a dirty cop until . . . well, until Monday night."

"Holy shit . . ." Hardy whispered. "Alberto? Agent Alberto Ramos? The guy pretending to be Beto?"

Jason nodded.

"Jason, did you know Beto was an undercover cop?" I asked.

"Yeah, I've known that for a few weeks now," Jason said. "Alberto approached me at the Body Farm get-together. You know, the day I went after Wes and threatened to kill him for getting Roxanne pregnant again. Alberto told me he was there to get evidence against Wes. And he asked me to help him. He said that with my help we could send Wes to prison for a long time. I wanted Wes out of Roxanne's life. That's the only reason I did it. To protect my sister and my nieces. But Alberto and Ethan had other plans."

"What is Alberto's connection to El Lobo?" Hardy asked.

Jason shrugged. "I don't know. I didn't even know they had a connection until last night. Alberto didn't tell me everything. Heck, he barely told me anything."

"Well, we better not keep Alberto and El Lobo waiting. This may be our only chance to get them," I said. I walked over to Ethan's patrol car and grabbed a gym bag off the passenger seat. Inside was a Devil mask and a set of black clothes. I tossed the bag to Hardy. "Put these on. You're about the same size as Ethan. As long as you don't talk, we can probably fool them."

After Hardy changed, we stripped Ethan down to his underwear and left him in a patch of poison oak that was growing near the side of the road. We then climbed into Ethan's car and headed back to the Body Farm. On the drive, Jason gave me and Hardy the condensed version of what all had been going on during the past few weeks.

After agreeing to help Alberto, Jason rekindled his friendship with Wesley to get close to him and gather more evidence. That was how Jason found out that Wesley had been talking to various drug dealers. Jason passed along that information to Alberto, and Alberto decided to use it to his advantage to set up Wesley. While Jason was part of the scheme to lure Wesley to the Roadhouse Motel, he was under the impression that Alberto was setting up a sting operation and was going to arrest Wesley. Jason swore he had no idea what Alberto and Ethan were planning to do until they had tied up the Three Stooges and transported them to the Torture Barn. Jason hadn't even known Ethan was involved until that night.

By the time Jason realized he was in over his head, it was too late to stop the assault. He swore he tried to keep Ethan from hurting Waylon or Hank. He also took credit for cutting off Wesley's pinkie—but he insisted that Alberto and Ethan forced him to do it.

In the days following the assault—when Jason's loyalty started to waiver and it looked like he might turn them in—Alberto and Ethan threatened to harm Roxanne, Summer, and Autumn. To keep his sister and his nieces safe, Jason continued to go along with Alberto's and Ethan's instructions. Lucky for me, he didn't exactly follow those instructions. Otherwise, the Molotov cocktail would have been thrown through my living room window opposed to the mausoleum.

As for Ethan, Jason informed me that he had become increasingly angry over the past few days as I had repeatedly rejected his advances. For whatever reason, Ethan had never gotten over his teenage obsession with me. And he most certainly had not forgiven me for shooting his father.

"There's one more thing, Carrie," Jason said as we pulled into the Body Farm's empty parking lot and parked near the entrance. "One of the kids from the Youth Group called me a while ago and told me that Thaddeus and some of the parishioners are planning to burn down parts of the Body Farm tonight. You know, in revenge for me, Roxanne, and Wynonna destroying the Hell House. It's possible they will chicken out. But . . . I warned Bubba and Elvin, so there's probably gonna be a bunch of Shatners hanging around. Hopefully they don't get in the way . . ."

"Now you tell me . . ."

"Not much we can do about it now," Hardy said as he opened one of the cruiser's rear doors and pulled me out. "Let's just hope they're smart enough to stay out of the crossfire."

"Ha! You've met my family, Jerrod. They're more likely to run into the crossfire than away from it."

Hardy and Jason both took me by an arm and pulled me towards the Body Farm's entertainment area. The overhead lights were off, but the clouds had drifted away, and the full moon moderately lit up the area.

"They're over there." Jason gestured towards two Devil mask-clad individuals sitting on top of the picnic table closest to the food trucks. "

"I don't have to worry about you going to the dark side again, do I, Jason?" I asked as we made our way over to Alberto and El Lobo.

"You can trust me, Carrie."

As we got closer, one of the Devils stood up and asked, "What took so long?" The Spanish accent was light, and I assumed it was Alberto.

"Carrie put up a fight, Facundo," Jason said. He shoved me backwards and I sat down hard on a bench. "She almost ripped my mask off."

"Good thing she didn't. Otherwise, I'd have to kill you, too," Alberto said. He clapped Jason on the back and then leaned closer to me. The tip of the Devil's nose brushed my forehead. "I'm sorry I have to do this, Carrie. But you gave me no choice. I told you to back off. But you failed to listen. Now you must suffer the consequences."

"And so do you." I raised my head and glared into the mask's eyeholes. "Alberto."

I raised my leg and drilled my foot into Alberto's private parts. As he stumbled backwards, Jason dove at him and tackled him over the table. Meanwhile, Hardy pulled out his gun and pointed it at El Lobo.

"Hands above your head, El Lobo."

El Lobo appeared to be complying to Hardy's command when the overhead lights came on, bathing the entertainment area with harsh artificial light.

"What the hell . . ." I watched as a group of weapon-bearing Shatners came barreling out from behind the game stands. I thought they were headed for us, but they veered towards the entrance where a group of torch-bearing individuals were attempting to set fire to the ticket booth. They were also wearing Devil masks. "You have got to be kidding me . . . They couldn't have waited five more minutes."

Chaos erupted around me. The stuffed animals at the basketball game went up in flames, as did one of the vinyl banners above the food trucks. There was also a gunshot, and someone screamed. The Shatners clashed with the Devil mask wearing induvial, Alberto and El Lobo got lost among them. I also lost sight of Hardy and Jason.

I spotted a short, stocky person hobbling towards the Carn-Evil of Chaos. It was either Alberto looking for a place to hide or a Calvary Baptist parishioner looking to do some damage. Regardless of who it was, the person had to be stopped.

I sprinted across the entertainment area and entered the Carn-Evil through the clown's gigantic mouth. Directly inside was a spinning tunnel that was meant to throw off the customers' equilibriums. Bubba— or someone else—had turned off the tunnel at the end of the night, and I easily passed through it.

On the other side of the tunnel was a small room featuring a dilapidated ticket booth. It is where the carnival barker would greet the customers before pulling aside the red and white striped curtain and sending them into the midway.

The midway part of the Carn-Evil of Chaos took up the entire center section of the barn, and the room was two-stories tall. On either side were three-story wings. The third floor connected the two wings. The midway would be the perfect place for someone to hide since it was full of small amusement rides, game booths, and food stands and trucks. I cautiously entered the midway. After passing through the curtain, I scooted behind the closest food truck and peered around the room. The overhead string lights were still on, as were the lights on the rides and stands. I could see, but not very well.

In the center of the midway, a miniature Ferris wheel reached towards the ceiling. A carousel with skeleton horses took up a chunk of floorspace, as did several small children's' rides. A rollercoaster track ran around the perimeter of the room. None of the rides were in operation now.

Scattered throughout the room were game and food stands. They were set up to form a twisting path that directed the customers through the midway. If I followed the path, I would be taken into one of the haunted house's wings. The first-floor room was set up as the carnival backlot. A set of stairs would take me up to the second-floor menagerie tent. The entire third floor was set up as a three-ring circus. Coming down the steps in the opposite wing, I would find myself in the freak show/sideshow on the second floor and then the funhouse on the first floor.

"I know you're in here, Alberto!" I yelled. "The gig is up. Jason told me everything."

"It seems I have an advantage on you, Carrie!" Alberto called back. His voice sounded close by. "You don't know where I am. But I know where you are."

A gunshot echoed in the room, and, off to my left, one of the windows in the food truck shattered. I dropped to the ground and rolled under the truck.

"I'm still one step ahead of you, Carrie!"

"But you're in my domain now," I shouted as I crawled past a spaceship shaped coin-operated kiddie ride. Once I was between two of the game stands, I took off running. "I helped build this place. I know where everything is."

I found one of the emergency switches hidden behind a banner. I ripped off the protective plastic case and slammed my palm against the button. Immediately, overhead lights flashed on and lit up the room. A siren also began to wail.

"I see you!" I shouted at Alberto. He was perched on top of the black and purple striped fiberglass canopy that covered the carousel. I pulled my gun out of my waistband and took a shot at him. Alberto ducked behind the massive skull that was at the peak of the canopy. My bullet struck one of the skull's glowing red eyeballs. "Damn it."

Alberto popped out from the other side of the skull and returned fire. The bullet thudded harmlessly into the wall above my head.

I sprinted a few feet along the wall and then threw myself through a hidden doorway that connected the midway to the funhouse. Multicolored flashing lights lit up the room, and a short, squat version of me stared back from a wavy mirror.

To escape the funhouse, I would have to wade through a ball pit, pass through the mirror maze and then the airbags, and walk across numerous sections of moving flooring. Then it was another spinning tunnel to the outside.

I had just stepped into the mirror maze when I was greeted by countless Albertos.

"You forget I've been spending a lot of time around the Body Farm. At this point, I probably know it as well as you do," Alberto said. The mirror next to me exploded into millions of pieces. "I've got you now, Carrie."

"No, Alberto. I've got you."

Alberto might have spent some time in the Carn-Evil of Chaos, but there was no way he had figured out the mirror maze. The people who acted in the mirror maze received extensive training so they would be able to make their way through without comically bumping into the walls. I might not have received that training, but I had helped create the mirror maze.

I took a deep breath and oriented myself. Meanwhile, another nearby mirror exploded. I couldn't let it get to me. I had one shot. I had to make the most of it.

Once I had myself centered, I turned slightly to my left, aimed at one of the countless Albertos—hopefully the real one and not a reflection—and pulled the trigger. Around me, all the Albertos screamed and grabbed at their chests.

"Bullseye!"

I scampered through the mirror maze to where Alberto lay on the ground. He had been less than ten feet away from me when I pulled the trigger. I kicked his gun away from him and then knelt. My shot had hit him in the upper left of his chest, and blood was heavily leaking from the wound.

"Don't you dare die on me, Alberto," I commanded as I applied pressure to the wound. Blood bubbled up between my fingers. "At least not until you've explained yourself. Why me? Why my family? And who is El Lobo? What is he to you?"

"Why not your family?" Alberto wheezed. He was quickly losing blood and was slipping away from me. "And you of all people should understand family loyalty. Everything I did was to protect my family."

"Family? Is El Lobo your family?"

Alberto weakly nodded. "*Él Lobo es mi hermano* . . . Well, half-brother. Same dad. Different moms. We grew up on different sides of the law. Like you, I used my job to protect him and *mi papá*. How else do you think El Lobo's gotten away with it for this long? I helped him."

"Oh my god, your father is the head of the Rio Cartel . . ."

"Like you, I had to protect my family."

"But why did you come after us? And why did you setup the boys?"

Alberto opened his mouth, but the only thing that came out was a wheeze followed by a stream of blood. After a few gasping, rattling breaths, Alberto lay still.

Covered in blood, I emerged from the Carn-Evil of Chaos. Hardy came running to meet me. Lieutenant Underwood and Lieutenant Schmitt were with him. While I had been inside dealing with Alberto, the fire department and Wyatt County deputies had arrived on scene to take control. The ticket booth and game stands were a smoldering ruin, and Shatners were seated at the picnic tables. Thaddeus and his congregants were over by the Manor.

"Are you okay?" Hardy asked.

"It's not my blood. It's Alberto's. He's dead." I turned to Schmitt and said, "I'm sorry. I didn't mean to kill him. I know you would have wanted to question him—"

Schmitt interrupted and said, "It's okay, Carrie. It came down to you and him. And I'm glad you're the one who walked out."

"Where is he?" Bubba asked. He was the only other Shatner on site who wasn't in handcuffs. "Where's Alberto?"

"Mirror maze."

Schmitt and Underwood headed towards the Carn-Evil of Chaos. Bubba led the way.

"You sure you're okay, Carrie?" Hardy asked.

I nodded. "Please tell me you got El Lobo?"

Hardy nodded. "Jason helped me. Poor kid took a bullet to the side for his trouble. The EMTs took him to the hospital, but he should be all right."

I went to rub my hands over my face, but remembered they were coated in sticky blood. I wanted to scream. I wanted to cry. I wanted to punch someone in the face.

"Where's El Lobo?"

"They've got him in a cruiser in the parking lot."

"I have a couple questions for him."

Hardy escorted me out to the parking lot. He must have sensed by desire to hit El Lobo because he held me back from the cruiser. El Lobo smirked at me from the backseat.

"Your brother is dead," I told him as I held up my blood covered hands. "He won't be able to protect you anymore."

El Lobo swore under his breath in Spanish.

"I have two questions for you," I said. "What's your real name?"

"*Mi nombre es Raul, Mamacita* . . . Raul Ramos. Raul means wolf."

"*El lobo* . . . Spanish for the wolf." I tilted my head back and groaned. "And why my family?"

"Why not your family?" El Lobo asked. "They messy. They a threat to me. Especially that Wesley. *Mi amigo pelirrojo* couldn't keep his mouth shut. He was going to get me in trouble. Nothing against you, *Mamacita*, but the boy had to be stopped."

"Y'all failed."

"Did we, *Mamacita*? Did we? Because it looks like your time is up."

With his chin, El Lobo gestured behind me. I glanced over my shoulder and watched as agents from the DPS, DEA, and ATF descended on my family.

"Time's up, *Mamacita*."

"We've been running on borrowed time for a while now . . ."

Hardy drew me away from the cruiser. "Come on, Carrie, let's get out of here. The shit can finish hitting the fan without you."

"It's really over, isn't it?"

"It's not completely over. But this is the beginning of the end . . ."

I pulled my sheriff's department badge out of my pocket and held it up to the moonlight. "I guess I won't be needing this anymore. My days of working for law enforcement are most likely over."

"You had a good run."

"A damn good run."

EPILOGUE

Two years later . . .

"**S**HERIFF JERROD HARDY . . . IT HAS A NICE RING TO IT, don't you think?"

Hardy pinned his shiny new badge to the front of his uniform and then leaned towards the bathroom mirror for a closer look. From the doorway, I had been watching him get ready for his first day on the job. The new black and gray Wyatt County Sheriff's Department uniform looked good on him. Hardy was starting his first term as sheriff with a new department building and a fresh batch of deputies. There were very few deputies left over from Uncle Murph's reign.

"Yeah, Sheriff Hardy has a nice ring to it," I admitted. "But Sergeant Jerrod Hardy of the Texas Rangers sounded better."

"Yeah, well . . ." Hardy turned to face me. "You and I both know that there was no way I could stay with the Texas Rangers after everything that happened. Besides, I'm happier here than I was with the Rangers. I get to come home to you almost every night."

"It has been nice having you around more often." I wrapped my arms around Hardy's waist and hugged him. "I don't know how I would have gotten through all this without you."

That night at the Body Farm might have been the beginning of the end, but the story was far from over. And—for several Shatners, Devereuxs, and Palmers—that story was not going to have a happy ending.

In the days following the shootout, the Department of Public Safety, Drug Enforcement Administration, and Bureau of Alcohol, Tobacco, Firearms and Explosives ramped up their investigation into the Shatners, Devereuxs, and Palmers. As time went on, other federal agencies joined in as well. Countless search warrants were served, and, one-by-one, we were all taken in for extensive questioning. A myriad of criminal charges were also filed—some stuck, some were dropped, and others were thrown out in court.

Despite my agreement with the DPS that absolved me of any wrong-doing and protected me from arrest, I was questioned about a dozen times by five different law enforcement agencies. The fact that I was questioned but never arrested caused some bad blood between me and some of my family members. Most of those fences had been mended in the past year, but I was still on the outs with certain Shatners. My great-aunts Mabel and Imogen refused to speak to me, as did my aunts Margaret and Loretta.

After realizing that the deal he had made with Alberto wasn't going to hold water with anyone, Uncle Houston selfishly scrambled to save himself. I don't know what changed his mind—maybe the knowledge that many of his family members were looking at extensive prison sentences—but, for probably the first time in his life, Uncle Houston did something unselfish. He eventually threw himself upon the grenade and sacrificed himself to protect the rest of the family. Uncle Houston took the blame for many crimes—including ones that he couldn't possibly have committed.

Uncle Houston's selfless act spared a few Shatners from prison, and probably saved others from a longer stay. He joined Uncle Ted and Cousin Randy who were already in prison—Uncle Ted for the marijuana and Randy for violating his parole. Also joining them were my uncles Bowie, Murph, Vernon, Delmar, Butch, and Kinky. Despite cleaning up after themselves, there was still enough evidence floating around of some of their crimes. Cousin Billy Bob was also arrested—as were Dale, Dickie, and Rooster.

Wesley was also in prison—and all five of his children would be out of high school before he was eligible for parole. As promised, he had married Roxanne after the birth of Wesley Jr. The same judge that arraigned him also performed the wedding ceremony.

It had taken time, but Waylon had almost completely recovered from the assault. He suffered some memory loss and was now prone to migraines. But he was alive, and, thanks to Wesley, a free man.

Oscar was the only male Palmer who avoided going to prison—and that was because he had been deemed mentally incompetent to stand trial. In the months following the attack on our family, Oscar's early onset dementia turned into Alzheimer's disease.

Catfish Devereux also escaped prosecution when he peacefully died in his sleep after suffering a massive heart attack. After he died, his sixth wife gave me a letter that she had found in one of Catfish's safety deposit boxes. In the letter, Catfish took the blame for gunning down my Uncle Benjamin all those years ago. He swore that Great Aunt Emily Morgan and Uncle Houston had not been involved, but I had my doubts.

More people than just Shatners, Devereuxs, and Palmers wound up going to jail. The ripple effect had been strong, and people were still feeling the effects. Numerous officers with the Holler, Wilder, and Mooresville police departments were forced to turn in their guns and badges to escape prosecution. Every judge in Wyatt County abruptly retired—and there were so many others—including ones I probably didn't even know about.

Hardy planted a kiss on my forehead and drew me back into the present.

"You know what else has a nice ring to it, Mrs. Hardy . . ."

"Yes, it is a very nice ring." I held up my left hand and admired my diamond and amethyst wedding ring. "And Mrs. Hardy sounds divine."

Mere days after the shootout at the Body Farm—as my world was crumbling around me—Hardy and I boarded a plane to Las Vegas. We were married in a super cheesy ceremony performed by a mediocre Elvis impersonator. Lieutenant Hugh Underwood hadn't been thrilled one of his sergeants had married the ex-head of a known criminal organization, but he allowed Hardy to keep his badge. It was Hardy's coworkers that shunned him and eventually drove him to quit the Rangers.

"What are your plans for the day?" Hardy asked.

"The same as every other day for the past two years," I said.

After turning in my badge, I dedicated myself to helping my family rebuild. Not everyone was going to prison, and we had several legal business ventures that we had to keep up and running. Uncle Vernon's construction company had been forced to shut down, but the rest of our businesses came out of the mess mostly intact.

"You ever miss working for the sheriff's department?"

"Of course. Aside from cleaning up after my family, I enjoyed my job. But that ship has sailed. No one in their right mind would ever give me a badge."

"Well, you've questioned my sanity plenty of times in the past couple years." Hardy reached into his back pocket and pulled out a badge. It was my old sheriff's department badge. "I could use a crime scene investigator at the sheriff's department, and I heard you're the best in the county. I could use you."

"You sure about this?" I plucked the badge out of Hardy's hand and pressed it against my chest. "You do know I'm related to a whole bunch of criminals, right? Once upon a time, I used this badge and my job to cover up their indiscretions."

"Yeah, but the troublemakers are in prison," Hardy said. "And the ones left aren't going to be breaking the law and asking you to cover for them."

"Yeah . . . Let's hope that's the case."

RANDEE GREEN IS THE AUTHOR of the Carrie Shatner Mystery series. Her passion for reading began in grade school with *Little House in the Big Woods* by Laura Ingalls Wilder. She has a bachelor's degree in English Literature, as well as a master's and an MFA in Creative Writing. When not writing, she's usually reading, indulging in her passion for Texas country music, traveling, or hanging out with her pets Daisy and Snookums.